8-2'23

Siege of Rage and Ruin

MORE BOOKS BY DJANGO WEXLER

THE WELLS OF SORCERY TRILOGY
for young adults

Ship of Smoke and Steel

City of Stone and Silence

THE SHADOW CAMPAIGNS
for adults

The Thousand Names

The Shadow Throne

The Price of Valor

The Guns of Empire

The Infernal Battalion

THE FORBIDDEN LIBRARY SERIES
for young readers

The Forbidden Library

The Mad Apprentice

The Palace of Glass

The Fall of the Readers

DJANGO WEXLER

Siege of Rage and Ruin

Book Three: The Wells of Sorcery Trilogy

TOR TEEN

A Tom Doherty Associates Book
New York

SIEGE OF RAGE AND RUIN

Copyright © 2020 by Django Wexler

Map by Jennifer Hanover

A Tor Teen Book
Published by Tom Doherty Associates
120 Broadway
New York, NY 10271

www.tor-forge.com

Tor® is a registered trademark of Macmillan Publishing Group, LLC.

The Library of Congress Cataloging-in-Publication Data
is available upon request.

ISBN 978-0-7653-9731-7 (hardcover)
ISBN 978-0-7653-9730-0 (ebook)

Our books may be purchased in bulk for promotional, educational, or
business use. Please contact your local bookseller or the Macmillan Corporate
and Premium Sales Department at 1-800-221-7945, extension 5442,
or by email at MacmillanSpecialMarkets@macmillan.com.

First Edition: January 2021

Printed in the United States of America

0 9 8 7 6 5 4 3 2 1

This book was largely produced during the COVID-19 pandemic and is dedicated to all the scientists, doctors, healthcare workers, and others who have worked so hard to keep us safe.

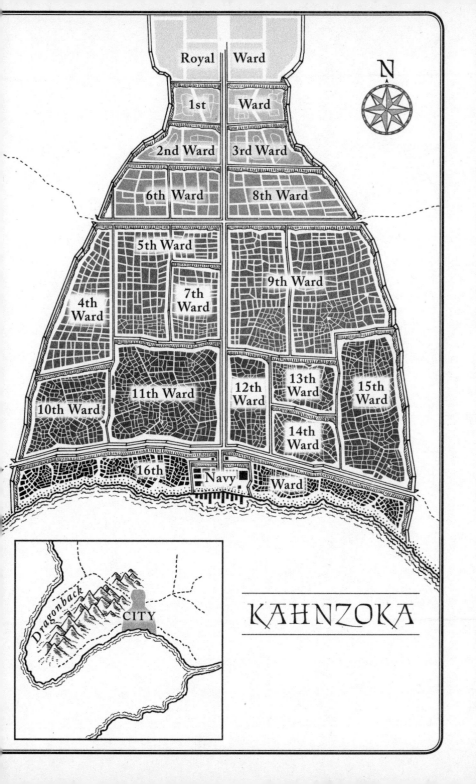

Siege of Rage
and Ruin

1

For days after it rains, water drips through the bowels of *Soliton*, running down cool metal walls and through ragged, rusty gaps. It beads on the surface of the pale shelf mushrooms, catching stray sunlight to gleam like a handful of diamonds, and gathers in muddy pools where algae blooms in a short-lived riot of color. The steady *plink plink plink* infiltrates its way into silent moments, the kind of sound you're certain is going to drive you mad but eventually just fades into the background.

I crouch at the junction of two corridors, my breathing as quiet as I can make it, and the dripping grows louder in my ears, like a parade's worth of kettledrums. The blueshell's footsteps are silent—soft, springy balls at the ends of its legs absorbing any noise—but segments of its chitinous armor brush against each other with a sound like shuffling paper. I hear it come closer, then stop. It know I'm here. This close, it can hear the heart pounding in my chest.

Time to get loud, then.

I spring to my feet, slapping the wall with one hand to produce a hollow *bong*. The blueshell comes forward, edging around the corner, eight feet of sky-colored crab with a mass of sharp-edged tentacles for a face. It reaches for me with a foreleg tipped with a big knobbly claw, but I'm already gone, boots ringing against the metal deck as I run down the corridor.

The blueshell gives chase, moving fast and quiet. I turn another corner, out into a wide corridor, and it comes with me, tendrils writhing. This one is hungry, and it thinks it has the scent of easy prey.

Sometimes it's easy to be wrong about who's hunting who.

Halfway down the corridor, I turn on my heel, skidding to a stop on the slimy metal. My armor comes up, green Melos energy crackling across me, and my blades ignite—glowing, spitting chunks of pure sorcery, springing from the backs of my wrists like extensions of my arms. A drop of water falls from the ceiling and splashes across them, evaporating with a steamy *hiss*.

The crab pulls up short as well. Whether it knows what the sight of those blades means, or whether it's just hesitating at something unfamiliar, I have no idea. Whatever the reason, its hunger quickly overcomes its caution, and it reaches for me with a claw. I duck under the limb, slashing across it with a blade, but energy screeches and leaves only a black scorch mark on the crab's blue armor. I dance in closer, near the tentacled maw, and it reaches for me. No armor *here,* and my flashing blades leave several tendrils severed and smoking, twitching on the deck. The crab recoils, backing away.

I first made my name on *Soliton* killing a blueshell single-handedly, but I'm not such a glutton for pain that I'm eager to repeat the experience. *Any rotting time, people.*

As though in answer, a figure steps from a doorway behind the crab, outlined in an aura of pale blue light. Lines of Tartak force reach out, expertly grabbing two of the blueshell's back legs just as it takes a step, lifting its sticky pads from the floor. The magic grabs the limbs and yanks backward, and the crab stumbles.

Shadows flicker, peeling away from the walls and swirling into a tall, lean shape. Jack usually fights with a spear, but for this she carries a short, heavy blade, with enough weight to crack crabshell. She lines up a two-handed swing with one of the pinioned legs and nails the joint expertly, crushing the thin armor and taking the leg off. It crashes to the deck, still twitching, and Jack spins to sever the other. The blueshell reaches for her with a claw, but she's already gone, vanished with a swirl of shadows and a mocking laugh.

Zarun releases his hold on the broken legs and steps forward, his own Melos armor glowing around him. The crab turns awkwardly, shifting on its remaining limbs, would-be prey forgotten in its effort to get at its tormentors. It tries to reach Zarun with its claws, but he grabs and holds them with Tartak force. It shoves closer, lashing him with its tentacles, their sharpened tips drawing bright green flares from his armor. I know, from painful experience, that each of those flares is matched by a bloom of heat across his skin, slowly increasing from mild to unbearable, but Zarun doesn't show any strain.

And he's got the crab's attention, which is all I need. I shift the flow of Melos power, letting one blade fade away while the other shortens and narrows into a thin, brutal spike. Energy collects in my fist, growing hotter by the moment. When I can barely stand it, I sprint forward, darting past the blueshell's ruined back legs and slipping underneath it. The armor is thick here, but it still has seams, and I drive the spike in between two plates. It breaks through with a *crunch,* and I release the energy I've gathered, a wave of coruscating fire that rips through the creature's vulnerable innards. I have to jump back as it collapses, twitching wildly.

Chalk up another one. This is getting almost *too* easy.

I let my armor fade away, and shake out my hand. Wisps of steam are still rising from between my fingers.

"You're getting better at that," Zarun says, hopping over the crab's outstretched claws. "I still can't get the hang of it."

He's in his hunting gear, ragged trousers and an open vest that shows off a well-muscled torso, his dark hair long enough that it's starting to curl, skin Jyashtani-copper and eyes a startling blue. For all that he's *toothsome,* as the late and unlamented Butcher might have put it, these days I find I can look at him and appreciate without being tempted. I have everything I need waiting for me, back in the Garden.

"Maybe too good," I say, shaking my hand again. My skin feels tender and raw, though without the muscle-ache of full power-burn. "I think I cooked myself a little."

"A little "burn is better than not killing the thing first try," Zarun says. "Nothing like a mortally wounded blueshell thrashing around to ruin your day."

"Don't remind me," I mutter.

"Brave companions! I see we are victorious once again!"

Shadows shiver and part to reveal Jack, who bows like a conjurer at the end of a trick. She's half a head taller than me, skinny as a pole, dressed in flowing, colorful silk. Her head is half-shaved, with the remaining hair dyed a brilliant purple. Her features make her look Imperial, but her accent careers wildly across the known world and beyond.

"Another triumph to add to our legend," she goes on. "Another mighty deed in a life replete with mighty deeds. Truly, no heroes have ever been so valorous as we three, pitting ourselves alone against the monsters of the Deeps, with no thought for our own safety—"

"We're only out here because *you* kept saying you were bored," Zarun says.

"And because you said you were tired of fruit and bread," I remind him.

"True." Zarun looks at the blueshell and licks his lips. "That's going to be some good eating."

"We have to get it home first," I say.

"Clever Jack will scout the way!" Jack says immediately, shadows rushing around her like dark water. Her voice fades gradually as she vanishes. "It would be terrible to be ambushed, after all. Many are the perils that haunt the dark places of *Soliton.* . . ."

Zarun and I exchange a look, and roll our eyes.

In truth, it's mostly Zarun who carries the dead blueshell, lifting it with his Tartak Well while I assist whenever there's a tricky doorway. It doesn't take long to get back to the Garden, the cylindrical hideout near the front of the ship where we'd first taken shelter from the Vile Rot. The great folding door at its base is closed, and I concentrate, reaching out through my Eddica Well into the fabric of the ship. After a moment, the door obediently slides open.

I'm getting better at that, too. I feel a burst of triumph, which is a little ridiculous for what is, after all, only a door. Having spent so long bashing my head against *Soliton*'s obstinate, inscrutable system, it still feels like a revelation when I can make it do anything like what I intend. In theory, the authority I was granted at the Harbor gives me complete control over the ship. In practice, things are . . . more difficult.

Hagan is better at it than I am. Of course, being dead, he has a lot more time to practice.

Jack is waiting for us, bouncing idly from one foot to another, animated as always by a manic energy that never seems to take a breath. As Zarun hauls the dead crab over the threshold and lays it out on the grassy meadow that occupies the first layer of the Garden, Jack follows close behind, practically drooling.

"Good eating, indeed," she says. "And none too soon, for Clever Jack has a hunger. And a thirst, come to think of it, if there's any wine left in that jug. But mostly a hunger."

"Let's get it properly butchered first," Zarun says, igniting his own Melos blades. "Otherwise half of it will go bad before we get the chance to cook it."

I ignite my blades as well, ignoring a twinge in my singed hand. "Show me where to cut."

"I'll take care of it," Zarun says. "Go upstairs and tend to your princess."

"Yes, go!" Jack says. "You, at least, should enjoy the voyage."

"But—"

"And by that," Jack interrupts, "I mean engage in the lustful press of flesh against warm, yielding flesh, skin against skin, tongue against—"

"*Jack*," Zarun says.

"Apologies." Jack bows, panting, her purple hair flopping

forward. "Every mile *Soliton* puts between Lovelorn Jack and dearest Thora is like a thorn in her heart, and every day that passes adds to her . . . frustration."

"I'm sorry," I mutter.

"Don't put that on Isoka," Zarun says. "You volunteered for this, same as I did. Now go and fetch the pick and the shell-spreader."

"Useful Jack will retrieve the tools of slaughter!" Jack says, bounding off toward the stairs.

Zarun shook his head. "Don't mind her."

"I try not to," I say. "But I can help with this, if you need me."

"Don't worry about it," Zarun said, stretching. "It keeps me busy, at least."

Keeping busy, I reflect as I ascend to the Garden's upper floors, really has been the biggest problem we've encountered so far. We spent the passage through the straits near the Vile Rot sealed up tight inside the Garden, and since then it's been a steady run northward, the temperature slowly rising as we parallel the coast of the Southern Kingdoms and make for Imperial shores. With control of the angels, crab attacks aren't a worry, and the Garden provides more than enough food now that the four of us are the only ones aboard.

Even my worry about Tori has receded a little. Not much, of course, but at least we're headed in the right direction at the best speed I can manage. When we arrive at Kahnzoka—another two days, according to Meroe's charts—I'll start to worry again. Until then, all I can do is wait, while mighty *Soliton* sweeps the miles under its keel.

Tori will be fine. She has to be. It's months, yet, until Kuon Naga's deadline.

And Kuon Naga would never lie to you? a traitor part of my mind whispers.

Meroe and I share a chamber in the highest part of the Garden. It's not large, but it feels positively luxurious compared to the voyage to the Harbor, when hundreds of us were crammed into these rooms. It's furnished haphazardly, out of the superstitious offerings of goods that have accumulated over decades all across *Soliton*. Our bed is a nest of cushions and thick carpets, our fire-pit is a brazen shield carved with a lion's head, and we eat off gold and silver plate that would be at home in the Imperial palace. When she's not looking through her telescope or plotting our course on her maps, Meroe makes herself clothes from scavenged fabric, strange hybrids of Imperial *kizen* and Jyashtani dresses that would draw attention on the street of any city in the world. She always looks beautiful, of course.

When I arrive, she's busy sketching something, sitting at a small desk we'd made from the remnants of a heavy sea chest, carefully husbanding a stub of a pencil from her small, precious stock. Her brow has a single, adorable furrow of concentration, and her tongue pokes ever so slightly out of the corner of her mouth. Back in Kahnzoka, I'm going to buy her a crate of pencils, and inks in every color she can imagine, and a bigger telescope and—

"Isoka!" She looks up and gives me that smile that makes my stomach wobble. "Everything went all right?"

"Fine," I say. "Zarun and Jack are butchering a blueshell downstairs."

"Nobody hurt?"

I grin and flex my hand. "I may have burned my fingers a little finishing it off."

"My mighty hunter." She gets to her feet, all smooth, automatic grace. She's wearing pale green, setting off her brown skin and the silver of the asymmetric armband that's her only jewelry. Her hair is tied into an untidy pile at the back of her head. "And you're not helping?"

"They told me to head upstairs and 'tend to you,'" I tell her. "Well. Zarun told me that. Jack specifically told me I should go and rut you. Something about the lustful press of flesh against warm, yielding flesh?"

Meroe laughs, covering her mouth with her hand. She steps closer, lively red-brown eyes flashing, one eyebrow quirked.

"Something like that," she says, "could be arranged." She halts, and sniffs. *"After* you wash, though. You smell like crab."

I sniff, and have to agree with her. I make a great show of an exasperated sigh, and she laughs again.

The Garden, it turns out, has *showers*. That's what Zarun calls them, anyway. In Kahnzoka we have baths, but apparently in Jyashtan the rich like to have warm water pumped up into the ceiling and drizzled on them like a kind of private rainstorm. Zarun says this is a recent invention, but the ancients who built *Soliton* must have had a similar idea, because there are little rooms adjacent to our chambers that produce a spray of hot water on demand. Just another benefit of finally achieving real control over the ship. I still prefer a nice hot soak to relax, but for getting yourself clean the shower beats dumping a bucket over your head.

I strip down and start the water with an Eddica command, leaning against the wall and letting it beat down on my shoulders. After a few moments, the tension goes out of my muscles, and I shiver.

Meroe leans her head around the corner, smiling wickedly. I raise my eyebrows.

"Can I help you?"

"Just watching," she says. "Pay no mind."

Frankly, I don't know what she's so eager to look at. I'm certainly no beauty, more muscle than curves, with my history written on my skin for all to see. Pale ridged scars on my back and thighs, from the Kahnzoka streets, a dozen overlapping cuts from various blades, healed into puckered lines; and of course the line of cross-hatched blue marks that cover my leg and run up my torso and across my face, legacy of the time Meroe's Ghul power saved my life in the Deeps.

But if she wants to watch, I'm hardly going to complain. I turn around under the shower, letting the sweat and crab blood sluice off my skin. When I look back, the green dress is puddled at Meroe's feet, with nothing beneath but smooth, curving brown skin.

"Sorry," she says. "I got impatient."

She pulls her hair loose, and it cascades down to her shoulders in a dark, thick mass. I start to object, then wonder why in the Rot I would do that, and by then she's kicked free of the dress and stepped into the shower with me. I lean down, just a little, and she kisses me.

"Patience," I murmur, "can be overrated."

She laughs, and pulls in tighter, her skin slick against mine, her warm, yielding flesh—

Well. What Jack said.

I've never been married, obviously.

When I was a girl on the streets of the Sixteenth Ward, the older teens would talk about being "hooked." This, I understood, meant a couple who were rutting on the regular, and had agreed not to do it with anyone else, at least until their partner got locked away by the Ward Guard or turned up bled white in some alley. There wasn't a lot of room for romance in the Sixteenth, at least not for kids with nothing to sell except their bodies and whatever they could steal.

Point is, I'd never been hooked, or particularly wanted to be. I'd rutted, when I got old enough to feel the need for it, with boys I'd paid for or taken a fancy to at Breda's tavern. I'd visited a Ghul-touched, an old woman, and suffered her bony fingers to touch me long enough to ward against any unwanted complications, but that was about all the thought I'd given to the consequences. The closest thing I'd had to a long-term relationship had been with Hagan, who'd worked with me as muscle as well as sharing my bed, and that had ended with me killing him to keep him from talking to Kuon Naga's interrogators. (Not that it made a difference in the end, and don't think I'm entirely free of guilt on the subject.)

Point is, what I have with Meroe is different. Obviously. But neither she nor I have a lot of experience with *being* with someone, in the most literal sense of the phrase, and what with the constant threat of being eaten by crabs or torn apart by Prime's walking corpses we hadn't gotten much chance to practice. Ever since we came back from the Deeps, the crew has been looking to us for leadership. We'd figured out that we liked kissing and everything that came after, but that was about as far as it went.

But the last few weeks, since we'd left the Harbor, had been . . . different. It's just her, me, Zarun, and Jack—and Hagan, if dead people count—alone in all the vastness of *Soliton*. The others have their own ways of amusing themselves—Jack scavenges for interesting tidbits, like a magpie, and Zarun reads the books he finds among the sacrifices—which has left Meroe and me mostly on our own. No one to lead, no one to take care of, just . . . living. Just for a while.

It's weird. But . . . in a good way. Waking up in the same bed. Eating the same meals. Falling asleep together, and knowing tomorrow will be more of the same.

Until it's not. And that time is getting closer, which is probably why I can't sleep.

For my practice sessions, I picked one of the angels that's not quite so distressing to look at—no screaming baby faces or ranks of grasping hands. This one is tall, six-legged, and vaguely leonine, with a complex pattern of blocky protrusions surrounding its single crystalline eye. That eye, the heart of the angel's connection to *Soliton*, glows a brilliant blue, throwing snaky shadows as the huge thing paces around the control room with its complicated interlocking conduits.

"See?" Hagan says. "You can manage."

I grit my teeth and bite back a sarcastic rejoinder. I hate being patronized, but after everything that's happened between us, Hagan of all people has earned a little restraint. He hangs in the air beside me, outlined in pale gray Eddica light that would be invisible to anyone without a connection to the Well of Spirits. I can see gray threads linking his form to the conduits throughout the room, and more threads running back up to the angel. All of *Soliton* is a single system, a complex construct of Eddica energy. Hagan doesn't *control* it, precisely; it's more like he inhabits it—or *haunts* it, I suppose—and he's learned to twist the threads to his own ends.

That's what he tells me, anyway. Honestly I don't understand half of what he and Silvoa talked about. Which is something of a problem, actually, since as far as anyone knows I'm the only living Eddica adept—the last Eddicant—which puts the fate of *Soliton* and the Harbor in my hands. Since I overrode the system at the Harbor and it acknowledged me as the highest authority, I theoretically have the power to make *Soliton* and its angels do whatever I want. Getting the ship to sail in a particular direction turned out to be easy enough, but controlling the angels is not.

"I've always been able to do it when I'm concentrating," I tell Hagan, trying not to lose my focus on the angel. It keeps walking around in circles, six legs moving smoothly, and I wonder if I *am* finally getting it. "It's setting the rotting things up so they keep doing what they're supposed to be doing that's the problem."

Hagan shakes his head, brushing back his long hair. His appearance has changed, become more *stylized*, as though he no longer bothers to re-create every detail of his living self. He's more like a sketch of what he was in life, a few bold lines roughing in a face, clothes vague and indistinct. I wonder if he'll eventually give up on a human form entirely, and what will happen to him when he does.

"I told you," he says, "it's all about patterns. You impress the pattern of what you want the angel to do into its mind, like it was a wax tablet you were sketching on with a stylus."

Patterns. I try to think a pattern at the angel, a simple circle. *Keep walking round and round.* I feel it respond, and slowly withdraw my control. For a moment, it seems to work, and the thing keeps moving at a steady pace. Then it shifts, one foot coming down awkwardly on the uneven floor. With the next step, it topples over, legs churning mindlessly in place as it lies on its side.

Hagan snorts a laugh, ignoring the death glare I shoot at him. I suppose it's hard to intimidate a ghost.

"You're pushing too hard," he says. "The angels aren't blank slates. They know how to walk already. You just have to tell them where you want them to go."

"You just told me to imagine a blank slate!" I protest.

"I didn't mean—" Hagan looks up. "Never mind. We'll try again later."

He disappears, vanishing like a candle flame in a sudden wind. I turn and find Meroe standing in the doorway, watching the fallen angel trying to walk.

"It looks a little bit like a clockwork soldier," Meroe says. "Do you have those in Kahnzoka? Where you wind the key and it marches around."

"I've seen one," I say, uncomfortably. There was a time when I'd aspired to be nothing more than a soldier like that, carrying out orders as the boss of the Sixteenth Ward and never thinking about anything but the next job and Tori's safety. I won't say I miss that life, but it was . . . easier.

"Something wrong?" Meroe says, coming into the room.

"Just a bad memory."

"Sorry I brought it up," she says, then cocks her head. "Actually, one of my brothers took *our* clockwork soldier apart until it was just a pair of legs that walked on their own, and he used it to scare my little sister half to death. They're creepy things when you think about it."

"I suppose they are." I reach out to the angel, and it stills. "So what are you doing up?"

"I woke in the middle of the night and found my partner missing," Meroe says. "What's *your* excuse?"

"I couldn't sleep."

It's hard to say more than that, but mercifully I don't have to. Meroe comes over to me and puts her arm around my shoulders, pulling me close. For a moment we stand in silence, here in the room where I fought the Scholar, where I nearly died and saved

Soliton's crew. The bloodstains are gone. I wonder if one of the angels cleaned them.

"She'll be all right," Meroe says.

"You don't know that," I say, very quietly. "You can't."

"I know she's related to *you*," Meroe says. "That means she can take care of herself."

"I didn't teach her to take care of herself," I say. "I never *wanted* her to take care of herself. I wanted her to grow up and be happy and not have to worry."

"We'll get there," Meroe says, a whisper in my ear.

"We'll get there," I repeat. *And then what?*

And then what? It's the central question, really.

Kuon Naga sent me to capture *Soliton* and bring it back for service in the navy of the Blessed Empire, in anticipation of another war against Jyashtan. He gave me a year, with my sister as hostage. I learned, later, that I wasn't the first agent he'd smuggled aboard the legendary ghost ship. How much he knows about *Soliton*, if any of his previous spies smuggled any information off, I have no idea.

Unlike any of his other agents, unlike anyone since the time of the ancients, I succeeded. *Soliton* goes where I want it to. Whether Naga can do anything with it is his problem—I've fulfilled my side of the bargain. I ought to be able to sail into Kahnzoka harbor, take Tori, and go.

Except—

Go rotting *where?* Back to my life in the Sixteenth Ward? It's hard to imagine, now. And hard to believe that Kuon Naga would let us live for long. The head of the Immortals, the Emperor's guards and secret police, didn't get to where he is by leaving loose ends. And even if I could return to the streets, would Meroe come with me? Would I want her to? How would she look at me if I spent my days cutting down small-time crooks who hadn't paid their protection money?

Options, options. We could leave Kahnzoka. Take Tori, take the money I've salted away, and go. Rot, we don't even need my savings—there's enough gold on *Soliton* for a hundred fortunes, no one is going to miss a bit. But that still leaves the question of *where* wide open. And there's Jack to consider. Her partner, Thora, is back at the Harbor, and *Soliton* is her only way back. I doubt Kuon Naga will give her a ride for the asking.

If I could make the angels do what I want—if I had the kind of control I *ought* to have—then I would hold all the cards. There are hundreds of angels aboard *Soliton*, maybe thousands. They're absurdly strong and nearly indestructible. No army in the world, not even the Invincible Legions, could stand against them. But I get a headache trying to control *two* angels at once, let alone thousands. And even if I could, Naga would have Tori as a hostage. If he hurts her, I'll tear him apart piece by bloody piece, but that would be small comfort.

What's left, then? Hope. Hope that Naga always figured this was a long-shot bet. He'll have people watching Tori, but if he hasn't actually put her under lock and key, the four of us can probably get to her and get away before he knows we're here. If we can get back to *Soliton*, we're safe; the entire Imperial Navy can't stop the ghost ship from going exactly where it wants to.

Therefore—

—I'm building a boat.

Or the angels are building a boat under Hagan's control. I'm supervising, Zarun is complaining, and Jack has gotten bored and wandered off.

"It still doesn't look like much," Zarun says. "The wood is all cracked and splintered. Are you sure this'll float?"

"It'll float," Hagan says. "I'm caulking it with sap from bluegill mushrooms."

"Hagan says he's caulking it with mushroom sap," I relay to

Zarun, who looks uncomfortable at the mention of Hagan's name, but pretends not to be.

"Was Hagan particularly familiar with boats?" he says. "When he was alive, I mean."

"Not really," I say, and glance at Hagan. He shrugs.

"*Soliton* has memories," he says. "Embedded in the system. People have done this before."

"Has it ever worked?" I send this via Eddica, so Zarun won't hear.

"The boat worked fine," he says. "Until they tried to leave and the angels wrecked it."

"Right." I sigh and raise my voice again. "Besides, the only other thing we have to use is scraps from the hull, and if anyone spots us in a rotting *metal* rowboat, there are going to be some serious questions." I still haven't quite gotten used to the idea that anything made of metal could float.

"If anyone gets a good look at any of this, there are going to be some questions," Zarun says.

He's right. What wood there is on *Soliton* comes from sacrifices, so the boat is being assembled from bits of furniture, chests, and other detritus. I don't doubt that it'll float, but it doesn't look like any another rowboat *I've* seen. Beside it is a small pile of sacks full of easily portable treasure—gold and silver, mostly, and a few gems and pearls. I don't know what we're going to find in Kahnzoka, but having full purses certainly won't hurt.

That night, according to Meroe's instruments, *Soliton* slips silently past Kahnzoka. We're well out to sea, too far to catch sight of the city, but I trust Meroe's skill, and that means it's time to put the plan into action. Following my instructions, the ghost ship executes a slow turn to starboard, running east under cover of darkness until the humped shapes of the Dragonback hills start blotting out the stars.

If we're going to steal Tori out from under Kuon Naga's nose, we need to make sure he doesn't know we're coming, which means keeping *Soliton* out of sight. The headlands that define the sweep of Kahnzoka's bay both have Imperial watchposts on them. It's hard to get past them in a blacked-out skiff, let alone a metal leviathan the size of a small mountain. The smugglers I know from my days as ward boss preferred to land on the coast north of the city, across the Dragonbacks. It means a couple of days on the road to get to the landward gate, but the chance to blend in to the endless civilian traffic makes it a safer bet. I remember directions to a couple of their favorite spots, or at least I've convinced myself that I do.

So, with the coast only a dark line in the distance, the same swinging pulley that first lifted me onto *Soliton* in an iron cage lowers our makeshift boat over the side, with Zarun, Jack, Meroe, and me aboard, plus a king's ransom in assorted gold and jewels. On a cord under my shirt, smooth against my skin, I carry a segment of the ship's conduit, charged with Eddica power. As the Scholar and I had discovered, cut fragments retained their connection to the system for quite some time, so until the energy decays I'll be able to use it to contact *Soliton* and Hagan.

I hope, anyway. There's a lot of hope involved in this endeavor.

Amazingly, the first part of the plan goes off without a hitch. We take turns pulling on oars carved from an oak tabletop, driving the furniture-boat through a mild surf as the stars wheel slowly above us. *Soliton* turns away, a rapidly diminishing shadow—I told Hagan to take the ship farther out to sea, to make sure it isn't spotted by some sharp-eyed lookout. After an hour, back and shoulders burning furiously, I hear the crash of waves, and Jack shouts excited directions to keep us aimed at a broad inlet lined with pebbled beaches. It's a calm night, and before long I can roll out of the boat and wade through waist-deep water, dragging our little craft in the rest of the way.

I pause for a moment, feet in the surf, as the others start unloading. *Kahnzoka.* I look out at the moonlight-dappled water and test my feelings. *Back to the Empire. Back to my home.*

It still doesn't feel real. The beach could be any beach. Maybe it's because of the way I left the city, trussed in a cage.

But Tori's here. She's close. After so many miles, I'm almost there. *Almost.*

It feels strange to abandon the boat, after spending so much effort putting it together, but it's served its purpose. We take up our packs full of treasure—more strain on my already scream-ing shoulders—and hike across the beach and up the low ridge beyond. That takes us to the coast road, a long, rutted dirt track that runs across the point and up to the farming and fishing villages of Kahnzoka's hinterland. We stop in a copse of trees and wait for the sun to rise. If my memory serves, there's a small town a few miles farther along, and in the morning we can hike in like any other group of travelers, on our way to the city to sell our wares.

So far, so good. *Right?*

The town is called Redtree, on account of having an enormous red tree in the square. Country folk are nothing if not rotting imaginative.

I had worried a little that the appearance of our party might at-tract some comment. In Kahnzoka itself, foreigners are a common sight, and almost any combination of costume and features would probably pass without notice. Out in the country, the fact that we are two Imperials, a Jyashtani, and a southerner in a weird combi-nation of silks and scraps could have been more notable.

As it turns out, though, I needn't have worried. Redtree is packed far beyond the town's modest capacity for visitors. There are carts everywhere, pulled by horses, mules, donkeys, oxen, or sweating porters, all of them making as much noise as they're capable of. Men and women with wheelbarrows make their way along the slow-moving mass of traffic, selling food, drink, and fodder at outrageous prices.

"I have to admit," Zarun says, "I always thought you Imperials were boasting when you called your capital the greatest city in the world. But even at Horimae you don't get stuck in traffic before you get to the walls."

"This is . . . not normal." I look over the lines of arguing carters and frown. Most of the loads are food, which is common enough, but there are other things, too, barrels and crates with a suspiciously uniform look. "Something's happening."

"Thirsty Jack suggests a drink," Jack says, pointing to the town's only tavern, creatively called The Redtree Tavern. And perhaps a wagging tongue will clarify matters."

I glance at Meroe, who gives a little nod. The next step in the plan involves hiring a wagon to take us to the city, and the tavern is as good a place as any to start looking. I clear my throat.

"Okay," I tell them. "Remember we're trying to avoid notice, though. Let me do the talking." I glare at Jack until she meets my gaze. "Understood?"

"Clever Jack will attempt to conceal her natural brilliance, lest we attract undue attention," Jack says. "But a true diamond can never be hidden for long."

Zarun snorts, but says nothing. I lead the way to the tavern.

The place is surprisingly crowded for mid-morning. In fact, judging by the spills and vomit on the floor, I doubt they got the chance to close last night. I edge my way around the worst of it and claim a corner table still sticky with wine. I send Zarun to get us drinks and settle in for some eavesdropping.

Most of the tables in the tavern are occupied with chattering traders, and the conversations revolve around goods and prices. I hear some numbers which make me raise an eyebrow—if people in Kahnzoka are paying that much for grain and salt fish, then something must be seriously wrong. Storms, maybe, or a failed harvest?

"If this is what you Imperials call wine," Zarun says when he returns, "I can see why you're always trying to steal from us. A Jyashtani dog wouldn't deign to piss in this stuff."

"Charming," I mutter, as he passes wooden mugs across the table. "Now sit down and be quiet."

"It does have a certain . . . piquancy," Meroe says, wrinkling her nose at her cup. Jack drains half of hers in a single swallow.

"We're not exactly in the Imperial Palace here," I say, feeling a need to defend my hometown. "And even a backcountry tavern isn't going to waste the good stuff on this lot." I push my chair back. "Stay here. I'm going to see if I can get us a ride."

A couple of tables up from us, a pair of young men have been discussing the day's plan in loud voices. I've gathered that they have a pair of wagons, and that they were loaded with barrels of salt slitfish. Nobody who can afford not to eats slitfish, so they have to be hauling to the lower wards, and probably won't mind carrying a few paying passengers.

The two of them look at me as I sit down, and it takes me a moment to place their expressions. I'm used to contempt from the rich and fear from the poor, at least if they know my reputation, but this is neither. They're staring, and I'm abruptly conscious of my mismatched clothes, my ragged hair, and most of all the blue cross-hatching that wanders across my face.

This is going to take some getting used to.

"Morning, sirs," I say. It takes an effort to speak pure Imperial, instead of the polyglot mess we use on *Soliton*. "My friends and I were hoping for a ride to the city, down to the Sixteenth." I open my hand to show the gleam of silver. "We can pay."

One of the pair, a gangly youth with a patchy beard, gives a derisive snort. The other, his older brother for a guess, looks at me with another strange expression.

"I can give you a ride," he says, slowly, "but I'm wondering what rock you've been hiding under, and if you know what you'll be riding into."

I feel a prickle on the back of my neck. "Meaning what?"

"Meaning there ain't no more Sixteenth," he says. "My uncle had a little flat there, and a shop, but it's all smoke and ashes now, and my uncle along with it. The Sixteenth is *gone*, friend."

I don't remember jumping to my feet, but I must have. The next thing I know, everyone in the room is looking at me, and the two traders are frozen in place. I feel Meroe touch me gently on the shoulder.

"Gentlemen," she says, her Imperial fluent and correct. "Can we buy you a few drinks, and hear the whole story?"

2

TORI

The headquarters of the Red Sash Rebellion—which is what they're calling us now—is the old Ward Guard barracks in the southwest corner of the Eighth Ward. It was built to house a central reserve that could move via the military highway to prevent an uprising in any of the lower wards. Having failed in that purpose, it turned out be to be useful to us for similar reasons. Three stories high, backed against the ward walls on two sides, it's built like a fortress. There's a large square in front, formerly the site of a daily market, now used by Red Sashes for drills and practice. The shops and apartments around the edges have been taken over by Hasaka's people for more living space, their owners fled or kicked out.

A line of Red Sashes waits at the edge of the square, keeping back a small crowd of civilians. There's not much to distinguish the two groups, except for the eponymous swathes of crimson fabric and the spears in the hands of the former. Both look dirty and threadbare, though the Red Sashes are perhaps a bit better fed.

I cross the square from the small apartment building I've claimed for my own. I don't wear a sash, but no one challenges me—even if they didn't know me by sight, the trio of Blues behind me is identification enough. Two men and a woman in nondescript clothing, wearing the red sash of the revolution crossed with a blue one. That band of blue cloth and their eerie, silent movement marks them out, and the rebels in the square give us a wide berth. I can taste the tang of discomfort and fear in their minds, and the steady pulse of obedience from the Blues.

Which is as it should be. It's hard to believe I used to keep my Kindre senses shut down most of the time. It's like going through life with your eyes closed tight, out of fear of the sun.

The two soldiers at the front door bow as I enter, and I give them a brief nod. Inside, people bustle about, but armed Red Sashes and civilians alike pause whatever they're doing and bow, too. I used to stop them, but I've given up trying. Let them bow, if it makes them feel like someone's in charge.

We use the map room on the second floor for our conferences. It's cramped, nearly filled with a big table bearing a large-scale map of Kahnzoka and its wards. The others are already waiting when I arrive, and with a silent pulse of Kindre power I order the Blues to stay outside.

There are four of us left, the commanders of the rebellion, since Hotara died in the battle for the Sixteenth Ward. One way or another, we're all tied to Grandma Tadeka, whose death was the spark that started everything. Hasaka watched the door at Grandma's hospital and mage-blood sanctuary, and was the unofficial head of her security. He's a tall, powerfully built man, long arms wrapped in dark tattoos, and his time in the Ward Guard makes him an invaluable resource. Unfortunately, the rigors of rebellion have brought out the worst in his gloomy nature, and a dour, sullen expression now seems permanently etched onto his features. Still, what discipline and training the Red Sashes have, they mostly owe to his efforts, and he commands our fighting soldiers.

His boyfriend, Jakibsa, sits beside him, a stack of paper sorting itself in midair in front of him with a faint glow of Tartak blue. A pen hovers by his ear, revolving slowly. Jakibsa is cheerier than his lover, though you wouldn't know it to look at him. Long hair brushed forward over one side of his face can't entirely hide the red-and-white burn scars that disfigure him, and his gloved hands are nearly useless, forcing him to rely on his Tartak Well. At Grandma's, Jakibsa managed a wing of the hospital, tracking meals and medicine and linens—now he's our quartermaster, overseeing the rebellion's food, weapons, and supplies.

Giniva, on the other side of the table, is engrossed in a study of the map, unconsciously coiling and uncoiling the end of her thick braid around her fingers. She's a mage-blood, who'd joined the sanctuary just before everything exploded. She has every right to hate me—her sister had tried to join along with her, but I'd seen a plan to betray us in her mind and told Grandma to send her away. In spite of that, Giniva has never shown any resentment, attacking any work we put before her with quiet, understated efficiency. She's shown a particular flair for gathering and organizing information, so she's our head of intelligence, if you can dignify the haphazard collection of watchposts and patrols with the name.

And then, of course, there's me. Gelmei Tori, a few months past my fourteenth birthday, raised in a Third Ward mansion since I was eight years old, carefully insulated by hired servants from everything that was wrong with the world. A spoiled little girl who until a few months ago had never earned a day's wage, never kissed a boy, never made her own supper.

Isoka had wanted me that way, free from pain and need, protected from the bloodstains she gladly took on herself. All I wanted was to make her happy. Now she's gone, probably never coming back, probably dead, and it's for the best. I'm not who she wanted me to be, who I was supposed to be. I stabbed a boy in the throat and felt his hot blood gush across my hands. I crushed a woman's mind like a butterfly in my palm, and watched as she died at my command. I pulled a terrified family out of hiding and used them like hunting dogs to bring down my prey. I burned the Sixteenth Ward to ash and bone.

Monster, the voice in my head says. *Monster, monster, monster.*

The Red Sashes are what I have left. The three in this room, and everyone fighting for us out in the city, are what's left of Grandma's sanctuary and the people who joined us in the streets. I will do what I can for them. And, maybe, for the chance to get my hands around Kuon Naga's throat, and squeeze until his eyeballs pop like grapes.

As Grandma Tadeka once told me, sometimes you have to do what you can with what you have.

The others are all staring at me, waiting. I realize I've drifted off again, lost in my own thoughts. It's happening more than it used to. *Maybe Kindre is driving me mad.* Not that it matters. None of us are likely to live long enough to worry about our long-term mental health.

"Sorry," I mutter. "Thinking. Give me the news."

Hasaka and Jakibsa look at one another, and I can hear tinny anxiety in their minds. Giniva just sits up, expectant, calm as ever.

"Well," Hasaka says. "Not much news on my front. Some hints that more militia troops are moving into position off the Fourth District, but they haven't tried anything beyond the usual skirmishing."

"'The usual skirmishing'" means arrows fired back and forth, people dying in pain and blood. Just not very many of them. Not enough to really matter, and anyway probably more of *them* dying than *us,* which has to be a good thing, right?

Kahnzoka is a city of walls. The main defenses face outward, protecting the capital against any outside force. Inside, the wards are divided from one another by an interlocking set of barriers, manned by the Ward Guard. This is supposed to stop rebellions like ours, but the city's architects hadn't expected a secret gang of mage-bloods, nor the assistance of the criminal underworld and their smugglers' paths. We'd taken the city, down to the water-front and up to the Second and Third Wards, and manned those same walls against the government's counterattack.

We'd done as well as we had because the Ward Guard are better at beating up dissidents and taking bribes than actually fighting, and the provincial militias they'd called on for reinforcements are little better. The Navy is another matter, which is why we had to abandon the waterfront and pull back behind the north wall of the Sixteenth Ward, but so far we've held the rest. But the real soldiers of the Empire, the Invincible Legions, are out there somewhere, and everyone knows they have to be coming. It's just a matter of time.

"They're not gathering there for the fun of it," Jakibsa says. "They must be planning something."

"Or else it's a bluff," Giniva says quietly. "Or a feint, and the real attack is elsewhere."

"Exactly." Hasaka rests his fingertips against his forehead. "We can't know. And we have to guess right, because if they break through . . ."

He didn't have to finish. If they break through, we won't be able to stop them. We don't have the numbers for a street fight, not now that the Ward Guard's been reinforced. We have to hold at the walls, or not at all.

"Assign extra patrols to the Fourth's walls," I tell them. "If they're going to try something, it's not going to be a straight-ahead attack. They must have an edge. A hidden gate, or a weak spot."

"Or a traitor," Giniva muses.

"Or a traitor." I resolve to walk the wall myself, as soon as I get the chance. Betrayal is hard to hide from a Kindre adept.

"If this goes on much longer, there are going to be a lot more traitors," Jakibsa says. A sheet of paper shuffles itself free of the mess in front of him. "We finished our sweep last night. Everything edible is now in the depots."

"And?" Hasaka says, though I can feel the answer in his gloomy mind.

"Four weeks," Jakibsa says. "That's on short rations for Red Sashes and half for the civilians."

"Four weeks is long enough," Hasaka says. "The Legions will crush us before we starve."

"There's already a black market for food," Giniva says. "And it'll get worse as people get hungrier."

"Rotting hoarders," Jakibsa says. "Selling out their neighbors for a handful of gold they won't have the chance to spend."

"We should have started rationing sooner," Giniva says. "If we'd gathered food before the fire . . ."

They don't look at me, but I feel the surge of guilt anyway. I was the one who burned the Sixteenth Ward. I should have seen this coming. We hadn't worried about food as long as we had access to the sea—Kahnzoka Bay produced fish in plenty. After the Sixteenth burned, the Navy had taken control of the ruined docks, and we'd been forced to rely on stocks left in the city.

"There's more under the temples," Jakibsa says. "A lot more. But the Returners have them all locked tight."

"I still say we should go in there and break some heads," Hasaka says. "If they're not going to fight, they can at least share their bread."

Another stab of guilt. *A monster is a monster. What does a little more blood matter?* But there are some lines I won't cross. *Not yet, anyway,* my inner voice taunts. *Not until you can convince yourself you don't have a choice.*

"I'll talk to Kosura again," I tell Hasaka. "Today."

He grunts and concedes the point, though his mind radiates skepticism. I turn to Giniva. "You're working on finding the hoarders?"

"As best I can," she says. "It's not easy."

"I know." I blow out a breath. "How many cases for me today?"

"Two."

"Let's get that over with," I decide. Better to have my plate clear before I go to butt heads with the cultists. "Anything else?"

Jakibsa and Hasaka shake their heads. Giniva gets up, and I follow her out, the three Blues falling into step behind me. We descend through the chaos of headquarters in a bubble of quiet, activity stilling as we turn a corner and resuming behind us. How much of that is me and how much is Giniva, I don't know. Dealing with traitors is part of her job, and that tends to make people cautious.

There's an extensive prison under the barracks, now mostly empty. A few guards hang around the near end, where two small holding cells are occupied by a man and a young woman. The man is middle-aged, with a patchy beard and ragged clothes, a rotten-egg stink of panic rising off him. He looks up at me as I stop in front of his cage, baring his teeth in a snarl.

"Here she is," he says. "Rotting Queen of the Ashes. Hunting for your harem, is it? I heard you like it good and hard up the—"

One of the guards slams the bars with the butt of a spear, and the man subsides, his eyes wild. I look at Giniva.

"Attempted rape," she says. "A couple of Red Sashes saw him pull a woman into an alley. He pulled a knife on them."

"Acting like you have any right to tell us what to do," the man says. "Queen of the Rotting Ashes. You're going to be so much cold meat when the Legion gets here, and you know it."

Probably. But you won't be around to see it. Once I would have felt guilty about thoughts like that, but not anymore. "Hang him," I tell Giniva. "With a notice of what he did."

She nods, both of us as calm as though we hadn't just condemned a man to death. He howls in incoherent protest as we leave his cage, until the guards get tired of it and start beating him with the butts of their spears.

The girl in the other cell is calm, the fear I can sense in her mind not visible on her face. She sits cross-legged, dark hair cut short. I guess that she's seventeen or eighteen, with the hard, underfed look of a street kid from the lower wards.

She looks like Isoka. Not really. Her face is wrong, more broad and square than my sister's, but there's a hint of Isoka in her ropy muscles, the set of her jaw. I glance at Giniva.

"Desertion," Giniva says. "She was a guard on the wall of the Fifteenth, and the others on her shift caught her climbing down a rope ladder."

"Do you deny it?" I ask the girl.

She shakes her head tightly. "Why would I? It's the only sane thing to do." Her eyes bore into me. "We're all going to die here."

"What's your name?" I ask.

She snorts, and says nothing.

"It's Krea," Giniva supplies.

Krea. She really doesn't look much like Isoka. "I'll take her."

A sudden flare of fear from Krea. She looks at the floor of the cell to cover it. Giniva nods.

"I'll have her sent over," she says.

"Let me know how it goes with the hoarders," I tell her. "We're going to need to make a few examples once we catch up with them."

"Of course."

I give her a nod, and head back upstairs. Once again, the crowd parts in front of me.

Sometimes I feel like I'm watching myself, as though an actor were playing me on a stage and I'm just in the audience. Passing judgment, ordering patrols, making examples.

How did I get here? I can answer the question, step by step, but it doesn't feel real. How did quiet little Tori, who only wanted to drink plum juice and eat dumplings with her sister, turn into this?

You were always this, the voice—my voice—tells me. *A monster. You just don't have to pretend anymore.*

I want to go back to my room, wrap myself in my blanket, and sleep for a hundred years. Or forever.

Instead, I turn my steps toward the Temple of the Blessed's Mercy, and try to figure out how to talk to a fanatic.

The Temple is also in the Eighth Ward, on the east side. It's the largest in the city, big enough that it distorts the neighborhood around it by virtue of its ecclesiastical gravity. There are dozens of cheap hostels catering to pilgrims, and plenty of winesinks and gambling houses for the less than completely pious. In better times, the Temple's weekly procession always brought a crowd eager to watch the masked and costumed dancers carrying colorful floats, while supplicators droned prayers and vendors sold fried dough and roast potatoes.

Everything is quiet now, of course. The inns are shuttered, the winesinks silent. Even most of the apartments are empty. The

Eighth Ward borders the Third, not more than a mile from the Temple. Many civilians figure that any Imperial offensive will come downhill from the palace, and this will be the first target. Hasaka's opinion is that this is unlikely, since the walls are stronger here, but that isn't enough to stop people from seeking safety farther south.

The Temple of the Blessed's Mercy, on the other hand, is bustling. It's set back from the streets, its grounds surrounded by a high, spiked fence. The central building, with its distinctive double-curved roof like a broken-down horse, is supposed to be over three hundred years old, but it's surrounded by more modern constructions spread out through a carefully tended garden patch. Now it seems like every inch of that garden has been covered by tents, and the smoke from dozens of cookfires rises to mix with the steady stream from the temple's chimneys.

The Returners—the Followers of the Blessed's Return, as they call themselves—have been growing steadily since the Sixteenth Ward burned. It's not just here. There's at least a dozen big temples throughout Kahnzoka that have been converted into camps, with thousands of people seeking shelter behind their fences. They're nearly a city within a city, and whether they fall under the authority of the Red Sashes is . . . disputed.

A single guard waits at the temple gate, though what a guard who has sworn not to fight is supposed to accomplish is beyond me. She's dressed in a gray robe with a white belt, like all the Returners, and she bows deep, her freshly shaven scalp gleaming. "Miss Gelmei," she says. They all call me that. "Welcome."

"I need to see her," I say.

"Of course." The guard straightens and looks at my escort of Blues. "Your companions will have to wait outside, or surrender their weapons."

She seems serenely confident that I'll obey, and I feel no hint otherwise from her mind. It's one of the reasons I have trouble dealing with these Returners. I've grown too used to hypocrisy;

sincerity is unsettling. I send a Kindre signal to the Blues, and they stand back, blank faced. The guard smiles and leads me into the complex.

There are people all around, in the tents that sprawl over the grass. I can see them staring at me, and feel the suspicion rising in their minds. Most of them are still in civilian clothes, rather than Returner robes, and there are a great many children. I wonder how many desperate families have ended up here, terrified mothers gambling that sheltering on temple ground is a safer bet for their kids than helping the Red Sashes. In all honestly, they're probably not wrong.

We head for the ancient part of the temple. The doors are polished wood, carved with scenes from the Blessed One's life rubbed into illegibility by centuries of fingers. Inside, the floors are old-style reed mats, the walls pure white, hung with ancient paintings. We're not going into the main worship hall, but into the warren of chambers that adjoins it, where the supplicators of the Temple lived and worked.

"The Teacher has instructed that you be admitted to see her at any time," my guide says, when we reach a small sitting room. "Please wait here, and I will tell her you've arrived."

She bows again and bustles off. There's no furniture, just cushions on the floor. Even by the standards of the Third Ward, this place is old-fashioned, but I suppose that's only to be expected. I sit, years of etiquette lessons falling into place automatically, and give a polite smile to the boy who comes in with a steaming pot of tea.

Kosura arrives a few moments after that, the boy holding the door open and sliding it closed behind her. She wears a rough black robe, belted in white, and the beautiful hair I remember is shaved peach-fuzz close. Her injuries have mostly healed, but there's a patchy white scar beside her left eye. Though she moves with her customary grace, there's still a detectable limp. I suspect there always will be.

My heart does a queer flop in my chest, as it always does when

I see her. Kosura was my best friend at Grandma Tadeka's. She was the only one I trusted enough to talk about my encounter with Garo, and I can still remember her blushing face as she teased me about opening my shirt to help out a boy. Her starstruck certainty as she declared Garo must be in love with me.

It's hard to imagine the young woman in front of me giggling about a flirtation. There's a quiet calm to her that belies the horror she's been through. She was captured by the Immortals, along with Grandma and the rest at the hospital, and was one of the few who survived the attentions of their interrogators long enough for us to rescue them. Even then, bruised and broken, she'd seemed more hurt by Grandma's death than her own suffering.

And now she's running a cult, with all these fanatics calling her Teacher. The cynical part of my mind can't help but sneer.

"Tori," she says, kneeling on the cushion opposite me and settling back on her heels. "It's so good to see you."

"You too," I say, already feeling awkward.

"You're well?"

"Well enough." I scratch the back of my head. "You?"

"Well, by the Blessed One's grace. We live each day in hope of His imminent return."

"Right," I mutter. "That."

Theology isn't my specialty, and I never paid as much attention to my supplicator as I probably should have. As best I understand it, some accounts of the Blessed One's life record that before his ascent to Heaven, he said he would be reunited with believers. While most supplicators have held this to mean that *we* would go to *him,* if we were good enough, the Returners have decided it's the other way around—that the Blessed One is coming back, to punish the wicked and reward the righteous. There are prophecies, apparently.

"You think I'm misguided," Kosura says quietly.

"I didn't say that."

"I know you, remember?" She smiles, and just for a moment she looks like the old Kosura again, laughing as we do laundry.

"Stay here with me, Tori. Just for a few days. If you read the texts yourself—"

"Unfortunately, I don't have a few days." I rub my eyes with my palms. It's barely noon, and I'm already exhausted. "The Legion is coming, the militia is already pressing us, and we're running out of food." I fix her with a level stare. "I need you to open the temple granaries. The soldiers on the wall are on short rations as it is."

Kosura chews her lip for a moment, then shakes her head. "I can't."

Anger flares in my chest. "This is no time for everyone to start looking out for themselves."

"It's not about looking out for ourselves. If the temples are well-supplied, it's because people have entrusted that food to us knowing it would be used in accordance with the Blessed's principles. If those in need come to us, of course we will help them, but only if they abide by the proscriptions the Blessed One laid down in his teachings."

"That they don't fight, in other words. That they don't defend the city against Kuon Naga's rotting Immortals."

"It's not *just* fighting, but yes." Kosura closes her eyes, and rubs at her scar. "I know better than anyone what the Immortals can do. But answering violence with violence is not what the Blessed One would have of us."

"Easy to say when the rest of us are fighting for you," I snap, and grit my teeth. "Do you really think Naga's going to respect the sanctity of the temples when he takes the city? He'll have the Grand Supplicator and all his acolytes ready to condemn your lot as heretics." I take a deep breath, and soften my voice. "You're all going to *die*, Kosura. We all are, unless we win this."

"We're all going to die, regardless," Kosura says. "All humans do. That is the will of Heaven. What matters is what happens afterward."

What happens *afterward* is that you lie in the dirt and rot. I take another deep breath, fighting down frustration. I can feel Kosura's mind, burning with a pure certainty, and—

—it would be so *easy* to reach out to it. Just a touch, a twist, an adjustment. She would agree with me. She would be *happy* about it.

No. I swallow hard. *No, no, no.*

There has to be a line I won't cross. That even monsters won't cross. Kosura is my friend. She was tortured because of me, because I came to Grandma's and drew Kuon Naga's attention. If I do that to her, I might as well twist the whole city into puppets and be done.

I dream about that, most nights. Puppet strings running from my fingers.

"I'm sorry," Kosura says. "I know this is difficult for you. I wish I could help you find peace."

"Yeah, well. That seems unlikely." I let out a sigh. "I don't want to threaten you, so please don't take this the wrong way. But if things get worse—and they will—and rumors go around that the temples still have food, sooner or later people's respect is going to run out. When that happens, you and your followers could get hurt."

"*If* that happens, it will be as the Blessed One wills." Kosura inclines her head. "Before his return, we are taught there will be a time of trials we must endure. What is all this if not the fulfillment of that prophecy?"

"Fine." I've taken about as much of this as I can stand, and I get abruptly to my feet. "Good luck."

"There is no luck," Kosura says. "Only the Blessed's favor. I pray that it go with you as well, Tori."

There's more to do. Posts to visit, reports to listen to, decisions to make. I don't have the faintest idea what I'm doing, of course, but what I've come to understand is that it hardly matters. The answers to many questions are obvious; the important thing is that *someone* make the decision. That's half my role—not a figurehead, exactly, but the person who officially tells everyone to do what they know they should be doing anyway.

By the time I get back to my rooms, night is falling, and exhaustion has thickened into a headache that throbs in a ring around my skull. The three Blues who have accompanied me uncomplaining throughout the day are still by my side. I make a mental note to rotate them out, lest someone collapse in the middle of the street.

More Blues guard my quarters. They're the only people I can really trust. I've taken over a small building on the same square as Red Sash headquarters, in a row of shops and houses now occupied by rebel officers. A couple of dozen Blues stay there with me, while the rest are spread throughout the city. When I close my eyes, I can feel them, a net of linked minds like a spider's web.

The ground floor was once a pastry shop, but the shelves and tables have all been ripped out and replaced with bedrolls. A dozen Blues wait there, watching me silently as I clomp up the stairs to the apartment above. There's not a lot here. My own bedroom, at the back, and a small common room with a table and cushions. A second bedroom, which we use as a holding cell.

A whimper reminds me that the cell is occupied. One more duty to perform before I can put my head down for the evening. Two Blues, a man and a woman, both well-muscled, watch the door. At my mental command, they slide it open. The girl, Krea, is sitting in the back corner, pressed against the wall as if she wants to worm her way through it with her shoulder blades.

She really doesn't look much like Isoka. It's just something about her hair, her build. I can feel the fear in her mind, the stink coming off her like rotting meat.

"What do you *want* from me?" she whispers.

"Nothing, really." I sit cross-legged on the floor in front of her. My head throbs.

"Then let me go." Her voice is soft. "Please. I didn't hurt anybody. I just want to get *out* of here before—"

"The problem," I cut her off, "is that if we let deserters go free, pretty soon everyone would desert."

"Because we don't have a *chance*." Her voice is a hiss. "What's the point of fighting if we're just waiting until the Legion gets here?"

I resist the urge to shrug. Anger rises for a moment in her mind, then dies, smothered by fear.

"What are you going to do to me?" she says.

"You're going to help me," I tell her.

"How?"

"Like this." And I reach out to her mind.

I've done this often enough, now, that it's routine. I can feel the structure of her thoughts, the overwhelming fear, with little coils of other emotions beneath it, joy and lust and hate and all the rest. My power presses down with the force of a drop hammer, grinding everything beneath into dust. I flatten her out, smooth all the delicate intricacy of her humanity into flat nothingness, and then on that clean canvas I sketch out what I need.

Obedience, first and foremost. Eagerness. Fearlessness. And the little twist that lets a mind receive my mental commands, linking it in to the rest of the Blues, another node in the spider's web.

My artificial fanatics. After the fall of the Sixteenth Ward, the rebellion nearly collapsed. We needed people we could trust, people who would fight on no matter the odds and help inspire others to do likewise. At first I'd thought of using volunteers—but people who would volunteer for *this* are exactly the sort of people who are unlikely to need it, aren't they? And then a whole company of Red Sashes plotted to open the gates to the Immortals. Giniva's informers turned them in, and we had to figure out what to do with them.

At first I made excuses. Only prisoners, only people who'd committed crimes that would otherwise see them hanged in the square. Deserters, traitors, murderers. The longer this goes on, though, the more I only keep to those rules out of habit. It's hard to convince myself to care anymore. No one is going to forgive me, either way. *Monster.*

Krea has stopped her trembling. She sits calmly, now, looking at me with the same respectful patience as the other Blues. I can feel her mind, smooth and untroubled by doubts.

"There," I mutter, pushing myself to my feet. "Better than a short, sharp drop, right?"

She doesn't answer, because I haven't instructed her to.

In my nightmare, I'm climbing a mountain of corpses.

They're slick and cold beneath me, uncertain footing. I stumble, going down on my hands and knees. I feel someone's face under my palm, features contorted in pain. A hand by my foot, fingers curled and stiff in death.

I get back up, and take another step, and another. Bone gives way with a *crunch* under my boot. I grab a loose *kizen* for a handhold, and the fabric tears. I snatch at a lock of long hair instead, and use it to pull myself forward.

Ahead of me are men and women in blue sashes, adding more bodies to the pile. It's not a mountain after all, but a stairway, and they're building the next level even as I struggle to climb to the top. I don't look at the fresh corpses, but I know I'd recognize them. Instead I keep my eyes up, looking past the end of the ghastly steps, toward—what?

There was a reason I was climbing, when I started. I know that, but I don't remember what it was. I was trying to get somewhere, but now all that's ahead of me is darkness. And when I look back, for just a moment—

I wake up with a gasp, ice cold, drenched in sweat, my heart hammering and my breath coming fast. My head pounds, as though someone were sinking nails in it. I fumble for a mug of water beside me, manage to spill most of it on the bedroll, and swallow what's left. A command ripples out to the Blues for more, inaudible, irresistible.

Krea glides in a few moments later, mug in hand. She must have been the closest to my door. She's still wearing the dirty tunic she was arrested in, but she's added the red and blue sashes all my

Blues wear. She kneels down beside me and offers the mug, gentle and careful. I take it with a shaking hand, and manage to get most of the water down my throat this time.

She doesn't look much like Isoka, but in the dark I can almost pretend. She bends forward, puts her arms around me, pulls me closer. I huddle against her, shivering, my eyes shut tight against tears, and wait for morning.

3

ISOKA

"Are you all right?" Meroe says, for the twentieth time. She's hovering over my shoulder, hand out like she wants to touch me but is afraid to.

"I'm all right." It comes out too fast, too harsh, and I glance at her face and see the worry. I force myself to take a breath, relax my shoulders. "I'm all right."

"We don't know how much of what they told us is true," Zarun says. "Rumors get exaggerated."

"Indeed," Jack says. "Why, Clever Jack once overheard a tale of her own exploits she hardly recognized."

Another deep breath. "I know."

Exaggerated or not, the story the traders had told is enough to get my heart pounding. A rebellion, born out of a gang of rebel mage-bloods and a draft riot, that had not only escaped the control of the Ward Guard but undermined the walls to spread throughout the city. For all intents and purposes, Kahnzoka was under siege by its own government, the rebel-held wards surrounded by camps of Ward Guard and militia troops. That explains all the traders here in Redtree—the Imperial Nrmy is buying supplies at generous rates.

And the Sixteenth Ward, my home, the brutal, familiar world of dock scum and kidcatchers, corner noodle shops and rickety tenements—gone. The traders disagreed about who had set the fire—one said it was the rebels, the other the Ward Guard—but were certain that it had consumed everything between the wall and the waterfront.

I wonder, briefly, how many of the people I remember died in the conflagration. If there's anyone left who remembers me.

Later. I press the feeling down. *Focus, Isoka.*

"Tori's house is in the Third District, on the north side of the city," I say. "The traders said that was definitely still on the Imperial side of the line. We just have to get there." *And hope that she's still there, that she's okay, that—*

Enough. My fists clench, Melos power throbbing under my skin, as though my blades want to emerge of their own accord. *First, get there.*

Meroe sits down on the narrow bed, brow furrowing. We're in one of the upstairs rooms of the Redtree Inn, rented for a few hours for an exorbitant fee. It's about the size of a coffin, with a bed that wouldn't fit two of us. Zarun and Jack lean against the door, and I pace in what little room is left.

"That's not going to be easy, I think," she says. "I can't imagine they want loose civilians wandering around."

"The traders are going somewhere," Zarun points out.

"There'll be a system of passes," I say. "The Ward Guard loves passes. Can't get from here to there without the right bit of paper and the right stamp."

"Could we fake one?" Meroe says.

"Not easily." I frown. "Not without getting ahold of one, anyway. And if we can do that, we might as well just use it for ourselves."

"That makes things easy, then," Jack says. "The town is teeming with fine fat fish. We just have to catch one and pluck its feathers."

"Fish don't normally have feathers," Meroe says. "But she has a point. If we can distract one of the traders, maybe get them drunk, we might be able to get hold of a pass."

I shake my head. "Takes too long. We just have to find someone on the road and convince them to hand it over."

Meroe looks troubled. "Actual highway robbery? I just—"

"I think there's an easier way," Zarun says. When we both look at him, he rattles the pouch in his pocket, which makes a dull jingle.

"Oh," Meroe and I say together, then smile at one another. I give Zarun an embarrassed grin. "That should work."

"—and it's only that my grandfather is *very* ill, and he can't be moved," Meroe says. "And I promised I'd be with him before the end. I'd do anything."

The merchant—a gawky boy with a prominent Adam's apple that bobs when he swallows—has gone wide-eyed. Not from Meroe's story, which I doubt he's even hearing, but at the weight of the gold coins Zarun is patiently counting into his outstretched palm. They bear the name and face of a monarch who lived a thousand miles and two centuries from here, but gold is gold, whatever's stamped on it.

"We'll need your cart and horses," I tell him. "And whatever paperwork you've got for your delivery."

I'm trying not to sound too eager, and I suppress a sigh of relief as he digs a leather folio out of his satchel and hands it over. The first document is an official pass, allowing the bearer to transport a cargo of miscellaneous foodstuffs into the siege lines around the Third District, illegibly signed and with a blurry stamp. I pretend to riffle through the rest of the papers, which direct us to bring the wagon to some headquarters or other.

"I'll make sure this gets there," I say.

The boy nods, although I'm certain he no longer gives a rotting fishhead whether his cargo arrives. He sets off on foot up the road with enough gold in his pocket to buy most of Redtree. The part of me that spent years as a ward boss cynically gives him a life expectancy of about two days, but maybe things are a little less cutthroat out in the country.

In exchange for a handful of *Soliton*'s treasure, we have bought ourselves a run-down farm cart, pulled by an equally run-down pair of horses, laden so heavily with bags, barrels, and crates that it looks ready to tip over. The reddening light of the setting sun filters through the trees; we're just off the coast road, east of Redtree, where our trader was resting his team and enjoying a quiet smoke before we ambushed him with a small fortune.

There's only room for Meroe and me on the box, but Zarun makes space for himself and Jack by hurling a few sacks of rice into the woods. Meroe pulls herself up and takes the reins, and I hop up beside her, eyeing the rumps of the horses distrustfully.

"You know how to make them go, right?" I ask.

She laughs. "Yes, I know how to make them go." She looks up at the sky, where the clouds are blazing crimson. "We're not going to get far before dark, though."

"If we go through the night—"

"Then one of the horses is going to step in a rut and break a leg," she says. "And if we show up with a trader's pass with no cart, people are going to ask questions."

I clench my jaw for a moment, then force out a breath. *Whether Tori's safe or not, it's not likely to change by tomorrow morning.* "Okay."

"I know how hard this is for you," she says, quietly. "But we're almost there."

I give a jerky nod. *Almost there. I sail halfway around the world, and come back to find they've burned the rotting place down. Typical.*

We put a few more miles between us and town before the sun sets behind the screen of trees and the sky goes from red to purple to black. We don't have proper camping gear, but it's a mild night, so we munch on food from our packs and huddle together under blankets. Meroe tends the horses, which seem grateful for her efforts, and I fall asleep with her head on my shoulder and their thick equine scent in my nostrils.

As soon as it's light, we start moving again, in spite of Jack's complaints about the "cursed and ungodly hour." She eventually falls asleep in the back, curled up around a barrel of salted squid and snoring loudly. Zarun occupies himself poking through the cargo, occasionally asking me to identify something. He seems bemused.

"Imperials really eat this stuff?" he says, holding up a morsel from Jack's pillow by one dangling tentacle.

I snatch it from his fingers and shove it into my mouth. The squid is flat as a sheet of paper, crunchy and chewy both at once. Not bad, actually, though the salt makes me thirsty. I wash it down with a drink from my canteen.

"You ate crab on *Soliton*," I point out. "And don't Jyashtani eat snakes and crickets?"

"Only mad southerners eat snakes," he says. "But candied crickets are delicious."

"In Nimar we have many delicacies," Meroe says. "But my favorite was always rhinoceros testicles." She cups her hands, indicating something the size of an apple. "They're served raw, with just a touch of butter and salt."

There's a long, contemplative silence.

"That was a joke," Meroe says, with a wicked grin. Then, as I exhale, she adds, "*Obviously* we cook them."

I don't know if the two of them agreed to try to distract me, but I'm glad of the opportunity not to be alone with my thoughts as the cart crawls, desperately slow, along the coast road. We climb steadily, until by noon we reach the top of a promontory, a long ridge that stretches out like a finger into the bay. Having ascended in a series of lazy switchbacks, the road crosses over its spine before going down in the same fashion. Meroe brings the horses to a halt for a moment. From here we can see all of Kahnzoka, spread out on its hill a half day's journey ahead of us.

I've never been far enough from my city to really *see* it, except for that last night, when the Immortals rowed me out to *Soliton* and the lights looked like distant fireflies. In daylight, it's a vast, sprawling thing, roughly triangular, wide where it meets the sea and narrowing progressively as it climbs the hill. At the top is the Royal Ward, visible at this distance as a scattering of black-and-red buildings amidst an expanse of green. The First Ward has a fair amount of green, too, as do the Second and Third, before gardens and ornamental ponds give way to endless rows of wood-and-plaster buildings packed cheek-by-jowl, their sloping slate roofs close enough to touch. The military highways run through the chaotic tangle like knife wounds, one top-to-bottom, the other left-to-right.

But it's the Sixteenth Ward that draws my eye. Or where the Sixteenth Ward used to be, because it's clear the traders weren't exaggerating at all. The whole long strip between the water and the southernmost wall is a blackened ruin, a few half-burned structures leaning drunkenly amid the wasteland of charred wood and fallen tiles.

Here and there I can see patches of fluttering white, which I realize must be the tents of the besieging army, camps cleared out amidst the debris. Other than that, the only repair work going on is around the docks, where new piers are already stretching into the sea. Even that has barely begun, though. A small section around the Imperial Navy dockyard has been cleared, but most of the waterfront is still a mess of canted, blackened masts and wrecked moorings.

No wonder they've got so many traders coming in. The whole fishing fleet must have burned. Kahnzoka had long since grown past the point where it could feed itself entirely from the bay, but for the poorer part of the citizenry fish has always been a staple. With the docks in ruins, everything has to be shipped in overland.

Not that there are *no* ships visible. At least a dozen Navy galleys cruise up and down the waterfront, their gold-trimmed sails gleaming, and there are more farther out in the bay. *Good thing we didn't try to bring* Soliton *in this way.* With half the Navy on patrol, Naga would have spotted us immediately.

"I don't know," Zarun says. "I thought it would be bigger."

I glance at him, and catch a teasing grin. I manage to smile back, fighting a sinking feeling in the pit of my stomach.

"It'll look big enough when we get up close," I tell him. Meroe clicks her tongue, and the horses start their slow plod forward.

We run into the first checkpoint at the crossroads, where the coast road splits, one branch following the sea down to the Sixteenth Ward, the other winding up the hill to eventually meet with the military highway. A Ward Guard officer sits by the side of the road, yawning, while a squad of a dozen militia with spears and wooden helmets checks passes. I present our borrowed credentials, trying to look as bored as everyone else. The militiaman, a weathered farmer with gray in his beard, gives us a once-over. He lingers a little on Meroe and Zarun, with their foreign looks, but he eventually waves us through.

There's another checkpoint at the military highway, and another where we have to veer off onto a local path to ascend toward the Third Ward. By this point the siege lines are in sight, rows of identical white tents milling with militia soldiers. A perimeter of ditches and sharpened stakes lines the city-facing side, and then there's a hundred yards or so of no-man's-land, full of mud, grass, and abandoned shacks. Beyond that is the city wall, with a few figures visible on the battlements. At this distance, all that marks them as rebels is the red sashes they wear.

Zarun has been looking more nervous the closer we get to the city, keeping a wary eye on the militia. As the horses strain up the sloping dirt road, he worms his way forward, until he's close enough to speak to me and Meroe.

"Are we sure this is a good idea?" he says, quietly.

"Of course not," I say. "But I didn't hear any better ones."

"Is something wrong?" Meroe says.

"Just a lot of soldiers," Zarun mutters. "Makes my palms itch."

I give him a curious look. I know Zarun is the bastard son of some princeling, which is what earned him a one-way trip to *Soliton* when he became inconvenient. Other than that, he hasn't talked much about the time before he came to the ship. I wonder if he had some run-ins with the Jyashtani equivalent of the Ward Guard.

My own history with the guardians of peace and order in Kahnzoka is certainly a checkered one. But they don't frighten me. The thing about the Ward Guard is that they're fundamentally there to defend people with money and power from people without; to manipulate them, you just have to convince them you're on the right side. That's part of why I set Tori up with a house in the Third Ward instead of living high in the Sixteenth. When you live in the Third Ward, the guards work for you.

Not that this was enough to keep the residents from bolting at the first sign of trouble. We finally pass through the city wall, & well beyond the border of the rebel control. Once again, a militiaman checks our papers, then directs us where to take our cargo. Meroe thanks him effusively, and we ignore his instructions as soon as we're out of sight, following the broad, curving streets of the Second Ward toward the Third. Night is coming on, but nearly all the houses are still dark, the lampposts that mark their long drives untended.

"Does anyone actually live in this city?" Jack says, as we pass through a deserted crossroad.

"You have to be rich to live in this part of it," I say. "And if you're rich, you probably don't want to hang around when a bunch of peasants start getting ideas. I imagine there's been a run on guest rooms at country estates."

"And this is where your sister lives?" Zarun says.

I nod, and he gives a low whistle. Something tightens in my chest. *It was supposed to be* safe *here.*

Meroe grips my hand and gives it a squeeze.

Another gate separates the Second and Third Wards, but this one is closed up. We wave to a couple of guards, and then we're *finally* on the streets I remember. These houses are abandoned, too, and it suddenly occurs to be that Tori may not even *be* here. *What would Ofalo do? He knows he has to keep her safe or he'll answer to me.* Maybe he's gotten her away from the city.

If so, he'll have left a note. Something. I swallow as we turn onto Tori's street, and the horses' hooves crunch on the gravel drive. *There has to be something.*

The house is just as I remember it, all understated style and traditional Imperial lines, and the knot in my chest relaxes fractionally. It's not burned, or obviously looted, though the shutters are tightly closed as though in expectation of a storm. Meroe brings the cart to a stop, and I hop down, not waiting for the others. The front walk is lined with stands of decorative bamboo, recently trimmed. *Someone's still here.* I stride up to the front door, rap loudly, and after a moment's silence try to slide it open. It rattles in its frame—locked.

"Hello?" I try hard to keep the anxiety out of my voice. "It's Isoka. Open up!"

No answer. Meroe has caught up, waiting a pace behind me, not sure what to do. I glare at the door, my hands tightening into fists. My blades would make short work of lock and bar, but—

"Hello?" The voice comes from around the side of the house. "Is someone there?"

A man pushes a wheelbarrow around the corner and stops, gawking. I recognize him—a skinny, ferret-looking gardener with too-large front teeth. I round on him, and my face must be thunderous, because he backs up a step in obvious alarm. Fortunately, Meroe is quickly beside him, speaking in soothing tones and slipping a silver coin into his hand. He looks down at it briefly, then back up at me, and raises his eyebrows.

"What happened here?" I ask him. "Where is everybody?"

"Dunno much," he says. "Master Ofalo took the staff north when the fighting started. Staying with friends in Jinzoka, I hear. Doubled my wage to stay on and keep the grounds up."

I stand still for a moment and absorb this information. On the one hand, it will slow us down—Jinzoka is at least two weeks' travel, well inland. On the other, it means we can get away from the mess here in Kahnzoka, and if Kuon Naga has a full-fledged rebellion in the capital to deal with, he may not have time to worry about us after all. On the whole, I think, the news is welcome. I catch Meroe's eye, and she gives a relieved nod.

"You're sure about that?" I ask the gardener. "He and Tori are in Jinzoka?"

The man blinks, then shakes his head. "Master Ofalo might be in Jinzoka, but Miss Tori surely isn't. She ran off before all this got going. Everyone says she's with the Red Sashes now—Master Ofalo said it was ridiculous, but Chen heard from his cousin that *she* heard—"

The tension that had been draining out of me rushes back. I step forward, and I can feel the prickle of Melos energy in my arms. The gardener quails again, and Meroe puts a warning hand on my chest.

"Tell me," I growl.

"There's . . . there's not much to tell," the man says, voice quivering. "Not for sure. Miss Tori was ill for a while, or at least spending a lot of time in her room. Then one day she was gone. Master Ofalo organized a search and had the Ward Guard out looking for her, and that's where we got rumors she was down in the Eleventh Ward, maybe with a young man. But before we could figure out where exactly, the riots started. The Ward Guard shut all the gates, and after the first big battle Master Ofalo said it wasn't safe for the girls and such to stay around here." He swallows hard. "That's all I know, I swear."

Rotting Ofalo. That was unfair, and I knew it, but I couldn't help myself. *I'll kill him. I'll rotting kill him.* I'd paid him—paid him a *fortune*, by Sixteenth Ward standards—to keep Tori safe. That he'd been unable to hide her from the Immortals was one thing. Letting her do something as stupid as running away to the Eleventh Ward—

"Isoka," Meroe says. "Not here."

I was *so close.* At Tori's front door. And now . . .

"She's *with* the Red Sashes?" I say. It takes an effort to keep my voice steady. "As in she's one of them?"

"Don't know that for sure," the gardener says. He clearly wants nothing more than to get away from this conversation, silver coin or no silver coin. "Just what Chen's cousin heard."

I snort and turn away, leaving Meroe to reassure the man and slip him another coin. I stalk across the drive, kicking at the gravel and desperately trying to keep myself on a leash. I want to scream, to summon my blades and chop something into kindling.

Finally, the gardener is gone. Meroe and I return to our cart, where Jack and Zarun are waiting.

"Perspicacious Jack senses that all has not gone as planned," Jack says.

"She's not here," I growl. I want to lash out, so badly, but my friends don't deserve it.

"Not here," Zarun says, "as in—"

"The household has fled the fighting," Meroe says. "But the groundskeeper was certain that Tori left before then, and that she's somewhere in the rebel part of the city."

"That doesn't make any rotting *sense*," I say. "Why in the Blessed's Name would she be down in the Eleventh Ward in the first place, much less joining a rebellion?"

"He said there might have been a boy involved," Meroe says.

"Tori's too young for that," I snap, then catch Zarun's look. "What?"

"You said she was fourteen?" he says. "Plenty of fourteen-year-olds have done stupid things for a pretty face."

"True enough," Jack says. "It may surprise you, but even Jack's own decisions have occasionally been less than perfect in the face of her . . . urges."

"I don't need to hear about my little sister's *urges*." I rub my hand over my face. "All right, fine. She's getting to that age. But she ought to have better sense. I mean . . ."

"You don't know what happened," Meroe says, putting her hand on my shoulder. "Or what things have been like while you've been gone."

"Or whether any of this is true." I shake my head. "Maybe the rotting gardener is wrong, and she's with Ofalo on the road to

Jinzoka." *Or maybe the story about the Red Sashes is a plant, and Naga's already snatched her and stuffed her in some dungeon cell*—I cut the thought off abruptly.

"He seemed honest," Meroe says. "But he may have been misinformed."

"So you want to head north, then?" Zarun says. "Find Ofalo and get the whole story?"

"We don't have the time." I grit my teeth. "Two weeks to Jinzoka, two weeks back. This rotting rebellion will be dead and buried by then, and if Tori *is* here, she could easily get killed with it. Not to mention that's nearly a month for Kuon Naga to figure out we're back and send the Immortals after us. We have to go inside now."

"That's not going to be easy," Zarun says. "In *or* out."

"I know. But it's the best chance we have." I shake my head. "I can go in alone. This is going to be much more dangerous than we thought—"

"Isoka," Meroe says, "please stop being ridiculous."

"Agreed," Jack says. "A few rebels do not frighten the bold conquerors of Prime's ziggurat."

"I always figured this would be a mess," Zarun says. "Everything seems to be, with you."

"Thanks." I take a deep breath, and try to let some of the tension out with it. *My friends.* At least something good has come out of all this.

"Any ideas on how we get past the lines and over the wall?" Meroe says.

"That shouldn't be the difficult part." I glance to the south, toward the ward wall, though from here it's invisible behind a screen of trees. "It's the Ward Guard running the show. And if there's one thing I learned in the Sixteenth, it's that a Ward Guard officer never met a rotting bribe he didn't like."

As the old joke goes: how do you find a corrupt Ward Guard officer?

First, throw a rock. Second, pay him off so he doesn't run you in for rock-tossing.

You might think that being in the middle of an actual siege against rebels would inspire an increased devotion to duty, but you would be wrong. At times like these, all the regular rules and procedures go out the window, which means even more opportunity to line one's own pocket. Sure enough, at the first section of wall we approach, the Ward Guard officer in charge proves willing to have a quiet conversation about the disposition of our cart full of supplies. With a little bit of *Soliton* gold in his hand, he readily agrees to slip us past his own sentries.

"Mind you, I can't guarantee that it'll be open," the man says, blowing at the corners of an enormous mustache. "And dealing with the rebels on the other side is your business. As is getting out again."

"Don't worry about that," I tell him. "The rebels pay well enough that we can afford it."

The officer gives a snort. "Not as though it's going to matter either way. The Legions will be here before they have the chance to starve."

He bids us to wait until nightfall, to reduce the chance of discovery—less because he's worried about getting in trouble, I gather, than because anyone who stumbles onto us would want a share of the bribe. The four of us pull the cart into a side street, out of sight of the troops camped below the wall, and we wait an hour for the sun to slip below the horizon.

Zarun is glaring in the direction of the Ward Guard officer and his men, looking disgusted.

"Is there a problem?" I ask him.

"Not for us," he says. "I'm just surprised that a soldier would let us supply his enemies for a pocketful of gold."

"Ward Guard aren't proper soldiers," I tell him. "They're just bullies in uniform, and the militia are farmers and tradesmen doing a month's service."

"Everyone seems confident the Legions will deal with the rebels when they arrive," Meroe says.

I shrug. "They've got good reason. If you're a commoner born a mage-blood and you're not taken by a noble family as breeding stock, you probably end up in the Legions. With that much sorcery, they can roll over any non–mage-blood force."

She grimaces. "The way you Imperials treat your mage-bloods is . . ." Meroe glances at me, and trails off.

"Barbaric?" I supply.

"I didn't want to be insulting."

"Go ahead. I spent half my life dodging the Immortals because of my Well, and when they caught up with me they threw me on *Soliton*. I'm not going to defend them."

"Jack has a similar tale of woe," Jack says, which makes me perk up a little. Jack has never shared much about her past. But she only adds, "On the other hand, if not for being exiled to *Soliton*, there would have been no relationship with the lovely Thora."

"What are we going to do when we're through the lines?" Zarun says.

"Try not to kill anyone," I tell him. "Apart from that, I'm going to improvise."

Eventually the walrus-faced officer returns and beckons us forward. Meroe drives the cart down a narrow street, running to the base of the wall, while the rest of us walk beside it on foot. A few stakes block the road, but they've been pulled aside, and two sentries with torches salute the Ward Guard officer as he waves us through. As easy as that, we're in no-man's-land, between the Imperial positions and the rebel-held fortification.

The gate is a small one, a double door in the base of the wall barely big enough for our cart. Like all the Third Ward's fortifications, it was designed to keep people *out*, and the rebels had to hastily fit it with a bar on the other side. I watch the wall overhead for the silhouette of night patrols, but if they're there they're keeping out of sight.

Meroe brings the horses to a halt in the shadow of the wall, and I go to the gate. Not much chance the rebels will open it for the asking, so I ignite my blades, first taking care that the cart is between me and anyone who might see the flare of green. It's the work of a few seconds to carve through the bar with Melos power, and the gate swings open to a push. Beyond is another side street, leading down into the Eighth Ward, where the buildings are packed tighter but still put up a respectable façade. Shops with glass fronts line both sides of the road, though many are boarded over now. Above them are apartments with darkened windows like empty eye sockets.

A small barricade has been set up, in case the enemy makes a push through this gate. Crates and furniture block the road, and a voice barks an order. Men and women rise up from behind the obstacle, at least a dozen of them, all with leveled crossbows. More lean out of the doorways of the nearest shops, and there's a few on the wall behind us.

All right. So the rebels aren't *completely* idiotic. *Probably better for us in the long run.* I spread my hands, cautiously, and raise my voice. "Who's in charge here?"

"That would be me." A short woman with her hair in a bun walks out from behind the line of crossbowmen, carrying a lantern. She has to be at least fifty. In the light, I can see she—and the rest of them—wear a crimson sash diagonally across their chests. "I have to say, if you lot are spies, chopping through a gate is a really stupid way to try to get through the lines."

"Which means we're probably not rotting spies, right?" I grin, hoping for a laugh, and don't get one.

"If you're not spies," the woman says, "how'd you get through Imperial lines?"

"Bribed 'em," I answer promptly. "You know Ward Guard."

"And what've you got in the cart?"

"Food, mostly," I say. "Originally meant for His Imperial Majesty's Nrmy, now our gift to the Red Sash rebels."

I can see the effect this produces on the faces of the rebel soldiers. There's a lean, pinched look to them: not starving exactly, but certainly not well fed. The officer with the lantern frowns.

"That's awfully generous of you," she says. "What are we expected to offer in return for this gift?"

"Nothing," I say. "Except to let us be on our way."

"Which is exactly the sort of thing a spy would say," she mutters. "You're not very good at this."

"Or I'm just being rotting honest."

She beckons two of her men over, and they start a conversation in low tones. I catch the words, "can't get much worse," and "rotting hungry."

"Think it'll work?" Zarun says in a whisper.

"Probably." I shift slightly. "If it doesn't, I'll take the ones on the left, you take the ones on the right, and do your best to cover Meroe."

He grunts acknowledgment. The argument among the rebels reaches some sort of conclusion, and the officer raises her lantern.

"Well," she says, "we agree that you're much too stupid to be spies. So—"

"What's happening here?"

A man's voice, utterly calm and devoid of emotion. The rebel officer freezes at the sight of three people coming down the street toward the blockade. The soldiers look over their shoulders, and a dark muttering passes among them. I hear the word "Blues," and several people make quick signs of blessing against evil.

The trio, once they come into the range of the lantern light, seem ordinary enough. Like the other rebel soldiers, they're dressed in everyday worker's clothes, running to ragged. In addition to the red sash, these three wear a blue sash running the other way. What that means, I have no idea, but the officer is instantly deferential.

"These four came through, sir," she says. "The one with the tattoos is Melos; she cut through the gate. Say they've got food in the cart for the cause."

The closest blue-sash looks us over. There's something strange about his eyes. Not vacant, exactly, but . . . unconcerned.

"We will bring them to headquarters for questioning," he says, in the same monotone. "And the wagon will be taken to our ration depot. Detail four soldiers for an escort, please."

"Of course, sir." The officer points to four of the crossbowmen, who get hurriedly to their feet. "The rest of you, clear a path! We need to get this cart to the depot."

"I don't like this," Meroe whispers.

"I'm not rotting crazy about it myself," I mutter.

"So we break out," Zarun says.

"Jack stands ready," Jack adds.

"I think we don't, for now," I tell them. "Keep nice and calm."

"You're sure?" Zarun says.

"They're taking us to their headquarters, which seems like a good place to ask questions," I tell him. "If we don't like the answers, *then* we can start a fight."

The rebel headquarters, it turns out, is in the old Ward Guard barracks, at the very far end of the Eighth Ward, which means we have a ways to walk. In spite of the late hour, once we get away from the vicinity of the wall there are signs of life in the streets. All the shops are closed, but there are fires at regular intervals, and small groups huddled around them. Makeshift shelters built of wood and canvas line the road. The sight of our cart draws people's attention, and they gawk, giving the blue-sashed soldiers a respectful distance. Most watch in silence, but a few call out.

"Spare something, sir?"

"My daughter—she's so hungry, please—"

"Just a handful—"

I'm sitting on the box with Meroe again, Jack and Zarun in the back, the blue-sashes and the crossbowmen walking alongside. Meroe's hand finds mine, and our fingers interlace. I give her a squeeze.

"They're starving," she says, quietly.

"That's sort of the point of a siege, yeah." I look over the sea of hollow faces. "I think these are Sixteenth District people." *My people.* "If the whole waterfront burned, and nobody wants to live near the outer walls, that's a lot of people without roofs."

"It's awful." She pulls in closer to me. Meroe being Meroe, I know her mind is racing, trying to figure out some way to help.

I should be thinking about that, too. This is my city, and it's tearing itself apart. But all I can do is scan the crowds for Tori's face. *Would I even recognize her?* It's only been a few months, but you just have to look at me to see how much a few months can change a person.

Eventually we reach the square outside the old Ward Guard barracks. A line of Red Sashes are on guard, and I look for Tori there, too, as they stand aside and let us through. The blue-sashed soldiers lead us past more guards at the front door, who stiffen. Zarun eyes the rebel soldiers, catches my gaze, and shrugs.

I hope we won't need to fight our way out. But I have to admit it's comforting having him along, just in case.

We're hustled through a confusing warren of passages and stairs into a plain room with a round table. A blue-sashed man has stayed with us, and he asks us to sit and wait. His companions have broken off somewhere along the way, presumably to tell someone important we're here. *So far, so good.* At least nobody's taking us to the dungeon.

A few minutes later, the door opens, admitting a big, burly man, his long arms heavily tattooed. I recognize a few bits of Ward Guard imagery, but those days are apparently behind him, because he's wearing a red sash and the other rebels salute as he comes in. He looks down at us, the bags under his narrowed eyes speaking of too many nights without sleep.

"Who in the Rot are you?" he says. "Thanks for the food, I suppose, but I'm not sure what you thought you were doing. If you haven't noticed, this is a rotting siege."

"We're aware of that," I tell him. "I'm here to find my sister. That's all."

"Oh, I see." He shakes his head and slides into a chair across from us. "I've heard that story before. Saving her from the horrors of war, is that it?"

"Something like that," I say. "If you can help me find her, then we'll be on our way."

"On your way?" He stares at me incredulously. "You *have* noticed that we're surrounded by the Imperial Nrmy?"

"Let me worry about that," I say. "Please. This doesn't have to be difficult."

"Even if I was inclined to help, do you know how many people are in hiding, just here in the Eighth Ward? We don't have the resources—

"Then just let us search," I cut in. "That's all we ask."

"And very conveniently give a bunch of potential spies the run of the city." He scratches his beard. "No, I think not. You'll spend the night in the cells, and in the morning Tori can have a look at you. She'll soon find out—"

"Tori." I'm on my feet, and the Red Sash guards level their spears. I put one hand on Meroe's shoulder, ready to shove her behind me, and I sensed Zarun tense. "Where is she?"

"Tori?" The Red Sash commander stares at me, incredulously. "*Tori* is your sister? That makes you—"

"Isoka!" The voice is muffled, outside the room. The blue-sashed guard slides the door open, then steps aside.

Standing in the doorway, gasping for breath, is my sister.

4

TORI

There's a long, long silence, broken by the rattle of breath in my lungs. I'd sprinted across the square from my quarters, and a stitch digs painfully into my side. I ignore it, and everything else, my eyes only on *her*.

"Hasaka," I say. "Take everyone downstairs, please, and leave us alone until I call for you."

"Are you certain?" His voice seems distant. "She might be dangerous—"

"*Rotting do it*, please. Now."

Isoka's eyes go a little wider at hearing such language from me. Of course they do. The Tori she knows wears a *kizen* and speaks quietly about pleasant things. What is she going to think of me now?

You know what she'll think. Monster, monster, monster—

People shuffle out of the room—Hasaka, the guards, a few others whose presence I hadn't even registered. The Blue slides the door shut behind them, and I feel the pulse of his mind as he positions himself outside. Then we're alone.

"Tori?" Isoka's voice is hesitant.

I take one step forward, then another. Then I'm running to her, throwing myself against her, already wracked with sobs.

Isoka puts her arms around me. I have this dream, some nights, where I see her again. Around this point, she usually tells me I'm a monster and kills me, splitting me on her Melos blades or slashing my throat. I don't know if this is a dream or not, and I don't care.

My heart thumps wildly against my ribs, as though trying to break through them and escape. Isoka's hands settle on my shuddering shoulders, tentatively, like wild birds.

I don't know how long we stay like that, the tears spilling out of me in a great ugly torrent, soaking the front of Isoka's shirt. She says nothing, just holds me, her chin pressed against my hair.

By the time I raise my head, I feel empty, wrung out, like laundry put through a mangle. Isoka looks down at me, and there are tears in her eyes, too.

"I thought you were dead." My voice sounds strange in my ears.

"I thought . . ." Her hand brushes over my face, down through my hair. "A lot of things."

"You look . . . different."

That is an understatement. Her hair is shorter, and some kind of tattoo stretches across her face, blue cross-hatches in a wandering line. There's something in her expression, too, something I can't quite place.

"It's been a long trip," Isoka says. "I'm sorry I wasn't here when . . . all this started. You must have thought I'd abandoned you."

"Of course not," I blurt out. "I thought—I found out what happened. That Kuon Naga took you, and sent you to *Soliton.*" Never mind exactly *how* I'd found that out—squeezed out of an Immortal captain, her mind crushed like soft fruit in the grip of my power. "Nobody ever comes back from that. I thought I'd never see you again."

"Nothing could stop me from coming back to you." There's an odd glitter in Isoka's eye. "Not if I had to go to the Vile Rot and back. Which, as a matter of fact, I did."

"The . . . the Rot?" I shake my head. "That's—"

"Like I said, it's been a long trip." Isoka's features take on a business-like calm. "We can talk about it later. Right now the most important thing is getting you out of here. Will the rebels let you use one of the gates into the Sixteenth District?"

"P . . . probably," I say, not quite keeping up. "But there are Imperial troops there."

"We can handle a few Ward Guard," she says. "At least long enough to get to the waterfront."

"The waterfront burned," I say. *I burned it.* "There aren't any ships. Even if we stole a boat, we'd never get past the Navy—"

"No need to worry about that," Isoka says. "I already stole one, and I'd like to see the Navy try and stop it. If we can get to the water, we're safe."

"What do you mean, we're safe?" I take a step back, shaking my head. The gleam in Isoka's eye is almost manic. "Isoka, why do you want to *go*? You just made it home!"

"Home is a pile of ashes," Isoka says. "But it's all right, Tori. It's hard to explain, but I've found somewhere we can go. Away from Kuon Naga, away from the Empire and the Jyashtani and *everyone*. A place where mage-bloods don't have to hide from the Immortals or anyone else." She grins, and reaches for me. "You don't have to worry about anything anymore, I promise. I know it must have been hard for you, while I was gone, but now I'm going to take care of everything."

I back away again, and Isoka frowns.

"What's wrong?"

"I'm not . . . you don't understand." I feel like I'm fighting for air. My heart is still hammering. "What about everyone *else*? The rebels?"

"What about them?" Isoka straightens up. "We can't save everyone. They made their choice, and they'll suffer the consequences."

"You mean they'll be killed."

"The rebellion will be crushed, like every other rebellion against the Empire," she says. "Which is all the more reason not to stick around."

There's a long silence, broken only by the pounding of my pulse in my ears.

"We," I say, quietly.

"What?"

"*We* made *our* choice. I was part of this from the beginning." *And my hands are soaked in blood.* "I can't just . . . leave." *I don't deserve to.*

"You can," Isoka says. "Just trust me."

"I need to . . . think." I turn to the door, fists clenching. "I'm sorry."

"Tori!" Isoka comes after me, and I pull the door open. The Blue waiting outside lets me pass, then steps between us. "Tori, wait!"

I flee.

ISOKA

"I'm telling you, someone's gotten to her." I pace across the carpeted floor, back and forth, in front of Meroe. "Hasaka or this Giniva or . . . *someone.* She didn't sound like herself."

"You don't know what she's been through," Meroe says.

"I know *her.*"

The insistence sounds hollow, even in my own ears. *Do I, really?* Who is this girl with Tori's face, who gives orders and accepts the salutes of grown men as her due?

"Isoka, stop." Meroe reaches out and grabs my elbow. "Please. You're giving me a headache."

"Sorry," I mutter. Then I pause, and look up at her. Her face is pale, and there's something hollow in her eyes. "Are you all right?"

"I don't know." Meroe swallows. "I wasn't expecting . . . this."

She gestures at the windows, and I take her meaning. We've been escorted, politely but firmly, to an apartment in one of the buildings adjoining the rebel headquarters. It's big enough for a family of four, with furniture hastily pushed aside to make room for miscellaneous supplies. I get the sense that the rebellion doesn't have a lot of practice with guests it can't stash in a prison cell.

Outside the window, the first fingers of dawn are creeping into the eastern sky, and people are gathering in the square. A queue is forming, policed by Red Sashes with spears, snaking back and forth across the cobbles. It grows by the hour, an endless line of people, mostly women and children in shabby, mismatched clothes.

"This is the central ration depot," Meroe says quietly. "Giniva told me on the way over. They start distributing food at dawn, but people line up all night. Everyone's scared they're going to run out before they get their share."

"There's nothing we can do," I tell her. "I'm not saying I like it, Blessed knows, but . . ."

"There ought to be *something*." She looks up at me. "You said there was nothing we could do to save *Soliton*'s crew, when you wanted me to run away to the Garden with you."

"That's different," I mutter. "We can't just take everybody with us this time."

I'd actually thought about that, after I'd calmed down. *Just march the whole rebellion down to* Soliton *and sail away, thumbing our noses at Kuon Naga. Maybe that would make Tori happy.* But the numbers just don't work out. There have to be thousands of Red Sashes, probably tens of thousands. If we try to move them all aboard ship at once, the Imperials will attack, and the result will be a massacre. And that says nothing of the civilians who would be left behind.

"I know," Meroe says. "I'm sorry. It's not that I have any answers. I just look out at that and . . . I can't bear it."

I wrap my arms around her, and she leans her head against my shoulder. For a moment, we just breathe.

"Jack requires sustenance!" Jack shouts, from the other room.

Meroe looks up at me, and we both break into giggles. She leans back, wiping her eyes.

"I suppose it has been a while since dinner," she says.

"Given that we brought them a wagonload of food, I imagine the rebels won't begrudge us a meal or two."

"I'll talk to Giniva," Meroe says. She seems to have formed a rapport with the soft-spoken rebel lieutenant into whose custody we've been given. We're not prisoners, exactly—the door isn't locked, but it *is* guarded, by two ordinary rebels and one of the strange soldiers they call Blues. One of the guards escorts Meroe away.

"We could still fight our way out," Zarun says. He's sitting on a couch in the front room, with his boots propped on a barrel and his hands behind his head. "There may be a few mage-bloods around, but most of the guards don't seem like anything special."

"Silent Jack could slip out to gather information." Jack, lying on her back in a corner, walks her feet up the wall, leaving black marks on the plaster. "Or seduce both guards at once!"

"Don't think Thora would like that," Zarun drawls.

"Thora would forgive a little seduction in the name of a daring escape," Jacks says. "She knows Jack's heart is forever hers, no matter how many fools declare themselves slaves of Jack's beauty and brilliance."

"Let's not do anything drastic quite yet," I tell them. "Tori and I just need to . . . talk."

But the clock is ticking, just like it was in the Harbor. *The longer we stay here, right under Naga's nose, the better the chance that he's going to catch on.*

I turn at the sound of footsteps outside, and the door slides open. Meroe's there, with Giniva. The rebel girl is our age, pretty and well built, with a long braid and a sense of quiet determination. She looks us over for a moment, then says, "A meal has been prepared. And Miss Tori would like to speak with you."

"Finally," I mutter.

"Jack agrees," Jack says, pushing away from the wall and rolling to her feet. "Her stomach growls fiercely!"

"The guards will show you the way," Giniva says. "Isoka, if I could speak to you alone for a moment?"

I'm not sure I like the sound of *that*, but I shrug. Meroe leads the others out of the room, and Giniva steps closer, lowering her voice.

"Tori told me about her sister," the girl says. "She practically worshiped her, but I always thought she sounded like a bit of a thug."

I find myself smiling, slow and dangerous. "You're not wrong."

"I don't know what you're doing here," Giniva says. "But if you've come to hurt her, just know that you're going to have to go through me first, and I won't be the only one. Tori saved all our lives, more than once."

I have a hard time imagining that; gossipy, friendly Tori saving lives by . . . what, chatting the enemy to death? But, as Meroe keeps reminding me, I don't know what she's been through. I give another shrug.

"She's my sister," I tell Giniva. "I'm here to help her, not hurt her."

"That may not be the way she sees it." Giniva frowns. "Anyway. Just so you know where you stand."

"I appreciate it," I say, dryly. Having been threatened by the likes of Prime or the Butcher, this girl's fierce little announcement is more cute than anything, but it wouldn't be diplomatic to tell her that. I try to act properly cowed as I follow her out and into the building, down a set of stairs to a dining room.

A big table has been laid with platters of food, basic but plentiful—rice, smoked fish, dumplings and soup, bowls of pickles and dried plums. Jack has already started in, eating with her bare hands, while Meroe helps herself a little more delicately and Zarun fumbles with a pair of chopsticks. Tori sits across the table, picking absently at a plate of plain rice. She looks exhausted, like all of the rebels, dressed in ragged worker's clothes, her long, beautiful hair pinned up in an untidy bun. There's a scar on her left arm, a knife wound. I've already sworn to find whoever gave it to her and twist their head off their body.

"Isoka," she says. "Giniva. Sit and have something to eat." When I hesitate, she meets my eyes. "Please."

Reluctantly, I take a seat beside Meroe, opposite a darkened window looking on the square. After a moment, I awkwardly clear my throat. "I suppose I should do introductions. Tori, these are my friends Meroe, Zarun, and Jack. Everyone, this is my sister Tori."

"We've heard quite a lot about you," Meroe says, diplomatically.

"Indeed," Jack says, mouth full.

"You met Hasaka," Tori says. "He's our military commander. Giniva runs intelligence and security. Jakibsa is still over working in the depot, but he's in charge of logistics."

"And what do you do?" I say.

Tori hesitates.

"She's in charge," Giniva cuts in.

"In charge?" Zarun raises an eyebrow. "Of the whole rebellion?"

"Yes," Giniva snaps. Tori blushes, silently. "Is that going to be a problem?"

"Oh, no," Zarun says, poking at his smoked fish with one chopstick. "I was just . . . curious."

"Tori," I say, trying to keep my voice level. "Maybe we should talk in private."

Giniva scowls, but Tori gets to her feet, and we retreat to the corner. Meroe gives me a curious look, which I do my best to ignore.

"You're in *charge*?" I say.

"It's a long story," Tori says.

"I'd be interested to hear it."

"Some other time." Tori looks anxious, unhappy. "But you see how it is. I'm *responsible* for this. I can't just leave."

"Look." I take a deep breath, fighting to keep my temper in check. I don't want her running off again. "I understand how everything can feel like your responsibility. But you can't take all of this on yourself. We have to *go,* before it's too late."

"You don't—" Tori bites off her response, frustrated. "You're not listening to me."

"I'm trying," I say. "What exactly do you want to do? Stay here and die?"

"Stay here and *fight*." Tori looks up at me. "If you help us, we might have a chance."

"If *I* help?" I choke off a laugh. "I'm just trying to get out of here before Kuon Naga and his Immortals find us."

"Why should we have to run away? This is our home." Tori gestures around her. "If you want to fight Kuon Naga, we'll be with you."

"I don't want to fight Kuon Naga," I growl. "I never did. I was happy when he left me alone, and all I ever wanted was—"

I cut off, and Tori glares at me. "What?"

"—to keep *you* safe. You know that, don't you?"

"Of course I do. But *safe* isn't good enough, Isoka. I'm not . . ." Tori swallows, and there are tears pricking her eyes. "It can't just be about me."

"Why not?" I feel my voice rising. "What rotting else was it all for?"

"I don't *know!*" Tori shakes her head violently, a few strands of hair escaping from her bun. "You don't—I mean, I'm—" Her voice is thick, and she fights for breath. "I'm not who you think I am."

"Don't be stupid." I try to smile. "I know exactly who you are."

Tori meets my eyes, and smiles too, very slightly. But there's something dark at the edges, and I don't like it. *What's happened to her?* If someone's hurt her, I'll—

"Miss Gelmei."

It's been long enough since anyone called me that that I don't even look up. But Tori does, and I follow her gaze to find two Blues standing in the doorway. One of them bows.

"A messenger has arrived, with urgent information," the man says, in their strange monotone. "You are needed downstairs."

"Right." Tori wipes her eyes with the back of her sleeve. "Duty calls. Eat something, Isoka. I'll be right back."

I watch in silence as the Blues escort her away, feeling Giniva's heated gaze from the table. When they're gone, I sit down next to Meroe, and help myself to a bowl of rice.

"It didn't sound like you were making progress," Meroe says.

I flick my eyes to Giniva. "Talk later."

Zarun looks up, frowning. "Is that—"

Then the window shatters, and three figures in black wearing chain-link veils join the party.

TORI

She doesn't understand. I blink away tears as I follow the Blues downstairs. *How could she?* She doesn't even know I'm a Kindre adept, much less the awful things I've done with that power. For a moment, I'd been on the verge of letting it all spill out. But the thought of the look on her face when she realizes that the perfect little girl she loves is gone, replaced with this . . .

Monster, my mind supplies. *Monster, monster, monster.*

I can't. I'd wanted to see Isoka again so badly it hurt like a hole carved out of my insides. And now she's *here,* and all I can think is that I wish she'd never come. If she's right, and we're all going to die when the Legions crush us, then better she never see how badly her little sister has ruined herself.

Deal with reality, Tori. She *is* here, and I have to live with that. Some part of me, the part that condemns prisoners and gives orders to confiscate food supplies, notes coldly that Isoka would be an incomparable asset to the Red Sashes if she could be relied on. *I just have to convince her . . . what, to stay and die with the rest of us?*

I push the whole mess aside as one of the Blues opens a door to a windowless interrogation room. Two more guards wait inside, along with a young woman in a red sash. She looks worn out, even more so than the rest of us, panting as though she'd sprinted all the way from the walls. At the sight of me, she gets to her feet.

"Sir." I feel the panic rising off her mind. "Someone's broken through the perimeter."

"Where?" I press down on the beginnings of a matching panic. If the Imperials have made a substantial lodgment in the wrong place, we could lose half the city. "How many enemy are over the wall? Has anyone ordered a counterattack?"

"It's not—" The messenger shakes her head. "It wasn't regular Imperial troops. My squad and I were moving to take our shift down at the southern wall, in the Eleventh Ward. When we got there, the torches were out and the wall was empty. No guards."

I frown. "Deserters?"

"My captain thought so at first, sir, but we searched and found blood and scorch marks all over. Someone took that section in a rush, with lots of sorcery, and then hid the bodies. As far as we can tell, they came into the city."

Lots of sorcery. There was only one thing *that* could mean. *Immortals.* We'd seen relatively little of Naga's elites thus far, and Hasaka and I had speculated that he was holding them back for some reason. It might be that they were never as numerous or as powerful as he'd let on. *Or else he has a plan, and he didn't want to spring it too soon.*

"How long has it been since the last shift went on duty?" I ask.

"Four hours, sir. I ran here as soon as we found the breach, but they could still be almost anywhere by now."

"We'll tighten security, start a search. Extra patrols on the walls."

I reach out with Kindre to the Blues, ready to relay orders. With their ability to communicate among themselves, they're a wonderful asset for spreading information quickly.

Or they would be, if I could reach them. Something is smothering my powers, like a thick, cottony pillow pressed across my mind. I've felt something like it only once before, the last time Kuon Naga sent a squad of Immortals after me. Another Kindre user, a powerful one and close by, using their own abilities to shut mine down. I feel abruptly blind and deaf, and jump up from the table in a panic.

"Here!" I shout. "They're here! Sound the alarm!"

Something explodes in the hallway outside, loud enough to shake dust from the walls. The door slams open, revealing a figure in black armor, face obscured by hanging chains. Shimmering green light outlines her body, and a pair of crackling energy blades emerge from her wrists.

There are two Blues in the doorway, two more guards inside the room, but it doesn't matter. The Blues don't even have time to draw their swords before they're cut down in sprays of blood and arcing green power. The first guard gets her spear leveled, but the Melos adept twists out of the way and contemptuously lops the head off the weapon before ramming her blade into the guard's gut. As the Red Sash falls, blood gushing from her lips, the second guard draws a knife and stabs the Immortal in the back. Green energy flares, stopping the blade short of her dark armor, and the Immortal spins and delivers a blow that opens the Red Sash from navel to sternum.

Then she's coming toward me, stalking across the room at an unhurried pace. The messenger lunges to her feet, weaponless but bravely trying to grab hold of the Immortal's arm. The soldier reaches out without looking and slashes her throat, leaving the girl staggering away spraying crimson. The Immortal lets one of her blades fade away and uses her free hand to raise her veil. I recognize her face—cruel, badly scarred on one side by Myrkai fire. The same woman who nearly captured me the last time, until I turned an innocent family into weapons.

No innocents here. No tools, no weapons. Nothing. Her lip, twisted at one corner by the scar, spreads into a half smile.

I don't even have a dagger. I stopped carrying it, after we burned the Sixteenth Ward. Not that it would do any good against a Melos Adept, but at least I could kill myself.

"It was a good trick, last time," she says. Her voice is harsh, as though her throat is damaged. "I respect that."

I ignore her, bearing down as hard as I can, trying to force my power through the enveloping fog. For a moment it *almost* works, the block shifting against my unexpected onslaught. Then it snaps back, as though the other adept has dug in their heels, and I'm shoved back into the confines of my own skull. Even so, I don't stop pushing. Heat ripples and shifts across my skin.

"That's quite enough of that." The Immortal glows golden for a moment, a flash of Rhema speed. All at once, she's behind me, one arm around my midsection. Before I can kick or twist to bite her, she shoves something across my face, a thick cloth with a strong, sour smell. I try to hold my breath, but I've already gotten a lungful, and suddenly my limbs feel like lead weights. I feel myself slumping against the woman's armor, limp as a doll.

"That's better," she purrs in my ear. "Kuon Naga very much wants to see you."

5

ISOKA

Immortals.

I slam my chair back from the table, armor coming up with a crackle. Glass sprays across the room, bouncing off me with a shower of green sparks. I hear someone scream, but I don't have time to figure out who.

There are three of them, coming out of a crouch beneath the window, black-armored and chain-veiled. We're on the third floor, so my guess is there's one more below, a Tartak adept who hurled his comrades upward. And Blessed knows how many in the rest of the building. *One thing at a time. Focus, Isoka.*

I step sideways, in front of Meroe, shoving her backward. The Immortal opposite is extending his hands, Myrkai fire gathering in his palm, so I summon a Melos shield on my left arm and raise it just in time. The bolt of flame splashes against solid green energy and washes past us, heat running across my skin as power flows through me.

Giniva is diving for cover under the table. *Sensible.* Another Immortal lashes out at us with a pulse of Tartak force, only to find Zarun blocking it with one of his own, waves of pale blue colliding over the table and scattering food and plates in all directions. The third Immortal, glowing golden with Rhema, draws a short sword and circles around, flashing from position to position like a poorly drawn flipbook.

There's the threat. "Meroe, down!"

She obeys, throwing herself flat. I block another Myrkai

projectile, then turn to engage the Rhema user, bulling in with my shield to spoil her strike. She backpedals, flickering golden, ducking under my blade.

Zarun is still locked in tight against the other Tartak adept, blue projections materializing one after another, like a wrestling match with a hundred arms. At this distance, there's no room for error, and his face is a mask of concentration. The Immortal's must be the same, but his expression is invisible under the chain veil. He's not watching his flank, at least, when shadows swirl and Jack steps out just behind him. Her short spear goes into the man's side, punching through the black armor, and the Immortal staggers away, blood gouting.

The Rhema user hacks at me, and I give ground. I take most of the blows on my shield, but a few get through and tag my armor, drawing fountains of sparks and waves of heat. It's a dangerous game for her, though, and I finally get the shot I need—she overcommits, in spite of her speed, and I sidestep and slash my blade along her arm. Melos power cuts through leather and chain, and blood wells underneath. She drops the sword, drawing a knife in her off-hand, chain veil jingling.

Zarun snarls in triumph as the other Tartak adept's constructs fail. A bolt of Myrkai fire from the third Immortal catches him in the chest, and his armor flares bright green, but it holds. He leaps up on the table, kicking a surviving bowl aside, and summons his blades, decapitating the Myrkai user in a scissor-like sweep. The Tartak adept tries to recover, blue light flickering, but Jack jabs him again with her spear and he doubles over.

My own opponent charges, desperate or enraged. I take her shield-on, her dagger skittering and scraping against Melos power, and jam my blade into her stomach. The tip emerges between her shoulders, blood smoking away from the crackling energy. I let the blade vanish and straighten up; she staggers sideways, hits the wall, and slides down it, leaving a streak of gore. Looking across the table, I catch Zarun finishing off the fallen Tartak user.

Meroe. I turn. She's already on her feet, face streaked with blood, a damp patch on her side binding her shirt to her skin. I rush to her, but she waves me off, shaking her head.

"I'll be all right," she says. "Just a few cuts from the glass. Everyone else okay?"

"Gonna have some 'burn in the morning, but I'll live," Zarun snarls.

"Mighty Jack is unscathed," Jack says, bending under the table. "And Jack believes Giniva to be unharmed as well."

"I'm fine," Giniva says, brushing glass from her clothes. She has a cut on her forehead, blood trickling down her cheek. "We have to find Tori. It's her they're here for."

Oh, rot and ruin. "You're sure?"

"The last time the Immortals came," she says through gritted teeth, "they came for her. Follow me."

She opens the door. There's a short corridor, then a large clear area, centered on the stairway. By the time we emerge, it's already a pandemonium of screams, flames, and the *crackle* and *crunch* of magic.

All the accessible furniture—a couple of sofas, three tables, and assorted chairs—has been yanked into a barricade by Tartak force. A half-dozen Immortals crouch behind it, defending a semi-circular perimeter that blocks the stairs. One more black-armored figure lies still, pinioned by a pair of crossbow bolts, but the floor outside the barricade is a carpet of rebel dead. Red-sashed bodies lie in heaps, or crawl desperately away from the fighting. Some, living and dead, are still on fire, and flames lick at the walls.

More rebels have converged, gathering in the doorways around the open space, where they have a modicum of cover. A rain of crossbow bolts rattles down on the Immortals, intercepted by a Tartak user who throws up barricades of pale blue force. Three Myrkai users return fire, hurling bolts of flames that shatter against the walls with a roar or catch an incautious rebel with a whoosh and a scream.

"Rot!" Giniva flattens herself against the wall before she attracts a bolt.

"They can't hold there long," Zarun says. "Anyone coming up the stairs will be behind them."

"Tori's downstairs, isn't she?" I say. When Giniva gives a grim nod, I curse. "They're buying time. Once they've got her, they'll pull out."

"Then we have to break through," Meroe says.

"I have a really bad idea," I say. "And I don't think we have time for a better one. I'll draw their fire, get close as soon as you can."

Jack gives a nod and vanishes in a swirl of shadow. I turn to Zarun.

"Throw me over the barricade."

He raises an eyebrow. "Really?"

"Unless you have a better plan after all?"

"Nope." Pale blue bands of force materialize around me, taking hold of my wrists and ankles. "Here goes." I lift, jerkily, into the air.

It's less of a throw and more of a controlled flight, for which I'm thankful. Zarun lets go when I'm near the ceiling, on a trajectory that will bring me down amidst the Immortals. I push my shield out as large as it will go and try to fit my body behind it. A Myrkai bolt explodes against it, then another, and then I hit the ground in a confusion of black armor and glowing sorcery.

I jump to my feet as the Immortals turn on me, blocking another firebolt with my shield. Tartak force grabs my sword arm, and I shift the shield back to a blade long enough to cut the Tartak constructs apart. The Tartak user, a heavyset woman, tries again, but this time I dodge and spin, closing with her. A steel blade licks my shoulder, drawing a flare of power from my armor, and another blast of flame explodes against my back. I feel the wash of heat, rapidly going from uncomfortable to excruciating, but I push forward and cut down their Tartak adept with a quick slash. Behind her, a young man hurls a knife at my eye—he must have Sahzim—and I flinch backward automatically. The blade hits my armor, heat flashing across my face, and skitters away.

Someone grabs me from behind. One of the Myrkai adepts,

grimacing as my armor sparks and flares against him, but working his hand around to press against my chest. Fire glows white-hot in his palm. Ahdron tried this trick on me, a lifetime ago, but that doesn't make it any less dangerous. I go limp in his grip, and he overbalances for a moment, long enough for me to twist and ram the Melos blade into his guts. His fire grazes my shoulder as he goes down, though, and my armor flares to match it. I fight a scream as I feel my skin blister.

By now, though, I've bought enough time. With the Tartak adept dead, the rebel crossbowmen have a chance, picking off another of the Myrkai users. Giniva is launching firebolts, too—I didn't know she was a mage-blood—and Zarun charges across the open space, ducking under a shot and leaping the barricade. The boy with the knives backs up, toward the stairway, and Jack material-izes behind him, his chain-veil jingling as she slashes his throat. A few seconds more, and all the Immortals are down.

I'm breathing hard, teeth gritted. Zarun reaches my side, and whistles at the sight of my shoulder.

"That's going to hurt in the morning," he says.

"It rotting hurts *now*," I snap. "Come on. We have to get to Tori."

Jack leads the way down the stairs, with the two of us close behind, followed by Giniva and a squad of Red Sashes. The stair-way switchbacks into another open room, similarly strewn with dead. Two Immortals guard the stairs farther down, hurling bolts of flame at more rebels on the first floor. Another, a frail-looking woman, stands motionless in the center of the room. And, by the window—

"Tori!" I level my blade. She's slung over the shoulder of yet another Immortal. This one has her chain veil pulled aside, re-vealing a face with the characteristic bubbling scar left by Myrkai fire. Tori hangs mostly limp, but her legs are still kicking weakly. *She's alive.*

The Immortal is at the window, which is already shattered. She looks at me for a moment, hesitates, then throws herself through the opening, taking Tori with her. I sprint after her, not wasting time or breath on a scream. Behind me, I'm barely aware of fire-bolts slamming into the walls and the *zip* of crossbows as the rebels rush the remaining Immortals.

The window looks out the back of the barracks, into a small court-yard between the main building and a wooden stable. Behind the stable is the ward wall, dividing the Eighth Ward from the Sixth, with the tops of several large apartment buildings visible beyond it. The scarred woman's jump has turned into an upward flight, Tartak constructs gripping her and hurling her skyward much as Zarun had thrown me at the Immortal barricade. She's soaring over the wall, and as I watch she lands with a *thump* on a rooftop beyond it. A glow forms around her, twisted auras of Rhema gold and Melos green, and she takes off at a pace faster than a normal human could attempt, easily making the jump between one building and the next.

She's getting away. She's *taking Tori* and there's nothing I can do—

Now I scream.

TORI

My body lies awkwardly across the scarred woman's shoulder, her armor pressing uncomfortably into my stomach, but all I can do is squirm. I can feel my mind dissolving under the influence of whatever chemical was in that rag, my eyelids horribly heavy. I fight back as hard as I can, trying to move, to *see*.

I catch a glimpse of green light, people coming down the stairs. *Isoka!*

Then we're flying, falling. My captor's boots hit the roof hard, and the shock is enough to make me bite my tongue. The taste of blood fills my mouth, but for a moment the pain revives me. I want to scream, but there's no breath in my lungs.

Then the veil around my mind lifts, shredding as though it

were merely a cloud in truth. I throw all my power at the scarred woman, but the drug still has me in its grip, and I can't muster the energy to do more than pry feebly at the edges of her mind. She's already moving again, running toward the next building, and I can feel the minds in the rebel headquarters getting farther away. Giniva, Isoka, the others—my Blues—

The Blues. With the last of my strength, I push a message into the ether, through the interlocking network that is the Blues' minds. It's the last thought I can manage before the drug's darkness closes in around me.

ISOKA

Zarun is standing over the body of the frail Immortal woman, looking at her with a frown.

"She was doing something," he says, touching his forehead. "I felt her . . . trying to talk to me."

"Kindre." My voice comes out in a croak. "The Well of Mind."

Zarun shudders, then looks up at me. "Are you—"

"One of them got away," I tell him. "She took Tori."

"Hells and rot." He shakes his head and runs to the window. "If we get after her—"

"She has Rhema and Melos," I say. "Jumping between rooftops. No way we can catch her now."

"Maybe the rebels can do something," he says, but I hear the despair in his voice. It matches the feeling running through my veins.

They took her. Naga *took her, just like he said he would.* It was possible, of course, that the Immortals wanted Tori only in her capacity as leader of this rebellion, and that they didn't even know I was here. *That doesn't sound like Naga, though.* We pushed our luck too far, stayed too long. *If she'd rotting come with me when we got here—*

I'm only vaguely aware of the room filling up with rebels, men and women in red sashes searching the buildings and gathering the bodies. All I can see is Naga, telling me what will happen to Tori if I don't do what he wants—beaten, sold to a brothel, tortured—

"Isoka!" Meroe's voice. I blink, and her face swims into focus.

"They took Tori," I say. It comes out as a whisper.

"I know." Meroe stands on her toes to press her forehead against mine. "We're going to get her back, you understand? We've come this far. We *will* get her back."

She squeezes my shoulders. This is probably meant to be reassuring, but since one of them is badly burned from the Immortal's attack, I double over in agony. Meroe gives a startled shriek, and starts trying to apologize, but I feel weirdly grateful for the pain. It's . . . clarifying.

We'll get her back. The task is still the same as it ever was. *If I have to go through every Immortal Naga has, we'll get her back.* Four of us, against an empire. *So rotting what?*

I straighten up, eyes brimming with tears, and grab Meroe's hands.

"You're right," I tell her. "As usual."

A commotion is rising, and it crests when Hasaka—the bearded ex–Ward Guard—arrives with an escort of more Red Sashes and a couple of Blues. He's accompanied by a young man I haven't seen before, with long hair pulled forward to partly conceal horrific burns on his face. Hasaka raises his hands for quiet, and gradually gets it, everyone in the room turning to look at him. Giniva pushes through the crowd to join him.

"We killed a Tartak adept in the courtyard," he says. "That's how they got in, and how one of them managed to get away. The building seems to be clear, otherwise. I want double patrols and perimeter guards, until we have a chance to rework security—"

I bark a bitter laugh. "A little late."

"I admit we weren't expecting this," Hasaka says, glaring at me. "I don't understand how the rest of their team was supposed to get away, but obviously it didn't go according to plan."

"It went exactly according to plan," Giniva says. "This was a suicide mission, except for the one woman whose task was to get Tori out. Naga clearly thinks taking her alive is worth the sacrifice of a dozen Immortals."

"That . . ." Hasaka shakes his head. "That may be. We underestimated him. But as to what we do now—"

"I have a message from Miss Gelmei."

Everyone pauses. The voice belongs to one of the Blues, standing quiet by Hasaka's side until now.

"A message?" Hasaka says. "How—"

"Shh." Giniva cuts him off. "Tell us."

"The message is: I am alive. Until I return, my sister Isoka is granted command of the Blues. Isoka, please help us, if you can. I will find a way out, and—" The Blue stops abruptly, then clarifies, "Message ends."

Eventually, I escape from the bedlam by brandishing my wounded shoulder and threatening to pass out if they don't leave me alone. Giniva finds a spare bedroom for me and Meroe, and promises to make sure Zarun and Jack are looked after. I sit down on the thin mat, my back to the wall, suddenly acutely aware that I haven't had any sleep in more than a day.

Meroe crouches opposite me, poking my shoulder with one finger. I wince, and she frowns.

"Shirt off," she says. "Let me have a look."

Jack wouldn't let that pass without a lewd comment, but I'm too tired to joke. I tug my rough traveling shirt over my head, gritting my teeth as it pulls away from the burned skin, and toss it in a wad in the corner. Meroe hisses at the sight of the wound.

"That's not just powerburn," she says.

"No," I mutter. "That Immortal was strong. An adept for certain."

"I need to wash this," she says. "Do you think you can bear it?"

I nod. She takes a wet cloth and starts brushing it lightly over my shoulder, which alternately stings and twinges. I feel tears prick my eyes, and wipe them away with my free hand. For some reason they won't stop.

"Isoka . . ." Meroe says.

"It just hurts," I say, through clenched teeth.

"Not that badly." She cocks her head with a sad smile, and I sigh.

Meroe pulls my head forward, careful of my shoulder this time, and I press my face into her chest. I feel my shoulders shake, silently.

"I was so close." My throat is thick. "I had her *in my arms*. And I still couldn't . . . I couldn't . . ."

"I know."

"What rotting good am I, if I can't keep her safe? What's the point of . . . of *any* of it?"

"We'll get her back."

"Maybe. Or maybe she's already dead. Maybe Kuon Naga's already tearing her fingernails out. Maybe—"

"Shhh." Meroe lets out a breath. "You're right. I can't make any promises. But let's think about this for a little while, okay?"

I don't answer.

"They city has been under siege for weeks. We arrive, and the next morning Naga's Immortals come for Tori." She pushes my head off her chest and looks down at me with a slight smile. "Does that coincidence seem likely to you?"

"No." My voice is barely audible.

"Which means . . . ?

"Naga knows we're here, and that's why he launched his raid now."

"Right." Meroe's smile widens. "Because?"

"Because he still wants *Soliton*." I take a deep breath. "Tori is his leverage to get it from me. To keep me from just sailing away."

"That was my thought, too. And that probably means Tori is safe, for the moment. If he wants to trade her for *Soliton*, he's got to produce her at some point, and not badly damaged, right?"

"There are still things he could do to her," I say, anger creeping into my voice. "If he—"

"She's *alive*, Isoka. That's what matters, because it means that we can still get her back."

"Right." Another deep breath. My chest seems to be opening up. "You're right. As usual."

"Thanks." Meroe's smile broadens, and she dips her cloth back in the basin. I reach out and grab her hands for a moment.

"My strange princess. What did I ever rotting do without you?"

"Gods only know," she says. "But I think a more important question is what we're going to do now."

"Find Tori. Get her back."

"Obviously." Meroe returns to cleaning my shoulder, and I wince again. "But finding her isn't going to be easy. Naga will expect us to come looking."

"Let him try to stop me."

"You can't fight the entire Imperial Nrmy, Isoka." She prods my wound, and I give a squeak of protest. "And that's what you're going to have to do if you go off alone."

My smile fades. "You still want me to help the rebels, don't you?"

"She asked you to. Your sister."

"If that message was even from her." I still hadn't wrapped my mind around the Blues, who remind me unpleasantly of Prime's walking corpses.

"And the rebels want to help her just as much as we do, I think. We stand a much better chance if we work together."

"Assuming they want to work with me at all," I say. "Hasaka didn't seem too friendly."

"We can try, at least," Meroe says. "If the rebellion falls apart and the Imperials march in, I think we'll have a much harder time finding Tori. In the worst case, if Naga manages to take you captive, he doesn't even have to bargain."

"He won't take me captive." I'd long ago promised myself that

I'd force him to kill me, if it came to that. *But,* my stupid, rotting mind supplies, *he could take* Meroe *away . . .*

I shake my head, refusing to entertain that thought. Meroe glares at me, and I hastily clear my throat.

"Even if I help them," I say, "it's not going to change anything in the long run. They're all still rutted when the Legions get here. And if we manage to get Tori away from Naga, she still won't want to leave, and we're back to where we started."

"One problem at a time," Meroe says. "I think somebody told me that once."

I chuckle weakly. "It's still impossible."

"Getting the crew all the way to the Garden was impossible. We did it anyway."

"Not all of them." I remember that march. The bodies we left behind.

"Not all of them," Meroe agrees. "But we saved something."

I turn it over for a minute, but it's just for show. You can't really argue with Meroe when she's made up her mind; not because she's stubborn, but just because she's always right.

"I think this will heal clean," she says, pulling the cloth away from my burn. "I'll leave it, unless it gets infected."

I give an absent nod. Meroe's control of her Ghul powers has improved considerably, but she's still very aware that every use is a risk. Those powers have saved my life, more than once; they also turned a friend of mine into a giant explosive tumor. She tries to use them only when it's life or death.

"All right," I tell her, as she starts winding a bandage. "I'll try and help, if they'll have me. If we can keep the rebellion going long enough, Naga will make some kind of offer to negotiate. That could be our chance."

"I think," Meroe says with a smile, "it sounds like a very sensible strategy." And she ties the bandage off, a little tighter than perhaps strictly necessary.

6

TORI

I wake up in perfect darkness.

My limbs are still numb, but slowly return to life, prickling with invisible pins and needles. I sit up as soon as I'm able to, gasping for breath, exploring the space around me with my hands. It's stone, cold against my skin, and I can hear the plink of water dripping somewhere nearby.

A dungeon, I assume. *Where else do you throw a captured rebel?*

Reaching out with my mind yields nothing. Kuon Naga has not neglected to provide a Kindre user—maybe the same one, for all I know—to smother my supernatural senses. Whatever else he is, the Emperor's spymaster is certainly thorough.

I follow the edges of the space, which is about what I expected—a cell a couple of yards square, ceiling low enough I can brush it with my fingertips. The lack of light is doing strange things to my eyes, and I keep thinking I see flickers of color.

Now what? They'll have to give me food and water eventually, unless they just mean to bury me alive. *That doesn't sound like Naga.* The Immortal could have killed me and didn't; therefore, he wants me for something.

Which maybe means I shouldn't oblige him. The thought makes my stomach flop, but it's logical. I remember Kosura, after we retrieved her from the Immortals, the marks they'd left on her. And she'd just been one prisoner among many, not important. Whatever Naga has planned for *me,* architect of the rebellion, can't be pleasant.

Unfortunately, no easy means of suicide presents itself, short of trying to crack my skull against the stone. I don't think I have the courage to go through with it anyway, even if they'd left me a convenient dagger.

A coward and *a monster.*

I feel . . . strange. Terrified, of course, but also in an odd way *released.* Whatever burdens were on my shoulders are gone. When I parse that thought, it brings a dark smile to my face.

I may be in a cell about to get tortured or worse, but at least I don't have to tell my sister the truth!

As my old supplicator would say, the Blessed's mercies come at unexpected hours.

Times passes. It's hard to judge how much, with nothing to go by but my breath and the beating of my heart. The air in the cell gets warm and thick, and I'm not sure I'm imagining feeling light-headed. *Kuon Naga wouldn't let me suffocate by accident, would he?* I'm just contemplating whether to try shouting for help when there's a grinding sound above me.

The entire roof of the cell lifts up, a solid stone block suspended with glimmering Tartak force. An Immortal jumps down beside me, armored and veiled. I can't see her face, but when she speaks I recognize the scarred Melos adept who took me from the rebels.

"Good men and women accepted their deaths to get you out of there," she says, in her harsh voice. "Soldiers loyal to the Emperor and the Blessed One. Each of them is worth a thousand of you rotting traitors."

"I'm sorry to hear it." I blink in the light. "Personally, I'd have preferred they not have bothered."

"You . . ." She pauses, breathing hard, the chains of her veil rasping softly. "The only reason you're not screaming in agony right now is because Master Naga requires you undamaged. For the moment. But by all means, continue joking at my expense, and we'll see if you have any unfortunate accidents."

It hadn't been a joke, really, but I take the hint and stay quiet.

The Immortal pulls a damp cloth from a pouch, and I back up a half step. She sighs.

"Make things easy on yourself, rotscum. This is the only way you're getting out of this cell."

There's not much room to retreat in any event. I force myself to hold still as she applies the drugged cloth to my face, the smell of it sharp in my nostrils.

"My name is Kadi," she whispers, as my consciousness fades. "When Master Naga is done with you, I'm going to take a personal interest in carving you to pieces as slowly as I know how." She leans close, chains pressing against my cheek. "Sweet dreams."

This time, I wake up on a sleeping mat.

For a few moments, while the pins and needles run through my arms and legs, I wonder if Kadi got the dosage on her drug wrong and killed me after all. It seems like the only explanation for my new surroundings, which have more in common with the supplicators' descriptions of Heaven than any dungeon I've ever heard of.

The sheets around me are the finest silk, dyed in swirling, expensive patterns, cool against my skin. As my vision clears, I can see the rest of the room, lined with carved hardwood polished to a gleam, the walls plastered and painted with understated murals in an archaic style. A wardrobe and a heavy chest sit against one wall, intricately carved with delicate reliefs, the details picked out in gold. A lamp made of beautiful colored glass hangs from a silver chain, puffing sweetly scented smoke.

Ultimately, I conclude it can't be Heaven, because I find myself in urgent need of a toilet. I'm pretty sure the truly righteous, sitting at the side of the Blessed, don't have to worry about such things. I sit up, still groggy, and try to get enough control of my limbs to go in search of one.

A door, cunningly disguised as part of the paneling, slides open. There's a woman behind it, already on her knees, wearing a robe in a delicate blue-and-green pattern like a butterfly's wings.

It's not quite a *kizen,* being cut closer to a servant's looser attire, but it still looks finer than any *kizen* I've ever owned. She carries a basin of water, which she pushes across the threshold, then looks up in alarm as I start struggling to my feet.

"Hey—" I manage.

She slides the door shut, and I hear hurried footsteps departing. *All right, then.*

A quick search of the room reveals no toilet, but an old-fashioned chamber pot tucked into a concealed closet. I use it with relief, then wash my hands in the basin, shaking my head. Everything looks like props out of a historical drama, except I'm pretty sure all the gold is *real.*

Where in the Blessed's name has Naga taken me?

That I *am* still in Naga's clutches, I confirm with a quick test of my Kindre powers. Somewhere nearby, another Kindre user is still pressing down on my mind, locking me in. I don't push too hard—my head hurts already—but it means that whatever this change of venue portends, I haven't escaped.

More footsteps from the corridor outside. I look around, not sure what to do. Unlike the stone cell, there are things in here I might be able to use as a weapon—I could bash someone over the head with the chamber pot—

The door slides open, and it's Garo.

His hair has grown since I saw him last, its curls tamed with oil and neat braids. Instead of the worker's clothes he wore when we met in the Eleventh Ward, he's in a loose, double-layered robe, wide-collared and belted at the waist, the classic casual look for an old-fashioned aristocrat. He kicks off a pair of lacquer sandals and rushes into the room before I have a chance to do more than gape, and throws his arms around me in a grip that crushes the air from my lungs.

"Thank the Blessed," he mutters, head bent to press against my shoulder. "Oh, thank the Blessed. You're all right."

"I'd be better," I manage in a strangled voice, "if I could breathe."

"Sorry! Sorry." He pulls away a step, and I can see there are tears in his eyes, cutting through the light dusting of powder on his cheeks. "I just . . . after everything that happened, I thought . . ."

"I can guess," I say. "But I'm . . . okay." I stare at him, wonderingly. "Unless I'm still in a cell somewhere, and this is a dream. Which actually seems pretty likely."

"It must be a shock, I know. But I promise it's not a dream."

"Then what is going *on*? Where am I? How are *you* here?" My voice is rising, slightly hysterical, and Garo smiles broadly and holds up a hand for patience.

"It's *all right*, Tori. You're safe, I promise." He waves at the splendor around us. "This is the Imperial Palace, in the Royal Ward."

I goggle. I think I would have been less surprised if he told me we were on the moon.

"As for *how*, that's down to my father." Garo blushes slightly under his powder. "I told him everything, and I begged him to do whatever he could for you. He prevailed on Kuon Naga to have you brought here after you were captured."

That, at least, makes a kind of sense. Garo's father, Lord Marka, is a powerful man, wealthy and well-connected at court. *But powerful enough to tell* Naga *what to do?* It doesn't strike me as likely. And yet here we are.

"It's still house arrest," Garo says, scratching the back of his head, a bit embarrassed. It's such a familiar gesture that I melt a little. "You can't leave, I mean. But it's better than a dungeon. I was . . . after the fighting started . . ." He shakes his head, and his voice is tight. "It's good to see you, Tori."

"It's good to see you, too," I say, dazed.

He grabs my hands and squeezes them.

"Now that you're awake," he says, "we need to go and see my father right away."

It turns out that this is a bit of an overstatement. One apparently does not just drop in on Lord Marka in sweat-stained work clothes, smelling like unwashed sheets. Garo summons a pair of colorfully robed servants, and they escort me to another room, down an apparently endless corridor.

The beauty of the palace takes my breath away. I can't help but compare it to the Black Flower, the den of vice in the Sixteenth Ward. There, the luxury had been exclusively on the surface, gaudy gold leaf and glass gemstones, already peeling to reveal the rot beneath. Here, things are *solid*, built to last. The palace gives the impression that every piece of it, every floorboard, every wall panel, was all individually installed by some grizzled master craftsman after much careful thought and consultation. The amount of *labor* lavished on every square yard is staggering, and must have taken generations—it looks archaic because it is.

The servants take me to a washroom, where an iron-footed tub on four clawed feet is full of water so hot it trails wisps of steam. Another servant waits beside it, with kettles of lukewarm water to cool it to my exact specifications.

Back in the Third Ward, I'd eventually been able to chase the servants away and win the right to bathe myself. There seems to be no chance of that here, so I resign myself to company. I strip down and test the water, then slip in, gasping as the heat hits my minor cuts and sores. It makes me dizzy, and for a moment I worry I'm going to pass out—hopefully the palace servants won't let me drown. They sit with apparently endless patience while I soak, feeling the pain slowly leaching out of my skin.

This still feels like a dream. Not long ago—I think, though I still have no idea exactly how long it's been—I was at rebel headquarters, trying to figure out what to say to my sister to get her to understand. Now I'm soaking in a tub at the *palace*, with most of the in-between spent either unconscious or certain I was about to suffer some dire torture. It would be enough to disorient anyone.

Part of my mind is screaming that I should make a plan, try to figure out what to do next. Isoka is still out there with the rebels, surrounded by the Imperial Nrmy, starving and threatened on all sides. But there's nothing I can do for them, not yet, and so I try not to begrudge myself a moment or two to float.

Anyway, I told them to listen to Isoka. She'll be a better rebel leader than I ever could, if only she decides to help.

When the water starts to cool, the servants move in, whisking soap in bowls with horsehair brushes and painting it gently over my skin. Another girl works on my hair, a task which is frankly long overdue, unpicking my braid and giving it a thorough wash. They take turns brushing it out and patting it dry, until it looks almost like it did when I left the Third Ward—a long curtain of silky darkness, only a little frayed from everything I've been through.

Clothes—a *kizen*, naturally, of fine, cool silk, in a delicate blue-and-white pattern. Powder and jewelry, more than I ever used on my own, but applied with an expert hand. They wheel in a long mirror, and I scarcely recognize myself. Or, rather, I *do*—I look like the girl I was *before*, before everything went wrong, before I learned I'm a person who lies and steals and kills.

If Isoka could see me like this, I can't help but think, *I wonder what she would say?*

Finally, with the full routine completed, a male servant arrives to escort me to the Markas'. By this point, between the warm water and the release of tension, I feel like I could use a nap, but I try to make myself focus as we walk down yet another beautifully appointed corridor toward another set of rooms.

This place must be a maze. I could never find my way back to the room I'd first woken up in on my own. Hopefully, I won't have to. There are other things on my mind.

All right. If Lord Marka asked for me to be brought here, and Kuon Naga allowed it, they both must have something to gain. What that could be, especially in the former case, I have no idea. Court politics are well beyond my ken. *But if I can find out, maybe I can use it to my advantage.*

We finally arrive, and the servant kneels and opens the door. Garo is waiting, sitting across a low table from an older man with a bald pate ringed by graying hair. He dresses plainly, at least by palace standards, and has a carefully groomed, pencil-thin mustache above lips that seem prone to curl in disappointment. This,

I assume, is Lord Marka, and I bow and shuffle into the room in the careful gait the *kizen* permits.

"Tori." Garo gets to his feet and takes my hand. "You look beautiful."

"Thanks." He helps me sit—it isn't easy to do, in a *kizen*—and I incline my head again to his father. Lord Marka looks back at me with a frankly curious eye.

"Well," he says eventually, "I can see why my son is so taken with you."

I'm not sure what to say to that, so I just smile. It seems to please him.

"Welcome, child," he goes on. "I am Lord Marka. Garo has told me a great deal about you."

"He's too kind," I murmur, old polite instincts automatically falling into place.

"He says that you saved his life, several times. I want you to know that I am most grateful."

Proper humility walks a fine line; argue with a compliment, and you can insult the giver. I incline my head again. "Thank you, my lord."

"He has explained to me the . . . circumstances that lead to your involvement in the current unpleasantness. I have prevailed on Kuon Naga to allow you to be held here for the duration."

"I am very grateful, my lord."

"Mmm. Yes." A slight smile crosses his face. "I imagine it's better than what he might have had planned for you."

Again, there's nothing I can quite think of to answer that.

"In return," Lord Marka says, "I expect good behavior from you. I have argued to Naga that you were led astray by others, and had good but misguided intentions. You will prove this by your cooperation now. Do you understand?"

Just a touch of the whip. Lord Marka would have gotten along well with some of my tutors. I bow my head. "Yes, my lord."

"Good. We can all hope this matter will be concluded soon."

I clear my throat, and he looks at me, eyes narrowed.

"Apologies, my lord," I say. "If I might ask a question, when this matter *is* concluded, what do you imagine might happen?"

"To you?" I see him reevaluating me, his eyes canny. "That rather depends on your behavior, I think. It may be that Naga will have some . . . questions, some requests, and I suggest you please him. If you do, he assures me that it should not be necessary to punish you further."

Ah. So that's the game. I bow my head again. "Thank you, my lord."

He waves a dismissal. "Garo, show her to her room."

"Yes, Father." He takes my hand again, and we return to the corridor. He glances at me, and I'm surprised to see relief on his face.

"What's wrong?" I ask him.

"You know how to talk to a lord," he says. "I was a little worried Father would find some way to take offense."

"I didn't ignore my etiquette tutors, if that's what you mean," I tell him. "You know I grew up in the Third Ward. Not exactly nobility, obviously—"

"I know," he says. "I just haven't seen you . . . like this."

That's true, I suppose. We'd always met in the Eleventh Ward, both of us in worker's clothes, and I'd spent our free time teaching him how to do things like a commoner—scrub laundry, order in restaurants, swear at carters. For obvious reasons, I'd never brought him home to Ofalo.

"You really are beautiful, you know," he adds, and flushes slightly. I find myself blushing, too.

"What I am," I say firmly, "is exhausted. If you can show me where I can lie down for a while?"

"Of course." Garo coughs. "Follow me."

I sleep for what turns out to be twelve hours, and wake up the following morning feeling ravenous and better than I have in weeks.

After devouring the breakfast the servants bring me and dressing in a lighter casual robe, I set out to explore the palace.

I'm still a captive, obviously, so I don't expect to be given the run of the place, but it's surprising how far I'm allowed to wander before I run into a guard who, apologetically, won't let me pass. I had vaguely pictured the palace as something like my house in the Third Ward, plus a few ceremonial chambers, but it's clearly much larger than that, almost a city unto itself. The part we're in—I hear the servants calling it the Pear Wing, and there is indeed a pear motif in some of the paneling and furniture—is bigger than our whole estate, and includes several sets of apartments, each with their own sitting rooms and dining chambers, with servants' passages woven around them. Rooms wrap around carefully tended courtyards, each a tiny jewel box of greenery, water, and stone.

More important, for my purposes, the place feels almost abandoned. Garo and his father are living here, and I catch glimpses of a few other nobles associated with the Marka clan, plus of course the innumerable, almost invisible, servants who make clean clothes and fresh food appear as if by magic. Even so, most of the time the corridors are empty, and I can walk for what feels like miles without seeing anyone.

I have a strong feeling, however, that I am not as unobserved as I might think. The fog of Kindre blindness is with me always, but when I open my mental senses I get a vague sensation of pressure. My suspicion is that whatever Immortal Kindre user Naga has suppressing my abilities is also tasked with keeping track of my movements. I've done that often enough with my own powers.

Exploring gives me some time to think, unfortunately, and I find I would rather not. My captivity is a fact, and I'm not naïve enough to imagine I might be able to escape now that I have Kuon Naga's attention. I should be grateful that I'm apparently going to be kept in pampered luxury instead of naked in some filthy hole, having my fingernails ripped out. But—

—my friends are still out there. Giniva, Hasaka, Jakibsa, even

Kosura. Everyone who believed in me, who followed when I told them to fight the Ward Guard. They're still fighting, and if nothing changes they're all going to die.

And *Isoka* is out there. My sister is alive, and she came back to take me with her. I had a chance, somehow, in spite of everything, and I threw it away.

It would have meant leaving your friends to die.

But if they're going to die anyway, why not?

My head feels like one of the Eleventh's cheap noodle shops, with a hundred customers bellowing arguments at the top of their lungs. It's a relief when, with evening coming on, I open yet another beautifully painted lacquer door and finally find something interesting.

The door is off a long corridor that winds away from the rest of the Pear Wing, and honestly I expected to run into more palace guards on the other side. Instead, I slide it open and find a large room, airy and well-lit by paper-screen windows, full of row after row of bookcases. *A library.*

That, in itself, is interesting. We had a small library at the house in the Third Ward, plus whatever my tutors assigned me, which was invariably deadly boring moral tracts and carefully composed histories. I don't know what they keep in the palace libraries, but it has to be better than that. Even more intriguing, though, is the young man sitting alone at a reading table in the central aisle, bent over a book with several more stacked up beside him, his lips pursed in a slight frown.

He's Isoka's age, I guess, or a little younger, with thin, intelligent features and long hair tied in a complicated queue. He plays with the end of it as he reads, swinging it back and forth, periodically licking his finger to turn a page. He's wearing a casual robe, but a very fine one, silk embroidered with fanciful wild beasts. He can't be a servant slacking off. But he's also not wearing the colors of the Marka household. *So what's he doing here?*

I approach, rustling my slippers against the floor mats so as not to startle him. This doesn't work, and he remains engrossed in the book, so I'm forced to resort to a cough. He jerks upright, looking around wildly, and I wonder if he's not supposed to be in here after all. *He looks like he's afraid of getting caught.* When he sees me, he relaxes a bit and smiles.

"Hello, miss," he says. "I don't believe I know you."

"I'm—" I hesitate. *A prisoner? Does everyone know that?* "A guest of the Markas. I was just . . . looking around. I hope it's all right."

"Of course." His smile widens. "The library is here for the use of the guests in the Pear Wing. Please, feel free."

He has a proprietary air, as though welcoming me to his home. *A servant after all, then? Maybe a senior one, out of uniform?* I give a slight bow in thanks. "I'll have to find something interesting."

"I can help you, if you like," he says. "Do you know what you're looking for?"

"Not . . . exactly." I find myself hesitant to admit I haven't given it much thought, and try to change the subject. "What are you reading?"

"Ancient history. The reign of the Emperor Rhioa."

"I've never heard of him."

"I'm not surprised. This was two hundred years before the birth of the Blessed One. The supplicators say that history before the Blessed has little to teach us, but I disagree. Rhioa, for example—" He pauses, cocking his head. There's something vaguely birdlike about his movements, quick and precise. "I'm sorry. Are you interested, or were you just being polite? I have a tendency to rattle on."

"I'm interested," I tell him, and take a seat across from him at the table. "I was just killing time anyway."

"Fair enough." He smiles again. "Emperor Rhioa had the misfortune to ascend the throne during a time of war with both the Southern Kings—this was when they'd formed the Dalsin League, you know—and the icelings, who'd carved out a protectorate in the north. Every year, Rhioa sent out his generals in both directions, but they kept losing battles, and every year things seemed to get worse. Rhioa stormed and raged at his advisors, and finally announced he was leading the southern army personally. They tried to talk him out of it, but he refused to listen."

"And he won?"

"Oh, no." The boy's smile fades. "He marched the army right into a trap laid by the Nimari general Sandro. A full third of the Empire's soldiers were killed, and Rhioa himself was captured. For a ransom, the southerners demanded all the land below the Girin River, and it took the Empire another two hundred years to get it back. As it turned out, Rhioa had caught some southern disease when he was in their camp, too, so he died within a year and nobody was very sorry about it."

"Ah." I shake my head. "Sounds like he would have been better off if he'd stayed in the palace."

"Indeed." The boy turns one more page, then closes the book with a sigh. "That's usually the lesson, I find."

"So why are you reading about ancient failures?"

"I think the failures are the most instructive. If you glance through the popular histories, you'd think we went from one great ruler to the next, but of course there's quite a lot of disasters between them. Otherwise, I suppose the Blessed Empire would have conquered the world by now."

"I see." I don't, really, but I still don't know what to make of this odd creature. I pause, trying to think of a polite way to ask what exactly he's doing here.

"I should go," he says, glancing at the windows. The light is starting to fade.

"So should I, actually."

"But it's lovely to make your acquaintance, Miss . . ." He pauses.

"Tori," I say. All at once, I remember the time I met Garo, and impulsively gave him my name. *If I hadn't done that, would everything else still have followed?* Probably. Kuon Naga was coming for me, whatever I did. "Gelmei Tori."

"Miss Gelmei. Perhaps I'll see you again."

He gets to his feet, and I follow suit. As he heads for the door,

I decide to risk being rude, and blurt out, "Wait. What's your name?"

"Me?" He half-turns with a frown, looking embarrassed. "I'm Avyntea." He pauses a moment, then adds, "The Emperor."

I bark out a laugh in disbelief. He smiles again, bows slightly, and slips out the door.

7

ISOKA

One more time, I tell myself. *I will try one more time.*

I do my best to keep my voice calm. "Will you please just listen to me?"

"I'm listening, Isoka," Hasaka says.

He's not. We're in the headquarters conference room, and he's going over the big map of the city, making notes. Jakibsa, the burned Tartak adept, sits beside him and assists with a floating pencil. If nobody had told me the pair are lovers, I would have guessed it from the way they bicker.

I grab a spare pencil and put a big ugly *X* on the map, up at the north end of rebel territory, where the wall separates the Third Ward from the Eighth. Jakibsa gives me a questioning glance, and Hasaka just sighs.

"This is where we came through, and we got a good look at the Imperial defenses," I tell them. "There's nothing there that would stand up to a real attack. It's a few Ward Guard officers in charge of conscripted peasants with sharpened sticks, and when they run away I'm not sure which is more likely to be at the front of the pack. I could punch through that rotting line myself."

"So you've mentioned," Hasaka says. "Several times."

"Because you don't seem to be paying attention. I'm telling you there's enemy territory ripe for the taking. We could push all the way up to the First Ward wall."

"And then what?" Hasaka's voice is controlled, but his face makes it clear he's only barely reining in his temper. I wish he would lose it, shout at me. Then I could shout back. "Say we capture the Second and Third Wards. Now we have a longer circuit of wall to defend, without the benefit of any the preparations we've made over the past few weeks."

"There'll be supplies there. Food. Maybe hostages."

"She has a point," Jakibsa says. "Those are big houses with deep cellars."

"Enough to matter?" Hasaka says. "For the whole city?"

"Probably not," Jakibsa concedes. Hasaka turns back to me, as though this proves his point.

"What's the alternative?" I shoot back at him. "What's your plan?"

"I've already explained it," he says. "You were here for the meeting."

I can't help but snort in disgust. *Some plan.* The Red Sash commanders filed into the conference room and listened in silence while Hasaka gave them assignments—shore up the wall here, keep an eye on a troop concentration there, move ammunition to one spot and food to another. Then they filed out, muttering to one another, no doubt asking what *I* was doing there, while I sat by ready to explode.

One more time.

"If not the north," I say, "then the waterfront. If we can—"

"*Isoka*," Hasaka growls. "Please. Leave this to us."

"Why? Because you're doing such a good job?" I find myself rising from my chair. "I'm only here because you let my little sister get rotting kidnapped under your nose—"

"Don't talk to me about Tori," Hasaka says, standing himself. "You weren't here. What in the Rot do you know—"

"I think," Jakibsa says, "that's about enough."

"That's for rotting sure." I manage to say it under my breath instead of at the top of my lungs, but I can't help shoving the chair aside with a clatter as I head for the door. Hasaka starts to reply, but Jakibsa cuts him off. I slam the door shut and stalk downstairs, fuming.

Rotting Red Sashes and their rotting stupidity. Guards and civilians alike hurry to get out of my way. I suppose word has gotten around that the beloved leader's rotscum sister isn't someone to mess with. *Tori, why in the Blessed's name did you get involved with these idiots?*

We're staying in Tori's old quarters, a building on the headquarters square given over to her and her Blues. Four of them guard the front door, watching with silent, emotionless stares as I approach. I ignore them, and they don't even twitch as I wrench the door open.

I can hear quiet conversation as I approach the rooms Meroe and I share. Another Blue steps aside to let me pass, and I find Meroe at the sitting room table with Giniva, going over a closely written report. Meroe takes a look at my face, raises an eyebrow, and gets up.

"I appreciate the information," she says to Giniva, who also rises. "Let me know if you come up with anything more."

"I will." Giniva looks from Meroe to me and back. "Good luck."

I'm practically shaking with the effort of holding still while Giniva leaves. When she finally shuts the door behind her, I take a deep breath, and Meroe holds up a hand.

"Not too loud, unless you want the rebel spymaster to hear you," she says. "The walls are thin here."

"Rutting bloody *rotscum*," I rasp, in a stage whisper. "Blessed's pustulant *boils*."

"Meeting went that well, did it?" Meroe says.

"Hasaka is—" I look around, breathing hard. I want to hit something. If we were on *Soliton*, I'd find the nearest crab, but all that offers itself here is some inoffensive furniture. "He doesn't understand how unutterably *screwed* he is, and that means he doesn't want to do anything about it. And nobody will tell him except for me, so he just thinks—I don't rotting care what he thinks, but he won't *listen*. None of them will."

"Tori didn't tell you to take command," Meroe says, fetching a pot of tea and pouring two cups. "She just asked you to help."

"I'm *trying* to help." I'm pacing again, brushing the walls of the room with my fingertips before turning on my heel. "The longer this goes on, the closer we get to the moment where the Legions show up and squash us like roaches. If this rebellion is going to get anywhere we have to *do* something, keep pushing on Naga until something breaks."

"You think attacking is going to convince him to back off?"

"No, I think we're all rotting doomed," I snap. "But sitting here behind the walls *definitely* isn't going to accomplish anything."

"Sit," Meroe says. "Drink tea. Please."

My face twists into a snarl, but I swallow it and throw myself onto the cushion. Meroe settles down, cupping a steaming mug in her hands.

"Hasaka is . . . afraid," she says. "Giniva was telling me about him. He's been part of this ever since it started, but he never asked to be in charge. Now that he is, I think it terrifies him."

"It should," I mutter. "I was rotting terrified of being in charge, too, remember?"

"And did a little bit of sulking as well." Meroe sips her tea thoughtfully. "Yes, I remember."

"And then you hit me." I shake my head. "Somehow I don't think me slugging Hasaka is going to be helpful."

"Probably not. But you might try to understand where he's coming from, at least a little."

"It's not that I don't understand." I lean back on my elbows, staring at the ceiling. "I get it. Everyone here is in an impossible position. They've climbed way out over the cliff and there's no way back. It's just a matter of time before the rocks give way, but they're holding on as hard as they can. I *get* it. But—"

"But?" Meroe raises an eyebrow again.

"There's nothing I can rotting do about it." I let my elbows slide out and end up lying on my back. "I'm trying to come up with something, and I *can't*. And every minute in the back of my mind, I'm wondering what Naga's doing to Tori, whether he's finally lost patience and he's going to start sending me her fingers."

That, of course, is what makes the situation unbearable, what pushes my temper so close to the surface. It's been three days, and we've had no word from Naga and the Immortals, no demand for *Soliton* or offer to negotiate. Nothing. And with every hour that passes, I imagine—

Well. In certain areas, I have a vivid imagination.

"All I want to do is find her," I say, closing my eyes. "And I feel like I can't even *try*, because I'm too busy patching all the holes in a sinking ship, and nobody else can see that we're already going down. . . ."

"That's probably enough metaphors," Meroe says, close by. "I get the picture."

I open my eyes and find her leaning over me, a soft smile on her face. She kisses me, and just for a moment I relax, feeling the muscles in my shoulders unknot.

What did I do to deserve her? Sometimes I really don't know.

There's a knock at the door. Meroe sits up, and I roll to my feet with a pang of regret. "Come in."

A couple of Blues enter, a man and a woman, dressed in simple workers' clothes, each carrying a sword. The woman's trousers are too long, I notice, and the cuffs are filthy. She doesn't appear to be bothered.

"Miss Gelmei," she says, in the flat tone they all use. "Miss Nimara. Masters Jack and Zarun have returned, and wish to see you."

"Send them up," I say.

She nods, and her eyes flicker for a moment. The Blues can *talk* to each other, instantly and silently. It reminds me of the link between Prime and his minions, and the comparison makes my stomach churn.

"I will escort them up," the woman says.

"Afterward, have someone do something about your pants," I tell her. "You're liable to trip."

She glances down. "Understood. If you'll excuse me."

The man, still silent, slides the door shut behind them. I let out a breath and glance at Meroe, whose brow is creased with a frown.

"Something wrong?" I ask her.

"I still don't like them," she says.

"Believe me, I'm not fond of them, either."

"It has to be Kindre."

I shrug, uncomfortably. I certainly can't think of a better explanation, but I know almost nothing about the strange Well of Mind. Supposedly, powerful users are rare, less common even than Ghul adepts, and their abilities are undetectable except to other Kindre users. I've also heard that the Immortals search them out almost as assiduously as ghulwitches, for all the obvious reasons.

"In Nimar," Meroe says, "Kindre users serve in a kind of holy order. They're required to use their abilities for the benefit of everyone, searching out lies in courts of law and the like. Actually altering someone else's mind is . . . an abomination."

"I assume they don't get a choice about whether to join."

Meroe shakes her head, and I force a smile.

"And the same set of rules," I add, "would condemn you, a Ghul adept, to immediate execution for having the power you've used to save my life at least twice."

"I know," Meroe says. "And Tori . . . probably had her reasons. But when I see them, I can't help but . . . I don't know."

"Tori?" My brow creases.

"The Blues served her, until she ordered them to serve you. And she sent that message. She has to be the Kindre adept, doesn't she?"

"Tori's not an adept. She's not even a mage-blood."

"She—" Meroe stops. "We can figure that out later, I suppose."

She turns away, searching for more tea mugs. I'm still lost in thought. *Tori couldn't really be an adept, could she? Even if she'd come into her powers late, I would have noticed something. Besides, why would she hide that from me?*

The door slides open again, and Jack and Zarun come in.

They've changed from their *Soliton*-made clothes into ordinary Imperial garb, the better to go unnoticed, and both bear the dust of a long day on the streets. Zarun accepts a cup of tea from Meroe with a grunt of thanks, and Jack gives a broad grin.

"Truly," she says, "you have a grace worthy of a queen. Thirsty Jack offers her thanks."

"And?" I ask, unable to contain my impatience. "Did you find anything?"

"We made some progress," Jack says, "but were ultimately stymied."

"People in this city aren't exactly eager to chat with strangers right now," Zarun says. "And even gold isn't as persuasive as it might be."

"I suppose there's not much to spend it on," Meroe says.

Jack nods, sipping her tea. "We sought out those who'd seen the Immortal's flight with Tori. They went north, for certain, and we tracked them to a cemetery in the Sixth Ward where they spent the night."

"They?" I'm trying to keep my voice level. "You're sure Tori was alive?"

"Certain," Zarun says quietly. "When we went there we found one of the old crypts opened and cleaned out. It'd make a fine cell to stash somebody for the night. A couple of beggars who live in the alley nearby saw an Immortal heading north again in the morning, carrying something."

"They passed over the ward wall into the Second Ward," Jack says. "After that, we couldn't follow, for which Jack is regretful."

"But I can't see them going to this much trouble to extract a body," Zarun says. "This was a kidnapping. They wanted her alive, and they got her."

"Yeah," I mutter. We'd guessed that much, but I try to take comfort in the confirmation. *Tori was alive two nights ago. They have no reason not to keep her that way.*

Meroe puts a hand on my shoulder, sensing my turmoil. "The

question," she says, "is what Naga is up to. If he intends to use Tori to threaten Isoka, why hasn't he sent us a message?"

"Maybe he just wants you to stew," Zarun says. "Or maybe we're wrong and he doesn't know you're here, but he's got some plan for her as leader of the Red Sashes."

"No." I take a deep breath. "Meroe was right the first time. He must know I'm here, or else why attack *then*? I think leaving me to stew is more likely. The bastard is good at twisting people. It's just like him to leave me waiting for—"

Another knock at the door. I jump, and Jack and Zarun look at one another. Hesitantly, Meroe says, "Yes?"

"A messenger," says a Blue's flat voice.

"From Naga?" I blurt out.

"No," the Blue says. "From the western defenses. The wall has been breached, and the Fourth Ward is under attack."

"'Under attack'" is an understatement. By the time we reach the scene, the Fourth has all but fallen.

From the top of one of the ward wall towers, we have a good view to the west, over the roughly triangular patch of city that makes up the Fourth Ward. It's a densely packed district, more orderly than the tenements of the Eleventh or the ramshackle slums of the Sixteenth, a neat grid of streets lined with four and five-story timber-and-plaster buildings, broken up by older stone structures. There's a gentle downward slope toward the outer wall, which sweeps diagonally across the grid from the military high-way gate in the north to a junction with the Tenth Ward wall in the south.

Somewhere along that long sweep of wall, something has gone badly wrong. Either a gate was broken or—more likely—opened from the inside. Either way, Imperial troops have flooded through, ascending the walls and taking the surprised defenders from behind. While they worked their way north and south to widen the breach, other columns pushed into the streets, engaging the hastily mobilized Red Sashes in a running fight across the ward.

I can track their progress by the columns of smoke. Thankfully, it rained last night, and most of the city is still too damp to burn, but here and there wisps of gray curl into the sky. The closest are no more than a few blocks from the inner wall.

Our position is getting crowded. Hasaka is here, of course, and Giniva, with me and Jack and Zarun, and a few other Red Sash officers. Meroe split off when we arrived, heading for the makeshift field hospital below the wall. To either side of us, men and women are pouring onto the battlements, armed with spears and crossbows. Hasaka has called out the reserves, obviously, but so far he seems content to watch. A young woman stands beside him with a spyglass, scanning the rooftops of the ward.

"Flags on the roof of the Grayrock, sir!" she says suddenly. "It's a message!"

I try to follow her line of sight. There's a huge, squat stone building in the middle distance, close to the center of the ward, and I can just make out a flicker of black-and-white semaphore flags atop it. I can't follow them, but the girl waits for a moment and says, "It's Ralobi, sir. He says he's holding but hard-pressed."

I glance at Hasaka, who doesn't seem inclined to explain. Instead I turn to Giniva, who steps closer and speaks in low tones.

"Ralobi is the commander in this sector," she says. "The Grayrock's an old prison, built like a fortress."

The girl has retrieved a pair of semaphore flags of her own, and holds them at her side, waiting for Hasaka's word. The old Ward Guard looks down at the fighting, mostly invisible in the narrow streets, and shakes his head.

"Ask her how many soldiers she has with her," he says eventually, "and how long she can hold out."

The girl wags the flags back and forth. A few moments later, the answer comes.

"A couple of hundred, she says," the girl repeats. "She says they can hold the prison, but they don't have any fresh water stored, so they can't last long."

Hasaka looks at the prison, and his lip twists. I can already tell what he's thinking. The soldiers on the walls seem badly shaken, and any attempt to rescue the people trapped in the prison is likely to meet with disaster. If the next wall falls, the Imperials could overrun the whole city before anyone could stop them.

Rot, rot, rot. I suck in a breath. *All right. Tori wanted me to help.* Maybe I can't command a rebellion, but *this* is something I can do. Hasaka is about to speak, but I cut him off.

"I'll get them out," I say.

Everyone turns to me. Jack is already grinning broadly.

"We can't spare the troops," Hasaka says. "I'm sorry, but a counterattack—"

"I won't need any support." *Not that I'd counted on him for any.* "Jack, Zarun, are you up for this?"

"Dashing Jack is always ready to spring to the aid of those in need," Jack says, spinning grandly on one foot.

"You know I'm with you," Zarun says. "Though Meroe might not approve."

"Meroe wouldn't want me to leave people to die," I tell him. Then I turn to the man in the blue sash standing behind me, so quiet everyone has forgotten his presence. "How many Blues can you get here in the next five minutes?"

He pauses only a few seconds. "Sixty-three."

"That'll do. Gather them at the gate. Weapons ready."

"Understood."

He doesn't move, but I imagine the orders rippling out through the weird connection the Blues share, men and women suddenly turning and heading in our direction, coming together in a silent mass. *Yeah. That* definitely *creeps me out.*

"Isoka—" Hasaka looks at me and shakes his head. "I can't stop you, can I?"

"Nope. Stay here and hold the wall. I'll bring those soldiers back."

I turn on my heel and head for the stairs, with Jack, Zarun, and the Blue following.

"Good luck!" Giniva calls after us, amid the silence.

The gate in the ward wall is still open, manned by nervous Red Sashes ready to swing it closed at the first sign of the enemy. Refugees and wounded stream through, screams and shouts overwhelming the barked orders of the rebel sergeants.

As promised, sixty-three Blues have gathered in the shadow of the gate, ordinary-looking men and women in plain, ragged clothing, each with a sword or spear. I beckon one of them forward, knowing that's as good as addressing them all, and huddle close with Jack and Zarun.

"Okay," I tell them. "It's chaos out there, so we shouldn't run into any really organized resistance until we get to the prison itself. The most important thing is to *keep moving*. We'll meet with this Ralobi and punch through back to the gate." I look at the Blue. "You all stay together, and focus on keeping our backs clear. Don't get bogged down, whatever happens. Got it?"

"Understood," the man says, as unconcerned as if I'd given him a dinner order.

"We'll clear a path," I tell Jack and Zarun. "And keep an eye out for Immortals or any other mage-bloods."

"A fresh hunt," Jack crows.

"I'm not sure if I'd rather be going after blueshell," Zarun says. "Crabs don't call for help."

"Just follow me and stay close," I tell them. "Here we go."

We press forward, breasting the stream of fleeing civilians. They shy out of the way, unsettled by the Blues, and before long we're into the street on the other side. The columns of smoke are all ahead of us—this area is, for the moment, held by the rebels, but that won't last. I take a moment to orient myself, pick the street that leads most directly toward the Grayrock, and start jogging.

For a few blocks we don't see anyone apart from more civilians hurrying in the opposite direction. Then I catch the flash and bang of Myrkai fire from up ahead, mixed with the shouts and screams of combat. I break into a run, Zarun on my left and Jack on my right, the mass of Blues pounding along behind me.

There's a barricade made of furniture blocking the street ahead of us. Two dozen rebels are fighting hand to hand with twice that many militia, the Red Sashes desperately fending off the Imperials' attempts to get up and over the obstacle. Five Ward Guard with crossbows bring up the rear of the Imperial assault, led by an officer whose hands glow with flames. As I watch, she hurls another bolt, which explodes at the top of the barricade in a shower of flaming splinters. The rebels duck for cover, and the Imperials surge forward.

"I'll take the officer," I bark, without looking back. The barricade is coming up fast, and some of the rebels have noticed us, gawking at this strange force charging to the rescue. I ignore them, too, and jump atop an upside-down couch, leaping from there to a chest of drawers badly scorched by sorcerous flame. Two militia with spears backpedal, not sure what to make of an unarmed girl coming at them full speed.

When I ignite my blades, they get the picture. One of them drops her spear and runs. The other thrusts his weapon at me, a panicked attack I twist away from easily. I hack the shaft in two with one swipe, then take his hand with the next, leaving him howling behind me.

Ahead, the Ward Guard are shouting to one another. Crossbows *twang*, but none of the bolts come close. I switch one blade to a shield and charge down the other side of the barricade. The Myrkai user unleashes a bolt, which slams into my shield without much effect, and barely has time to snarl an oath before I'm on top of her, gutting her with my blade. She falls away, choking, and I move to the next Ward Guard, cutting him down as he struggles to load his crossbow. Jack appears in front of me, stepping from a shadow to spit another man on her spear.

Behind me, the Blues are cresting the barricade, laying into the shocked militia. Zarun is with them, pulling Imperial troops into the air with Tartak and flinging them aside, like a child playing with dolls. I see one Blue woman take a crossbow bolt to the chest and collapse, but in only a few seconds the militia are running for their lives, scrambling away down side streets.

"Leave them!" I shout. "Keep moving to the prison!"

We run. We should be past the front line, now, but a fight like this doesn't *have* a front line, and we keep running into both Red Sashes and Imperial troops. It's hard to say who's more surprised to see us. Most of the Imperials take one look and scatter, but a few try to fight, and we cut them to pieces. The rebels mostly flee, too, but some take it into their heads to follow—when I look back, the crowd behind me has grown, Red Sashes mixed in with the Blues. *I suppose they think following me is as safe as anything else.*

Block by block, the prison gets closer. Crossbowmen fire at us from the upper windows of nearby buildings, and Zarun grabs them with Tartak and plucks them out to fall screaming to the street below. An officer on a horse bellows to a crowd of fleeing conscripts, trying to rally a defense, until Jack materializes out of his shadow and slits his throat.

We turn a corner, and Grayrock is suddenly there, a looming mass of stone that takes up most of a block. Giniva was right about it being a fortress—it's a single solid building, with one main door and a stable gate around the side, but no other entrances and only slits for windows. The Imperials aren't even trying to attack it—they've settled down for a quick siege, several hundred of them gathered in the streets outside, just waiting.

Or at least, they were just waiting. Someone must have managed to beat our little army there with a message, because when we arrive whoever's in command is drawing up his forces for battle. These troops aren't as scattered as those that have fanned out through the ward, and they line the street in neat ranks, spearmen in front, crossbows behind. Officers on horseback canter back and forth behind the line, swords drawn.

We're about a block away. I hesitate, but we can't wait for

long—if the Imperials get too organized, they'll surrounded us. *No way out but through.*

"Zarun! Can you stop crossbow bolts?"

He grimaces. "Not well. I've never been too agile with Tartak."

"Clever Jack has an idea!" Jack says, spinning out of Zarun's shadow. She points to a wagon loaded with barrels, its team long since cut away, sitting abandoned by the side of the street.

"Right," Zarun says, with a smile. "*That* I can handle."

He spreads his hands, and pale blue light grips the wagon. It starts to roll, slowly at first but gathering momentum, headed for the Imperial lines.

No time for much in the way of battle cries. I wave to the mob of rebels behind me—more Red Sashes than Blues now, somehow—and gesture with my blade. "Follow me!"

Zarun jogs to keep up with the wagon, and I follow. As we get closer, he makes a fist, and the wagon flips up on its side, scattering its barrels. They roll into the Imperial lines like projectiles, causing chaos, while the flat bed screens us. When the crossbowmen open fire, the wagon shudders under the impact of dozens of bolts. Some Imperials aim high, and those on the wings shoot around the barrier, bolts finding men and women in the mass and sending them spinning to the ground.

It's not enough to stop us, though. Zarun shoves his palm out, and the pincushioned wagon flies forward, bouncing end over end across the cobbles until it collides with the Imperial line. Soldiers dive aside or are knocked flat, the neat ranks of spearmen breaking up. I lower my head into a sprint, a blade on each arm, and dive into the melee with Zarun at my side.

Once we're in close, it's almost too easy. There's no shortage of targets, terrified militia scrambling to bring their clumsy weapons to bear. I twist, turn, and dodge, blades crackling and smoking as they slash through flimsy armor and flesh. Stray blows send waves of heat washing across me, drawing bursts of shimmering green energy. A head goes flying, and blood sprays, drops pattering on my face.

It's every fight I ever had in the Sixteenth Ward, all rolled into one. The criminals and thugs I exterminated for the organization were never a real threat to me—a few knives and clubs, occasionally a crossbow or a weak Myrkai touch. Since boarding *Soliton*, I've nearly died more times than I can count—against monstrous crabs, Prime's walking corpses, the Scholar's angel, or vicious mage-blood fighters like the Butcher. Now I feel like I've stepped back in time, to the days when I walked through the street trash like a god, sheathed in Melos armor and invincible.

It gives me a thrill, I can't deny it. The rush of power. I'd almost forgotten what it's like. But something has changed. I see the faces of the people around me, eyes wide with terror under their cheap mass-issue helmets, knuckles white on their cheap mass-issue weapons, and they feel like—*people*.

A girl swings at me, desperately, with the butt of her spear. She has a pug nose, red hair, and freckles, evidence of non-Imperial blood. Maybe her mother was from the islands, or her father was a Jyashtani trader. She grew up on a farm, most likely, did chores and tended animals. Has she found a boy or a girl she likes, kissed them, gotten tangled and sweaty in some hayloft?

And then, one day, someone with an Imperial seal comes to the farm and tell her there's an emergency levy. They hand her a spear and helmet, take her to the capital, tell her to wait, dig here, march there, line up with the rest. Then there's *me*, soaked in blood, glowing green, coruscating sparks arcing off my skin, crackling blades of otherworldly power on my arms. There's not even room to jab with her spear, so she swings the butt. It glances off my thigh, deflected by my armor, I barely notice as I turn—

—and this is how her story ends, this girl, this *person*, with a family and a life and a heart, throat torn out by a sorcerous blade, choking and drowning in her own blood and not even understanding a little bit of what's happening. One story after another, extinguished, left to litter the streets like garbage.

The understanding, the strange sense of identification with my enemies, comes and goes in an instant. I pull the blow that's already headed for the red-haired girl's throat, cracking her in the face with my elbow instead; her nose breaks with a *crunch*, and her eyes roll back in her head as she slumps to the cobbles, hidden at once by the press of battle. I stand still for a moment, not sure what comes next. I want to shout, but no one would hear me. And then another militiaman is coming at me with a spear, teeth bared in a snarl, and the moment is gone. My blades once again crackle and spit as they sever flesh and bone.

I can't stop. Not now. But Meroe is right. I've changed—she's changed me. *Even if the Sixteenth Ward hadn't burned, I could never have gone home again.*

I'm not sure if it's a comforting thought or a terrifying one.

The militia breaks, in spite of having twice our numbers. Their officers are dead, cut down by a slim girl who laughs as she dances in and out of the shadows, and nothing they have can stand up to the pair of Melos adepts who chop through everyone their weapons reach with horrible, effortless ease. Within a few minutes of the first blows, the Imperials are scattering, dropping their weapons and running, and in a few minutes more the street is empty except for us, the wounded, and the dead.

I resist the urge to try to find the red-haired girl. She matters no more and no less than any of the others sprawled in the dirt or curled around pools of blood. There are plenty of Red Sashes on the ground, too, and quite a few Blues, though the latter don't scream or whimper.

A small postern beside the prison's massive main gate swings open, and a squad of a half-dozen Red Sashes emerges, cautiously. I stride over to them, and they flinch from the sight of me. I can only imagine what I look like, scarred and marked and sodden with blood.

"What's going on?" one of the rebels manages. "Are we taking the ward back?"

I shake my head. "The ward's lost. We don't have much time before the Imperials regroup. We're getting everyone back to the inner wall."

The man shakes his head. "Ralobi will have to give the order—"

"Then rotting *get her out here*," I growl. "*Now.*"

He swallows hard and ducks back inside.

Fortunately Ralobi, when she emerges, turns out to be eminently reasonable. She's an older woman, heavyset and well-muscled, with the leathery skin of someone who has spent a lifetime laboring in the sun. I'm half-convinced she became an officer by sheer volume—her voice carries from one end of the prison to the other. Red Sashes start spilling out of the building and forming up in the street. We gather our wounded, hastily triaging those who might survive and leaving the rest behind, and start back toward the wall.

No organized Imperial force tries to stop us. I'm not sure if their commanders have decided it's not worth it, or if there's still such confusion in the ward that nobody really understands what's happened. Either way, we retrace our steps and encounter only the occasional band of militia, all of whom flee immediately at the sight of three hundred rebel soldiers moving with purpose. More Red Sashes fall in with us as we go, emerging from hiding places.

It can't be more than a fraction of those who were fighting to defend the district. But it's something, and the cheers and shouts of joy when we reach the gate ring loud in my ears. I wait for the rest to stream through before following, Jack and Zarun still with me.

Meroe is waiting on the other side with Hasaka, Giniva, and Jakibsa. I ignore the three rebel leaders for the moment, and wait for Meroe to reprimand me for running off on my own again. But she only smiles and kisses me, thoroughly, before slipping away to help deal with the wounded.

Maybe I'm finally getting the hang of this.

Reluctantly, I turn to the Red Sashes. Hasaka glares at me, then looks away, flushing.

"That was an impressive performance," Giniva says. "I can see why Tori was so interested in getting you on our side."

I shrug. "It needed doing."

"Rot," Hasaka mutters to himself, then looks up at me. "You're right. You saved a lot of lives. I . . . thank you. I know I haven't been . . . that is . . ."

"It's all right. I get it." I look up at the wall behind us, now thick with rebel soldiers. "Do you think you can hold the inner wall?"

"Probably," Hasaka says, his frown returning. He looks at Jakibsa. "But that may not be our biggest problem."

"What now?"

Jakibsa sighs, running his gloved hand through the fringe of hair that hangs over his burned face. "The grain store. The Fourth Ward is the site of the city's biggest rice and wheat wholesalers, and has most of the storehouses. We relocated as much of the supply as we could when we took the city, but for the most part there wasn't anywhere else to put it."

"So how much did we lose?" Giniva says.

"A lot," Jakibsa says. "Everyone's on half rations, as of now. And even that won't last. Another couple of weeks, at the outside, and we'll be down to eating rats."

8

TORI

The gardens of the Imperial Palace are, of course, the very epitome of the art. As sunlight fades in the western sky and the clouds glow delicate shades of orange and pink, fireflies emerge, hovering over the little stream that wends its careful way through the sculpted grounds. I feel like there's a pattern to the lights, and it makes me wonder if there's an Imperial Insect Manager somewhere, painstakingly breeding fireflies in different colors and training them to blink in unison.

Garo walks beside me. Some time ago, he reached out and took my hand in his. His fingers are soft, his palm slightly damp with sweat. He's nervous; I can tell by the way he won't stop talking.

"And then there's the ministries. The Ministry of Taxation will be abolished, of course."

"Of course," I murmur.

"Its functions will be taken over by a new Ministry of the Interior, which will also assume the role of the Ministry of Farmland, although my father wants to preserve some of the provincial bureaucracy—"

It's been three days. Or possibly four—time got a little hazy when the Immortal drugged me into unconsciousness. In that time, the palace servants have treated me like an honored guest. Meals are delivered to my rooms, arranged—of course—as miniature works of art, on plates hand glazed by masters of the form. More clothes arrived, tailored for me as if by magic, gorgeous silk *kizen* and casual robes, shoes and slippers and jewels and combs for my hair.

As dungeons go, it's certainly a comfortable one.

And Garo himself has extended every courtesy. He seems oddly unsettled around me, which I attribute to the fact that the last time I saw him I practically pushed him out a window. I haven't seen much of Lord Marka, thankfully, but every evening after dinner I find Garo outside my room, asking politely if I'd like to walk in the gardens. Today is the first time I've said yes, and that's made him even more flustered. He's been telling me for an hour about his father's plans for reforming the government, while I listen with half an ear and stare up at the darkening sky.

"What's that?" I say, interrupting a discussion of the expanded role of the Navy in maritime trade management. "The building with the silver roof."

It's just visible over the wall of the garden, catching the vanishing sun and momentarily lighting up in a blaze of gleaming red. Garo follows my pointing finger, and smiles.

"That's the Imperial Temple, where the Emperor personally worships with the Grand Supplicator. It's just behind the Imperial Residence."

I try to gauge the distance. It must be at least half a mile away—the palace is *huge*, with buildings widely spaced across the grounds. *The Imperial Residence has to have its own walls and guards. So it's not like I could just run into the Emperor in, say, a library. Right?*

"Have you ever met him?"

Garo blinks, confused. "Who?"

"The Emperor." I shrug. "It's just strange to think he's . . . right over there, you know. The actual Emperor of the whole Blessed Empire."

"It's easy to forget," Garo says. "He doesn't come out much. My father and I were granted an audience when we first arrived, but we didn't actually *meet* him. It was all ceremony."

"You saw him, though? What does he look like?" By tradition, the Emperors are never depicted during their lifetimes. Cartoonists use a stylized sketch of the Imperial regalia, and in plays he's always represented as a voice from offstage.

"Honestly? Just a young man." Garo shrugs. "A bit older than me, maybe, with a long queue."

That does match the boy I'd seen in the library. *And probably half the other noble sons.* I purse my lips.

"Something wrong?" Garo says.

"Just . . . thinking." I turn to him. "Are there many nobles staying at the palace?"

He chuckles. "There aren't many nobles left in the *city*. You and your Red Sashes put the fear of the Blessed into them. All the mansions in the First Ward are empty."

"But you're here."

"My father . . . came to terms with Kuon Naga. After the rebels rejected his first offer." He coughs, uncomfortably. That had been about the time I threw him out the window. "They made an agreement around changes to the government once the rebellion is finished. Reforms. Even Naga realizes things can't go on as they were before. My father brought us to the palace to show his support."

A bold move, I realize. Coming to the palace put Lord Marka in Kuon Naga's power, when he presumably could have fled to his country estates and the safety of his own retainers. *I wonder what Naga promised him.*

"Tori," Garo says, coming abruptly to a halt. He's still holding my hand, and his grip pulls me around to face him.

"Yes?"

"I know you were . . . involved in all of this. Deeply involved. But now . . ." He shook his head. "Being here, in the palace, and being privy to a little bit of what's gone on between Naga and my father made me realize how naïve some of my ideas were. I don't think what we fought for was wrong, exactly, but we didn't do it the right way."

The right way. Begging the government for a few scraps of reform. I try to recall the fury I'd felt, back at the beginning. It's distant now, the fire banked, layered over with everything that had happened since. *The things I did.*

"We need to . . . step back," Garo says. "Grow up a little. Someday, it will be our turn."

"Our turn," I echo.

"Right." Garo takes a deep breath. "You let me kiss you once, Tori. Do you . . . that is . . . would you mind terribly if I did it again?"

It's my turn to blink, and really focus on him. I've been so lost in my own thoughts I haven't paid enough attention. Now Garo is facing me, standing just a little too close, his eyes boring into mine. The last reds of the sky are behind him, and the soft lights of the fireflies flicker all around us. A stream burbles quietly to itself, but otherwise the great palace is silent.

And I think, *why not?*

"No," I say, then hurriedly, as his face falls, "I mean, no, I wouldn't mind."

"Ah." Garo swallows, and grins. "I . . . thank you."

He takes my other hand, and comes forward a step. Our lips brush, gently at first, then more firmly. My lips part under his, and I press closer against him. He's strong, and warm. My heart beats fast.

Even monsters can enjoy a kiss. *Can't we?*

"It nearly killed me to leave you behind," he says, when he pulls away for a moment. His breath is warm against my cheek as he speaks in a whisper. "I imagined . . . so many terrible things. But you're safe now. I'll keep you safe. I promise."

The next morning, as has become my habit, I return to the library.

The last two times I came here, the carved reading tables and long, dusty stacks were empty, looking as though they'd been abandoned for centuries. I tried waiting, choosing a book at random to pass the time—a treatise on the animal life of southern Jyashtan which turned out to be fascinating, if not particularly relevant. Today, though, a familiar figure is bent over one of the tables, with a stack of books beside him.

"Avyntea?" The name sounds strange, as archaic as the rest of the palace. It takes him a moment to respond; he looks around, puzzled, then breaks into a wide smile when he sees me.

"Miss Tori," he says. "My apologies. People mostly don't call me by name."

"Because you're the Emperor," I deadpan.

"Indeed."

"Shouldn't you be angry with me for not knowing the right etiquette, then?" I cross the room, and he pushes his book aside and turns to me.

"Probably," he says. "But it's refreshing. Call me Avyn, if you like."

"All right." I sit down across from him. "You can call me just Tori, then."

"Tori." He looks genuinely pleased. "I was hoping to see you again."

"Likewise." I smile back. "I was hoping I could ask you some questions."

"Of course! What about?"

I blink. I hadn't imagined, talking to someone who claimed to be the *Emperor*, there could be another topic of conversation, but apparently he expects me to ask him about the mating habits of Jyashtani canids or something. I shake my head. "You say you're the Emperor—"

"I don't *say* it," he says, frowning slightly. "I just am. I—" He pauses, and his face lights up with sudden delight. "You don't believe me!"

"It's a pretty wild thing to claim, isn't it?"

"Is it? I wouldn't know." He plays idly with the end of his braid, thinking. "Men have impersonated the Emperor before, I suppose. Three hundred years ago a young man got most of the way into the Vault of the Imperial Regalia with a crew of actors and a forged pass."

"*If* you're the Emperor," I ask him, "then what are you doing here?"

"Here in the palace? Where else would you expect to find the Emperor?" There's a slight edge to his smile that tells me he knows he's being annoying.

"Here in the *library*. Specifically, the library in a wing of the palace that I can wander into, even though I'm a . . . guest." I gesture at the quiet all around us. "The Emperor should have . . . guards. Attendants."

"Ah. I can see how that would be troubling." He leans forward across the table. "Can you keep a secret?"

I nod, skeptically. He grins again.

"I'm sneaking out," he says. "I have guards and attendants and so on, and they all think I'm asleep in my chambers right now."

"You snuck out of your own chambers? How?"

"I have my ways," he says, waggling his eyebrows. "No one knows the palace better than I do. I've lived here my whole life."

"All right, *why*? You must have a library of your own."

"This is the best one in the palace, actually. At least for the things I'm interested in. Everything in *my* library is so carefully vetted and expurgated that I don't even have to open a book to know what it's going to say. My tutors mean well, but they're a bit overzealous." He waves at the books around us. "Whereas *this* is where they stick all the books we get given as gifts that nobody really wants. It's not in much order, but you can find some fascinating gems."

The funny thing is, it sounds almost plausible. At the house in the Third Ward, our supplicator always watched my tutors carefully, making sure they didn't teach anything that would be bad for my moral development. (Clearly, *that* worked out well.) For the actual Emperor, it has to be so much worse.

But . . . still. I look at Avyn. *Really?*

"Let's say I believe you," I say slowly. "You really are the Emperor."

"For the sake of argument," he says, agreeably.

"If that were true, I'd want to say . . ." A bubble of anger rises up inside me. "What in the *Rot* are you doing sitting in a library? Do you have any idea what's happening outside?"

The smile fades from his face, slowly. I stare at him and shake my head.

"You don't know, do you? They haven't told you anything."

"They don't give me the details," Avyn says quietly. "And I don't ask. But if you mean, do I know about the rebellion, the fighting, then yes."

"And you approve?"

He presses his lips together. "It doesn't matter whether or not I approve."

"But—" I raise my hands, helplessly. "Why?"

I'm not really sure what I'm expecting. When I'd imagined our enemy, I'd always pictured Kuon Naga, the cruel, omniscient spymaster everyone knew dominated the government. It was hard to connect this handsome, charming boy to the slaughter at Grandma's hospital, or the assault on the Sixteenth Ward that had claimed so many lives. But, ultimately—always assuming I believe him, of course—he has to be responsible for all of it, doesn't he? Everything Naga does, he does in the Emperor's name.

"You're not a noble," he says, staring at me. "Not a guest like the Markas."

"No," I mutter. No point in pretending now. "I was—*am*—a rebel leader. Gelmei Tori. Unless that was a *detail* that got left out."

"That explains a few things." He cocks his head. "You must hate me. Should I be afraid?"

"Afraid?" It takes me a moment to get it. "I'm not about to assassinate you with a book, if that's what you mean. And . . . I don't know. Everyone outside assumes Kuon Naga is running the show. No one ever mentions the Emperor *doing* anything."

"That's the answer, more or less." He shakes his head. "Emperors doing things always leads to disaster."

"What do you mean?"

"I told you the story of Emperor Rhioa, didn't I?"

"Who took charge of his troops and got everybody killed?"

"Exactly. And here I've been reading about Emperor Valenga. In his time, there was a schism among the priests of the Blessed, with two different Grand Supplicators, each supported by their own faction. Valenga tried to stay out of it, but his advisors eventually convinced him to pick a side."

"And it went badly, I suppose."

"Catastrophically badly. The population turned on him, and there was fighting in every major city. Eventually Valenga was forced into suicide so his son could take over and renounce his decision. Tens of thousands died because he'd made the wrong choice."

"Things don't *always* go wrong, though," I protest.

"Of course not. Who's the best emperor you've ever heard of?"

"Uh . . . Gatlin the Great, I suppose?" I feel suddenly ignorant— the history of the Empire has never been a particular interest.

"Certainly. Defeated the Jyashtani, added two provinces in the north, reformed the coinage and ushered in a boom in trade."

"Right—"

"Never left the palace. Barely left his chambers, in fact, after his ascension. His wars were fought by generals, his Minister of Currency saw to the coins. Whereas Emperor Corund the Blind personally oversaw the redesign of the Imperial Mint, and bankrupted the state within a year."

"So . . . what?" I glare at him. "You're not doing anything about what's going on in the city because you're worried you'll get it wrong?"

"It's not just *worry*. I've studied our history, ever since I was a boy. My father died when I was young, you know, and I grew up knowing that all this was my responsibility. I just wanted to be . . . good at it. And what I discovered is that often means doing nothing at all."

"*Often*, maybe, but this is hardly ordinary circumstances." I take a deep breath. At some point, I started taking this seriously. *If he really is . . . I mean . . . what if I can get through to him?* "You could end this tomorrow! Tell Naga to call off the troops, cancel the draft, pardon the fugitive mage-bloods—"

"And then what?" He shakes his head. "That's the trouble, what comes *after*. Cancel the draft, lose the war. Give in to the rebels, and in ten years time there's another rebellion, twice as bad.

It's like—being emperor is like being a giant. You've got all this strength, all this power, but if you actually *use* it people are going to get trampled underfoot. You're big and clumsy and you're going to break things."

"So instead you sit in here reading ancient history while people are dying?"

"People are always dying, Tori." Avyn fixes me with his bird-like gaze. "That's the other lesson of all this. There are always wars, plagues, famines. No matter what, people are dying. I've spent ten years trying to teach myself how not to make it worse."

I get to my feet, my hands trembling on the tabletop. "That's horrible. You're horrible."

"From your point of view, I suppose I am." He smiles at me again, a little sad this time. "I guess you won't want me to recommend you any books after all?"

I storm out of the library before he has the chance to say another word.

I brood on the conversation all afternoon.

People are always dying.

It can't be that simple, that stark. There has to be *something* he can do.

And how well have you *done?* asks the traitor part of my mind, the dark slithering shameful thing in its depths. *With* your *power. You decided to wield it, in the end, and look where that's gotten you. If you'd stayed at home, been the good girl that Isoka wanted you to, none of this would have happened.*

Or it would have happened anyway. But it wouldn't have been my fault.

I'd thought Isoka needed my help. *Idiot.* She'd made it home without any effort from me. Of course she had. She's *unstoppable,* my sister, I was rotting stupid to doubt her. *If I'd only done nothing*—

Grandma Tadeka might be alive. The others from the sanctuary. Thousands in the Sixteenth Ward.

Monster, monster, monster—

I throw myself on my mat, facedown in my pillow, trying to blot out the voices coming from inside my head. Kindre pressure bears down on me, as always, like I'm wrapped in cotton wool. I try to push back on it, but it's like punching fog.

I do my best to ignore the soft rapping at the door. After a few minutes, though, I hear it slide open, and the soft rustle of a servant shuffling forward.

"Mistress Tori," a woman says, very quietly. "Dinner is in half an hour."

"I'm not feeling well," I say.

"Your presence has been requested," the servant says, then hesitates. "Master Kuon Naga will be joining us."

I sit up abruptly. "Naga's coming here?"

"Yes, mistress." The servant woman is bowed over in the entrance. "Please allow us to assist you in getting dressed."

I do, standing like a cloth-shop mannequin while three young woman bustle around me, pinning and arranging under an older servant's critical eye. I'm not sure how much the staff here are aware of my situation, but they obviously understand the importance of a visit from Kuon Naga. I'm soon swathed in the finest of everything—silk cool and smooth against my skin, embroidered in colorful patterns that would put butterflies to shame, hair artfully pinned and arranged with jeweled combs, face delicately painted.

Naga. I want to vomit, or sleep for a hundred years. Instead I smile at the servants, and follow them out to the main dining room.

I haven't looked in here, but it fits with the rest of palace—old-fashioned, expensive, beautiful. A long, low table has been laid for twelve people, with tasseled silken cushions at each place. Garo and his father are already here, along with a half-dozen other men I know are Marka cousins or close allies. They're talking in low tones, but fall silent as I enter, every eye directed my way.

Garo gets to his feet, gesturing to an empty seat beside him at the end of the table. I take it, gratefully, glad to have him between me and all those stares. It's only natural, of course. They must know who I am, and why I'm here.

"Are you all right?" he says quietly, squeezing my hand for a moment. "Father was worried you'd be late."

"It's been a long day," I admit.

Before he can respond, the door slides open, and another man enters. He's short and slim, with a bald dome of a skull and circular wire-frame eyeglasses. His robe is plain gray, unadorned, with long sleeves that hide his hands. You might take him for a clerk, except that everyone in the room turns to him and bows, including Lord Marka. I follow suit, trying to watch his face out of the corner of my eye.

This, then, is Kuon Naga. When he waves a hand to let us up, I see that he has long, lacquered fingernails, like claws hidden in the folds of his robe. He crosses the room, and I realize with a start that the only available seat is directly opposite me. Naga folds himself onto the cushion, and greets me with a smile and a nod.

Servants rush in, bearing trays with plates of jellied rock-eel and small cups of sweet liquor for the first course. No one moves, not daring to touch anything until Naga does. Finally, he reaches out one hand for his cup, lifts it delicately, and brushes it against his lips. Apparently this is some kind of signal, because all of a sudden everyone is eating in a clatter of chopsticks and porcelain.

"Master Naga," Lord Marka says. "It is an honor to have you with us."

"Thank you for welcoming me, my lord." Naga's smile is polite, his eyes unreadable behind thick lenses. "His Imperial Majesty wishes me to convey once again his appreciation for the support of his staunchest allies in this time of crisis."

"The House of Marka has ever been a friend to the throne," Lord Marka says. "I am thankful to have the opportunity to prove this once again."

"Indeed." Naga gestures at Garo with a lazy claw. "I do not believe I have met your son."

"I am Marka Garo, Master Naga," Garo says. He sounds wary. "As my father says, it is an honor for us all."

"It is a good thing to see such fine manners in a young man," Naga says. "Too many of the current generation are prone to frivolousness and strange passions."

I know I'm not catching everything that goes on here. Like the formal structure of a religious play, there are layers to this conversation reaching far beneath the surface. I'm guessing, though, that Naga's last words constitute a threat to Lord Marka—he must know about Garo's role in the rebellion. If Lord Marka is worried, he doesn't show it.

"And you, young lady, must be Miss Gelmei Tori," Naga says to me. All at once, conversation goes quiet along the table. "I have followed your career with interest, but I don't believe we've been introduced."

I bow my head, blood thundering in my ears. *What does he expect me to say? What does he want from me?* I reach for my anger, but all I can find is fear. I feel hollowed out.

"Miss Tori has been an exemplary guest," Lord Marka says.

"I'm glad to hear it," Naga says. That smile again, thin and bloodless. Everyone else starts talking at once, and I blow out a long breath.

Dinner proceeds, course after course. It is probably the finest meal I've ever had, but I barely notice the taste of it. I take a few bites of each dish, a swallow of liquor or wine for politeness' sake, and listen to the chatter that passes among the Marka clan. Mostly, it's gossip about other nobles—who has fled to the country, who is staying with whom, what it might mean in terms of alliances or romantic liaisons. Naga listens in silence, not eating much more than I am.

Every so often, Garo reaches for my hand. I think he means to comfort me, but I suspect he needs reassurance as much as I do.

We've reached the sweet pastry course, near the end, when Naga clears his throat. Instantly, everything goes quiet.

"I do have a little news from the city, as it happens," he says. He glances around, eyes running over Lord Marka and Garo and finally coming to rest on me. "Our loyal militia, led by the Ward Guard, launched an offensive against the rebels and won a tremendous victory. The Fourth Ward has been freed, and the traitors are falling back in disarray."

There's a brief, shocked silence. Then one of the cousins snatches up his cup and raises it high, proclaiming a toast to the Emperor and his loyal soldiers, and afterward everyone else has to compete to find the most ostentatious way to proclaim his loyalty. Lord Marka quiets everyone by raising a glass to those brave men and women who have fallen in the struggle, while expressing his hopes that the Blessed will cast the rebel dead into oblivion. Naga smiles and nods, approvingly.

The Fourth Ward. How did they get over the wall? All I can think about are the grain storehouses, the lines of hungry people who were already gathered outside rebel headquarters. *They won't even have to wait for the Legions. The Red Sashes will starve in a few weeks. Unless Jakibsa cuts off supplies to the civilians entirely—but in that case, we're guaranteed to have traitors—*

Garo nudges me in the ribs. I blink and look up to find Naga and the rest looking at me, cups in hand. *I guess it's my turn.* I nearly fumble my own cup and manage to get it raised.

"To an end of the violence," I offer, "with no more bloodshed."

Lord Marka narrows his eyes, and the cousins look at one another. But Naga raises his glass and murmurs, "To an end of the violence," and then everyone joins in a chorus. I sip from my cup—a strong cherry spirit, alcohol thick in my nose—and set it down again.

The mints that traditionally end a feast are produced, and I start to hope the ordeal is finally over. Naga picks one off the silver tray with two fingernails, turning it over with surprising deftness before popping it into his mouth. He gets to his feet and adjusts his eyeglasses.

"Your hospitality is remarkable, Lord Marka," he says, as though Marka had provided any of this himself. "Once again, let me convey His Imperial Majesty's gratitude for your service."

"I am honored beyond measure," Lord Marka says, with a bow.

"Now, unfortunately, I must return to my duties." He looks around the room, and his eyes catch mine. As if as an afterthought, he says, "Miss Gelmei, do you think we might have a few words alone before I go?"

"Of course," Lord Marka jumps in, before I can respond.

So I walk back to my chamber with the most powerful man in the Empire, the head of the Immortals, personally responsible for the deaths of many of my friends. We're escorted by a couple of servants, and I catch a glimpse of Garo trailing us at a distance. I open the door and bow to invite Naga inside, and once we're over the threshold he dismisses the servants with a wave.

I try to calm my pounding heart. *If Naga wanted me dead, or tortured, he doesn't have to come here personally to do it.* But then, why *is* he here?

"Can I . . ." My voice trembles a little, and I cough. After a deep breath, it's steadier. "Can I fetch you something, my lord?"

"No, I believe we will keep this brief." He folds his hands inside his long sleeves. The lamps are reflected in his glasses, like tiny fireflies. "And I am not a lord, as men like Lord Marka take pains to remind me. Master Naga will do."

"Master Naga." I turn to face him. "Then what are you doing here?"

"You *are* a bold little thing, aren't you?" That thin smile again. "Pretty, but with steel under the surface. An interesting combination. So unlike your sister, who is jagged iron through and through."

"I haven't seen my sister in months—" I begin.

"Spare me. I'm not going to insult your loyalty to her or your rebel friends by trying to turn you, so in return please don't insult my intelligence with stupid lies. Your sister returned to Kahnzoka four days ago and made contact with you immediately."

"And in response you had me kidnapped."

"Indeed." Naga's smile broadens, showing teeth. "I want you to help me, Gelmei Tori."

Anger breaks through the fear, just for a moment. "And why would I do that?"

"I think I can convince you it's in your best interests. That is, in part, why you're here, instead of stuck down some horrible rathole—and I assure you I have a wide selection of horrible ratholes at my disposal."

I roll my eyes. "So you think you can turn me against my sister with nice clothes and sweets?"

"Nothing quite so crude." He waves, sleeve flapping. "Do you know why the Empire—and every civilized nation, I might add—executes Ghul adepts?"

I blink at the sudden change in topic. "Because they're dangerous. They can create plagues, kill people with a touch."

"Exactly. But why are Kindre users not treated the same way? To command a man's mind is no less horrifying than giving him some rotting disease, and equally difficult to guard against. A true adept might even simply order a victim to die."

I shake my head, swallowing hard.

"There are two reasons, in truth," Naga goes on. "The first is that Kindre power is rare, rarer than any other well. Kindre touched or talents may never even know their abilities exist. But more importantly, Kindre has the property that defense is easier than attack—a simple talent, properly instructed, can fend off the mental assault of an adept, even block that adept's senses. Since there are many more talents than adepts, it means Kindre users are amenable to control." He leans closer. "This is, of course, the only reason I am able to stand in the same room with you. The only reason you are still alive."

"What does that have to do with wanting my help?"

"Just that I want you to understand it is feasible for your present situation to continue . . . indefinitely. If you thought I could keep your power contained only with serious effort, it would be no great leap to conclude that eventually I would have to kill you. Whereas I hope that, ultimately, you will be willing to trust me."

I fight back a laugh. "That seems unlikely."

"I do prefer to deal honestly." He shrugs. "The situation is this. Your sister came to Kahnzoka aboard a most unusual vessel."

"*Soliton*," I tell him. "The ghost ship. The one *you* sent her to steal."

He raises an eyebrow. "My, you *are* well informed. I suppose I should expect that of a Kindre adept. Yes, *Soliton*. She brought it back here, and it follows that she has control of it. From the beginning, our deal was that she would trade the ship for your life, and I see no reason why that should change. She, however, may be . . . difficult."

"Isoka does have that tendency," I say.

"And thus I need your help. If anyone can convince her, you can."

"And if I do—what, you'll let me go?" I have to admit, it doesn't seem likely, and Naga shakes his head with another smile.

"Unfortunately, your abilities make that impossible. No, the deal is this. Your sister surrenders *Soliton*. She will be permitted to leave Kahnzoka unmolested, never to return. *You* will remain here, as a guest of the palace, supervised by my Immortals but otherwise kept in luxury." He leans forward. "That is, after all, what your sister always wanted for you, isn't it? A life of comfort and ease, far from the danger and filth of the streets where you grew up."

"I—" The rotting awful thing is, he might be right. "What if she doesn't take the deal?"

Naga's smile fades. "Then we will have to move on to more distasteful methods. I'm sure I don't have to tell you that I employ specialists in . . . unpleasantness. I would hate to order them to go to work on you, but if your sister refuses . . ." He shrugs. "Let us say it is greatly in your interest to convince her to take the deal. It is the best you are likely to get."

I sit on the sofa in my chambers, head in my hands. Naga is gone, and all the lanterns have guttered out but one, leaving the room half in shadow. Voices echo in my head, like distant monks chanting.

Monster, monster, monster . . .

Again, there's a soft knock at the door.

"I don't need any help getting to bed," I mumble.

"It's me," Garo says. "Can I come in?"

After a long moment, I sit up with a groan. "Go ahead."

He slides the door open, outlined momentarily against the corridor, then closes it behind him. He's changed since dinner into something more casual. I'm still in my finery, the powder on my face messy with sweat and tears.

"I just wanted to make sure you were all right," he says, coming to stand in front of the couch. "Naga didn't hurt you?"

"No." I push down a hysterical giggle. "He didn't hurt me."

"Thank the Blessed." Garo sits on the couch beside me, bends forward to examine my face in the dim light. "You look . . ."

"Awful?" I force a smile. "Like I said. It's been a long day."

"I understand," Garo says. "Dinner was . . . difficult. Watching my father with Naga . . ."

"It must be difficult for him," I mutter. "Bowing and scraping to a jumped-up bureaucrat."

"He does what he needs to do for the family," Garo says. "Regardless of his pride. I never . . . understood that, before."

"An admirable man." My voice feels distant.

"I used to hate him," Garo says. "Now . . . I don't know." He takes a deep breath. "I know this, though. If Naga wants to harm you, I will fight him, regardless of what my father wants."

"Thank you, Garo." I turn to face him. "That's . . . very kind."

He hesitates. "Tori . . ."

I can tell he's about to say something stupid, so I kiss him. I want to shut him up, to shut up the voices in my head, and he's warm and solid. He leans into me, and my hands slide up his chest. He works his fingers into my braided hair, pulling me tighter against him.

Naga's right, about what Isoka wants. That's why she put me in the house in the Third Ward, pampered and protected, and cut herself off from me. She never understood that all *I* wanted was to be with her, whether it was in the upper wards or down on the bloody streets of the Sixteenth. Even when she held a knife to my throat, the only thing that ever frightened me was the thought that we might be separated.

But why should you get what you want? The voices mock me, shrieking and cackling. *Monster, monster, monster.* If I stay here, if I take Naga's deal, then that will make *Isoka* happy, won't it? She can go away, knowing I'll be safe. Leave me behind. That's all she wants. It's all she *should* want.

If I take the deal, I never have to tell her the things that I've done. Never have to watch her face as she realizes that her little sister isn't perfect, isn't pure. That Tori can live in her mind, untainted, and *I* can . . . fade away.

"Tori," Garo murmurs. His hands slide down my back, brushing the silk of my *kizen* against my skin. I break away from his lips, gasping for air, and he kisses my cheek, the hollow of my throat, across my collarbone. His fingers work their way up my flanks.

I lace my hands behind his head and pull him to me, kissing him with a desperate fever, as though I can lose myself in *this* and escape my thoughts. He matches me, breath for breath. I feel his hands on my sides, palms warm through the silk. His thumbs brush over my ribs, upward, and move across my breasts.

He pauses, lips still against mine. Waiting, I realize, for my approval. I feel his heartbeat jumping in his throat.

I know what comes next, of course. I'm not a child. And my skin is fever hot, the silk *kizen* like a blanket I'm eager to kick off, the heat running down through my belly and between my legs. And Garo is *Garo,* handsome and loyal and smart and funny, who helped me without question when I told him I needed it. And he's here, strong and warm, and—

He's part of the deal, I realize. Part of Naga's bargain. Not that he would agree to such a thing, of course. But that's why I'm *here,* with the Markas, instead of in some other secluded retreat. Naga is offering me a *life,* this life—luxury, safety, endless books, and a boy who loves me. I can stay here—I can stay with *him*—and everything will work out. Isoka will escape, the rebels will be crushed, and men like Lord Marka will tweak a few laws and proclaim what wonderful things they've done for the people of the Empire.

While men like Naga will still be in control.

That smile of his. As though he knows everything.

For some reason, I think of Avyn. *People are always dying.*

That's how Naga wants me to think. Stay safe. Don't act out. *People are always dying.* Why bother trying to change anything? Take the beautiful life, the beautiful boy, and be happy. *And Isoka never needs to know you're a monster.*

Monster, monster, monster—

Enough.

Just for a moment, I feel . . . clarity.

"Garo," I murmur, pulling my lips away from his. "Stop."

His hands fall away. "Sorry. I didn't—"

"It's all right." I take a deep breath and push myself away from him. Part of me still aches to be touched. "I'm just . . . tired."

"I understand." He gets to his feet. His face is flushed. "I'll see you tomorrow, then?"

"Tomorrow." I smile at him. "Thank you, Garo."

"Good night, Tori."

The door slides open and shut, and he's gone.

I sit back on the couch, staring at the ceiling. The last lantern flickers out, leaving me in darkness.

People are always dying.

I close my eyes, and open my mind. Fog pushes in all around me, blocking my senses. Somewhere, some Kindre talent in a black chain-veil is pressing down on me.

I gather all my strength, and start pushing back.

9

ISOKA

The crowd fills the square outside rebel headquarters.

They've been there since the news went out, two days ago, that rations were going to be cut again—half normal for Red Sashes, and a quarter for everyone else. That amounts to a few handfuls of rice or a crusted corner of bread. Not enough to fill anyone's belly, let alone people who are already hungry.

At first the Red Sash sentries tried to keep everyone out, but the sheer weight of the crowds threatened to trample them underfoot. Hasaka ordered them to retreat to the headquarters itself, barring the doors. So now we sit in the old Ward Guard barracks, a siege within a siege, and every hour the muttering outside grows louder.

My own stomach reminds me with a grumble that we're feeling the pinch, too. I've gone soft in recent years—time was, on the street, that a couple of days without food was only to be expected. I'd been an expert in gorging myself when meals were available and tightening my belt when they weren't. I'd eaten better as a ward boss, though, and even better on *Soliton,* once I'd accustomed myself to crab.

I was the one who insisted that we all had to share the reduced rations, even the commanders. Not out of any moral solidarity, of course. There's no faster way to bring on a riot then for people to find out their leaders are still living fat while they starve. Another thing I'd learned on the streets, watching more than one gang tear itself to pieces.

When we gather in the conference room, faces are grim. Jakibsa sits with Meroe, going over figures and tables. Hasaka stares off into the middle distance, as though looking beyond the far wall, while Zarun sits in a corner and glowers. Only Jack looks cheery. Sometimes I think Jack would look cheery while her liver was being devoured by wolves; the only time I've seen her break down was when she thought Thora was dying, after our first foray into Prime's bloody ziggurat.

Giniva is the last to arrive, a sheaf of paper under her arm. She looks us over, her lips a thin line, and says what everyone is already thinking.

"This isn't going to work."

When no one responds, she sits down at the table, tossing her paperwork carelessly in front of her. Her eyes are bloodshot, and there's more emotion in her voice than I ever remember hearing. We're all hungry, but she looks as though she's added sleepless nights into the bargain.

"Morale is collapsing," she says. "Especially among the civilians. We've had to pull fighters off the walls to guard the ration posts and prevent riots. I've had a dozen deserters arrested in the last day, and probably a dozen more that we missed. Between the loss of the Fourth and the lack of food, nobody expects us to be able to hold out for a week, much less win."

"Unfortunately, they may be right," Jakibsa says. He exchanges a look with Meroe. "Even at this rate, we'll run through what supplies we have in another six days. We could stretch it a bit longer if we cut off the civilians entirely—"

Meroe shakes her head. "You might as well surrender and save a few lives if it comes to that."

"She's right," Giniva says. "We don't have the numbers to garrison the city *and* defend it. We only have a chance if the people are behind us."

"They should be behind us," Hasaka mutters. "It's the Imperials who are starving them."

"They don't care, as long as they're starving," I say. "So going on like this isn't an option. What choices do we have?"

"The black markets are still open," Hasaka says. "We find the hoarders, execute them, and distribute their caches. That ought to buy us some goodwill."

"We've been searching," Giniva says. "Any hoarders still out there are *very* well hidden. And they can't have much—prices on the black market have tripled. Even the criminals are running out of food."

"What about retaking the depot in the Fourth Ward?" I ask.

"They'll be expecting us to try that," Hasaka says. "It'll be heavily defended."

"From what little information we have, that's correct," Giniva says. "And even if we got there, it's not defensible. Unless we retake the whole Fourth Ward, which we don't have the manpower to do, they'd just cut us off."

"That leaves the temples," Jakibsa says, with a significant look at Hasaka and Giniva.

I frown. "What about the temples?"

Giniva looks surprised for a moment. "I suppose there's no reason you'd know. Most of the city's large temples have been taken over by a . . . fringe group."

"A cult," Hasaka says. "Who believe the Blessed One is going to come back any minute now and smite the wicked."

"Broadly, yes," Giniva says. "They swear themselves to total nonviolence and spend all their in prayer and contemplation, to prepare for His return."

"And they have food?" I say, incredulously.

"We don't know how much," Jakibsa says slowly. "But there were significant caches at the major temples, and the early converts brought their own supplies."

"They're not on half rations, at least," Giniva adds.

"Then this seems pretty rotting simple to me," I say. "We tell them they have to share, like everybody else."

"We tried that," Jakibsa says. "They refused."

"Then we have all the weapons, and they're sworn not to fight," I snap. "If push comes to shove it's going to be a pretty short contest." I look from one of the Red Sash leaders to the other. "What am I missing here?"

There's a long pause.

"The leader of the Returners is a girl named Kosura," Hasaka says, uncomfortably. "She worked with us back when we were at Grandma Tadeka's hospital. She was . . . a good person."

"She and Tori were close," Giniva says. "During the rebellion, Kosura was captured by the Immortals. Tortured. Afterward, Tori felt . . . responsible. She would never listen to any talk of using force against her and the Returners."

Oh, Blessed defend. That sounds like the Tori I remembered. *But that's always been my job, hasn't it? Being hard so she wouldn't have to be.* I clear my throat.

"Well," I mutter. "Circumstances have changed. If Kosura can see that, fine. If she can't . . ." I shrug. "Meroe, will you come with me? Maybe you can talk some sense into her."

"Of course."

Jack and Zarun, silent so far, follow us out of the conference room. The hall outside is empty, like most of headquarters—everyone who can be spared is out on the walls or on the streets. I turn to the pair of them.

"Stay here," I tell them. "Try and keep them from doing anything catastrophic until we get back."

"Diplomatic Jack will endeavor to use her silver tongue," Jack says. "Although in this case she admits the situation might be getting out of hand."

"Right," Zarun growls. "Just hurry."

I pause at the harsh tone in his voice. "Are you okay?"

He purses his lips and sighs. "Just . . . bad memories. I spent a lot of time hungry in my younger days. I'm not enjoying the reminder."

"Neither am I, believe me." I search for something encouraging to say, and my obvious inability to find anything makes him smile.

"Don't worry about me. Worst comes to worst, I can always roast Jack."

"Tender Jack would no doubt be delectable, but opines that she would hardly be a morsel," Jack says. "If anyone is to be eaten, Zarun seems the better candidate."

"Hard to argue with that logic," I say, grinning at the two of them.

To leave headquarters, we enlist the help of a group of Blues, who still command a superstitious fear from the crowds. Also, if there's any trouble, the Blues at least can be relied on to obey orders and not lose their heads. Watching them silently push the crowd back with their spears, I feel the quiver of unease I always get in their presence, and I know without looking that Meroe feels the same.

Kindre. It seems impossible, but it has to be. *But* Tori? *Really?*

I shake my head and put it out of my mind. *We have more immediate problems.* The Blues surround us in a bubble of open space, but they don't block the shouts and stares. The people in the square are mostly from the poorer districts, refugees from the Sixteenth with their clothes in rags or laborers from slightly higher up the hill. But there are men in dirty but respectable robes mixed in, too, and women with colorfully patterned cloth stained with sweat. Many people have brought rice bowls with them, which they wave in the air in silent accusation.

We're trying, rot you. Screaming at them would be worse than useless, so I only grimace as the Blues shove their way through. When we finally reach the edge of the square, the crowd thins out, and we manage to break into a jog until we've turned a few corners. Here, the streets are eerily empty—everyone who isn't gathered at rebel headquarters or standing in line for rations is hunkered down, waiting for the worst.

Meroe pauses, leaning on a wall for support. I motion the Blues to give us some space and take her hand.

"What's wrong?" I ask her.

"I just . . . wasn't expecting that." She swallows hard and looks up at me. "They're angry at us."

"They're hungry," I say. "They're angry at everyone."

"I've never seen a crowd like that." Her eyes look haunted. "Back at home, when people filled the square, it was to cheer for my father."

"He must have been a good king," I say. "Apart from having you kidnapped and sacrificed to a ghost ship."

"Apart from that." She gives me a wry smile. "Sorry. I'll be all right."

"Take as long as you need."

Seeing Meroe unsettled shakes something in me at a deep level. Since practically the day we met, she's been the one I lean on, the unflappable, indomitable one. She straightens up and stretches out, then gives a decisive nod, but I can't help but watch her more closely. I tend to forget how much strain she's under, how much she takes on herself. Everywhere we've been, she wants to save everybody. *Even if they want to kill her.* But not even Meroe can save all of Kahnzoka.

We have to get out of here.

Moving north and east, we make our way through the Eighth Ward, toward the Temple of the Blessed's Mercy. It looks ancient, with bronze work on the outer fence that's gone green with the passage of centuries. The wide grounds are covered in tall, gnarled trees. The main gate leads onto a path that wanders up to a great hall with a double-curved roof, surrounded by lower, newer buildings. Every available space is covered in canvas, tents and makeshift shelters set up side by side. People are everywhere, sitting in group prayers, doing chores, or minding the dozens of children who run freely.

A pair of young women guard the gate, if guard is in fact the right word. They're unarmed, and at our approach they straighten up. They both wear plain gray robes with white belts, and their heads are shaven.

"Welcome," one of them says. "Do you seek the Teacher's wisdom?"

"I need to see Kosura," I tell them.

"The Teacher is very busy," the other girl says. "But lay down your weapons, and you are free to come into our sanctuary. She will attend to you as her duties allow."

"I'm here as a representative of the Red Sashes." I step closer to the guards. "Please tell your Teacher that I want her out here *now*."

"The Red Sashes have no authority within these grounds," the girl says. Her hands are trembling a little, but her voice is firm. I have to admire her nerve.

"If I come in," I grate, "how do you propose to stop me?"

Her eyes are very wide. "I will put my body in your path."

"And when you're dead?"

"I will add mine," her partner says. "And when I fall, another will take my place, and another."

"I have to say, if I were you, I wouldn't be thrilled with this plan."

The first girl swallows. "If we die, then we will be brought into the presence of the Blessed One, as he has promised."

Oh Blessed, do I hate fanatics. After a moment I realize the contradiction in that thought. Before I can try to formulate another threat, Meroe steps forward.

"This is Gelmei Isoka," she says. "Older sister of Gelmei Tori. I understand your Teacher was close friends with her. She'll want to see us, believe me."

The two girls look at one another. The name has clearly sparked some recognition.

"I will enquire," one of them says eventually. "Wait here."

I'm already on the point of just pushing past them, but Meroe lays a hand on my arm, and I grudgingly settle down. It isn't long until the girl returns, accompanied by an older man. He gives us a bow and a smile.

"The Teacher will speak with you," he says. "Your escort must remain here."

"Fine." I snap an order to the Blues, and Meroe and I follow him across the threshold, dodging gangs of running children as we make our way up the path.

"Isoka . . ." Meroe says, quietly.

"Don't say it," I mutter. "I wouldn't have actually killed anybody."

"I didn't think you would have," Meroe says. "But I'm not sure threats are going to get us anywhere."

"Fanatics." I snort. "Maybe they'll challenge me to a meditation contest like the last lot. No ice floes here, so we'll have to lock ourselves naked in a cage over a fire or something."

Meroe stifles a laugh. "That's certainly an image to treasure."

"The problem is," I say, glancing at our guide, "other than threats, I'm not sure what leverage we have."

"We'll have to see," Meroe says.

The great hall's main doors are open, so I can see that the place is full of believers, chanting prayers in front of an enormous bronze statue of the Blessed One. The man leading us turns off the path, heading for one of the other buildings, and brings us through a smaller doorway into a comfortable sitting room. Another shaven-headed believer lays a low table with steaming mugs of tea and a tray of crackers, which is enough to make my stomach rumble.

"The Teacher will join you soon," our guide says, as he withdraws. Meroe and I sit at the table, trying not to stare at the food.

"Would it compromise our negotiating position to eat them?" I ask.

"Probably . . . not," she says.

"Good enough for me."

I grab a handful and force myself to eat them one at a time, washing them down with tea. They're dry and tasteless, but food is food. Meroe is only a little less enthusiastic. By the time the door opens again, we've left only crumbs on the tray.

"I apologize for our hospitality," a young woman says. "But times being what they are, I hope you'll forgive us."

The Teacher is probably a year or two older than Tori, and her shaven head makes her look younger. She's a pale, delicate thing, pretty and graceful, though a fairly recent scar mars her face and she carries herself with a slight limp. The smile she gives us is bright and genuine, and she gestures for us to keep our seats as she comes and sits across from us at the table.

"Isoka," she says. "Tori spoke of you often."

"I can't say she ever mentioned you," I deadpan, "but I've been out of touch."

"She thinks the world of you," Kosura says. "They tell me you're also with the Red Sashes, now."

"We're not so much with them as providing temporary assistance," I mutter. "But yeah, that's about the shape of it."

"And who might this be?"

"I am Meroe hait Gevora Nimara, First Princess of Nimar," Meroe says, bowing. "It's an honor."

"The honor is mine," Kosura says with a slight smile. "I didn't realize we were entertaining royalty."

"You've heard what happened in the Fourth Ward, I assume," I put in.

"Yes," Kosura says. "We're not quite as isolated as that. And a number of those who fled have entreated us for protection."

"Then you know that the Imperials captured much of our remaining food supply," I say. "At this rate, we won't be able to defend the walls."

"And you know there are supplies under this temple, and others." Kosura gives a gentle sigh. "Tori and I have had this argument before. I imagine she sent you because she was too frustrated with me to come herself."

I blink. *She hasn't heard.* We hadn't exactly publicized the fact that Tori had been captured, though I know rumors have been spreading.

"Tori is gone," I say, surprised at how much the simple statement of fact hurts. *We'll get her back. We will.* "She was captured by the Immortals, almost a week ago."

"Oh." Kosura sits in silence for a moment, absorbing that information. "I . . . didn't know."

"Tori begged Isoka to help the rebels before she was taken,"

Meroe says, leaving out the exact circumstances. "We've have been doing our best to keep things together. But now that the Fourth Ward has fallen, we can't last more than another few days. If you do have food, we need your help. The city needs your help. It's not just the Red Sashes who are starving."

"I . . ." Kosura shakes her head, and I see tears in her eyes. "I'm sorry. Give me a moment."

She cares about Tori. And it's cruel of me to press an advantage, but I do it anyway. I lean forward and lower my voice. "We're pretty sure Tori is all right, for the moment. As long as the city holds out, Naga needs her for negotiations, and we have a chance at getting her back. But if the rebels surrender, then all bets are off. I'm just trying to keep my sister alive, Kosura."

"I understand." She sniffs, wiping her eyes, then touches the still-tender scar on her face. "Better than you can imagine, believe me. But . . ." She sucks in a breath, composing herself. "It isn't that simple."

"It certainly seems that simple to me," I grate.

"The food isn't mine to give," Kosura says. "It was cached by the faithful, and brought here in the early days of the rebellion, specifically to make sure we could stay *out* of this conflict. If I offer it to the rebels, I will be breaking the trust placed in me, and endangering the opportunity of every one of us to sit by the Blessed One's side."

I can feel my temper rising. "I don't think you're going to have much chance to repent and pray if the Imperials sack the city, or a hungry mob tears this place down around your ears."

"If that happens, it is also the Blessed's will." Kosura's face is calm now. "I'm not sure you understand why we're here. None of us expects to live out another month in the world as it is. These are the trials leading up to the Blessed's return—we are being tested, and if we maintain our faith, we will be rewarded."

"You know we don't have to ask," I say. "We can come in here and take what we want."

"And we will stand in your way," Kosura says calmly. "What then, Gelmei Isoka? Will you cut us down?"

"If I rotting have to," I growl. "I've done much worse, believe me."

"Then that is between you and the Blessed One," Kosura says. "My path is clear."

Meroe touches my arm, gently, and I bite back my retort and grind my teeth as she clears her throat.

"I wonder," she says, "if you've fully understood the nature of the test being presented to you."

"The sacred texts are clear," Kosura says, with a note of condescension. "I don't know how familiar you are with our ways in Nimar, but if you wish to learn—"

"In The Dialogues, Fasila writes that 'those who remain true to the path will be reunited with the Blessed One, and share his bounty in Heaven.' Correct?"

It's Kosura's turn to be taken aback. She blinks and says, "That's the modern translation. We believe it would be more accurate to render it as 'under Heaven,' implying that the reunion takes place in the physical realm."

"Interesting." Meroe grins, and I suspect only I would see a hint of the shark in her smile. "I admit I'm not familiar enough with Old Imperial to venture an opinion there. But I'm more interested in what it means to be 'true to the path.'"

"It means holding to faith in the Blessed One and his redemption, in spite of the tribulations of the times," Kosura says. "As I said—"

"But surely," Meroe interrupts, "it must *also* refer to living by the Blessed One's precepts?"

"Of course." Kosura gestures at the temple. "That is why we refuse violence, as He taught us, and spend our time in contemplation."

"And in Parallels, chapter nine, the Blessed One instructs us to 'provide food for the hungry, aid to the sick, and comfort to the dying, for this is the whole of the path.' Unless you prefer a different translation?"

"That is . . ." Kosura shakes her head. "You cannot simply pick out a passage from the sacred texts. They form a whole."

"I understand. I just want to establish that feeding the hungry is *among* the things the Blessed One commands." Meroe nods toward the city. "There are a great many hungry people out there."

"I know." Kosura looks genuinely anguished. "As I said, it is not that simple. I cannot endanger my people's souls."

"What if that's exactly what you're doing?" Meroe leans forward. "Have you considered that *this* may be the test?"

"This—" Kosura blinks, and falls silent.

"When the trials afflict us, it is to test our faith. And we demonstrate our faith in the Blessed One by *following his path,* not hiding ourselves away in prayer. If sharing food with the hungry seems to endanger us, isn't that what makes it more demanding of our faith?"

There's a long pause.

This can't possibly work, can it?

"I need to . . . consult." Kosura gets to her feet, not really looking at us. "Will you excuse me for a moment?"

Without waiting for an answer, she leaves the room, closing the door behind her.

I glance at Meroe. "I suppose you had comparative religion growing up in the palace in Nimar."

"Of course," she says, grinning. "We were intended for diplomatic roles, after all. Although I admit I did a fair bit of private reading. I always found the subject fascinating."

"But you don't actually believe any of that." I hesitate, a little uncomfortable. Meroe has never discussed what she *does* believe in, and I've never asked. "The Blessed One's teachings, I mean."

"They're not all that different from what our gods teach us. Or anyone else's, for that matter. Be kind, obey the law, respect authority." She shrugs. "I suppose the gods who teach 'kill whoever you want and don't pay your taxes' don't have followers who build empires, do they?"

"But Kosura . . ."

"She'll help." Meroe is confident. "She *wants* to help, but she felt like her duty required her not to. I just showed her a way to square the two. That's another thing we learned about diplomacy—the easiest trick is talking someone into doing something they already want to do."

"You can be terrifying sometimes, you know that?" I lace my fingers through hers and smile. "My strange princess."

"Thanks." She cocks her head. "I think?"

As Meroe predicted, Kosura agrees. We're summoned to another room, where she sits between a dozen shaven-headed believers, all looking at her with reverence. She gives me a nod, and then a deeper bow for Meroe.

"My apologies for keeping you waiting," she says. "And my gratitude for your . . . insight. Our stores are not unlimited, but we will offer what we can spare, to be used only by civilians."

That rankles, a little, but it amounts to the same thing—if the Red Sashes don't have to feed the civilians, that means more for the soldiers.

"The people will be grateful," Meroe says. "As are we."

"Gelmei Isoka," she says.

I sit up a little straighter. "Yes?"

"I know you will find your sister. I believe . . ." She hesitates. For a moment her face loses its serenity, and she looks like a scared teenager. "I believe that the Blessed One will not allow her to come to harm. But please. Help her."

"I will. Count on it."

"Princess Meroe," Kosura says. "We would like your assistance arranging distribution of the food. Given the number of people involved, it will be trying, I imagine."

"Of course." Meroe turns to me. "I'll stay here and start putting a plan together. You need to get back to headquarters as soon as you can."

"Are you sure?" I glance around at the Returners. I have to admit they don't seem like they present much of a threat.

"I'll be fine. When you get back, send Giniva to help. We're going to need to be careful if we want to hand out food without starting a riot."

"No kidding," I mutter. "*Be* careful, will you?"

"Of course." She leans forward and kisses me. "Go on. I'll be fine."

"All right." I glance at Kosura. "I'll send some more help when I can."

"Thank you." Kosura inclines her head. "May the Blessed favor you."

It feels strange leaving Meroe behind, but I remind myself again this isn't exactly a den of thieves. Back at the front gate, I'm reunited with my escort of Blues. I pick four of them out and tell them to stash their weapons, go into the temple, and find Meroe, then keep her safe until I come and relieve them. The blank-eyed soldiers nod, detached as always, and stack their spears neatly in the street.

"Anything important happening at headquarters?" I ask one of the others, as we set off back through the Eighth Ward.

There's a brief pause, as she consults through the weird mental link they share. I'm not expecting much, but she says, "There is a messenger waiting for you."

My heart jumps, but I try to restrain myself, remembering last time. "A messenger from who?"

"From Kuon Naga. He has refused to say anything more than that."

Rotting finally. I take a deep breath and look down the empty street.

"All right," I tell them. "Let's run."

Never bet against a Blue in a footrace, is all I can say. They just keep going, with a mechanical stride impervious to cramps or pain, and I imagine they wouldn't stop until they literally keeled over.

Did Tori really do *this to people?* Part of me still refuses to believe it. *Maybe she . . . found them, somehow, and took control?*

A light rain has begun by the time I get back, and the crowd in front of the headquarters has thinned, people heading to the ration depots to pick up their pitiful allotments or else going home to hunker down. The Blues clear a path, and I ignore the shouts that follow me up to the gates. The Red Sash woman guarding the door salutes.

"There's a messenger?" I ask her.

She nods. "He's upstairs."

"Take me to him."

We leave the Blues and hurry up. I take a moment to catch my breath, standing in front of the door to what was once an officer's bedroom. *Okay. Let's see what Naga has to say.* I wish Meroe was here. At the same time, though, I'm glad she's not—I've piled enough on her back. *This is my problem, not hers.*

I open the door.

The messenger is a young man in an Immortal's blacks, but with no chain-veil. He's dark-haired and pleasant-looking, with an aristocratic air, and he gives me a careful appraisal as I enter. I shut the door behind me, after checking to make sure no one is in a position to eavesdrop.

"Gelmei Isoka, I assume?" he says.

I rub the blue mark that runs across my cheek. "It's hard for me to deny it. You work for Naga?"

"My name is Rakol, and I'm here to speak for Master Naga and the Emperor."

"Where is my sister?" I try to keep my voice steady.

"She's safe. At the moment she's in the company of her companion Master Marka Garo, living as our guest in the palace. She has every comfort, believe me."

Garo. Giniva gave me a brief summary of his role in the rebellion, and said that he and Tori had been close. *Is he the one who led her into all this insanity?* The Marka family was powerful enough that even I knew their name, one of the half-dozen noble clans who provide the high bureaucrats who run the Empire.

Naga could be lying about any of this, of course. But it gives me a sliver of hope. *Tori's alive, at least, or he wouldn't be here trying to bargain.*

"All right," I say. "If that's true, your master has bought himself a couple of minutes to make his case. I assume you've brought some kind of deal?"

"Indeed." Rakol smiles placidly. "Master Naga abides by his commitments. The arrangement he offers is the same as what you were told at the very beginning. You will deliver the ghost ship *Soliton* into his control. In return, your sister will be allowed to live unmolested."

"I want her back."

"I'm afraid that won't be possible. But she will continue to live at the palace, under the lightest of house arrests, and in the company of the Marka family. Master Naga notes that in view of her frankly treasonous behavior since your departure, he considers this extremely generous."

I grit my teeth. "And what fate does your *generous* master have in mind for me?"

"You will leave Kahnzoka and not return," Rakol says. "It would be better for everyone, in fact, if you left the Empire entirely. Aside from that, he isn't concerned."

"So exile for me, and my sister is a prisoner forever."

"Tori will be *protected* forever," Rakol says. His smile is slick, and I can hear Naga's voice echoing through his words. "Isn't that what you wanted for her to begin with? A better life? She'll have the chance to live in the palace, with the family of a high noble. You couldn't have done as much for her in a century of slaughtering street thugs."

I've given up being surprised when Naga knows my secrets. I glare at Rakol, and shake my head slowly.

"How could I possibly trust you?"

"That's one reason Master Naga has allowed Tori to stay with Garo and his family. Lord Marka has considerable influence. If he takes it on himself to defend Tori, she will be safe."

"From Naga?" I snort. "Don't expect me to believe that."

"It would be . . . more difficult, at least." Rakol spreads his hands. "And Master Naga has no reason to lie. He cares little about either of you. It's *Soliton* that he wants."

"And the rebels? What happens to the Red Sashes?"

"Not your concern, and it never was. Leave the city, and leave the politics of the Empire to those who understand them."

His smile is getting on my nerves.

"When does Naga want an answer?"

"Within a day. If I don't return to the palace by then, there are . . . other contingencies. I hope I don't have to spell them out."

"If anything happens to Tori—"

"You'll take a terrible revenge on me, I'm sure." Rakol shrugs. "Hazards of the job."

I want to spit in his face. Instead I control myself long enough to say, "Stay here, then. I'll have food brought to you. And an answer, when we're ready."

I leave the room, closing the door hard enough that it clatters against the frame. A couple of Blues are waiting for me.

"I want this door guarded," I tell them. "Nobody speaks to the man inside. Deliver his meals yourselves."

"Understood," one of them says, and they take up positions.

However creepy they are, they're rotting useful. It's nice to have someone I can count on to do exactly as they're told.

I return to the chambers Meroe and I have been sharing, chase out the waiting orderly, and start pacing. Naga's offer is . . . not completely unexpected, but I still have a hard time parsing my feelings.

What I *want*, of course, is to tear the rotting bastard into tiny scraps. To charge in, find Tori, kill anyone in my way. But . . .

The palace. Of course. In addition to being on the other side of the siege lines, the Imperial Palace is naturally one of the most heavily guarded places in the Empire. While they've assumed the duties of a secret police, the Immortals were originally constituted as the Emperor's personal guards. No doubt a healthy contingent still protects the palace along with detachments from the Legions, all soldiers of a different caliber than the poor conscripts we'd cut through in the Fourth Ward. Much as it appeals to me, an assault would be doomed.

Plus, of course, Naga would never let me rescue Tori alive.

The same goes for entering the palace by stealth. Sahzim users make unparalleled watchmen. *And sneaking around was never my strong suit.*

Which leaves me with . . . what? *Either let Naga torture Tori, or take the deal and hope he keeps up his end of the bargain?*

It would mean never seeing Tori again. *But that's the point, isn't it?* Maybe it would be better, in a way. Before all this started, I'd tried to limit how often I visited Tori, knowing every contact put her in danger. I'd never been able to stay away for too long, though. I *needed* her, needed to see her face to remind myself that every-thing I was doing down in the Sixteenth Ward was worthwhile. That I wasn't *just* a monster.

But things have changed. *I* have changed. I felt that, in the fight in the Fourth Ward.

Meroe and I could leave. Go beyond the Empire. We probably can't go back to Nimar, considering her father tried to kill her, but there are other kingdoms in the south. Or we could visit Jyashtan with Zarun. Either way, we could certainly help ourselves to a fortune from *Soliton* before leaving.

And Tori would be safe.

I try to make it fit in my head, this vision of Meroe and I just . . . living. Not fighting for our lives every moment. It reminds me of our trip north, those precious few liminal days between one crisis and the next, when we'd had the chance to breathe. The image is a blur, but a powerfully attractive one. *I don't know what it would be like, but I wouldn't mind finding out.*

And Tori would be safe.

But . . .

There are a hundred buts. I reach the opposite wall, slap my hand against it for the tenth time, and start back the other way. I've been pacing long enough that the sun is setting, the light gray and fading under a layer of clouds. Rain still patters gently against the waxed-paper windows.

A knock at the door.

"I don't need anything."

"There's a report . . ." someone says, hesitantly.

"Take it to Hasaka," I snarl. "I'm busy."

"Miss Meroe requested that it be delivered to you." This is the flat, affectless voice of one of the Blues.

I stalk back to the door and wrench it open. The Blue, an older woman, stands with their usual calm, beside an obviously agitated boy in a red sash.

"What did she say?"

"She says not to do anything hasty," the Blue replies.

"What?" I frown. "What is that supposed to mean?"

"It's the food distribution," the boy squeaks. "The Returners announced they would be giving away rice at the old Eighth Ward market. But so many people showed up that the square was packed, and then someone started a rumor that there wouldn't be enough to go around—"

"Oh, Blessed's rotting *arsehole*," I shout, and the boy cringes away. The Blue stares at me, unmoved. "Meroe's all right?"

"She is unharmed," the Blue says. "Three of us are with her. But she and the Returners have been trapped in a storefront with Giniva and her guards. Several people have been killed, and the building is surrounded by a crowd."

"Hasaka says he's organizing a force to break it up," the boy says, "but they're outside headquarters, too, and—"

I ignore him and address the Blue. "Get everyone you can to the outskirts of the mob. Find Zarun and Jack and have them meet me downstairs."

"Understood," the Blue says, and her eyes go distant.

"What are you going to do?" the boy says.

I'm trying very hard not to imagine what could happen to Meroe at any moment. "Whatever I rotting need to," I snarl.

The mob is, if anything, bigger than the one that had gathered outside rebel headquarters. The shops of the Eighth Ward market, once a mix of cheap food and religious curio-sellers catering to pilgrims, are now shuttered and dark. But the irregular cobbled space between them is packed with people, many of them carrying torches, so it looks like a bobbing sea of lights. The rain has gotten harder, slicking hair and soaking clothes. Here and there, wood-and-paper umbrellas shift about like buoys in a rough storm.

At the periphery, most of those gathered are quiet, or even curious. The more frantic and energetic have pushed their way to the center, where several bonfires are raging, consuming piles of window shutters and furniture. The tightest knot of the crowd surrounds an older stone building, pounding at the door and throwing themselves against the windows. There's a wagon parked outside, which I guess delivered the first of the food Kosura had shared—its bed is empty now, and the team is gone. *Probably butchered for meat.*

Behind me are Zarun, Jack, and a squad of thirty or forty Blues. More are converging from across the city, but not enough.

"Is Hasaka sending soldiers?" I ask.

The closest Blue nods. "He says it will take several hours to gather a sufficient force without weakening the defenses on the walls."

"Then we're not waiting." I look at Zarun. "We're getting Meroe and the others out. Zarun, can you clear a path?"

"I . . . could." Zarun looks grim, his hair hanging and sodden, skin slick with rain. "But not gently."

"I don't give a rotting toss about gently," I growl. "Wait for my signal. But if they come at us, *break* them."

He nods. I turn to Jack.

"You get to Meroe and stay with her, whatever happens. Even if I get dragged down. Leave me behind. Understand?"

Jack, her purple hair hanging in a fringe in front of her eyes, gives a solemn nod. "Faithful Jack will protect fair Meroe with her life. But she trusts it will not come to that."

"I don't rotting trust anything. Not today." To the Blue, I say, "Have your people stay here and form a line. Watch our way out."

"Understood," the soldier says. The closest parts of the crowd shy away as they form up, leveling spears.

I gesture the line to open, and step through. Rain splashes all around me, rivulets running between the cobbles, puddles already forming. I can feel Zarun and Jack at my back, and I face the wall of bodies with a snarl. I draw in a breath and shout.

"*Everyone clear a path!*"

As I expected, this doesn't get much response. A few people edge sideways, misliking the look of the Blues, but most aren't paying attention. The air is full of shouts and the pounding of the rain.

Fair enough.

I ignite my blades with a *snap-hiss*. They stand out in the gray darkness, two flares of brilliant green, hissing and spitting as I raise them over my head. I shape them, making them longer and narrower, closer to spears than swords. Then I bring them together, one across the other.

There's a horrible sound, a sorcerous screech like a nail scraping across glass. Energy crackles and arcs, green lightning playing over me and leaping out to ground itself on everything nearby. A wave of heat washes through me, welcome in the wet and the chill. *Now* everyone is watching, the strobing, coruscating display of sorcery drawing all eyes, and when I separate my blades what follows is as close to silence as I'm going to get.

"*Clear a path!*" My voice is a hoarse scream. "*Now!*"

This time, people scramble to obey. But mobs have a mind of their own—or, rather, each individual person can only do so much, hemmed in by the weight of the crowd. The cobbles open up in front of us, but only halfway to the besieged shop, a broad semicircle of clear space. I start forward, blades at my side, trying to look confident.

"Rotting rebel bastards!" someone shouts, safe in the anonymity of the crowd. "We're rotting starving!"

"We need food, and they don't care!"

"Naga should hang you all!"

The circle of fear moves with us, the mob opening in front and closing behind. Some of the more excitable people in the crowd try to move closer, coming up on my rear, but Zarun takes position there and ignites his own blades. They fall back again, shouting abuse. A rock strikes my shoulder, making my Melos armor crackle.

Directly in front of the shop, a few people carry swords and spears. They've taken them from the bodies that are sprawled in the street around the wagon and the doorway. Most of these have been pummeled so badly they're nearly unrecognizable, literally beaten to a pulp. There are four soldiers, one wearing a blue sash and three wearing red, and another half-dozen in the gray robes of the Returners. A couple of civilians are dead, too.

The closer we get, the more the mob melts away, but the people at the very front have their blood up. Two men and a woman have been hacking at the shop door with wood axes, reducing it half to splinters. They turn to face us, rain-slick skin gleaming in the flickering green glow.

"You Red Sashes think you own the city," the woman says, stepping forward. "But we're the ones who suffer. Now you've made a deal with the Returners, and they're going to feed you while we starve—"

"Get out of my way," I tell her. "You have to the count of three. One. Two."

"You won't get away with it!" she screeches. "We won't let you!"

"Three."

She plants her feet and hefts her axe. I bring my blades across from both sides, intersecting like scissors. Her head and her axe both fall away, and for a moment a spray of warm blood joins the cold water raining down on us. Her body topples into the street, axe-handle bouncing off the cobbles. I look at the two men behind her.

"Count of three."

They run for it, joining the mass of the crowd. I step over the body.

And what was her *story?* I can't help but wonder. *Why did it have to end here and now?* But I crush the guilt before it has a chance to flower. *She wanted to hurt Meroe.* I come face-to-face with the broken door, and let my blades fade away.

"Meroe?" I hope someone inside is watching. "It's Isoka. We're getting you out of here."

The door opens. The shop interior is dark, and in the shadows I only get glimpses of shuffling figures. A couple of dozen in all—three Blues, some Red Sashes, more Returners. Finally, Meroe comes into view, helping a limping Giniva. Meroe's face is spattered with blood, and her dress is soaked.

"You all right?" I ask her.

"No." She looks at the woman I beheaded, then at the other bodies. "Not really. But I can walk."

"What about the rest of you?"

"Giniva's hurt worst," Meroe says.

"There's food in here," one of the Red Sashes says. "We were unloading it when they came after us."

"Leave it," I snap.

"They'll fight for it," Meroe says. "Tear each other to pieces—"

"Leave it." I turn away. "We're getting out of here."

We go back the way we came. Jack fades into being at Meroe's shoulder, and Zarun takes the lead. The crowd still won't come close enough to risk our blades, but more missiles pelt down on us, rocks and dirt and shit. A cobble narrowly misses Meroe, and I step in front of her. The next one is gripped in a blue aura as Zarun sends it sailing out over the crowd, and we hear a scream.

It seems like an eternity before we reach the edge, where the line of Blues is still waiting. The crowd could easily rush them, a mere two dozen spearmen, but fear holds them back. Meroe waits with Giniva until all the rest of the refugees have passed, and I stay beside them. Then, finally, we begin our retreat, while shouts indicate the crowd has discovered the shop's contents. As we turn the corner, I hear the first screams.

"You're not hurt." I repeat it to myself, trying to calm the pounding of my heart. We're back in our rooms, finally. "You're not hurt."

"I'm not hurt," Meroe says. There's a hitch in her voice. "Could you hold still a moment?"

"Sorry." I hadn't even realized I was pacing. Meroe comes over to me and leans against my chest, head on my shoulder. Hesitantly, I put my arms around her, and she presses in tighter. I pull her close, and I never want to let go.

"We were trying to help them." Her voice is muffled. "I kept telling them. Shouting it at them. That there was enough, that they just had to wait and they'd all . . . and then they just . . ."

"Rotscum," I say, very quietly.

"The Returners saved us," she says. "Giniva got everyone running, but we weren't going to make it inside until some of them just . . . stood in front of the crowd. People hit them with cobbles until they were just . . . mush."

"I saw." *Rot, rot,* rot. *Rot this bastard city and everyone in it.*

For a long while we just stand there. Meroc shakes in my arms, quietly, with the dignity of a princess. I hold her tight and make myself breathe.

"I'm sorry," she says, eventually. "I know you need me to be . . . strong. I just—"

"Rot *that*," I snarl. "Take as long as you like. If anyone comes in here to bother you I'll kill them myself."

Meroe chuckles weakly. "Maybe not *exactly* what I had in mind." She takes a deep breath, looking up at me. "This was just . . . they were just *people*. Not monster crabs or walking corpses or those horrible lizards. Just people."

"Yeah." I shake my head. "When I was fighting, in the Fourth Ward, there was a moment . . ." I grit my teeth. "It's hard to explain. But we shouldn't be here, Meroe. We don't belong here."

"Tori needs our help," Meroe says. She pulls away from me and goes to the table, pours herself a mug of water, drinks greedily. "They all need our help."

"They can go to the Rot." I feel my fists clench. "I'll take Naga's deal, and we'll be shot of this place for good."

"Naga's deal?" Meroe pauses, mug halfway to her lips. "He sent a message?"

"Yeah." I take a deep breath. "He wants *Soliton*."

"Of course he does. What are his terms?"

I explain, briefly. Meroe exhales.

"That's . . ." She looks at me, as though trying to decide what to say.

"It's what I wanted from the beginning," I say. "I hate his rotting guts, but he's *right*. It's a better life for Tori."

"You'd never see her again," Meroe says softly.

"So rotting what?" I shake my head, feeling tears prick my eyes. "That was the *point*. I should have never gone to see her in the first place. Had Ofalo tell her I was dead. She doesn't need me in her life. She's pure and perfect, and I'm . . . me."

"You don't believe that," Meroe says. She sips calmly. "About her, or about you."

"I let myself think it could be different." I look down at my clenched fists. "I was wrong."

Meroe crosses the room, covers my hands with her own. "You're not wrong. Not about this." When I look up, she meets my eye. "You may be wrong about Tori, though. Does the girl that everyone here knows sound like your innocent flower?" She cocks her head. "You've talked to Giniva and the others. Do you still think someone forced her into all this?"

"I . . . I don't know." I let my hands fall. "When I saw her, she was always . . ."

"Perfect?" Meroe smiles.

"But—"

I shake my head. "What does it matter? She's away from me now, and she'll have a better life."

"I don't think that would make her happy," Meroe says. "Giniva told me how she looked for you, when she found out you were taken by the Immortals. If you left her here, I don't know if she'd ever forgive you." She shrugs. "Besides, you know we can't give

Soliton to Naga. We need it to get back to the Harbor. We can't strand Jack and Zarun here, can we?"

I hadn't even thought about them. Or the friends I'd left behind in the Harbor—without *Soliton* bringing in more Eddica energy, eventually the city will shut down again, freezing itself in time to wait for the return of a ship that will never come.

She's right. As usual.

"So what, then?" I ask. "Try to convince Hasaka to attack the palace, and hope we can get to Tori before Naga's people kill her?"

"From what you've told me, I don't think that would work," Meroe says. "But there may be a more . . . subtle option. How much does Naga know about *Soliton*?"

"A lot more than he told *me*, that's for certain," I say. "One of his other agents must have managed to get some information overboard. The Scholar told me he's been trying for this for a long time."

"So he knows something about the ship, and what it can do," Meroe says. I can practically *see* the wheels turning behind her eyes. "But he doesn't know what *you* can do."

I look back at her for a moment, and then, slowly, start to smile.

10

TORI

I go back to the library to see the Emperor.

The last few times, he hasn't been around. That's fine with me, since I've had some reading to do to prepare for our next meeting. This time, it's a gray, cloudy day, and I can see the light of a covered lantern flickering from the table as I approach the door. I take a deep breath, straighten my *kizen*, and go in.

Here goes nothing.

He's sitting in his usual spot, with the usual stack of books beside him. The joy on his face when he hears me is almost painful to see. Most of all, I've realized, Avyn is *lonely*. I wonder how long he spent among these books by himself before I wandered in. If there's anyone, back in his official residence, he can really talk to.

Probably not. Who but an imprisoned traitor would risk actually *talking* to the Emperor? Safer to hide behind formal obeisances.

"Hello, Tori." He clears his throat. "I'm sorry if our last meeting got . . . a little heated. I hoped . . ." He looks pained. "If you want me to leave you alone to use the library, I'll go."

"You're the Emperor," I tell him, smiling to take the sting out of it. "It's your library."

"I suppose." He looks so relieved. "You seemed angry with me."

"I *seemed* angry?"

"To be honest I don't have much experience with people being angry with me," Avyn says. The slight twinkle is back in his eye. "But I definitely got that impression."

"Your impression was correct," I tell him. "Congratulations."

"I know from your perspective what I said might seem cruel, but I didn't mean—"

"I understand. It took me a while to realize it, but I do." I put on a slight smile. "Can you keep a secret?"

He grins back. "Naturally."

"I have never told anyone this. Not *anyone*. Not even my sister." It's surprisingly hard to get the actual words out. "I'm a mageblood. An adept."

He raises an eyebrow. "Really? Of what Well?"

I swallow. "Kindre."

His eyes widen slightly.

"Kuon Naga knows, of course," I go on quickly. "One of his Immortals is around here"—I gesture vaguely—"somewhere, smothering anything I might try to do."

"Hard to keep you a prisoner otherwise," Avyn murmurs. "A commoner Kindre adept. How extraordinary. If you'd been found out—"

"They would have taken me for the Immortals. Or killed me, if they thought I couldn't be controlled." I let my face go hard. "Or given me to some noble family, to be raped and bear children to add strength to their bloodline—"

He winces. "It's a barbaric practice."

So why not do *something about it?* This time I don't say it out loud, but he can see it in my face, and he looks away. *And it's not as though the Imperial family never needed its blood strengthened. How many of your ancestors were chained to their beds, do you think?*

I clear my throat. "The point is," I say aloud. "Do you know what it's like, being a Kindre adept? If no one knows what you are?"

He shakes his head, fascinated.

"You can reach out to anyone around you, whenever you want, and *twist* them." I close my eyes for a moment. "Always get your way. Always win an argument. And they wouldn't even know it. It would be wrong, I *know* it would be wrong, but sometimes the world feels like trying to walk on a bed of eggshells. It would be so easy. But once you start . . . there's nothing left. Nothing real."

My dreams come back to me, the whole world transformed into a puppeteer's stage, with the strings wrapped around my fingers.

"I imagine," I tell Avyn, "that it's a little bit like being Emperor."

Very slowly, he nods.

"So I do understand," I go on. "I spent most of my life hiding from my power. And the times when I did use it . . . I don't know if it was the right choice. If I made things better instead of worse."

Another nod. "Clumsy giants."

"Right." I take a deep breath. "But I've been doing some reading, too. Have you heard of the Emperor Gengjo?"

Avyn looks a little thrown by this change of topic, but he's willing to play along. His forehead creases in thought. "Pre-Blessed by about five hundred years, wasn't he? Made a mess of things, if I remember correctly."

"More or less. Back in those days, the Emperor could have multiple wives, and Gengjo had two. They were both political marriages—one was Jyashtani, the other was from Nimar. Poor Gengjo was a quiet soul, as best I can tell. He just wanted to stay in his garden and look at the stars with a telescope—which he basically invented, incidentally. But both the Empresses were ambitious, and they hated each other like poison. So while Gengjo hid himself in his garden, the court split into two factions, and it very nearly came to civil war. The Empire ended up fighting both Jyashtan and Nimar before the decade was out. Tens of thousands died."

"Remind me not to marry two ambitious women," Avyn said, with a half smile.

"Or take the Emperor Curoa," I say, ignoring him. "He had a finance minister who was exceeding his authority, squeezing the people until they were forced off their land so his cronies could expand their holdings. Representatives from the farmers came to plead with the Emperor, and he sympathized. But the minister was from an influential family, and the Emperor needed him.

"When the peasants finally rose in rebellion, the Emperor knew they'd been wronged, so he wouldn't let the Legions restore order. But he couldn't give in to their demands and remove the finance minister, either. So things just got worse and worse. A rebel army nearly burned Kahnzoka before one of Curoa's generals took matters into his own hands."

"I sense that you're trying to make a point."

"I am." My palms are sweating, and I rub them against my *kizen*. "I'm not the historian you are, I'm sure, but I can follow an argument. When you told me about Rhioa and Valenga, you meant to show me that when the Emperor intervenes—when he makes a choice—things go badly."

"Exactly—"

"But what that ignores is that doing nothing is *also a choice*. Once you know what's happening, it's not just a matter of which side you come down on, because not picking a side is using your power just the same. It's not always the wrong move, but that doesn't mean it's always the right one, either." I'm talking too fast, and I force myself to breathe. "Do you need more examples? I have more examples."

"I think I get the gist," he says. His eyes are hooded, now, giving away nothing. "But it's not that simple. My position—"

"Of course. That's what I realized, when it came to *my* power. I could use it, and maybe help people, but it would put me at risk. I could pick a side, or—"

"Be a coward?" His face is dark, and I wonder if I've gone too far.

"It's *not that simple*. If a plan has a small chance of accomplishing a little good, you'd be a fool to bet your life on it. If it's certain to accomplish a great deal, it would be equally foolish not to accept a bit of risk. It all comes down to the circumstances."

"Now you sound like a merchant, calculating percentages and odds."

"Better a merchant than a supplicator chanting *thou shalt not*. Merchants get things done. Who was the last supplicator who accomplished anything useful?"

That makes him smile, at least. "A touch," he murmurs. "If I could get back every hour I've spent listening to the Grand Supplicator drone on, I could do . . . well, just about anything."

"Then you appreciate my point?"

"In a manner of speaking." He sighs and waves at the books around us. "In the end, though, it's all so much hot air rustling dusty pages."

"It doesn't have to be."

His eyes narrow. "Meaning what?"

"Hypothetically. If you were so inclined. You could help me get out of here."

There's a long silence. Too long. My heart thumps, painfully loud.

"I can't just tell Kuon Naga to release you," he says. "If even he knew I'd *met* you . . ."

"I understand," I say hastily. "I know you can't move against him openly. But you must have a way in and out, one that gets you past the guards. Otherwise they wouldn't let you alone, would they?" I wipe my hands on my *kizen* again. "You once told me that you know the palace better than anyone."

"I do," he says. "Though there's a bit more to it than that. But why should I help you? You want me to intervene—why is *this* the right way?"

"I . . ." I hesitate, and Avyn sighs.

"You'd make a good scholar, Tori," he says. "But this . . ." He shakes his head. "I don't know. I need to think."

"Think, then." I fix his gaze with my own. "But not for too long."

It's not going to work.

I should never have expected to get Avyn to help. Of course a few citations from ancient history aren't going to overcome a lifetime of caution. Emperor or not, he's a schoolboy like any other, coming up with convenient justifications for why he shouldn't take any risks.

There has to be another way. Maybe I can find whatever secret passages he uses for myself. *But I'm running out of time. . . .*

I pass through a courtyard, staying to the covered path to keep out of the spitting rain, and find myself facing a trio of palace servants. They bow, deep and respectful, and one of them steps forward.

"Miss Gelmei," she says. "Master Naga requests your presence."

"Naga's here?"

"Yes, miss." She bows again. "Please, come with me."

And just like that, there may be no time left at all. My mouth goes dry, and I lick my lips as I make my own bow and follow them. The servants lead me to a small sitting room, sliding the door open and shuffling out of the way. Naga is waiting inside, legs crossed on a cushion, peeling an orange with his long, claw-like fingernails. Standing behind him is an Immortal, motionless in black leather and a chain-veil. I freeze as I recognize the Melos and Rhema adept who kidnapped me from rebel headquarters. *Kadi.* I hear her rasping voice. *The only reason you're not screaming in agony right now is because Master Naga requires you undamaged. For the moment.*

"Miss Gelmei," Naga says pleasantly. "So glad you found time to see me. You have been difficult to locate this afternoon."

"I went for a walk," I manage. "There are some wonderful gardens here."

"I'm sure there are." He gives his joyless smile. "I wanted to give you the good news. Your sister has agreed to . . . a discussion."

Isoka. I wonder what took so long. *Probably had to decide whether it was really worth getting me back.* I try to squash that thought, but it lingers like an unwanted guest.

"As you can imagine," Naga says, "she is not inclined to trust me. She is coming to the palace tomorrow, to verify that you are in good health. You will have the opportunity to help convince her to accept the deal. I suggest you take it."

"Isoka isn't going to listen to me," I say.

"I think she will. And it is in your best interest to be persuasive. If she refuses . . ." He nods at Kadi, who crosses her arms. "Well. Various of my employees are quite cross with you, and I might be inclined to let them relieve their frustrations."

"Very subtle," I tell him.

"I am only subtle when that is what the task requires, Miss Gelmei," Naga says. "Some objectives require a scalpel. Others call for a hammer."

"Or a bonesaw," Kadi says, in her raspy voice. "Or a branding iron."

"I get it, all right?" I hug myself, protectively, showing Naga a little bit of the weakness he wants to see, letting my voice quiver a little. It's not hard. "I'll get Isoka to go along."

"Very good." Naga pops the last of the orange slices into his mouth, leaving a neat coil of peel on the table. "Then I will see you tomorrow."

He gets up, nods to me, and moves to the door. Kadi falls in behind him, chain-veil jingling gently. As she passes me she gives a grunt that's as good as a threat, and chuckles as I flinch away.

Tomorrow. My mind is racing. *Rot rot* rot. There might be another way out, but I'm not going to find it. Not in time. *It has to be Avyn.*

"Tori?" Garo's voice. He peers around the corner, catches sight of me, and hurries over. "I heard Naga wanted to see you. Are you okay?"

"For now." I look past him to make sure he's alone, and lower my voice. "He asked me to convince Isoka to surrender."

"That's what I thought." He lets out a breath. "If you do what he wants, he'll let you stay here. My father will see to it, I promise. You'll be safe."

"I know." I give Garo a wan smile. "You've been so kind to me. I feel . . ."

"Please." Garo steps closer, hesitantly, and when I don't back away he folds me in his arms. "I told you I'd take care of you."

I feel guilty, I finish to myself, *because you've done your best, and I'm going to turn away.* In another life, maybe, we could have made it work—the nobleman and the street girl, like something from a romantic play. *But not here. Not with blood spilled in the streets. Not with everything I've done.*

Garo would stay here, with his father and his comfortable life, telling himself he was supporting everything our rebellion had wanted. Maybe they'd manage to get the draft quotas lowered by half a percent, or prosecute some of the corruption in the Ward Guard. *And Naga will get his war with Jyashtan. Poor bastards who can't afford a bribe will be shipped off to die in the fleet. And mage-blood commoners like Isoka and me will keep getting dragged away by the Immortals.*

"I know what I need to do," I tell him. "I'm just scared, is all."

"You're strong enough." Garo hugs me a little tighter. "I know you are."

The Emperor is waiting for me the next morning. I had a feeling he would be. This time he's turned his chair around and placed another one beside it with a stack of books between them, ready for a debate. He's grinning broadly.

"I found a few more examples to consider," he says, patting the tomes. "The question of whether *inaction* can be viewed as a true course in and of itself, rather than a default—"

"Avyn."

He blinks. "Yes?"

"Listen to me very carefully."

The Emperor straightens up in his chair. "All right."

"If you don't help me, right now, then Kuon Naga is going to have me tortured to death."

It's not *precisely* a lie. More like a strong probability. I certainly don't think that Isoka is likely to turn over *Soliton*, whatever I say to her. And in the end I can't bring myself to sing Naga's tune. *Which means Kadi will get her chance.*

"He—what?" Avyn shakes his head. "He can't."

"He can. Of course he can. What do you think he *does* with people when they disappear?"

The Emperor draws himself up. "I'm not a *child*. I know that the realities of governing can be unpleasant. But you're a guest of the palace. He wouldn't just—"

"I'm only a guest of the palace because he thought that was the best way to get me to play along," I say. "He doesn't know I've been sharing a library with the Emperor."

"But—"

I watch his face, his eyes darting as he looks for a way out. I feel a pang of sympathy for him, this young man who takes his responsibility so seriously. He knows, as he said, that the realities of governing can be unpleasant. But they're supposed to happen *out there*, beyond the walls, to faceless people he can imagine but never meet.

After a long moment, he slumps back in his chair.

"What am I supposed to do?" he says. "Order Naga to arrest himself?" He shakes his head. "Replace him as chief of the Immortals, perhaps. If there was someone else—"

"It won't work," I tell him. "You know that. The Immortals are loyal to Naga." Naga's not so foolish that he'd have it any other way. "If we had more time, there might be some way to undermine him, but—"

"Then what?"

"What I told you before. You have to help me sneak out of the palace."

"If they find us . . ."

"They'll kill me," I say, matter-of-factly. "And I imagine Naga will find a way to keep *you* from wandering."

"He's had me confined to my rooms before," Avyn whispers. "For months. Told everyone I was ill. I nearly went mad."

"I know it's a lot to ask," I say. "But I don't have any other choices."

"No." He takes a deep breath. "You don't, do you?"

There's a pause, silence balanced on the edge of a knife. Then he stands up, squaring his shoulders.

"Follow me."

11

ISOKA

"You have everything you need?" Meroe says.

I touch my collar, where the piece of *Soliton* conduit hangs on a cord beneath my shirt. It still pulses reassuringly with Eddica energy. "Got it."

"And you'll be careful." It's not a question, not a suggestion, just a statement of fact.

"Of course," I tell her. "You, too. Your part may be more dangerous than mine, you know."

"I seriously doubt that," Meroe says, running her hands through the curls of her hair. She ties it back with a knotted cord, then leans forward to kiss me. "But I'll be careful, too."

Zarun, Jack, and Giniva are waiting for me outside, along with a dozen Blues. Zarun looks better fed and in considerably better humor. Jack's purple hair is starting to show black at the roots. Giniva still walks with a slight limp, but otherwise seems recovered from the disastrous first attempt to distribute food. Since then, Hasaka and Jakibsa have organized a more careful dispersal of Kosura's gifts, with plenty of warning and heavy guard. For now, the square in front of rebel headquarters is empty again, though Kosura warns me her stores won't last long.

Hopefully we'll take care of that today, too. The audacity of what we're trying to pull still takes my breath away. *It's like walking a tightrope. Just keep moving and don't look down.*

"Have Naga's messengers arrived yet?" I ask the nearest Blue.

She looks into the distance for a moment, then nods. "They

have approached the wall carrying a flag of truce. As instructed, they have not been fired on."

"Tell the local commander we'll be there soon, and to keep his eyes on them." I turn to the others. "Everyone still sure you want to be a part of this?"

"You're going to need backup in case something goes wrong," Zarun says. "That's why I'm here."

"Likewise," Jack agrees. "And Curious Jack has always wanted to see the Imperial Palace."

I glance at Giniva, who nods. "One of us needs to be there," she says. "And the opportunity to observe Naga up close might be useful."

"Fair enough." I had to ask. "Let's get moving, then."

It's a long hike up the military highway, between the abandoned ward walls of the Sixth and Eighth, tramping steadily uphill toward the front line—the east-west wall dividing those districts from the Second and Third Wards. As I'd observed the night we arrived, most civilians have already evacuated the area, crowding into the "safer" wards farther south. *It must have gotten worse since the fall of the Fourth Ward.* We see almost no one as we move north.

Eventually, the wall comes into sight. I used to make this trip to visit Tori by carriage, and I never quite realized how long it is on foot. *Or maybe I'm just getting soft.* A large squad of Red Sashes comes out, commanded by a nervous sergeant who encourages us to hurry to the wall.

"Is there a problem?" I ask her.

"Not yet," she mutters. "But I don't like having Imperials so close, and neither do the rest. There are a lot of itchy trigger fingers."

Let's not get my little sister killed with your itchy rotting fingers. I restrain myself and just hurry along. The ward walls are high and strong here, to protect the wealthy at the city's height from the rotscum below. Now they've been awkwardly turned to the opposite purpose, wooden hoardings and mantlets providing cover where the original designers hadn't intended any. Red Sashes with crossbows are everywhere, staring down at the no-man's-land that extends from the base of the wall to the edge of bowshot.

The big gates are closed, but a team has already lifted the bar out of the way. A score of spearmen stand by, ready to block the gap if the Imperials try a sudden rush. *Paranoia.* I approve. I give the sergeant a nod, and she shouts orders. Four men haul the gates open, and everyone holds their breath.

On the other side of the wall is the Imperial truce party. Four soldiers in Ward Guard uniforms, one of them holding a white flag. Some ways back, I see a line of militia spearmen, waiting in case something goes wrong.

I find myself smiling, in spite of it all. I recognize the tension in the air, the moment of standoff, when no one is certain if all the poised violence is going to come rushing out or stay bottled up. When I was boss of the Sixteenth Ward, this was the moment after I'd kicked in someone's door, and they had to decide whether to pay up or take their chances with a blade. A surprising number went the latter route, even once the bodies started to pile up. I suppose anyone who thinks they can cheat the underworld of its cut is by definition a hopeless optimist.

Today, of course, I'm hoping things *don't* get violent. But I put on the same cocky smile I wore back in the old days as I stride out to meet Naga's embassy. *It can't hurt to put them on edge.* We pass through the gate, and it begins grinding shut behind us.

"Gelmei Isoka?" the Ward Guard officer calls.

"That's me," I say.

"We have instructions to take you to meet Master Naga," the man says. His eyes roam uncertainly over the people behind me. "I wasn't aware you were bringing an . . . escort."

"I wouldn't want Master Naga to get the impression that I trust him," I say.

"We've brought a carriage," the officer says, "but some of you are going to have to walk."

"We'll all walk." No way am I letting them put me in a wooden box heading who-knows-where. "Lead the way."

The man frowns. "As you say. Follow me, please."

We walk farther up the hill, following the boundary between the Second and Third Wards. The houses around us get grander as we ascend, set back from the streets amidst their lawns and gardens, peaked roofs rising over protective screens of pine and willow trees. Big circular stones marked with family crests start to appear, denoting the minor nobility, who share this tier of the city with those poorer in blood but better endowed with gold. The four Ward Guard lead the way, still carrying the white flag, while the troop of militia fall in behind us. They keep a good distance back, giving us a wide berth.

"This looks more like the Empire you see in paintings and woodcuts," Zarun says, approvingly. "Why do some of the houses have silver birds on the roofs?"

"They're falcons. Supposed to bring good luck." I shrug.

"From a pre-Blessed tradition of honoring local spirits!" Jack puts in. When we both look at her, she only shrugs. "What? Jack reads a bit in her spare time."

Soon enough, we come to the next ward wall, even larger than the last. This one blocks off the First Ward, and I'm not surprised to see it fully manned by well-equipped soldiers. Our guide has to yell explanations for some time before the gates reluctantly open, and the road beyond is lined with neatly turned out crossbowmen.

Here the houses, big as they must be, are invisible. The military highway drives straight through what might as well be a park, endless gardens separated by hedges, decorative fences, and neat little streams. Bridges arch over, cleverly wrought in the shape of leaping fish, and elegant lean-tos provide shady alcoves. Somewhere at the end of the long driveways, vast mansions lurk, visible only in snatches behind screens of trees. But every turnoff has a crest stone now, and the families are the most prestigious in the Empire. No merchants *here*, and no one who doesn't know the name of their great-great-grandfather.

The slope gets steeper as we climb. I can look over my shoulder and see the top of the ward wall behind and below us, and past that the city spreading out like a warren, stretching down until it meets the thin sparkling line of the sea. I'm sweating freely now, and everyone but Jack is breathing hard.

Finally, we reach another gate, this one in a lower, red-painted wall crowned with fantastic carved beasts, picked out with gold leaf. The Imperial Palace hasn't been a real fortress for centuries, and its defenses are symbolic. But there are guards everywhere, soldiers of the palace regiment with halberds and long tunics embroidered with more gold. More ominous are a pair of dark, armored shapes with their faces hidden behind chain-veils, waiting beside the arched gateway that leads onto the palace grounds. *Immortals*. I feel myself tense, and work to keep up my cocky smile.

The palace itself sprawls behind its walls, huge and ancient. It's not tall, only a single story in most places, but from here we can get only a sense of its vastness—the walls extend in both directions, sweeping out to take in an area bigger that the Second and Third Wards combined, and the whole of it is occupied by this single complex. The Palace is a city unto itself, with roads, stables, dormitories for servants, and of course the endless gardens and apartments of its denizens. Tucked away at its edges are the offices of the civil servants who do the actual work of running the Empire.

So I'm told, anyway. All that's obvious now, beyond the gateway, is a broad, circular drive, covered in raked gravel, with paths leading off it in all directions. Directly ahead is a platform, roofed but open at the front, with a curtain at the back. Somewhere for the Emperor or other high officials to stand, I presume, while greeting visitors or reviewing troops. For now, it's empty.

"Wait here," one of the Immortals tells us, a woman with a harsh rasp of a voice. She and her partner vanish, though there are still easily forty palace guardsmen scattered around the yard.

I glance over my shoulder again. The whole city is visible, down to the burned-out harbor. I can even see the ships of the Imperial Navy, sleek and shark-like, triangular sails furled as they row back and forth across the bay.

Thank the Blessed for good weather. I close my eyes for a moment. *And a little luck wouldn't go amiss, either . . .*

TORI

Avyn leads me to the back of the library. There's no dust—the palace servants would never allow that—but this section has the feel of a place undisturbed for decades. The Emperor goes to the end of an aisle and touches part of the decorative molding. It shifts with a *click,* and a small door swings out smoothly.

"These passages lead all over," he says. "But I don't know if I can get you out of the palace entirely."

"Just getting me out of the wing should do it," I tell him. "I think."

I've been putting my attention into my Kindre senses, pushing back slowly and carefully against the Immortal whose power is blanketing mine. Over the past few days, I've found that while Naga is right about defense being easier than offense, that works both ways—by pressing outward, I can clear a space where I *think* my minder won't be able to keep track of my movements. They shouldn't even be aware I'm doing it. *And if I can get far enough away, I can break out entirely.* With access to my power, escaping the palace should be simple enough. *I hope.*

"I'll take you as far as I can." He grimaces. "The problem is the passages don't connect. We'll have to get past a few guards."

"How do you normally do it?"

He raises a hand, and shadows stream toward him, flowing around his feet like water. They rise up in front of him, a shifting screen of darkness that fades out, leaving him hidden from view.

"Xenos." His voice comes from nowhere for a moment, and then the shadows swirl away. "My Well. A fairly weak form of it, I'm told, but it suffices."

"Can you cover both of us?"

"I've never tried, but I think so. At least for a while." He takes a deep breath. "We'll find out."

He looks nervous. I remind myself that while it's my life literally on the line here, Avyn is still taking a serious risk—if Naga discovers his ability to move around the palace, he could lose his only vestige of freedom. I give him an encouraging nod, most of my concentration on keeping up the subtle pressure that hides me from the watcher's mental view.

We duck to pass through the low doorway, and he closes the door behind us. The corridor is narrow, plain, and thick with dust—no servants have been cleaning *here*. It intersects another identical corridor in a four-way junction, and I would have no idea how to proceed, but the Emperor moves with confidence. We leave footprints behind us, and a swirl of disturbed dust in our wake.

At times, only the thickness of a plaster wall separates the hidden corridor from the inhabited rooms and halls of the palace, and we can hear everything, muffled as though through a thick curtain. I keep my steps careful and quiet. This place is an eavesdropper's dream—I catch snatches of conversation, scrapes and clangs of laundry basins and kitchens, the soft grunts and moans of a couple rutting in some quiet back room. I flush slightly, but Avyn pads onward in silence. No doubt he's heard everything the palace has to offer.

Before long we come to a dead end with a door—obvious from this side, but presumably concealed on the other. Avyn steps up and puts his eye to a peephole, then nods at me.

"Ready? We need to move quickly and quietly."

"Ready."

He thumbs the latch, and the door swings open. We emerge into an empty hallway. It's unfamiliar to me, so it must be outside the Pear Wing, but I still feel the pressure in my mind. *Not far enough away yet.*

The Emperor raises his hand, and shadows swirl around us. When they settle, it's like being draped with thick, dark gauze—I can see, but only dimly. Avyn lets out a low grunt with the effort, then shakes his head and takes my hand. We start walking.

Around the corner is a corridor junction, with four palace guards standing by. They're only yards away, and my breath catches in my throat, but Avyn moves at a slow, steady pace and I follow. Keeping up the Kindre pressure is starting to wear on me, and I can feel a headache building. The temptation to move faster is strong, but I stay behind Avyn, and eventually we're past and into another empty corridor. He lets the shadows drop away with a gasp, leaning on the wall.

"Are you all right?"

"I . . . think so." He takes a deep breath, sweat rolling down his face. "I've never tried that with two people before."

"It worked perfectly." I look around. "Where are we?"

"Lotus Wing," he says, wiping his brow. "Next one out from Pear. It's up against the inner wall of the palace."

"Can we get past?"

"The inner wall, yes. There's another passage that will take us to the outer courtyards. From there, though . . ." He shakes his head. "There's *supposed* to be an escape tunnel, but I've never actually tried to find it."

"One thing at a time," I tell him. I try to persuade myself that the pressure on my mind is weaker. "Which way to the secret door?"

ISOKA

The curtain on the platform shifts, and Kuon Naga emerges.

He looks much the same as the last time I saw him. Plain, casual robe, wire-rimmed glasses, long fingernails like a cat's claws. He steeples his hands, sleeves falling together, and comes to the front of the platform.

Perhaps fifteen yards separate us. A few heartbeats. I could summon my blades, my armor, and cut him down—

Don't be an idiot. A half-dozen Immortals have filed in behind Naga, men and women in dark armor and chain-veils. *At least one of them will be a Tartak adept. They'd stop you in your tracks. And besides, then you'd get Tori and your friends killed.*

All of which is perfectly sensible. But my hands still itch, looking at Naga's bland smile. I'd had a *life*—not a perfect life, or even a good life, but one that was my own. And he'd taken it from me, just because he thought I was a tool fit for his purpose. The fact that he'd turned out to be *right* rankled all the harder.

"Hello, Miss Gelmei," Naga says, voice carrying easily across the distance. "I'm afraid I don't know most of your companions."

"It's better that way," I say. I give Zarun and Jack a careful look, then come forward a few steps. "I did what you asked me to do. I stole *Soliton.*"

"So I gather." Naga smiles wider. "A feat worthy of legend, I'm sure. It's a pity the story will never be told."

"I wasn't the first person you sent," I go on. "Some of them smuggled information out, I assume?"

"I am not entirely ignorant, if that's what you mean."

"In that case, you know turning over control of *Soliton* isn't a matter of handing you a key. The Eddica system acknowledges me, so I control the ship and the angels."

"Indeed." There's a slight edge to Naga's voice, a *hunger*, breaking through his polished veneer. "I have a . . . suitable candidate to be the ship's master."

Another Eddica user. It shouldn't surprise me. *Probably the poor bastard he had lined up to go onboard once I died.* I wonder how many like me are out there, just unaware of the power that they can tap. Unlike lifting rocks or setting things on fire, it's easy for the power of the Well of Spirit to go unnoticed, even by the wielder. *All I ever had were strange dreams.*

"From what I understand," Naga goes on, "you can transfer the authority you possess to another, and thus place the ship under my command. Is that correct?"

"More or less," I say. No need to fill him in on exactly how the system works, or the presence of Hagan within it. "Assuming you've kept up your side of the bargain. I want to see my sister."

"Why is it so hard for people to trust one another?" Naga lets out an exaggerated sigh. "I've never dealt less than honestly with you, have I?"

"I want to see Tori," I growl. "If you've hurt her—"

If she's hurt—*not dead, she can't be dead, please Blessed please*—I don't know if I'll be able to restrain myself from taking Naga's head. On the other hand, he has to know this, so if Tori's hurt then this is a trap and none of us are walking out of here.

"Peace, Miss Gelmei." Naga holds out a hand. "I'm only having a bit of fun. Your sister is well, of course." He looks over his shoulder. "Fetch the girl."

There's a long pause. It stretches, silence building on itself, like a rickety tower rising higher and higher, making the final collapse ever louder. The curtain behind Naga rustles, and I see someone whispering inaudibly.

Oh, rot. I badly want to step back and put myself shoulder to shoulder with Jack and Zarun, but I feel pinned to the spot. I clench my hands, and power crackles along my arms, barely held in check. *Come on, come on . . .*

"There appears to be . . . some difficulty." The frustration in Naga's voice is evident. He turns to his Immortals and speaks in low tones. Someone replies. I catch his muffled order. "Then *find her!*"

I look away from Naga and out across the bulk of the palace. It does seem like it would be a difficult place to find *anyone. Tori?*

TORI

The second set of passages are considerably less pleasant. We follow a tunnel that slopes downward, burrowing under the inner wall. As it passes belowground, it grows damp, and pools of filthy water have collected between the flagstones. We pick our way carefully, and I wish I had better footwear than the delicate slippers from my Pear Wing wardrobe.

"This is as far as I've come," Avyn says when we reach the next junction. "I never needed to visit the outer palace."

"You can turn back." I try to keep the hesitation out of my voice—I'm not sure I can find my way out alone—but he shakes his head.

"I've studied the map. I can get you to the outer courtyard, at least."

That has to be far enough. The pressure in my head is definitely slackening. *Just a little longer . . .*

He points the way at the junction with only a moment's hesitation, and we continue onward. A set of stairs takes us back to ground level, and a door lets us out into a wood-floored corridor, not as secret as the tunnels but still clearly disused. Slits between the boards in the wall give a rotoscoping view of the palace outside. It's different from the Pear Wing, less landscaped and more business-like. I see vast stables, carts outside overflowing with dung, dirt courtyards trampled by many feet, and high, narrow buildings with a minimum of ornamentation.

"We're getting close to the main gate," Avyn says. "There should be an exit in a lower yard up ahead. If we can cross it, there's a way up to the wall-walk that won't be guarded during the day."

I nod, breathlessly. He gives me a tentative smile as we round the corner and face another door. There's a crack in the wall beside it, and I apply my eye. Outside is a square dirt yard, hard up against a wooden wall decorated with fanciful creatures. As Avyn promised, there's a ladder that leads up to the top of the wall, and a narrow walkway above where we can probably go unnoticed.

Unfortunately, between us and the ladder is a good thirty yards of courtyard, and there are at least ten guards hanging around. Only a few are armed—the rest appear to be on break, squatting in the shadow of a building playing at dice. *It doesn't matter, though. For us, a scream is as bad as a stab.*

"I'll cloak us in shadow," Avyn says.

"Are you sure?" I eye the distance doubtfully. "That's a long way."

"I'll manage." He takes my hand again. "Stay close."

Shadows wind themselves noiselessly around us, and the world is shrouded in semidarkness. Avyn eases open the door and we shuffle out so I can close it behind us. He starts to walk, and I follow, certain that every eye is on us. The men playing dice don't look up, and their shouts and laughter are enough to cover our footsteps. But several more guards wait by the base of the wall, spears on their shoulders, with the blank, distant expressions of men used to spending long periods of time staring into space.

They'll see us. The dust from our footsteps. *Something.* My back starts to itch, and I glance over at the Emperor.

He's sweating, breathing hard. I can see energy rippling over his skin, wraiths of shimmering power chasing themselves up and down his body. His hand is warm, too warm, the power coursing through him starting to burn itself into his skin.

We're not going to make it. We're in the middle of the courtyard. "Halfway there," I murmur, very quietly. "Come on."

"I . . ." He takes a step, then another. "I'm not sure I . . ."

His eyes roll up in his head, and he slumps forward. I barely have a chance to catch him before he plants his face in the dust.

Oh, rot.

The shadows shred like smoke in a strong wind. We're standing in the middle of the courtyard, in full view of ten astonished guards. One of the men at the wall lowers his spear and opens his mouth, ready to shout for an alarm—

STOP. I push for all I'm worth, tearing through the last shreds of the Kindre fog, and the command ripples out in a soundless rush. The guard freezes in place, along with his companions. Back by the dice game, men who were starting to stand up and look around are caught in awkward squatting poses. One of them, off balance, falls onto his side without so much as twitching a muscle.

I breathe out. Kindre blazes in my senses, every mind around me as visible as a bright lantern on a dark night. It feels like reaching the surface after a long swim underwater, or stepping out of a sauna into a cold wind. After so long, my energy is pent-up, over-flowing. It practically crackles as I move.

Avyn groans, and I help him sit up. He blinks, looking up at me, then around at the guards.

"You . . ."

"You got me far enough." I pull him to his feet. "I can make it from here."

"But—"

"You need to go. Now." More guards would walk through here, sooner or later, and I can't hold them all. More important, I can already tell I haven't gotten away clean. Pushing through the Kindre fog has alerted the Immortal projecting it, and he's no doubt rushing to tell Kuon Naga to hunt me down. "Get back to your rooms, and nobody will know you were involved."

It's what he promised to do, but he hesitates. "Are you sure?"

"I'll be fine," I say, with more conviction than I really feel. "*Go.* I can't hold them forever." I pause. "And . . . thank you."

"I . . ." Whatever he's going to say, he swallows the rest. He looks at the guards again, then runs for the secret doorway. Actually, right now, I feel like I *could* hold them forever. The enforced rest has apparently done wonders for my stamina after weeks of bad food and no sleep. Once Avyn is through the door and away, I run for the ladder. I send another pulse of Kindre power to quiet the minds of the guards, and as one man they slump to the ground, deep asleep. *Hopefully I'll be long gone before anyone finds them.*

Scrambling up to the wall-walk, I try to get my bearings. From here, I can see most of the palace, and in the other direction almost the entirety of Kahnzoka stretching down the hill toward the bay. There's no easy way to get over the wall and down the other side, though, and I can sense more guards scattered through the grounds.

A gate, then. Speed counts for more than stealth at this point. The palace guards are one thing—I can probably get past them. *Once Naga's Immortals get here . . .*

I spot the gate off to my left and start jogging in that direction.

My senses probe for minds, feeling the guards and servants in the courtyards I pass. Whenever one of them glances at me, I send them a light caress, twisting their attention elsewhere. I don't have shadows to cloak my progress, but I don't need them. I can hide in plain sight.

Up ahead, I feel a whole cluster of minds. Soldiers, and lots of them. They're waiting in a courtyard, attention focused on a path leading out to a wide gravel drive. Palace troops with halberds are backed up by Ward Guard with crossbows, and the dark-armored figures of a trio of Immortals. They stink of the vanilla-bean scent of violent readiness. Farther ahead, on the other side of the drive, I can feel another cluster, also waiting.

An ambush? It feels like a trap, ready to spring. *But who are they waiting for—*

My senses run over the drive, between the two ambush parties, and my heart leaps in my chest. There are people I *recognize* there. A dozen of the flat, placid minds of my Blues, Giniva's cloudy sparkle, and the prickly, sour shape of—

Isoka! And she's walking right into it.

ISOKA

Another messenger arrives behind the curtain. Naga listens to the frantic whispers, snaps something in return.

I'm running out of patience. "Where is my sister, Naga? If you ever want to see your rotting ship—"

Not that I plan to give it to him. But it's nice to see him flustered, though he quickly smooths his features.

"Your sister," he says, "appears to be causing the guards some . . . difficulty. She will be with us momentarily."

"Isoka!"

I blink, because that *sounds* like Tori's voice. One of Naga's Immortals shouts and points, and the guards are suddenly going for their weapons. I turn to see Tori lowering herself down from the

wall-walk, hanging by her fingertips for a moment before dropping the last few feet to the ground.

For a moment, I'm frozen as surely as if I'd spent the night
beyond the Harbor's protective embrace. Then Naga starts shouting, and that breaks the spell. Zarun and Jack have already moved
to flank Tori, thank the Blessed, and in a few moments the Blues
gather around her as well. I sprint over in a spray of gravel, bringing up my armor.

My sister looks . . . fine. Better than fine, actually. She's wearing an embroidered silk *kizen* of truly remarkable quality, with
matching ribbons, jewels, and slippers, though the latter are a bit
worse for wear. Her hair is carefully washed and braided, and her
face isn't as hollow as the night I arrived. More important, she
doesn't seem to be missing any pieces, which is all I could hope for
after a stay in Naga's company.

"Isoka!" She runs to meet me. We collide a little too fast, nearly
falling over, and she wraps her arm around my midsection. "Isoka,
it's a trap. There are soldiers everywhere—"

"I figured," I tell her. "I'll handle it. Are you all right?"

"Yeah." She pulls away, wiping tears from her eyes. "Long story.
Let's get *out* of here."

I spin to face Naga, fighting a smile. "It seems like I've got what
I came for."

"But our deal is not yet complete." Naga has used the few
moments to recover his composure. At a gesture, soldiers start fil-
ing into the courtyard from both sides, spearmen in palace guard
uniforms and Ward Guard with crossbows. A rotting *lot* of them.
Sounds behind me indicate more squads moving to cut off our retreat. "The terms remain the same. Deliver *Soliton*, or you and your
sister will not leave the palace. One way or the other."

It's still a hell of a bluff we're trying to pull. But Tori is alive, unharmed, standing next me. It makes me feel like I can do anything.

I pull the little bit of conduit up from my collar, clenching it
in my fist. I can feel the Eddica current inside, weaker now, but

still tied to where I'd take it from on *Soliton*. Through it, I send a message down across the city and out over the water.

Hagan? Are you there?

His response comes after a moment. *I hear you.*

Bring her in.

As you wish. I hear the slightest hint of amusement in his tone.

"You want me to deliver *Soliton*?" I give Naga my cockiest grin, then turn to gesture through the gate. "Here she is."

Gasps and oaths echo through the courtyard.

At this distance, it's hard to see much detail down in the harbor. The Navy galleys look like insects, crawling across the foreshortened surface of the glittering sea. But *Soliton* is impossible to miss as it comes around the headland, more like a mountain than a vessel. Even I, who have spent so many months on board, have a difficult time grasping the sheer size of the thing. If the Navy galleys *were* bugs, *Soliton* would be the size of an ox.

And, though the mind wants to insist that anything so large should be slow and lumbering, the great ship is *fast*. Hagan has driven *Soliton* as quickly as I've ever seen her move, a huge wave building up around the vast double-bow. Most of the Navy ships scramble to get out of the way as fast as their oars can pull them. A few don't, caught unawares or foolishly thinking to *attack* the behemoth, and they simply disappear into the froth of *Soliton*'s slipstream. I picture wrecked spars and drowned bodies surfacing in the great ship's wake.

Soliton is heading for Kahnzoka, and no force in the Empire is going to stop it.

"What exactly," Naga says acidly, "is this supposed to accomplish?"

"It's supposed to demonstrate to you that I can transmit orders to the ship from here," I tell him, holding up the conduit. "I wasn't sure if your spies had reported that little detail. And, of course, it's supposed to get your attention." I close the conduit in my fist. "Here are *my* terms. In a few minutes, *Soliton* will reach the docks.

If Tori and I, and the rest of our party, are not on our way back to the city by then, the angels will be unleashed on Kahnzoka."

There's a long pause. I fix Naga with a steady gaze.

"When you first *kidnapped* me," I go on, "and threatened my sister with rape and torture if I didn't take on your suicide mission, you mentioned what happened to a port in Jyashtan that refused to offer sacrifices. So I know that *you* know what I mean. The orders are already given. If I don't countermand them . . ."

"You're bluffing," he says.

I have to admit, my heart skips a beat. Because I *am* bluffing, but . . .

"You wouldn't do it," Naga continues, and all of a sudden I'm smiling wider. "This is your home. Unleashing that kind of destruction here would wreck the Blessed Empire."

"You read my rotting file when you recruited me." I let my anger seep into my voice, turning it into a snarl. "I assume it told you how much I believe in the rotting *Empire*. That's why you sent me out there, because you knew that Tori was the only thing I cared about. So don't tell me what I *wouldn't do* if you hurt her."

And the rotting heart of it is, back then, I would have been telling the truth. If I'd had a choice between losing Tori and watching the city burn, I would have helped light the match. Now . . . well, I don't know. The bluff isn't my intentions. The bluff is that I've never been able to get *one* angel to do what I want for very long, much less turn the whole lot of them on the city.

But Naga doesn't know that, does he?

"Come on," I tell our people. "We're leaving."

It's hard, turning my back on all those crossbows. But Naga stays silent as we push through the ranks of soldiers outside the palace, and no one pulls the trigger.

12

ISOKA

A ragged cheer rises from the battlements as we come into sight of the ward wall. A few minutes later, we're passing through the gates, back into the dubious safety of rebel territory. The Imperial forces have stayed behind, out of bowshot of the defenders, hundreds of militia and Ward Guard watching as Red Sashes scream taunts and make cheerfully obscene gestures.

Word has spread down the hill at the speed of rumor, racing ahead of us. My confrontation with Naga happened in front of a thousand soldiers, impossible to keep quiet. If the whole city doesn't yet know that the vast, strange ship pulling up to Kahnzoka's docks is commanded by Gelmei Isoka, it soon will. For the Red Sashes, it's the first bit of good news they've had in weeks, and they're willing to take it. I'd worried that *Soliton*'s appearance might provoke more fear than jubilation.

We made it. I can still scarcely believe it. Tori is walking beside me, waving at the rebels who recognize her and send up fresh cheers. *We didn't even have to cross blades with anyone.*

It won't last. *Which is why we need to move quickly.*

"Is the cart ready?" I shout.

The sergeant fights through the press of cheering men and manages a salute. "Ready and waiting!"

"Meroe's down by the harbor," I tell Tori. "I need to make sure things are going all right—you can wait here, if—"

"I'm staying with you," Tori says.

I start to object, then look at her fierce, exhausted face, and stop.

My heart gives a weak flop. *Blessed knows I never want to let her out of my sight again.* So we all pile into the cart, an old, unsprung farmer's wagon drawn by a pair of scrawny-looking mules. Given that most of the livestock in the city has been eaten by now, I'm surprised the rebels were able to find even this much. The Blues stay behind, except for a driver, and we bounce out of the court-yard and onto the smoother military highway. It runs straight as an arrow from here to the harbor.

Tori is huddled with Giniva, who I assume is filling her in on everything that happened while she was a captive. Jack is dis-tracted trying to charm the mules, but Zarun sits next to me and gives me a questioning look.

"That went . . . more or less according to plan," he says.

"For once," I agree. "I don't think the bluff will hold Naga for long, though. When I don't bring the angels ashore and use them to help the rebels, he'll figure it out."

"He may have a hard time convincing his soldiers of that," Zarun says. "I'd say we'll get a few days' grace. It's something."

A few days. I shake my head. "Then what?"

"That's up to you, 'fearless leader.'" This is a joke at Jack's ex-pense, but she doesn't seem to notice. "And your sister, I suppose."

I look at Tori, deep in conversation with Giniva. She looks more like the Tori I used to know, clean and well-dressed, but there's a hardness in her face I barely recognize.

Or, rather, recognize too well. I see it in the mirror.

"What would you do?" I say softly. "If it were you, and we were in Jyashtan?"

"Bash her over the head and drag her on the ship," Zarun says cheerfully. "Get out of here and never look back."

"And leave the rebels?"

"Like you said. They made their bed, they can lie in it."

I close my eyes. "Tori would never forgive me."

"'Never' is a long time. At least you'd both be alive to find out."

The next time I look back, Tori has her eyes closed, her head resting on Giniva's shoulder. I lean closer and lower my voice.

"Is she all right?"

Giniva nods. "Just exhausted, I think."

"After we get to the waterfront, you can take her back to headquarters to rest."

I watch Tori, and brood. It has the advantage of keeping me from worrying about Meroe, at least until we get down toward the bottom of the hill and the huge, dark bow of *Soliton* looms against the sky, its enormous folding ramp gaping open.

I hold my breath for a moment as we pass through the Sixteenth Ward gate. Last time I'd come this way, there'd been an Imperial army camped outside the wall, amid the burned-out wreckage of the district that had been my home. I'd *guessed* they wouldn't hang around when the legendary ghost ship sailed up, rail lined with bizarre-looking angels, but it's a relief to see I was right. There are no Ward Guard or militia in sight, just empty lines of tents and abandoned campfires. At the base of the ramp, several dozen Blues have gathered. Some of the Red Sashes are starting to venture out, staring up at the ship in awe.

More follow as our cart rumbles past, taking courage from my presence. I don't know if the rumors have gotten this far, or if they simply assume Tori and I have things under control. Either is fine with me—they need to get over their fear of the ship sooner rather than later for this to work.

As we approach, Meroe comes down the ramp, followed by a squad of Blues. They're all carrying containers of food—not crates and sacks but the familiar-but-alien makeshifts of *Soliton*, crab-shell tied together with sinew. Each is full to overflowing with grain, or fruit, or other products of the Garden.

"The path is clear," Meroe says to the Blues. "Take everything you can out of the storeroom and pile it out here, please."

Whether they appreciate the politeness is not clear, but the Blues obey, as I'd ordered them to. They tramp up and disappear into *Soliton*'s vast, dark interior.

I vault down from the cart before it pulls to a stop and run to Meroe. She grins at me, and I wrap her in my arms and kiss her.

We're okay. Tori, her, me. I wouldn't have laid odds on that this morning, and I feel a knot inside me unravel. *Thank the Blessed.*

"It worked?" she murmurs, forehead pressed against mine.

"It worked. You're a genius."

"Well. Half a genius. You helped some." She gives me another kiss. "Things are coming along here, but we need more hands, and people to transport everything inside the walls. I tried to get some of the Red Sashes to help, but nobody was willing." She looks up at the towering ship and sighs. "I suppose I can't blame them."

"I'll see what I can do," I tell her.

"How's Tori?"

I look over my shoulder, but she's still asleep. "Worn out, but surprisingly good, all things considered."

"That's something. I'm so glad you found her."

"We have to figure out what to do once Naga catches on—"

"Later," Meroe says firmly. "Let's get this done."

This being the second part of the plan. Kosura's stores helped keep the city from outright starvation, but that's all. If the defenders are going to get their strength back—and more important, their will to fight—back, they're going to need more. And *Soliton* has food in plenty, everything we harvested from the Garden and stashed in its storerooms.

Plus, of course, there's crabs. I take hold of the conduit. *We made it, Hagan. I'm just outside.*

I can see that. There are angels lining the rail up on deck, made small by the distance. I wave. *I've got plenty of meat, if you're ready.*

It's going to be a matter of finding people to carry it, I tell him. *Can you use the angels to bring it into the city?*

I tried that. Unfortunately, I can only command the angels indirectly, through the ship's system. They won't go ashore. Your authority may work better.

I can use one at a time, at least. I grit my teeth. If I *could* command all the angels, all our problems would be over. *Load one of them up, and I'll take it from there.*

Got it.

Try to pick one that's . . . less threatening. Most of the angels look like nightmare agglomerations of human and animal parts, anatomy sketches prepared by a mad artist. *I don't want the rebels to run screaming.*

I'll do my best, Hagan says, with a chuckle.

Bringing the angel outside goes about as well as you'd expect.

Meroe has put together a steady routine by then, Blues running back and forth hauling the strange foodstuffs from the Garden storerooms to the dock. Jakibsa, arriving from headquarters, has taken charge of things on the Red Sashes' side, organizing another relay to load up carts, wagons, and wheelbarrows and get the stuff inside the walls. The main difficulty is the shortage of draft animals, so Red Sashes and teams of civilian volunteers are strapping into the harnesses and hauling the food themselves. Hunger, unsurprisingly, is a powerful motivator.

Being back aboard the ship is oddly nostalgic. There's a smell to the air, the ozone tang of rusted metal, that has become something like home to me. I find myself smiling at the drip of water and the shelves of mushrooms that cling to the walls. In the maze of passages between the ramp and the Garden, I find a large empty space that Hagan and the angels have turned into an abattoir. The constructs have been hunting crabs, tearing the beasts apart into manageable chunks, and stacking them here to drain.

The sight of all that meat, the smell of it, makes my mouth water. It's been days since I've had anything but rice or stale bread. For the rest of the citizens of Kahnzoka, crab may be a bit strange, but I imagine they'll get over it. *I certainly did.*

Getting it out of the ship may be more difficult. The angel Hagan has chosen as "non-threatening" is a huge humpback thing, with six legs on one side and eight on the other. It has no visible head, just the pair of humps, so it's impossible to tell if it's coming or going. The blue crystal "eye" that all angels bear shines from the center of its stony body.

This one seemed a less aggressive design, Hagan says in my head. His voice is strong again now that I'm aboard. *And it is well-shaped for cargo transport.*

Again, the touch of dry humor. Hagan has changed, I reflect, in the months since his death.

Other angels, smaller and more agile, are fashioning a kind of harness to the big double-humped one out of rope and scraps of crabshell. The work goes surprisingly quickly, and they start loading it up with meat, until the angel itself is almost invisible under its burden. If the weight bothers the construct, though, there's no sign of it.

Once I let my mind sink into the streams of Eddica energy and take control of the humped angel, it's all I can do to get it moving while I walk slowly alongside. We wind our way out, back to the ramp, where a number of the more daring Red Sashes have started helping Meroe and the Blues unload food. Even these brave souls retreat at the sight of the angel; in retrospect, I realize I may have negated Hagan's choice of a non-threatening shape by covering it in torn scraps of monster crabs.

"It's all right!" I shout, running ahead of the angel. "It's a sort of . . . beast, from the ship. I've got it under control."

Everyone seems dubious about that, but once the angel is on the shore and I bring it to a halt, they're willing to come forward and start unloading the meat into carts, to be hauled into the city. More people are emerging from the gate as the work goes on, which is good—we need all the hands we can get to move food inside before Naga recovers his nerve.

That takes longer than I might have guessed, or else the militia commanders have to work hard to regain control over their frightened men. Either way, it's after sundown when scouts report that detachments of Imperial soldiery are closing in along the waterfront from both sides. One angel might be enough to send them running again, but I'll save that threat for another day. Instead, Hagan closes up *Soliton*'s ramp, and we retreat back inside the walls, leaving the baffled Imperial troops to pick through the scraps of crabshell and meat left on the docks.

Naga should know better than to try to have any of his men board *Soliton*. If he doesn't, well . . .

Headquarters is mostly deserted, except for the Blues. I'm exhausted, sweaty, and stinking with crab guts, so a bath is clearly in order. I grab one of the Blues first.

"Is my sister awake?" I can only imagine she has a lot of questions.

The Blue's eyes go distant for a moment. "No," he says. "She is still asleep in her quarters. Four of us are with her."

"In that case *I* am going to get some sleep. But if Tori asks for me, wake me anytime."

"Understood."

All in all, I tell myself as I head for my own quarters, *not a bad day's work.*

TORI

For a moment after I wake up, I don't know where I am.

Not at home in the Third Ward, on my comfortably worn sleeping mat with thick blankets. *Is that house still standing? Are Ofalo and the rest still there?* Not at Grandma's, with ancient mats and threadbare sheets. *Gone, burned and gone.* Not in the Pear Wing, swathed in silk, the room around me engraved and gilded like a jewel-box. *Was that a dream?*

I'm in my own quarters, adjacent to rebel headquarters in the Eighth Ward. Old, expensive furniture, chests and drawers standing empty, looted by fleeing residents or opportunists thereafter. Home, I suppose, though it has never felt like anything more than a temporary expedient. More shocking is when I extend my Kindre senses and no numbing fog blocks me. Quite the opposite—there are four Blues in the room, ordinary-looking men and women whose minds respond to my mental touch with perfect obedience.

Ow. Reaching out with Kindre brings another sensation to the fore, pain running down from my temple, over my face and down my neck. It's not agonizing but closer to *tender*, like an injury that's mostly healed but still makes its presence known.

It must be powerburn, or something close to it. I've never pulled enough energy to hurt myself that way before—it's harder with some Wells than others, I understand—but I know the theory. Apparently the effort of breaking through the Immortal's Kindre block was more draining than I realized. *That explains why I fell asleep after we left, I suppose.* Memory is slowly returning.

I sit up, and cautiously look around. The four Blues are in the corners of the room, motionless, but otherwise I'm alone. Careful not to strain myself, I reach out to them with Kindre, asking for information. My request ripples outward, repeated through the network, responses flowing back to me. There are fewer Blues than I remember—given the fighting, there must have been casualties, and I wasn't here to replace them. I wonder if Giniva has a queue of deserters and traitors waiting for me.

The Blues report that the front lines are quiet, for now. Outside, in the square in front of rebel headquarters, some kind of celebration seems to be in progress. I frown at this. *What do we have to celebrate?* Other than me being alive, I suppose, but that hardly seems likely to get the civilians excited.

But I am alive. That seems to have taken a moment to sink in. *I did it. I got away.* I send up a silent prayer that the Emperor managed to get back to his rooms before anyone noticed he was gone. *Whatever else he's responsible for, he helped me, and he didn't have to.*

I get up and dress quickly, shucking off the sweat-stained palace silks and putting on something more practical. When I emerge into the corridor, I can hear shouts from outside, but for the first time in weeks they're excited instead of threatening. I make my way downstairs, taking one of the Blues for escort, and emerge blinking into the midmorning sun to find something like a carnival underway.

The centerpiece is a row of bonfires, each holding a large iron pot. Half the inns in the ward must have surrendered their stewpots, which are bubbling away merrily. People poke through the steam with long wooden spoons to examine the contents. Nearby, others are working to prepare more ingredients, chopping odd-looking vegetables. Beside them, there are stacks of—

Meat? When I'd been captured, practically every animal in the city had already been killed and eaten, and I can't imagine the situation has improved. And the meat doesn't look like it came from any animal I recognize. It's orange and white, with the puffy texture of crab or shrimp, but piled in thick slabs as long as my arm. A woman drops off another load, and I follow her to a third station, which looks like it came from one of my more distressing nightmares.

There's a . . . thing, sitting (*Standing? Lying?*) in the square. It's twice my height, longer than a cart, with weird multi-jointed legs on each side and no face, just a glimmering blue crystal set into its stony flesh. It has two large humps, with a crude harness strung around them. Hanging from the harness are . . . pieces.

I spent enough time in Grandma's hospital to numb any squeamishness I had around blood or torn flesh, and I've been in butcher shops where sides of beef or pig carcasses wait for the cleaver. But whatever was dismembered and torn apart to make *these* bits had long, jointed limbs, covered in a hard exoskeleton, more like a giant insect than a cow or pig. They had either been huge, there had been a rotting lot of them, or both, because the humped thing is absolutely draped with shredded remains. People are happily grabbing them by the handful, cracking the shells with hammers and picking out the fragments, then hauling the meat over to be boiled.

For a moment I wonder if I'm still asleep, and this is all some kind of incredibly elaborate dreamscape, as though I'd woken up and found the entire population of the city cheerfully subsisting on giant spiders. I blink and touch my temples, feeling the beginnings of a headache.

"Tori!" I see Giniva fighting through the crowd of civilians and Red Sashes and waving in my direction. She's thinner than I remember, hollow-eyed, but smiling. "You're up!"

"That's what I thought, too," I say. "But I'm starting to doubt it."

She glances at the dismembered-giant-bug operation and chuckles. "I suppose it does look a bit . . . off. Your sister had a hard time convincing everyone at the start."

"My sister did all this?"

Giniva nods, and fills me in—the ration shortage, Kosura's change of heart, and the arrival of *Soliton*. All the strange food is from aboard the ship, apparently, including the monstrous-but-edible beasts Isoka calls "crabs." They still look more like giant bugs to me, but I don't press the point.

The sudden influx of food has done wonders for morale. I turn to take in the square beyond the cooking stations. It's packed, Red Sashes and civilians mingling in a way we wouldn't have dared allow before. People are singing and even playing instruments, and makeshift dance floors have opened up. Apparently everyone has been saving a bottle of something or other, and they've all come out now, passed freely from hand to hand. In the center of it all, a skinny woman with faded purple hair is dishing up bowl after bowl of the stuff from the kettles, what looks like soup thick with shredded bits of crabmeat.

I have to admit, it smells delicious. *But . . .*

"It's not going to change things. Not in the long term." I frown and look at how much meat is left on the thing Giniva called an "angel." At best it buys us a couple of days. Without what we had stored in the Fourth Ward—"

"I know," Giniva said. "Jakibsa tried to enforce rationing, but once everyone saw what was happening, we couldn't keep them away without turning it into a bloodbath. Isoka decided we might as well make a party out of it."

Isoka decided. I suppose I should be glad she listened to my plea to help the rebels, but . . . *No but*, I admonish myself sternly. *This is what I wanted.*

"We need to talk," I tell Giniva. "Hasaka, Jakibsa, Isoka, whoever else needs to be there."

"Agreed," Giniva says. "We've been waiting for you to wake up. Are you sure you're ready for it?"

I nod. "Where's Isoka now?"

"Not sure," Giniva says. "Ask Zarun—the Jyashtani, there. I'll round up Hasaka and the others." She hesitates, then puts a hand on my shoulder. "It's good to have you back."

"Thanks." For Giniva, this counts as a significant show of emotion. I smile at her, then head for the cook pots.

The Jyashtani is helping the purple-haired woman distribute soup. I remember them, vaguely, from when Isoka arrived, but drugs and terror have mostly reduced that day to a blur. They obviously recognize *me*, though, and they both smile broadly as I come over.

"Brave Tori!" the purple-haired woman says. "Stalwart Jack is relieved to see you returned to us. Even so sturdy a soul as she quailed at the prospect of your absence!"

"Jack . . . did?" I glance around. "Who is Jack?"

"She's Jack," Zarun says. He's handsome, with an easy smile and a Jyashtani accent. "She's just weird."

"Honest Jack freely accepts the label, which is bestowed by a society insufficiently advanced to appreciate her better qualities."

"I'm Zarun." He bows, awkwardly. "It's good to meet you properly."

"Likewise." I look dubiously at the bowl of soup in his hand. "You can really eat this stuff?"

Zarun laughs and hands it to me. "Try it. I promise, I lived on crab soup for years, with nothing but mushrooms and spice to fill it out."

I'm not as hungry as I was before the Pear Wing, but it has been at least a day since I've had anything substantial. I put the bowl to my lips and drink. It's good, hot and salty, thick with fat. When it's drained, I pop the chunks of vegetable and crab into my mouth with my fingers, trying my best not to think about where they came from. Pretending it's ordinary crab, I find, goes a long way toward making it palatable.

"Well?"

"Not bad at all." I raise an eyebrow. "You were on *Soliton,* then? With Isoka?"

He nods. "I suppose we're not keeping that secret anymore, with the ship in the harbor."

"Mysterious Jack no longer needs to conceal her origin story!" Jack puts in.

"And you were all . . . friends?"

"Well . . . eventually." Zarun glances upward, ticking off points on his fingers. "First she wanted to kill me. Then she agreed to work with me, then she rutted with me, then she drugged me and betrayed me, then we locked her up and were going to execute her. *Then* she saved everybody on the ship a couple of times and I decided I was done second-guessing her."

"I see," I manage.

"It's a little more complicated than that, of course," Zarun says, "but I'll leave it to her to explain. Jack and I just came to provide backup when she rescued you."

Jack grins and nods along. I shake my head.

"Where *is* Isoka, anyway?"

"Last I saw, over there." Zarun points toward one of the dance circles. "Do you want me to fetch her?"

"You're busy," I tell him. "I'll find her."

I don't have to push through the crowd. With my faithful Blue silent at my shoulder, they open in front of me and close behind, a bubble of awkward discomfort and murmured apologies as people shuffle aside. I make my way to the dancing and find my sister is standing at the edge, watching with rapt attention.

It's not hard to see what she's staring at. There's a girl about her age among the dancers, with the dark skin of a southerner and an elaborately wrapped green dress, a silver bangle on one arm gleaming in the light of the fires. The dance is an energetic one, all spinning and bouncing, not the carefully formal style I was taught as part of my Third Ward education. Circles of dancers rotate and split, according to some scheme I can't fathom, but

Isoka's eyes never leave the girl in green as the music whirls faster and faster.

Finally, it reaches a breathless crescendo and crashes into silence, and the dancers shout and raise their arms in unison. Then the group is breaking up, laughing, partners stumbling away with arms around one another's shoulders. The girl in green runs to Isoka, who takes her in her arms and hugs her tight. They kiss, thoroughly enough that I feel my cheeks flush.

That's . . . new. I'd known a few of Isoka's lovers, when we'd been on the streets together. Mostly she'd chosen them by what they could offer us, street kids forging alliances like the most ruthless politicians, picking partners with money or connections or skills they were willing to teach. I'd always assumed she'd continued in that vein after she installed me in the Third Ward. They'd all been boys, though. And she'd never looked at any of them the way she looked at this girl, as though for a moment there was nothing else in the universe.

The girl in green spots me, and pulls away from Isoka, who looks around. My sister startles, then grabs me in a hug.

"Tori!" she says. "You're feeling okay?"

I'm already getting tired of everyone asking that. "I'm fine. Just needed some rest." My eyes must have gone to the girl in green, because Isoka gives another start and then a sheepish grin.

"Right," she says. "We didn't have much time for introductions. Meroe, this is my little sister Tori. Tori, this is Meroe, my . . . ah . . . princess."

Meroe gives me an elegant bow. "It's a pleasure to meet you, Tori."

"Likewise," I tell her, feeling a little intimidated. For someone who's just been whirling madly on the dance floor, Meroe is perfectly composed, skin damp with sweat but otherwise barely mussed. She gives me a quick, secret smile, and I feel a little warmer.

"This is all kind of a long story," Isoka says, gesturing at the cook pots.

"I've had some of it from Giniva and Zarun," I tell her. "But we need to talk, all of us, about what comes next."

"Yeah." Isoka scratches her head. "I suppose we do."

She looks chagrined at the prospect. I try to soften my expression.

"Thank you," I tell her. "For coming to get me."

"What?" Isoka grins. "Of course. I'll always come for you, Tori. I told you that, didn't I?"

13

TORI

It takes almost an hour before we can extract everyone from the party. Zarun and Jack stay with the crab soup, but Meroe joins us, along with me, Isoka, Giniva, Hasaka, and Jakibsa.

Hasaka does not look well. I still remember him as the burly ex-soldier who guarded Grandma Tadeka's door, but my enforced absence makes me realize how much he's changed. He looks like an old man, skin hanging loose on a shrunken frame, eyes deep-sunk in their sockets. Jakibsa walks beside him, but now he seems like the solid one in spite of his wounds, with Hasaka holding on to him for support. They both perk up a little at the sight of me, and I try to conceal my worry.

The conference room, I can't help but notice, still bears the scars of the Immortals' attack. Someone has mopped up the bloodstains, but there's a burned notch in the table left by Isoka's blades, and soot on the plaster from a stray Myrkai bolt.

Let's hope this goes better than last time. There are four Blues in the room, and more all over the building and out in the city. *We should have some warning, at least.* And it had cost Naga a half-dozen of his precious Immortals to capture me once. I can't imagine him paying the price a second time.

Isoka and Meroe sit down, and there's a moment of awkward silence. Hasaka looks between Isoka and me, not sure where to begin. I clear my throat.

"So I'm back," I tell them. "Yes, I'm okay. Naga was trying to start off playing nice, and I got away before he changed his mind.

With Isoka's help, obviously." I turn to Jakibsa. "Giniva filled me in on what's been happening. How bad is it?"

"Pretty bad," Jakibsa admits. "The storehouse in the Fourth Ward had a lot of rice and flour we were counting on for staples. Kosura's sharing what she can, but the temples didn't have as much as we assumed."

"Unless she's lying to us," Giniva puts in. "But I don't think she is."

I nod. Kosura might refuse to feed people, if she thought it served some higher purpose, but I doubt she'd actually *lie*. *I need to ask Isoka how in the Blessed's Name she talked her into helping.* It rankled, a little. *Or maybe Kosura just knew I wouldn't turn the mob loose on her.*

Jakibsa continues. "The food we brought up from . . . ah, *Soliton*"—there's a hitch of disbelief at the name of the legendary ghost ship—"also helps. But since we haven't been able to ration it—"

"Didn't have a choice," Isoka says gruffly. "Not unless you wanted me to start slaughtering civilians."

"I understand," Jakibsa says apologetically. "And it's done wonders for morale. But it hasn't increased our overall stocks much. It'll take a little while to organize the supplies, but if we stay on short rations, we have maybe a week or so. Longer if we go to half, or cut the civilians out altogether, but . . ." He glances at Hasaka for a moment. "I think we learned that's not sustainable."

"And the walls?" I address Hasaka directly. "Are we having any problems holding them?"

He blinks, slowly, and shakes his head. "Not at the moment. My people are . . ." He mumbles something, and frowns. "They're holding."

He's broken. Whatever happened while I was gone, the toxic combination of hunger and stress has eaten away at him, and now he's a shell of his former self. He might recover, with enough rest, but I don't know if we have the time. *I'll have to talk to Jakibsa. Get someone else to take over.*

"There haven't been many attacks," Giniva says, cutting through the embarrassing moment of silence. "I think the Imperials shifted most of their reserves down to the waterfront once *Soliton* docked. Everywhere else they've been content to just sit and wait."

"I told Naga that I would have *Soliton* destroy the city if he stopped us from leaving the palace," Isoka says.

"Can you actually do that?" Jakibsa says.

Isoka shakes her head. "He'll figure it out eventually. But for now it may be holding him back, and that buys us time."

"Time for what?" Hasaka says. His voice is shaky. "To wait until the Legions get here and squash us?"

The words hang in the air for a moment, ugly and awkward, like a fart at a funeral. Giniva, again, hesitantly breaks the silence.

"That may be why the Imperials haven't attacked," she says. "If the Legions are coming, and now we have the unknown power of *Soliton*, then why risk a bloodbath?"

"That's one way to think about at it." I take a deep breath. "But I think there's another possibility."

Everyone looks at me, my sister included. Her eyes are hooded, though Meroe gives me an encouraging smile.

"What if the Legions aren't coming?" I ask them. "What if Naga is holding back because this is all he has, and now he doesn't know if it's enough?"

Another silence.

"Doesn't make sense," Hasaka mutters. "Of course the Legions are coming. That's the point of them, to defend the Empire."

"It does seem like a bit of wishful thinking," Jakibsa says.

"It was the draft that set off all of this," I tell them. "And they were drafting rowers for the fleet because Naga wants to go to war with Jyashtan, in the *south*. Maybe all the soldiers he can rely on are down *there*, and militia and Ward Guard are all he has to throw at us."

"What if they are?" Jakibsa says. "What difference does it make?"

"It makes all the difference." I put my hands on the table, pushing myself out of my seat. "We've all been so sure the Legions were coming for us, we spent our time worrying about how long we could hold out, just like Naga wanted. But if they're not coming, then it's Naga who should be worried, not us. And I think he is." I remember his casual threats, the brief break in his façade. *He's getting desperate.* "We need to attack."

"We can't attack," Hasaka says immediately, rubbing his hands against his forehead. "We don't have the strength . . ."

"If the Imperials aren't pushing on the walls, we can strip men from the quiet sections. Go back into the Fourth Ward and push all the way to the outer wall again, take back the storehouse. That solves two problems in one step."

"For a while—" Jakibsa says.

"Then the waterfront," I go on, face flushed with excitement. "We pulled back because the Navy could land troops anywhere along the shore, and we couldn't stop them. But *Soliton* is keeping the Navy back, now. All we have to do is retake the walls to the shoreline, and every soldier in the Sixteenth will be cut off. *We* can starve *them* out. And once they retreat or surrender, we'll have access to the bay again, and we can fish."

"Most of the fishing fleet burned," Giniva muses, "but I'm sure people can improvise. Plenty of material with all the ruined buildings."

"It's not *possible*," Hasaka moans. "We'll be crushed."

"The alternative is that we sit here until we starve," I snap. "And Kuon Naga is laughing at us for being scared of our own shadows."

Isoka coughs, and everyone turns to her. She hesitates a moment, then shakes her head.

"I agree with Hasaka," she says. "It's too much of a risk."

You agree with Hasaka? I blink. For a moment, it feels like someone's elbowed me in the stomach, taking my breath away. *That doesn't make sense.* Hasaka and Isoka have been at odds since she got here, and Giniva said that continued after I left—that Isoka was always the one pushing for more action, while Hasaka carped and hesitated.

Calm. I take a deep breath. *I'm sure she has her reasons.*

"Those angels," I ask her. "You said you can't use them to destroy the city. But you got that humped one to carry meat. Could you use it in a fight?"

Reluctantly, Isoka nods. "Commanding just one of them takes all my attention, though."

"One would be enough. With that thing leading the way, we could take the Fourth Ward back easily."

"And Naga would know I was bluffing," Isoka says. "Once he sees we're using the angels, but only *one*, he'll understand. If he orders an attack on the walls, he could take the city."

"*If* he has the strength. *If* he figures it out in time."

"It's too big a risk."

We stare at each other. Part of my mind, a distant part, marvels at my behavior. *Talking back to Isoka!* I never would have dared, before. Not even *dared*, it wasn't out of fear; I never would have *wanted* to, couldn't have imagined the circumstances that would make it necessary. Isoka knew what was best, always.

But she doesn't, now. She hasn't been here since the beginning, however much she's been giving orders while I was kidnapped. *And if we're too afraid of taking action, we'll end up like Avyn, stuck in his library and afraid of his own shadow.*

I look away from her and take a breath. "I need to talk to my sister," I tell them. "Jakibsa, work on better numbers for the food we have left. Giniva, give me an estimate of how many soldiers we'd have to work with if we reduced all the defenses to the bare minimum."

Everyone mutters agreement. They leave with unseemly haste, sensing the tension between me and Isoka. Meroe stays behind for a moment, exchanging a glance with Isoka, then follows the others out. Only the Blues remain, as silent as furniture.

"We have to attack," I tell her. "If we don't take the Fourth Ward and the waterfront, we're going to starve."

"It doesn't do us much good to take them if Naga storms the city," she says. The anger in her voice makes me flinch, but I try not to show it. "If we stay quiet it might buy another week before he figures out I was bluffing."

"And in that week, he'll get that much stronger, and we'll get that much weaker," I shoot back. "Right now, everyone's bellies are full of crab soup, and they believe we have a chance. Let that leak away and we'll never get it back again."

"*They* believe we have a chance," Isoka says.

"*I* believe it! I'm not just going to roll over and die without a fight."

"You don't have to—" Isoka bites the words off and looks away.

"That's right, I could run away with you and leave everyone *else* to die. Betray everything I'm supposed to be fighting for."

Isoka's voice is a soft growl. "You can't. Save. Everyone."

"So I shouldn't try?"

There's a long pause.

"You asked for my help," she says.

"I did. But this isn't helping."

"You want me to just salute and carry on?" She waves at the Blues. "Why not make me into one of your rotting zombies, then?"

The words feel like a slap. Of course she knows. I haven't exactly kept my Kindre powers a secret, but somehow I didn't think Isoka would figure it out. *But now she knows,* the voice in my head chitters, *and she knows what you've done. Monster, monster, monster.*

"You had better go," I mutter stiffly. "The others and I have work to do."

"Of course." Isoka stands up abruptly, chair scraping across the floor. "Just shout when you need someone to save your life. Again."

ISOKA

I slam the door to my quarters open hard enough that it shakes chips of ancient plaster from the wall. Meroe, sitting at the small table with a stack of papers, looks up and raises an eyebrow.

"It went that well, did it?" she says.

"I don't want to talk about it," I mutter. I stalk over to the hearth, where there's a half-full kettle of cold tea, and pour myself a cup without bothering to heat it. I stare down into the dead ashes for a moment, sipping the bitter stuff, until I hear the soft pad of Meroe's feet behind me. She puts her arms on my shoulders, gently lacing them across my neck. I feel the swell of her breasts pressed into my back.

"You're sure?" she says quietly.

"Very sure."

I set the teacup down and turn to face her inside the circle of her arms. Our lips meet, and her mouth opens under mine, warm and hungry. My hands slide up from the small of her back, slipping along the folds in her dress, pressing my thumbs along her shoulder blades. She gives a soft gasp, and I kiss the line of her jaw, down along her neck, across her collarbone, tasting salt on her beautiful brown skin. Her fingers dig into my shirt.

It's been too long. We haven't had much time to be alone, between my work with Hasaka and hers with Jakibsa, and in any case fretting that Naga might be torturing my sister didn't exactly set the right mood. And last night we'd both been too exhausted to do more than flop into bed together.

And if Tori gets her way, it's not going to get any better. An attack on the Fourth Ward *might* succeed, but it would bring a raft of new problems, and—

Meroe stops and gently disentangles herself. I straighten up, blinking.

"What's wrong?"

"You need to talk about it," she says with a wry grin, and points to a chair. "Sit. I'll make fresh tea."

"Not all problems can be solved with tea." I mean to say it under my breath, but Meroe has good hearing.

"You'd be surprised." She raises her eyebrows. "*Sit.*"

I sit. Meroe busies herself for a while poking the embers of the fire back to life, adding fuel as it grows, and filling the kettle. By the time she hangs it above the flames, my foot is tapping.

"You really do have a hard time sitting still when you're worried," Meroe says, taking the cushion opposite.

"It comes from a life where being worried usually meant I was going to have to kill somebody." I sigh, running a hand through my hair. "What am I supposed to do with her?"

"With Tori?"

"Of course with Tori." I wince. "Sorry. I'm just . . . I thought that getting her back from Naga was going to be the hard part."

"It wasn't the *easy* part," Meroe says.

"I was ready to have to rescue her," I say. "But *she* wants to rescue the whole city, and she wants me to help her. And it just means more of . . . this." I wave a hand. "More people dead. On both sides. These aren't crabs or corpses or the rotting Butcher. When we were fighting to save the Red Sashes at the prison, there was this girl . . ."

Meroe waits. She's good at waiting.

"She wasn't anyone special," I say, slowly. "She was just some . . . some *kid*. A farm girl. They'd given her a dull spear and some useless armor and told her to march, and then I came along and I was going to kill her and she probably didn't even know why. It just . . . got to me, all of a sudden."

"Did you kill her?"

"I don't know. Probably not. I punched her in the face and she went down." I shake my head. "It doesn't matter."

"It probably matters to *her*."

"I suppose." I take a deep breath. "You know me. You know what my life has been like. I keep thinking . . . this shouldn't bother me. Rot, I killed Hagan when the Immortals came for us, just because I was worried he would talk. I killed people just because they'd seen me use my blades, and I couldn't let that get around. I've done things . . ." My throat has gone thick, and I grit my teeth, fighting the emotion. "I don't *get* to be the one who feels this way."

"Isoka . . ." Meroe reaches across the table, puts her hand over mine. I weave my fingers into hers, and squeeze tight. We stay there for a long moment, until the shriek of the kettle interrupts.

"Tea," I mumble.

"Tea." Meroe gets up, and there's a pause for measuring and pouring. She puts a steaming pot between us, then sits back down. "Okay. Tea."

"I'm sorry." I shake my head. "I feel like I'm falling apart when everyone needs me."

"Please, Isoka. I have some idea what you've been carrying." She smiles at me. "You don't have to worry about showing yourself in front of me. Gods know I fell apart in front of you. We take turns being the strong one."

I chuckle, weakly. She takes my hand again.

"Tori wants to fight," she says.

I nod.

"Why?"

"Because she thinks we can win."

"And you don't?"

"Of course I don't." I look up at her. "You're the one with the history tutors. When the commoners stand up to the throne, it doesn't end well."

"Sometimes." Meroe shrugs. "Sometimes the throne backs down. Or they reach a compromise."

"Maybe in Nimar. Not in the Empire."

"At least two Emperors have stepped down in the face of popular uprisings in the last two centuries," Meroe says. "Though maybe they don't teach you about that here."

"It wasn't in any of the plays I watched, anyway." I take a breath. "Then, what? You believe Tori that the Legions aren't coming?"

"I don't know." She nods at the paperwork. "I've been trying to figure it out. But Tori . . ." She hesitates, then fixes my gaze. "Do you trust her?"

"*Trust* her?" I shake my head. "You think she's working for Naga, or—"

"That's not what I mean." Meroe lets go of my hand and starts pouring the tea. "When we first got here, you didn't believe that Tori was as important to the Red Sashes as they said she was. That she put all this together. Do you believe it now?"

"I mean . . ." I accept the steaming teacup, blowing absently across it. "I suppose I have to. Everyone really listens to her. And . . ." I pause. "She's a Kindre adept."

"She is." Meroe's own discomfort with the idea is visible only as a quick movement of her throat. "So she should know better than anyone what the odds are. What I mean is, do you trust her to make the right decision?" She cocks her head. "The way everyone trusted *you*, back at the Harbor."

"I would have been the first to admit I had no idea what I was doing," I say. "But Tori's . . . *Tori*. When I left, she was this . . . *innocent* little girl. She'd talk to me about . . . gossip from the servants, and which dog had just had puppies. We'd eat dumplings and drink plum juice and I would think, this is what I'm doing it for. This is the point." I take a deep breath. "It's why I never could bring myself to stop seeing her. But now I get back and she's—"

"Not that girl," Meroe says. "You think she ever was?"

"I don't know." My hand curls around the teacup. "Why would she lie to me?"

Meroe barks a startled laugh. I stare at her, disconcerted.

"Sorry." She sips her tea. "I just can't believe—Isoka, she *loves* you. She was trying to make you happy."

"I never asked her to," I say. "I just wanted *her* to be happy—"

"You wanted her to be innocent, and safe, and protected."

"Right. Happy."

She shakes her head. "It's not the same thing. But she let you think it was, because that was what you needed."

"Rot," I mutter, sipping my tea.

"Rot, you don't believe me?" Meroe says. "Or—"

"Rot, I think I've been an idiot."

"Probably. We're all idiots from time to time."

"When did you figure this out?"

"Oh, before we landed," Meroe says, waving a hand. "I told you, didn't I? Tori's related to you. I didn't think she could be as different as you made her out to be."

"You—" I shake my head. "Really?"

"Just a guess, of course." She sips her tea again. "But princesses need to be good at this sort of thing."

"Nimari princesses have to be good at a rotting lot of things," I mutter. "So what do I do?"

"Listen to her."

"I tried that. I ended up shouting at her."

"So stop shouting and *listen*. And believe what she tells you."

"Fine." I rub my forehead, fighting an incipient headache. "And once I've done that, then what? We still have to figure out how to save the rebellion without getting everybody killed."

"Of course," Meroe says. "But that'll be a lot easier with the two of you on the same side."

TORI

"Miss Gelmei," one of the Blues says. "Your sister would like to speak with you."

"If it's about the attack on the Fourth Ward—"

"She says that it is not." The Blue, a stout woman with graying hair, looks distant. "She says she would like to apologize."

"Apologize? Isoka?" I sigh. "Tell her to come in."

I'm still in the conference room, looking over the map. Notes are scattered across it. By rights, Hasaka ought to be here, too, but I told Jakibsa to make him rest. So I'm alone, adding up numbers from reports, trying to decide how many soldiers we could afford to send to their deaths to take a section of wall. Your usual fourteen-year-old-girl stuff.

A Blue opens the door, and Isoka enters. I gesture to one of the chairs without meeting her eye, and she sits. A pause stretches out, awkwardly.

"I'm sorry," she says. "For what I said."

"Which part?"

"All of it, I suppose." She grimaces. "I just . . ."

"It's all right." I give a sigh. "I asked you to help, and you held things together here."

"Barely."

"Barely is all we've ever managed."

Another silence. Isoka looks across the map table.

"Hasaka needs to go," she says finally. "He's not up to this."

"He needs a rest," I agree. "I'm trying to figure out how to break it to him."

"Yeah." Isoka stares at me, working her jaw. "This is who you are now, isn't it?"

"'This'?"

"Making plans. Giving orders." She leans back in her chair. "When I first got here, I was convinced someone else had to be running the show from behind the scenes. Trying to do it myself showed me how wrong I was."

"I . . . did what needed to be done." I shrug, looking down at the table. "That's all."

"I know how that feels. You take a step, because it's the only thing you can think of. Then you take another step, and another, and before long people are looking at you for orders and telling you about your rotting *responsibility*." She eyes me for a moment, with a faint smile. "I fell in love with a princess. What's your excuse?"

"I just wanted to help people. Grandma Tadeka—"

"Giniva told me," Isoka says. "You were doing this before I left."

I fight the urge to squirm, as though my tutor had caught me goofing off. "For years."

"Why?"

It's not the question I expected, but she seems genuinely interested. I hesitate for a moment.

"You took me off the streets," I tell her. "Let me live in comfort. After a while I couldn't stop thinking about people who didn't have someone like you helping them. It wasn't . . . fair."

"Nothing is ever fair," Isoka says mildly.

"No. But I thought I could do . . . something." I pause. "And I thought the mage-blood sanctuary might come in handy someday, if we needed a place to hide."

The ghost of a smile passes across her face. "You didn't tell me any of this."

"How could I?" More emotion wells up into my voice than I intend. "What was I supposed to say? 'Thanks for keeping me safe, Isoka, but I'm going to risk it all to help some poor sick rotscum'? What would you have done?"

"Told Ofalo to post guards and make sure you stayed in the house," Isoka says.

"Exactly. I just—"

"Not that it would have stopped you," Isoka interrupts. "Not a Kindre adept."

There's a long silence.

"How long have you known?" she says.

"A long time." I swallow. "In retrospect, since I was a girl. I always knew I could feel . . . something. It wasn't until I was studying that I really understood, though."

"You didn't tell me about that, either."

"I didn't *want* it." The chorus in my head chitters. *Monster, monster, monster.* My voice is low and thick. "I know it's wrong. It's *sick*, what I can do. But I . . ."

"Didn't have a choice." Isoka leans forward again. "I get it."

Her expression is tight, guarded. My chest feels like a clenched fist.

"We have to move." I force the words out. "Take the Fourth Ward, take the waterfront, take the palace. We can't just sit back and hope for the best."

"You mentioned," Isoka says.

"If you want to help, fine. If not, get on your ghost ship and go." I can barely force the words out. "Like you said. We rebels made our choice, and we'll suffer the consequences."

Isoka is silent a moment. I can't read her face, and I won't open my Kindre senses and look into her mind. Not her.

"I'll take over for Hasaka," she says. "You need someone to

organize the military side. Between the last battle in the Fourth Ward and the food we brought in, I think the Red Sashes trust me."

"That doesn't help if you're going to push against me."

"I won't." She takes a deep breath. "I'm going to take Meroe's advice."

"What's that?"

"I'm going to trust my little sister." She grins. "You're the one with some experience in this revolution business, after all."

14

ISOKA

Definitely been too long.

I lie facedown on my pillow, panting through the fabric, body warm and shivery. Meroe lies beside me, gloriously naked, beads of sweat trickling across her skin tracing her curves. She stretches contentedly, catlike, and rolls over to throw an arm and a leg across me.

The danger, of course, is that I don't want to move. Possibly not ever again, but definitely not as long as she's pressed against me, warm against my skin, her breath tickling my ear.

"I have to go," I tell her, muffled through the pillow.

"I know." Her hand tightens on my back, fingernails dimpling my skin. "I hate this."

"You didn't sound like you hated it."

"The rutting is fine. I hate the part where you get up and leave and I sit around waiting to find out if you're coming back."

"'Fine,' she says. I'm going to have to try harder."

"Isoka, *please.*"

"Sorry." I shift so I'm looking at her, her wide eyes only a few inches away. "What do you want me to say?"

"I don't *know.*" Her throat works as she swallows. "I just can't keep doing this."

"I know." I close my eyes for a moment. "Somehow, we're going to fix this. Tori will come with us, back to the Harbor, and I will never leave you behind again."

"I'll hold you to that," Meroe says.

"You should."

"It's going to make going to the toilet a little awkward."

I snort. She's smiling, but it doesn't reach her eyes.

A moment longer, and then I extract myself. In the bathroom I pour lukewarm water from a bucket over my head to sluice the sweat from my skin. I dress in my crab-shell armor, the suit Meroe made for me back on *Soliton,* in what feels like another life. It's decorative—Melos is all the armor I really need—but it highlights the blue marks her power left on my skin, the very first time she saved my life and I saved hers. On *Soliton,* it marked me as the Deepwalker.

Here, I suppose, it just looks strange, but at least I'll be easy to pick out in a melee. I add a red sash in the rebel style and head back out. Meroe is asleep, breath whistling faintly through her nose in the adorable way it sometimes does. I ease the door closed, and head downstairs.

In the square outside rebel headquarters, the Red Sashes are mustering. I honestly didn't know there were so many of them—Kahnzoka has a lot of walls, and the rebel forces have been spread thin defending them. Now Tori and I have pulled all but the bare minimum here, ready for what might be our last gamble. They don't look like much—several hundred men and women in ragged clothes and fraying red sashes, most armed with spears, others with swords or crossbows. They form up in small bands, under their individual commanders. I recognize Ralobi, from the Grayrock, and she gives me a salute.

There's a little cheering when I emerge, but most of them just stare. I don't blame them. *In a little bit I'll give them something to really stare at.*

Tori is already there, talking with Jakibsa and Giniva. Zarun and Jack are waiting for me. Zarun is in his usual loose shirt and trousers, while Jack has found a *cape* somewhere and is delightedly spinning in place to make it twirl behind her.

"It adds dash," she says, before I can ask. "And verve. And other things."

"Okay."

"Jack always felt she had need of a cape to complete her ensemble."

"Okay."

"Look at the way it—"

"We get it," Zarun says. "You like the cape."

Jack subsides, still muttering. Zarun turns to me and lowers his voice.

"You think this lot is going to stand·up?" He jerks his head at the Red Sashes in the square.

"They're going to have to." I look past them, at the huge shape looming behind the extinguished bonfires. "Besides, if this goes how we want it to, they won't have to do much more than run across the ward."

"That's a big if."

"That's what we're there for, isn't it?"

"Right." He gives me a smile, but I can tell his heart isn't in the banter, any more than Meroe's was.

My friends, my lover. Here not because they believe in a cause, or have a stake, but just for *me*. That I didn't ask them to come doesn't lessen the weight of responsibility. *If one of them gets hurt . . .*

I put it out of my mind. *Not today.*

"We should move," I tell Tori. "We don't want to wait too long with the walls stripped bare."

She says a few more quiet words. Jakibsa makes a sour face, but nods and heads back inside, and Giniva follows. Tori looks back to me.

"I'm ready."

"You could stay behind, you know."

"I can help." Tori taps the side of her head. "You'll see."

"Keep well back, then."

"Of course." She gives a shaky laugh.

All right. I step forward and raise my voice, speaking to the assembled rebels.

"If you don't know me, I'm Gelmei Isoka, Tori's older sister. I'm not going to try for any fancy speeches here. We're taking back the Fourth Ward and the grain storehouse. If we win, it means full bellies for weeks. Everyone got that?"

A hesitant cheer answers.

"We'll have . . . a little help." I gesture past the dead bonfires. "It's on our side, but stay out of its way. I don't want anyone getting stepped on. Apart from Imperials, that is."

There's a wave of nervous laughter. I close my eyes, and reach out with Eddica.

The double-humped angel in its rope-and-crab-shell harness is still there, dormant, spirit energy roiling gently inside it. When it feels my attention, its blue crystal eye flares with light, and its limbs shiver into readiness. I bring it forward, getting used to its weird multi-legged gait, passing between the lines of wide-eyed Red Sashes until its stands directly in front of us. Returning my attention to my physical body, I take hold of the harness and climb up, sitting between the humps. Jack swarms up after me, mounting the angel's highest point with her cape streaming, while Zarun take his place somewhat more reluctantly.

"You want a ride?" I say to Tori.

"I suppose you gallop around on these things all the time on *Soliton*," she says, looking up at me dubiously.

"This is my first time, actually." I think of riding the dog-angel Hagan possessed back at the Harbor. "Well, my first time with the reins, at least."

She purses her lips, but ultimately grabs hold of the ropes and makes her way up, waving to acknowledge shouts and cheers from the soldiers. Once she's settled opposite me, I close my eyes again.

"It takes all my concentration to run this thing," I tell her, "so please don't distract me."

The angel barely fits down the street leading west from the square, and I have to stay on the main roads lest we smash through a building. The Red Sashes follow, squad by squad, keeping a respectful distance behind the lumbering construct. When we reach the military highway, we head south, the angel's rolling gait taking the slope effortlessly in stride. At the junction, we turn west again, moving toward the city's main western gate at the very north tip of the Fourth Ward.

The plan, in essence, is simple. Use the angel to burst through whatever defenders are watching the gate, get atop the outer wall, then sweep south through the district, pushing the Imperials in front of us. With any luck, we'll catch them off balance, and have the Fourth back in our control before Naga can send reinforcements.

At the edge of rebel territory, the Blues are waiting for us, a group of fifty or more Tori has gathered from across the city. Beyond them is the gate into the Fourth Ward, still in our hands. Past that is the thin strip of no-man's-land, and then the Imperial defenses.

The angel, I estimate, should *just* fit through the gate. I open my eyes and let it come to a halt.

"Everybody off," I tell the others.

"Dauntless Jack will ride into battle atop this mighty steed!" Jack protests, whipping her cloak boldly back and forth.

"Brainless Jack is asking for an arrow to the face," Zarun growls. "Come on, get down here."

She grumbles, but complies. I glance at Tori.

"Stay close," I tell her. "And keep an eye out for Imperials trying to get behind us."

Tori nods. She's wearing her usual laborer's clothes, with a long knife thrust through her belt, and for a weird moment I feel like this *can't* be my sister. It has to be someone else, this calm, competent creature, at home amid the blood and death of a battlefield, just like—

Well. Just like me.

But then she looks back, and her face is so familiar my heart wants to break. The Blues will protect her, I know, and every soldier of the Red Sashes. But that didn't stop Naga from grabbing her once already, and I send up a silent prayer to the Blessed One. *Not that I suppose I have much credit in Heaven.*

The gates swing open. The highway leads out straight and clear, through a broad stretch of grass in front of the wall. Beyond that, the buildings of the Fourth District cluster close, and the road is blocked with wooden spikes. I can see the caps of militia soldiers crouched behind a barricade, and I can only imagine their confusion at the sight of the angel in the gateway.

I pull my armor up, and devote my attention to getting the angel moving. I can see through its crystal eye, though it turns the world black-and-white and queerly flat, like a moving pencil sketch. As the construct shuffles forward, a wave of consternation runs through the conscripts blocking the way. The angel clears the gateway and gathers speed, and they open fire. Crossbow bolts rise with a hiss and descend all around me. Mostly they miss, sticking in the road. Some manage to hit the angel, and glance away as though they'd struck a stone wall, with as little effect. One, by pure chance, catches my arm, drawing a brief flare from my armor.

The angel keeps moving, faster and faster, it's off-kilter gait rocking back and forth. I hear sergeants screaming at their troops to reload, but the construct is moving faster than a charging horse. They realize they're not going to have the time for another shot before I reach them, and they run.

I can't blame them. It's the only sensible thing to do—the angel is a ton of moving stone, like a runaway cart full of rocks, and as little inclined to show mercy to anything that gets in its way. The soldiers abandon their barricades and sprint down the street, ducking into alleys wherever they can find them. The angel hits their fortifications and crushes them like so many toothpicks, sending heavy pieces hurtling merrily through the air. More crossbow bolts rain down on me, and I can't help laughing out loud.

Eventually, no doubt, they'd figure out some way to get me off my unstoppable mount. It doesn't turn very well at top speed, so they might be able to circle in behind it and get a handhold on the harness. The plan, however, is not to give them any time for that, and in my wake the Red Sashes come boiling out of the gate, shouting for all they're worth. When men have started to run, their instinct is to *keep* running, and the militia who had manned the barricades need little more encouragement.

In less than a minute, we've reached the first major intersection, where the military highway meets the Fourth Ward's major north–south artery. A force of Red Sashes rushes to guard us from the south, and I keep the angel moving west, toward the outer wall. The district narrows to a point at the north end, and we're not far from there, so there's only a few blocks to cover.

As expected, the Imperials try to make another stand. There's a square in front of the outer wall gate, normally a market, now fortified with more barricades. Another volley of crossbow bolts greets me, and again one bounces off my armor, but the angel's charge scatters these soldiers as effectively as the first group. Unfortunately, here crossbow fire continues from the wall itself—the gatehouse and the wall-walk have a good view of the square, and the troops up there are safe from the angel.

It could probably take the wall down, if I went straight at it. The rogue angels we call dredwurms can rip right through *Soliton*'s metal decks. I wouldn't want to be anywhere near such a collision, though, and in any case we need the wall intact. I push instructions at the angel through Eddica, making it slew around ninety degrees in a spray of dirt, then settle down on its haunches. It makes a solid barrier across the square, only a few yards from the walls, and the Red Sashes coming after me sprint for it. Crossbow bolts fall among them, some finding their mark, but dozens of soldiers reach the shelter of the angel's bulk.

Zarun and Jack are among the leaders, and I slide off the angel's back to meet them. Red Sashes with bows are firing back, but the troops on the wall have the advantage of height. We need to push them off, and quickly. Fortunately, the outer wall isn't designed to be defended from an attack coming from inside the city—there are two wide staircases leading to the top of the gatehouse, the better for Ward Guard to man their posts quickly in an emergency.

"I'll take left, you take right," I tell Zarun. "Jack, get up there and stop those crossbows."

"Aye-aye!" Jack says, twirling her spear. She folds shadows around herself with a flourish of her new cape and vanishes. Zarun gives me a grunt and a nod, and we run in opposite directions, circling around the ends of the angel.

Militia soldiers are waiting for me on the staircase, trying to present a wall of spearpoints. I'm not close enough to see their faces, but I'm sure they're terrified. *Poor bloody rotscum.* I can end their stories now, like the red-haired girl, and for what? *But what else am I supposed to do?*

Crossbow bolts land all around me. One glances away from my armor just shy of my forehead, heat wrapping around my skull like a blast from an open oven. I snarl, and ignite my blades, green energy crackling and popping around me.

"*Run*," I shout at the top of my lungs. "*Or die!*"

It's all I can think of, my concession to the fact that these boys and girls don't want to be here any more than I do, don't want to die for the sake of Naga's ambition. Somewhat to my surprise, most of them *do* run, throwing down their spears, bowling over the furious Ward Guard officers who try to shout them back into line. Only a couple are still on the stairs by the time I get there, an older man and woman standing side by side.

I don't know if they're husband and wife, brother and sister, or just drinking buddies, but they've worked together before—the man thrusts his spear at me, and when I dodge the woman sweeps her blade across my legs. The tip slides across my armor with a scraped-glass screech, but it's enough to make me stumble, going to one knee on the stairs. She reverses her swing, but this time I see it coming and duck, ignoring the man's spearpoint as it goes for my ribs and slides away with a screech. I slash upward, my blade opening the woman diagonally from hip to breast, Melos power cutting through leather, skin, and bone. She falls in a welter of gore, and the man screams until I parry his wild thrust and put my other blade through his throat.

Another story ended. I pull away, letting him topple off the stairs, and keep climbing. The Ward Guard sergeant, left behind by his men, fumbles for the sword at his belt, and I cut him down without a pause and move on. *That*, at least, troubles my conscience not at all.

By the time I reach the top, it's all but over. A half-dozen crossbowmen lie in pools of blood, cut down before they even knew they were in danger. Jack stands watch over another dozen, who wait on their knees with their hands raised. Zarun has reached the top of the wall on the other side of the gate, leaving more bodies behind him, and the rest of the soldiers there are throwing down their arms, too. A few are still running, scrambling south along the wall-walk.

So far, so good. The Red Sashes are close behind us, swarming up the steps to take possession of the prisoners and the gatehouse. They swing the big gates closed and bar them, cutting off any troops still on the outside of the wall from coming to the assistance of those within. There are perhaps a half-dozen rebels lying in the courtyard, curled around crossbow bolts. *Fewer than we expected.* The Imperials had been quick to run for it.

Tori enters the yard, amid a phalanx of Blues, and I descend to meet her.

"Any trouble back at the intersection?" I ask one of the blank-faced women.

"No difficulty yet," she says, after a moment's pause. "The Imperials seem confused."

"It won't last." I look at Tori. "I'm going to take the angel and lead the drive south. The next place they'll probably try to seriously stop us is the Onion Market. Do you want to follow, or push along the wall?" *Or stay behind.* I don't doubt Tori's Kindre powers have their uses, but they won't stand up to a crossbow bolt.

"I'll stay with you." Tori seems a little winded, but looks determined.

"Then let's go." I raise my voice. "Jack! You take the drive along the wall! Keep them moving!"

"As you say, bold leader!" Jack raises her spear, cape whipping in the wind, and I have to admit she cuts a dashing figure. "Fearless rebels, with me! To death and glory!"

"It's supposed to be 'death *or* glory,'" Tori murmurs, under the resulting cheer.

I give a little shrug. *You* try to explain Jack.

Zarun returns, spattered with blood but otherwise unharmed, and I get back up to my place aboard the angel. Its crystal eye flashes blue and it lumbers to its feet, shedding a few crossbow bolts lodged in the harness. Carefully, I turn the thing around, heading back to the intersection. The respectful rebels clear a wide path.

The Onion Market is roughly in the center of the Fourth Ward, close to the grain storehouse and somewhat to the north of the Grayrock. The main road, sometimes called the Onion Way, runs into it from the north and south. As its name suggests, in better times it's a place for farmers in the city's hinterland to bring their produce. The Imperial siege lines put a stop to that, so the market is just a large dirt square surrounded by warehouses. According to Giniva's information, the Imperials use it as a mustering ground, and it's one of the only places in the Fourth large enough to form up a significant body of soldiers. If they're going to try to make a real stand, it has to be there.

I keep the angel's speed low as we move south, to let the troops on foot keep up. Zarun hangs from the harness with one hand, watching the surrounding buildings, while Tori walks at the center of her Blues. Behind them are the Red Sashes, their cheers growing quieter as we move through the ward. It feels empty, ghostly—if there are any civilians still here, they've hidden themselves away, and the streets are deserted.

"The square is coming up," Zarun says, as we round a slight curve. "And there they are." He gives a low whistle. "That's more than we expected."

I focus the angel's vision, and suppress a moment of panic. There are indeed Imperials waiting for us, and a rotting *lot* of them. Militia infantry are drawn up in a triple line, all across the square, spears at the ready, with a double line of crossbowmen behind them. On the wings are squadrons of Ward Guard cavalry, with real armor and sabers, waiting to swing around the ends of the undisciplined rebel mass as soon as we emerge into the open.

This may have been a bad idea. I can drive the angel right through the spearmen, of course, but then what? I glance over my shoulder and guess we have a few hundred Red Sashes with us, against easily a thousand Imperials in the square. *They'll be slaughtered. Rot, rot, rot.* I bring the angel to a halt, well back from where the road opens up into the market. Behind me, the soldiers come to a halt as well, with confused noises.

Tori comes forward, trailing a string of Blues, as I return my attention to my own body. She climbs halfway up the harness and waves me over.

"What's going on?"

I gesture at the Imperials waiting for us. "There's too many. We have to pull back."

She shakes her head. "You said yourself that if we give them a chance to get organized, they'll cut us to pieces."

"If they have this many soldiers here, there can't be many left at the wall." My mind is racing. "If we cut them off from supplies—"

"We can't hold the wall from the inside," Tori says. "We have to break them *now*."

"If we go in there, they'll slaughter us, even with the angel leading the charge. See the cavalry?" I've never fought men on horseback, but I can easily imagine the impact they would have at a gallop.

"I'll handle it," Tori says. "Just go straight down the middle."

"Tori—"

She gives me a look.

Trust her, Meroe said. *Is this what that means? Letting her lead a charge to certain death?*

But what other options have I got, right now?

"Okay," I tell her. "But you stay well back from the front."

She nods, and I can see the grim determination on her face. I wait for her to climb back down, out of earshot, before leaning over Zarun.

"Stay with Tori," I tell him. "If this goes bad, get her out of here."

"Got it. You'll be following, of course?"

"Don't worry about me." I pat the angel, and he nods, then jumps down to go after Tori.

I hear her shouting something to the Red Sashes, and getting a cheer in response. I'm busy with Eddica, sinking once again into the angel's senses, pushing the huge construct into a run.

Straight down the middle, she said. The angel isn't agile enough to try much else. It accelerates slowly but implacably, building momentum, moving first faster than a man can walk and then faster than a horse can run. Through the black-and-white view from the crystal eye, I can see Ward Guard officers shouting at their conscripts, ordering them to move aside. At least someone from the first encounter must have made it here, because they don't waste their crossbow fire on me.

It's not going to work. The officers are right—at full speed, the angel can hardly change direction, so all the Imperials need to do is clear out of its immediate path and close in behind me. By the time I can get turned around, the Red Sashes—and Tori—will be in the square, under the withering fire of those crossbows and being charged by the cavalry. *Blessed Above, it's going to be a rotting massacre—*

Except the officers are no longer shouting. They've gone quiet, standing stock still, and the militia are shifting in place, waiting for a signal that hasn't come. Spearpoints start to waver, all across the line, and the men and women in the rear shuffle backward, looking over their shoulders. I would dearly like to look over *mine,* but I don't dare—keeping the angel's complicated gait going requires all my attention.

But through its eyes, I see the first militiawoman run, throwing down her spear and sprinting past her suddenly paralyzed officer. She's followed by another, and another, and all at once the whole line is coming apart. The officers, suddenly reanimated, scream at their conscripts, but there's nothing to be done, not now. Horses rear and shriek, suddenly wild with fear, their swearing riders fighting desperately to keep them under control.

And then there *is* no Imperial line anymore, just a mass of men and women fleeing for their lives, streaming out of the square by every road and alley. I slow the angel's advance—no need to trample people already on their way out of the fight—and stare around uncertainly.

They had us dead to rights. *And they clearly knew what to expect.* So why—

I look over my shoulder. The Red Sashes are advancing into the square, spears waving. Tori follows, in the middle of the block of Blues, Zarun by her side.

Kindre. The Well of Mind. *Could she have done this?* A shiver runs through me.

The Red Sash captains are leading their companies onward, according to plan. Some of them are going straight to the grain storehouse, to make sure the Imperials don't try to burn it as they fall back. Others turn east and west, to link up with the rest of our forces, while most continue south, keeping up the pressure and making sure the militia don't have a chance to rally.

We might get this district back after all.

All at once, the angel seizes up. It's halfway through a step, and off balance—for a moment, it sways precariously, then settles sideways at an angle, as motionless as if it were a statue in truth. I'm tipped from my perch, too surprised to get a hold on the harness, and end up falling into the dirt.

I roll away, swearing, and pop back to my feet in time to see dark, armored figures dropping from the roof of a warehouse. The one in the lead is coming straight at me, and green energy crackles across her as blades ignite on her forearms.

The Immortals have arrived.

15

ISOKA

Not much time to think. There never is.

From the top of the building, a flight of crossbow bolts hiss out, scything down on Tori and the Blues. Men and women fall, and I catch a crackle of green from Zarun's armor. A moment later, the cluster of Blues is sprinting for cover, tightly grouped around Tori. They leave a dozen casualties behind them, lying still in the dirt or crawling doggedly after the rest.

Most of the Red Sashes have moved on already. A few return fire, and the Immortals on the roof shift their aim to cut down this opposition. The air is suddenly alive with the crack and hiss of crossbows, but up above pale blue shields drop into existence to deflect the bolts, while the rebels in the square have no such protection. I hear screams and curses.

That's about all I have the chance to take in before the Melos adept reaches me. She's shed her chain-veil, and I recognize the scarred face of the woman who abducted Tori. A wave of anger runs through me, and I ignite my own blades, a fat spark of green energy arcing between them as I charge her. She grins as she comes to meet me, and for a moment four blades cross, sorcery screaming against sorcery. Bolts of Melos power crackle between us, earthing all around as we form the eye of a maelstrom of barely contained power.

I pull back, hoping to draw her off-balance, but she follows without hesitation, blocking my underhand cut and slicing at my face. I duck, twisting inside, but she's ahead of me, bring her other blade down to block and forcing me to throw myself backward. She comes on with an overhand cut, which I let pass over my shoulder, drawing my blade the length of her forearm. Her armor flares, green energy spitting and popping, and at the same time her blade scores the side of my leg. Heat runs across my skin, and then she's twisting away.

I've only fought other Melos users twice, both times in the Ring on *Soliton*. I never learned the technique of using Melos energy to disrupt someone else's armor, so that leaves breaking through it, or doing enough damage that the powerburn cooks her alive. The Immortal, of course, is trying to do the same thing to me. But I have the advantage of having spent the last half year fighting armored monsters, and I've learned a few tricks.

I let my blade shrink, narrowing to an armor-piercing spike on one arm. I gather power there, enough that my skin grows warm, ready for a single devastating release. My opponent, watching, raises her eyebrows.

"An interesting style." Her voice is a rasp. "Master Naga is very cross with you, Isoka. He wants me to teach you a lesson in humility."

"Tell him to come out here and teach it himself." I close my fist, and green lightning crackles across my arm.

"Why would I want him to have all the fun?" She smiles, a twisted expression on her half-melted features. "He needs you alive to turn over *Soliton*, but alive doesn't mean intact. You'll be a little more biddable with no hands or feet."

"Get on with it, then." I drop deeper into my crouch, waiting.

Her smile widens. More light shimmers across her body, a golden glow joining the green, twisting through it. When she comes forward, she's so fast I can barely track her.

Melos *and* Rhema. *Rot.*

I may be in trouble.

TORI

The Imperials break and run, and I exhale, relaxing my mental grip.

I've done this before, but never on this scale. The principle is simple—reach out to their minds, suppress the duty and camaraderie that keeps them in their places, and replace it with an overwhelming, atavistic fear. Pushing so many at once strains my power, sending tendrils of warmth creeping across my scalp, but it helps that the fear is there *anyway*. These are conscripts, not professional soldiers, and it doesn't take much of a shove to turn an organized army into a mob.

Once the seeds are planted, I take hold of their officers, freezing them in place until the flight becomes a rout. Then I turn my attention to the cavalry, which is even easier—the horses don't have any duty to worry about, only training and habit, and the strangeness and noise of the angel already has them on edge. I drive the poor beasts into a frenzy, and leave the riders to try to handle them.

Now they're running, and the Red Sashes are following, spreading out across the square. Isoka reins in her bizarre mount on the other side of the market, and a mental touch brings the Blues to a halt around me. Zarun, Isoka's companion, is standing by my side, radiating a mix of cinnamon determination and twanging confusion at the Imperial flight. I imagine Isoka sent him to keep me safe. *Maybe now she'll understand.* Her sister is a monster, but a useful one—

My mind fills with fog. A Kindre user, somewhere close, flooding the mental plane with obscuring static. At the same time, I see the angel collapse, sending Isoka spilling to the ground. There's a drawn-out *hiss*, and black dots resolve abruptly into a flight of crossbow bolts descending on us.

The Blues don't shout or scream. A young woman steps in front of me and takes three bolts in the chest in rapid succession, tumbling backward with blood foaming from her mouth. More bolts stick in the dirt around me, and other Blues are falling as they try to interpose their bodies. Zarun is faster, and no sooner has he positioned himself over me than his armor flares brightly under multiple impacts. I see him grimace, but he grabs my hand.

"Cover," he growls. "Over there. Move!"

I need no urging. Every Blue still standing comes with us, contracting into a tight knot as we run for the edge of the square. A shop front overhangs the street, providing a small measure of shelter. As we run, blue lines of force reach out, grabbing planters and a table from in front of a neighboring shop and pulling them toward us. We reach this makeshift barricade just before the next volley lands, bolts thudding into wood in front of us and cutting down a couple of Blues who straggled behind.

Naga was waiting for us. Or, at least, once we'd come through the gate, he'd organized this ambush. The presence of a Kindre adept makes it clear it's me he's hunting for. *And something stopped that angel.* Isoka hasn't explained enough for me to understand how that was possible, but it has to be Naga's doing.

"They're on the roof," Zarun says. "Across the square. And Isoka's fighting another Melos adept."

More bolts land around us. I risk a quick look out between volleys, and see the rooftop he means, lined with armored figures. There's a whole squad of Ward Guard crossbowmen up there, and three Immortals in black armor and chain-veils. Beside the motionless angel, Isoka and another Immortal are a blur of coruscating green light.

"Rotting hell," Zarun says. "That woman's got Rhema, too. Isoka's in trouble." He straightens up. "Stay here. I'm going to help her."

Rhema. That makes it Kadi, the woman who'd kidnapped me. I grit my teeth. "I have a better idea."

"Better than helping your sister?" he snaps.

"One of those Immortals is keeping her from controlling the angel." I point at the rooftop. "If we can chase them off, then Isoka can use it." Or, if it comes down to it, I can handle Kadi myself once there's no Kindre fog protecting her.

Zarun bites his lip. "You're sure?"

I nod vigorously. He hesitates, then grabs my hand again, waiting for a volley of bolts to land and then darting toward the shop. The door shatters under Tartak force, and we duck into the darkened interior. The air is thick with spices.

The Blues follow, a half-dozen of them making it before one man catches a bolt in the temple and drops.

"Get the rest of them to stay," Zarun says. "It'll split their fire."

I relay the message, and we hurry into the back of the shop, finding a narrow stairway up into the apartment above. It's a single room, laid with several sleeping mats, now abandoned. There's no obvious way onto the roof, so Zarun simply ignites his blades and carves a hole, flinging the debris away with Tartak. Bands of pale blue grab me and lift me up until I can catch the edge, and he follows with a standing jump. The Blues swarm up after us.

We're about a quarter of the way around the square from the Immortals. The buildings are close together, with only a few alleys separating them, easily leaped. But the slate tiles are uncertain footing, and they'll be shooting at us the whole way.

I see Zarun making the same calculation, and I wonder if he wants me to stay behind. He doesn't say anything, only sets off at a run, tiles clattering and shifting underfoot. I order the Blues to stay between me and the Immortals, and run after him.

It doesn't take long for them to notice us. At a shouted command, the Ward Guard loose a volley in our direction. It's a hard shot, and bolts clatter around us without coming close. Zarun leaps an alley, landing catlike on the other side, and extends a Tartak tendril to help me over. More bolts start landing, and one of the Blues is caught in the leg just as she tries to make the jump. She trips and plummets to the earth below, her mental connection winking out.

Isoka is still fighting, green flashes blazing around her as Kadi hacks away, a blur of green and gold. *Move, Tori!* She said she'd trust me. *So do something!*

Another alley. My legs are burning, and there's a stitch in my side. Pale blue energy lifts me over, but I stumble on landing, sliding toward the edge of the roof. Two Blues swing down to catch my arms, keeping me from going over but pinning us all in place. Bolts hiss and clatter, and another of my defenders falls, all in silence. I get my feet under me and keep moving.

We're nearly there. The Ward Guard aim a final volley, too close to miss, but Zarun throws out his hand and a wave of Tartak force proceeds us, scattering the bolts like stalks of wheat in a windstorm. One of the three Immortals turns, a big, broad-shouldered man, and Tartak blooms around him. He meets Zarun head-on, force slamming against force, the two of them shoving like a pair of grappling wrestlers.

The Blues run past, drawing their weapons and engaging the Ward Guard, who drop their crossbows to fight back. It'll only buy a few moments—there aren't enough Blues. I focus on the other two Immortals, two women standing side by side. One, whose long golden hair falls in a thick braid from the back of her helmet, is focused on the angel and the fight below. The other stares straight at me from behind her chain-veil, and I feel the fog in my mind redouble.

I wonder if she was the one who kept me locked down in the Pear Wing. One of a few, perhaps, taking shifts. *How many Kindre users can Naga have?* I'd pushed through there, eventually, though not before I'd put a significant amount of distance between me and my minder. Now we're separated by only yards.

Naga said defense is easier than attack. But he also said that I'm an *adept*. I gather all the strength I can muster and throw it at the veiled Immortal, a hammerblow of mental energy. I see her flinch, and the fog recedes for an instant, then returns. I bear down, and so does she.

It's a raw contest of strength, of will. I don't know my abilities well enough for anything more subtle. The air between us starts to flicker with subtle power, invisible waves becoming almost tangible as they thrash against each other in shimmering rainbow patterns. Beside us, Zarun and the Tartak-wielding Immortal fight their own battle, lines of blue colliding and breaking apart at breathtaking speed, and down below green flares against green.

Heat rolls over me, pricking my skin. I clench my teeth so hard my jaw aches. Pain starts to spike inside my skull, beating inward from my ears. If I let up, I won't have anything left to try again. So I don't let up. I see the Immortal stagger, falling to one knee and tearing off her helmet. She's Isoka's age, with short dark hair, and *steam* is starting to waft off her. When she looks up, her eyes are stained crimson from burst capillaries.

"I can't hold her," she says. Her voice rises into a scream. "I can't hold her!"

My face is a rictus. I keep pressing, until all at once resistance collapses. The Immortal falls backward to the tiles, steaming all over. I fold up around a stitch in my gut, fighting for breath.

The big man claps his hands together, and a wave of Tartak power blows off him, pushing Zarun back for a moment. Before he can recover, the Immortal is backing away, grabbing the two women with blue energy and vanishing over the peak of the roof. The Ward Guard, who have cut down the Blues, seem bewildered to be thus abandoned, but not for long. Zarun grins, ignites his blades, and leaps among them. Terrified screams rise.

As soon as I can move, I turn to Isoka. She and Kadi are still fighting—Isoka has a shield on one arm, and she's huddled against the bulk of the angel, trying to protect herself from the other woman's breathtakingly fast assault. I reach for Kadi's mind, and nearly get a grip, but it's too far and I'm too tired to hold on.

She trusted you. I crawl toward the edge of the roof. *Do something.*

The third Immortal must have been the one who interfered with Isoka's control over the angel. I try to gather breath for a shout, but my lungs won't work. Finally, desperately, I reach out for my sister's mind.

ISOKA

"I may be in trouble" has been upgraded to "Rot rot rot, I am definitely going to die."

If the Immortal isn't a Rhema adept, she can't be far short. Being an adept in two Wells isn't impossible—I qualify in Melos and Eddica—but the latter has been disabled, somehow, while this woman has all the power of Melos and Rhema to draw on. She's as fast as a hornet, darting and striking with horrifying speed and precision, and her armor means the few counterblows I've been able to land haven't done much to slow her down.

My right hand still bears the armor-piercing spike, though I haven't gotten close to landing a finishing blow. On my left I've stretched the blade into a shield, desperately intercepting attack after attack. It's better than taking the hits directly on my armor, but it still drains power, and my left arm is in agony, slowly cooking from the inside out. Sweat is pouring down my face, and the padding of my armor is soaked, as though I've been fighting in a sauna.

She's sweating, too. But when she comes to a halt for a moment, she smiles her half-melted smile.

"Have to say I'm disappointed," she rasps. "The way Master Naga talked about you, I thought this would be harder."

"We're not done yet," I manage to gasp out. Bravado, from my ward boss days. *Defiant to the end.*

"Aren't we?" She raises her blades, and the golden aura around her flares. Her form flickers.

Isoka! The voice is Tori's, but it doesn't come through my ears. It rings in my skull like a bell, and a flood of emotion comes with it. Fear, determination, and a weight of crushing guilt that forces the air from my lungs. *The angel! Use the angel!*

The Immortal is coming. A cut glances off my shield, and she's already blurring away, trying to get between me and the stone flank of the construct. I haven't tried contacting the angel since it collapsed—I haven't had the time or concentration. Distract myself for a moment, and I'm likely to get skewered—

Trust her, Meroe said. My little sister is *in my head.* The thought makes me shudder. *Trust her.*

I reach out with Eddica, and the angel responds.

It surges forward, pushing itself upright, catching the Immortal completely off guard. One shoulder of the massive construct slams into her, drawing a brilliant flare from her armor and sending her flying. She hits the front of the closest building with another burst of green, then drops to her knees, blades vanishing.

"Not. Done. Yet." I let my shield and armor fade, feeling blessedly cool air wash over my burning skin, and push Eddica commands into the angel. It moves forward, enormous and implacable.

The Immortal woman gets to her feet, and our eyes meet for a moment. Her smile is gone. She gives me a small nod, as though in acknowledgment, and then golden light flares around her again. Between blinks, she's gone, leaving a trail of gold sparks lingering behind her.

Tori and I reunite atop the outer wall.

My arm is agony, matched by spots all over my body where flares scorched my skin. For now I can still move, but bitter experience tells me that by tomorrow powerburn will have me feverish and nearly immobile. Meroe has an ointment, prepared from *Soliton* mushrooms, that eases the pain, but it's never a pleasant experience.

Better than being chopped to bits, though.

After the Immortals retreated, the rest of the Fourth Ward fell without serious fighting. The panic of the main Imperial force in the Onion Market sapped the morale of the rest of the defenders, who mostly abandoned their positions and poured back out through the gates. We have a few hundred prisoners, militia cut off when the Red Sashes took the wall, and probably hundreds more scattered in hiding through the district. Many will probably just throw off their uniforms and blend in with the civilians. Any that surrender, I've made it clear, are to be treated well. The conscripts, at least, aren't our enemies.

Once I caught my breath in the square, I got hold of one of the Blues and told Tori and Zarun to go to the gatehouse while I followed the troops pushing south. Now, satisfied that there are no major pockets of Imperial resistance remaining, I head back to meet them. The surviving Blues—less than half of the force that had accompanied Tori this morning—are waiting at the bottom of the steps, which keeps the rest of the Red Sashes away.

I watch one woman bind up her hand, missing three fingers and spurting blood, with all the careful calm of someone dressing a chicken. *Poor bastards.* My skull still itches from Tori's phantom touch. I have to believe she wouldn't hurt me, but the *strength* of her voice—

Trust her. I swallow, and ascend the stairs.

Zarun is sitting on the top step, his shirt open, reddening tracks of powerburn visible across his smooth brown skin. He looks at my arm, which I cradle carefully against my body, and raises his eyebrows.

"Rough day?" he says.

"We've had rougher," I say, and he chuckles. "Have you heard from Jack?"

"Yeah. She's fine. Someone gave her a flag and she's running back and forth along the wall waving it at everybody."

"Fair enough." I pause. "Are you all right?"

"Just a little burn," he says. "I went head-to-head with an Immortal who turned out to be a Tartak adept. Just about held my own for a while, but I wouldn't have lasted much longer. Tori was the one who broke through." He shakes his head. "Your sister's a lot tougher than she looks. One of them must have been Kindre. Tori got cooked pretty bad, too, but she beat her."

There had been a third Immortal, the one with a long blond braid. By process of elimination, she must be Naga's Eddica user. Whatever she'd done to cut me off from the angel, it had been shockingly effective. It reminded me, a little, of my fight with Prime, where we'd struggled to block one another from accessing the power of the Harbor system. But there was no store of Eddica energy here.

I give Zarun a nod and move past him, up onto the battlements.

Most of the wall is lined with Red Sashes, looking down at the Imperial siege camp and making rude gestures. Here, though, Tori sits alone except for a couple of Blues. Her legs are crossed, eyes closed, but she looks around as I come closer.

"Please don't hug me this time," I say, raising my injured arm.

"I'm too tired to hug anyone." She's showing signs of power-burn, too, red lines forming across her face and neck. "And I'm aching already."

"Just wait until tomorrow," I say, wearily taking a seat beside her. "We've got some stuff that will help, but it smells awful. Meroe can show you how to put it on."

"Something to look forward to." She cocks her head, looking at me out of the corner of her eye. "But we made it."

"We made it," I agree. "And without many losses. The Imperials just dissolved after the line broke in the market."

"A lot of Blues died," Tori says. "I'll ask Giniva if she has anyone waiting."

"Waiting?" I shift uncomfortably. "They're—"

"Criminals," Tori says. "Murderers, hoarders, deserters, that sort of thing. People who would be executed otherwise. I take them and . . . make use of them."

"Oh." I pause a moment to digest that.

"It's not an excuse," Tori says. "I don't ask them to volunteer. Most of them would probably rather die." She lets out a breath and looks up at me. "Like I told you. I know what I can do is wrong. But—"

"But it's all you have." I remember the brief connection between us, the surge of guilt. "It's what you had to do."

"You don't know everything."

"I don't need to. I know you." I sigh. "At least, I'm starting to feel like I do."

There's a long pause.

"You saved my life," I tell her. "That Immortal—"

"Kadi," Tori says. "She was the one who kidnapped me."

"She doesn't like us very much."

"She mentioned that," Tori says.

"Anyway." I shrug awkwardly. "Thanks."

She doesn't seem to know what to say to that. We sit for a while in silence, almost comfortably. I'm going to have to move soon, before my aches solidify into a screaming mass of pain, but for the moment I don't want to go anywhere.

That moment is shattered by Jack, running along the battlements toward us, cloak flapping behind her.

"Sisters Gelmei!" she shouts. "Perspicacious Jack has made a discovery of ominous portent that she needs assistance interpreting!"

Tori looks at me. "Is she always like this?"

"Pretty much." I raise my voice. "What's going on, Jack?"

"Movement on the horizon!" Jack waves her spyglass in my direction. "Jack is not sufficiently well versed to guess at the meaning. Here, observe!"

I clamber painfully to my feet, and she hands me the spyglass. I get it focused and look out past the Imperial siege camps, up the rising hillsides beyond, in the direction of Dragonback.

"What exactly am I looking for?" I ask.

"Riders," Jack says, shading her eyes against the afternoon sun. "There!" She grabs my arm and pivots me until I catch a glimpse of a cloud of dust and zero in.

Riders. A column of them, in a neat three-abreast formation, coming down from the hills. The line snakes back up the road until it vanishes from sight into a cloud of dust that promises many more marching feet following behind. Flapping over the head of the lead riders is a long banner, black-and-silver with the heraldry of the Empire.

Silently, I hand the spyglass to Tori. I hear her breath catch.

"Well?" Jack says. "Whose is this formidable-looking vanguard?"

"I'm not an expert," I tell her. "But it looks like the Legion has arrived."

16

TORI

Despair spreads across the city like a cloak. I can *feel* it, filling my Kindre senses with the taste of ash.

The fear is not surprising. We all grow up hearing the stories of the Empire's Invincible Legions. For as long as I can remember, they have been faraway things, out in the northern borderlands, along the southern frontier, in the disputed islands. But the government assures us that our safety depends on their continued bravery and prowess, which are fortunately undisputed. Even the Emperor offers gratitude to the Legions, and prayers for their victory.

The Ward Guard are one thing. Everyone knows they would rather collect bribes than fight. And the militia are just peasants with spears pressed into their hands. But the Legions are the true strength of the Empire, trained and disciplined soldiers. Their ranks are thick with mage-bloods, officers drawn from the noble houses and commoners drafted after their abilities were discovered. Whatever hope we felt after the recapture of the Fourth Ward and its vital stores evaporates like smoke.

Isoka and I return to headquarters, but she stays barely an hour, just long enough to let Meroe spread ointment across her powerburn. Then she's off again, back to the western wall, to organize defenses in the newly reclaimed territory and start moving food out of the Fourth Ward storehouses. She must be in enormous pain, but her energy seems limitless.

She tells me to get some rest, and I make a show of reluctance, when in fact all I want to do is retreat to my bed and curl up into a ball. Meroe applies her medicine to my face and shoulders, and it's cool and earthy-smelling on my skin. She admonishes me to rest as well, with a gentle smile. I return to my room, burrow under my blankets, and press my face into the pillow before letting out a muffled sob.

The Legion.

I'd convinced the others they weren't coming. I'd half-convinced myself—at least, we had to *act* like they weren't, because if this was only going to end with us getting crushed, what was the point of *anything?* Now they're here, settling in on the western rim of the city, ready to storm our walls at their leisure. *And there's nothing we can rotting do about it.*

Naga had been right. Garo had been right. *Rot,* Isoka *was right, the first night she came.* She'd been able to see clearly what was going to happen. *Stupid, naïve little Tori didn't get it. Didn't understand that you can struggle all you like, but none of it is going to matter once the Empire brings the hammer down.* Now we're all going to get smashed flat.

I should have stayed in the palace. Talked Isoka into leaving. *Let Garo rut me.* It might have ended the same way, for the other rebels, but I might have been able to convince Lord Marka to advocate for leniency. And afterward, Garo and I could have pushed for reforms, slow and sensible, just like he wanted. *It wouldn't have done anything for the poor rotscum shipped off to die in this war, but we might have stopped the next one.* And those same poor rotscum, because they'd believed in what I told them, were now going to die trying to put up a fight against an unstoppable force. *So what did I really do for them, after all?*

At some point, I fall asleep. When I wake up, it's night, and my skin is a dull agony. Lines of itchy fire run across my scalp, and my face and shoulders still throb. My chamber feels icy cold, and I wrap the blankets tightly and still shiver.

More sleep. Bad dreams. I'm burning, fire consuming my flesh, blackening my skin, shriveling my hair, and no one seems to notice. They talk, joke, laugh as I walk among them, and when I scream for help they only look confused. Even Isoka.

I wake again in the morning, desperately thirsty, my skin damp with cool sweat. At least the pain has subsided, though my scalp still itches. I send mental orders to the Blues, and one of them fetches me a pitcher of cool water while the others draw a bath. Between blood, sweat, and Meroe's goop, I feel disgusting, and cleansing myself in the lukewarm tub helps a lot.

Out of habit, I dress, then realize I don't know where I'm going. I don't know anything about what's happened in the past day. *It might all be over by now.* It would be a relief, in a way, to slide the door aside and find myself facing an armored legionary. *No more decisions to make.*

Instead, there's nothing more alarming in the corridor than a waiting Blue, who bows slightly as I come out.

"Miss Gelmei. Miss Giniva requested to be told when you were awake. Shall I inform her?"

"Go ahead," I say. "Tell her I'm headed over to headquarters." I hesitate, then add, "Where's my sister?"

"Asleep," the Blue responds. "Shall I wake her? Miss Meroe requested she not be disturbed."

"Let her sleep." If Isoka's resting, the situation can't be *that* critical. "Just tell me when she gets up."

"Understood."

By the time I make it over to the old barracks, I can almost feign normality. The square is empty, no crowds cheering or hurling abuse, and the building itself feels mostly deserted. A few guards are on duty, but the constant back-and-forth of rushing messengers is gone. I see Red Sashes huddled in corners, talking in low tones, conversations that break up as soon as I come into sight.

Giniva is waiting for me in the conference room, which we have to ourselves. She's standing over the big map, which has been annotated in crimson pencil with the positions of the Legion along the western wall.

"Tori," she says. "It's good to see you. How are you feeling?"

"Itchy," I answer honestly. "But better than I expected. Meroe's ointment must really work."

"That's good to hear." Giniva smiles slightly. "Meroe dragged Isoka back by her ear to put her to bed. Not a person I would want to cross."

I smile, too, at that image. Then my eyes fall on the red marks on the map, and all the energy seems to drain out of me. Giniva follows my gaze, and her face falls, too.

"How bad is it?" I ask quietly.

"Bad," she says. "Our best guess is five or six thousand infantry and a couple of thousand cavalry. Even if they were more militia, that would probably double what the Imperials have around the city. But—"

"They're not just militia," I finish. "Are they taking over the siege lines?"

She shakes her head, touching the map. "They're all camped near where we first saw them, in the west. As far as I can tell they plan on taking the walls by storm."

"Or tearing them down." Get enough Tartak users in one place, and it's not an idle fancy.

"We've also had a message from their commander. Lord General Gymoto. He offers mercy to anyone who throws down their arms, and says the Emperor is prepared to be generous to all but the leaders."

"Which is a small comfort to *us*," I murmur. "Have there been desertions?"

"Not many, thus far," Giniva says. "But the reports I'm getting say that it's pretty close. If we don't do something soon . . ."

"Maybe it's time to let it go." I look away from the map, refusing to meet Giniva's eyes. "We can't stop a Legion. The more we fight, the more people are going to die for no reason."

"What's the alternative?" Giniva says. Her features, normally as calm as a Blue's, take on a hint of animation. "Throw ourselves on Kuon Naga's mercy?"

"He hasn't got any," I say. "But maybe this Gymoto does. Or maybe the Emperor will intervene."

"I can't . . ." Giniva trails off and is silent for a long while. When she finally speaks, her voice is thick. "You may be right. The ordinary soldiers will probably be pardoned."

"And Legion troops are less likely to hurt civilians than the Ward Guard and militia, at least."

"If you think it's the best we can hope for . . ." Giniva stops again, and swallows. "I would ask you for one favor."

"Of course."

"Have one of the Blues kill me quickly." Giniva looks up and meets my eyes, calm again. "My sister and I came to Grandma Tadeka's mage-blood sanctuary because we knew what would happen to us if we fell into the hands of the Immortals. I do not intend to face that, whatever happens."

"It won't come to that," I tell her. "Isoka has been trying to convince me to leave with her on *Soliton* since she got here. If I agree to go, and ask her to take a few others with me . . ."

"Take us where?" Giniva says.

"I honestly don't know," I say. "But it'll be away from here, at least." I stand up, unable to look at the map any longer. "I'll talk to Meroe about it right now."

"Thank you," Giniva says, as I slip away.

I can't get her look of quiet determination out of my mind. I'd thought of killing myself, when Kadi had me stuck in a hole. But there hadn't really been any chance I'd go through with it, even knowing what horrors might be waiting for me when the Immortal returned. Giniva faces the same choice, but she's stronger than I ever was.

I find Meroe in the sitting room of her quarters, with the bedroom door closed behind her. She's crushing mushrooms with a mortar and pestle, making up more of the powerburn ointment, but she gets up and gives me a bow as I come in.

I return it, uncertainly. I don't quite know what to make of Meroe, to be honest. The way she carries herself and her foreign features make her feel strange, inscrutable, but that all seems to melt away when she's laughing with Isoka. *Or kissing her.*

"How do you feel?" she says. Her Imperial is flawless, with only a hint of an accent. "Do you need more ointment?"

"I think I'll be all right," I tell her. "I was feverish last night, but it seems to have broken. But there's something else I want to talk to you about."

"Of course. Have a seat." She takes her place behind the mortar. "I hope you don't mind if I work. Isoka may need more when she wakes up."

"How is she?"

"Pushing herself too hard, as usual. Hurting herself trying to do things that she could safely leave to others." She grinds a little harder for a moment, then sighs. "I heard what happened in the Fourth Ward. You and Zarun saved her. Thank you."

"I . . . had to do something." I shift uncomfortably. "I should be the one thanking you, I think."

"For this?" Meroe raises the pestle. "It's nothing."

"Not just that. Isoka's . . . we talked a little bit, after the fighting. She's . . . different." I settle into the cushion, as she rhythmically scrapes stone against stone. "How much did she tell you about our life here?"

"Most of it, I think."

Isoka must really trust her. As far as I knew, she'd never told anyone the *whole* truth, not even Hagan or Ofalo. Everyone had half a story, the better to keep me safe. *For all the good that did against Naga.*

"She would . . . come to me," I say, carefully. "To visit. She'd be dressed up in a *kizen*, nothing like the sister I remembered, and we'd sit in the big house in the Third Ward and . . . pretend, I guess. That this was normal. That this was actually what our life was like, this *safety*, with plum juice and dumplings."

"Your sister loves you," Meroe says. "She told me, on *Soliton*, that she knew she ought to stay away for your sake, but she couldn't bear not seeing you."

"I know," I say. "I'm not sure I ever really understood *why* she needed that from me, that little bit of playing pretend, but I always knew it. I was happy to play along. After everything she's done for me . . ." I take a deep breath. "But talking to her now, she's *different*. She still cares about me, but there isn't that *need*. At first I was terrified that when she realized I wasn't the perfect little girl she remembered, she wouldn't want me anymore. But . . ."

"Isoka loves you no matter what," Meroe says. "Please believe that."

I nod. "There's a difference, I think. Between love, and that need. Whatever it is, I think it's because of you."

"Maybe." Meroe lifts the pestle, frowns, and tosses in another chunk of mushroom. "I can't say I haven't done my best. But she saved me first, before she had any reason to. I think I've just had to help her understand who she really is. That she's not a monster."

Monster. The voices chitter in the back of my mind. *Monster, monster, monster.* "Of course she's not. She did what she had to do."

"She did. So did you, I imagine."

I blink at her, wide-eyed. Meroe giggles, and leans forward to pat my shoulder.

"I'm sorry," she says. "You're just . . . you have an honest face, we'd say back home. It shows what you're feeling. At least to me." She gives me a sympathetic shrug. "Don't worry. I have special training."

"Training as a mind-reader?"

That makes her stop for a moment, wearing an odd expression. I'm tempted to reach out with Kindre, but I restrain myself.

"No," she says. "Training as a princess."

I eye her suspiciously. "Does that mean something different where you come from?"

"It means the daughter of a king."

"But—you're really—"

She nods cheerily, attacking the mushroom with extra vigor. I boggle quietly—Isoka had called Meroe her princess, but I hadn't realized she'd meant it *literally*. It takes me a few moments to figure out what to say.

"How did you end up here, then?"

"Long story." She pauses, cocking her head. "Well, not that long. My father found out I'm a Ghul adept, had me kidnapped and sacrificed to *Soliton*. Isoka saved my life and then I saved hers. I wanted to kiss her *really* badly but it took me a while to figure out that she wanted the same thing. We took over the ship and"—she waves a hand vaguely—"some more things happened, and then I came with her to come pick you up. Oh, and somewhere in there I realized I'd fallen in love with her."

"I . . ." I focus on the most obvious thing. "You're a Ghul adept?"

"Yeah. Please don't scream. I promise not to give you bleeding tumors."

"I'm not. . . ." I shake my head. "I worked at a hospital for a long time run by a woman we called Grandma Tadeka. She . . . was . . . a Ghul user. Probably only a talent, but she saved so many people. I know we're supposed to be afraid of ghulwitches, but I couldn't be, after that."

Meroe breathes out, looking down into her mortar. "Well, that's something. It still scares me, admitting it out loud." She swallows. "And you're a Kindre adept."

I give a small nod.

"In Nimar," Meroe says, still not looking up, "we're more afraid of people like you than we are of ghulwitches. There are horror stories about what you can do."

"They're probably true."

"Isoka told me about the Blues. How you would use people who were going to be executed." She raises her head, finally, and gives me a smile. "After what happened when we first tried to hand out food, the riot, I really thought what it must be like for you. Stuck in the middle of this, people behaving horribly, and you could just . . ."

"Reach out and fix them," I whisper. "It would be so easy."

"But you haven't." She goes back to grinding. "Like I said, you did what you had to. Just like Isoka."

"I don't . . ." I swallow, and fall silent while she raises the pestle with a satisfied look and starts scraping the ground bits into a clay jug. "I wanted to ask you something."

"You mentioned," Meroe says cheerfully. "What is it?"

"If I tell Isoka I'm willing to go with her, on *Soliton*, do you think she'd agree to take some of the others along? Not everyone, just the people who . . . would do badly, if we left them behind."

Meroe blinks. "Of course she would. It's not like there isn't room on *Soliton*, or at the Harbor. But I don't know if she'll want to leave."

"That was all she wanted, when you first got here. She tried to get me to abandon the rebels."

"Well." Meroe looks a little guilty. "I may have reminded her that helping you was the right thing to do."

"She's done more than I could have hoped," I say. "But now it's finished. We can't fight the Legions. They'll get over the wall, and whoever tries to stop them is going to die. It's time to save what we can."

Meroe regards me with wide, bright eyes. "I've been thinking about that. Maybe you can answer a question for me."

"If I can."

"Why did it take the Legion so long to get here? Why isn't there one stationed near the capital? In Nimar, the Royal Guard Regiments are always barracked near the palace, so they're close by if the king needs them."

"It's different in the Empire," I say. "All our enemies are a long way from Kahnzoka, up in the north or down on the southern border."

"And the Emperors don't worry about rebellions? They used to, at least." Meroe nods at the closest window. "Look at this city. It has more walls *inside* than it does around the outside. The whole place is built to defend the top of the hill from the bottom."

"There's a long history of rebellion in Kahnzoka." I'd learned a little bit about that in my studies, and more when I was going through the Pear Wing library looking for material to argue with Avyn. "It just seems to happen two or three times a century, like major fires."

"That was my impression," Meroe says. "But the Emperor still doesn't want to keep a Legion nearby, just in case?"

"I don't think the Emperor has much say in the matter," I mutter. It's an off-hand comment, but I freeze in place. "Wait."

"Hmm?" Meroe raises an eyebrow.

"There *used* to be a Legion based near the capital. Just on the other side of Dragonback. I remember reading about it. That was in the reign of Emperor Farada, the current Emperor's grandfather." He'd been a quiet, mostly ineffectual ruler, according to the histories. But he'd lived a long time, and after his death—

That was when Kuon Naga came to power. The Immortals had always been a palace guard, but it was Naga who'd made them into a secret police, aimed at political dominance as well as rooting out rogue mage-bloods.

"The Legion *was* here," I say, slowly. "It was sent away sometime after Emperor Farada's death. About forty years ago."

"Do you know why?"

I shake my head. "Probably it was needed at the frontiers." But the timing doesn't fit. The last war with Jyashtan had been ten years before that, and—"*Naga.* It has to be Naga."

"Isoka describes him as something of a power behind the throne."

"Exactly." My mind is racing ahead to a conclusion. "And he wouldn't want a Legion nearby, because they're the only force in the Empire that can stand up to the Immortals. And the Immortals might be loyal to Naga, but the Legions are sworn to obey the *Emperor.*"

"You sound like someone who's just had a dangerous idea," Meroe says, with a sly smile.

I feel suddenly breathless. "A *very* dangerous idea, I think."

ISOKA

I wake up feeling like a blueshell used my left arm as a chew toy, which is a considerable improvement over how I felt last night.

Night? Day? I've lost track. It's midmorning now, and we're not all dead, so not *too* much time can have passed.

I sit up with a groan, clenching my left fist experimentally. I can feel the tug of healing skin, and my grip seems a bit weaker than normal, but the pain is manageable. Thank the Blessed for the ointment Meroe got from Sister Cadua. I wonder, for a moment, how Sister Cadua is faring, and Shiara, Lady Catoria, and the others we left behind at the Harbor. With Prime gone, there shouldn't be any danger in that ancient, overgrown city. *Or so I hope.*

I force myself out of bed, and spend a few moments breathing deep, fighting the bands of pain around my chest. That Immortal—Kadi—had delivered a beating worse than anything I've had since I fought my first hammerhead.

"Isoka?" Meroe's voice, from outside the door. "Are you up?"

"More or less."

"Tori's here. We need to talk to you about something."

Oh, rot. What's happened now? Things had been bad enough last night when Meroe frog-marched me back to headquarters to rest. I'd been busy arranging the defenses on the western wall, putting every soldier the Red Sashes could spare into position, with archers up top and teams ready to counterattack the inevitable breaches. I didn't fool myself into thinking it would be enough. Everyone knew the Legions had plenty of mage-bloods, and Jack, Zarun, and I had demonstrated for ourselves what just a few adepts could do against masses of ordinary soldiers.

But what else can I do? Abandon my home city and the people I'd fought alongside, force Tori to flee, and make sure my sister hated me? We had a moment of connection, up on the battlements, something new and fragile. I want to let it grow, not stomp it underfoot. *Try to negotiate with Naga?* Hard enough before we'd shown our cards, but now he held the winning hand. Why should he bother?

I feel trapped, like I was back in the Ring with the Butcher closing in—no way to run without surrendering everything, and no way to fight and hope to win. *So now what?*

Meroe and Tori come in. Faint lines stripe Tori's face and shoulders, the familiar marks of powerburn. Whatever invisible contest she'd had with Kuon Naga's Kindre user, it had been nearly as fierce as my own. She seems full of energy, though, practically bouncing on her feet. Meroe fixes me with a knowing grin.

"Are we under attack?" I ask them.

"Not yet," Tori says. "Giniva tells me the Legion is still moving into place. We're expecting them at dawn tomorrow."

One more day, then, to build a sandcastle and hope it can hold back the sea. "So what's going on?"

"We have an idea," Tori says. "A plan. Kind of a plan."

"Tori made a friend in the palace," Meroe says.

"Oh?" I'm not sure where they're going with this. "Can they give us any useful information?"

"In a way," Tori says. "His name is Avyn, and he's . . . um . . . the Emperor."

"The Emperor." I look between them. "You just . . . made friends with the Emperor."

"More or less," Tori says.

"How did you even get to *see* the Emperor?"

"We met in the library," Tori says. "Listen, I know it sounds crazy. He's practically a prisoner in his own palace. Kuon Naga runs everything. But Avyn knows all these secret passages, and he's got a Xenos Well power that lets him hide, so he sneaks out. He was the one who helped me escape when you came for me."

"You didn't think this was worth mentioning earlier?" I ask incredulously.

"We haven't exactly had a lot of time to catch up," Tori says. "And I promised him I wouldn't tell anybody. If he gets caught they'll throw him in a box 'for his own safety.' But he's willing to listen, I swear."

"I can certainly believe that Naga's running things," I mutter. "But what does this actually change? Even if . . . Avyn were inclined to listen to us, you just said he's not actually in charge of anything."

"Because Naga controls the Immortals, and nobody can stand up to the Immortals," Tori says. She's speaking too fast, almost tripping over her words. "But the *Legion* can. And the Legion might listen to what the Emperor has to say."

"It makes sense," Meroe says, putting a hand on Tori's shoulder as she stops for breath. "It explains why Naga has taken so long to bring in the Legion. He's been afraid of destabilizing his position politically."

"And you think you can convince the Emperor to help?" My eyes narrow. "You don't mean—"

"Not with Kindre," Tori says, flushing a little. "Naga's Immortals would stop me anyway. I don't know if Avyn *agrees* with the rebellion, but he's certainly eager to be out from under Naga's thumb. If we offer him a chance at that, I think he'll take it."

"All right." I take a deep breath. "So that means, what? We have to break into the palace, then somehow get the Emperor to a place where he can appeal to the Legion before tomorrow morning? And hope Naga doesn't get in the way?"

"I had . . . some thoughts on that," Meroe says. "Trying to get the Emperor to the Legion camp won't work. He wouldn't be able to reach everyone before the Immortals counterattack. I think our best chance is to have him talk to them when they're formed up for battle tomorrow morning."

"Except that if we break into the palace and steal the Emperor—which, let me add, is a pretty rotting crazy thing to try—then Naga will know what's happening and change his plans."

"Right." Meroe's eyes are bright. "So we wait until the Legion is getting ready to attack, stall them at the walls, and *then* get the Emperor. Naga won't have time to react."

"Meroe." I shake my head. "It's a good plan, except that *both parts of it are impossible*. We can't stop the Legion at the walls, and we *certainly* can't abduct the Emperor."

"That's what I've been working on." She looks at Tori, who gives a hesitant nod. "I think I know how to do it. But it's going to be . . . well . . ."

She explains. I listen, my brow creasing deeper as she goes on. Now and then Meroe glances at Tori for backup, and my sister gives another nod. She seems reluctant to meet my eye.

When they're finished, I take a deep breath.

"Tori," I say, "can I speak with Meroe alone for a moment?"

Tori gives another wordless nod and slips out the door. I stare at Meroe.

"It'll work," Meroe says. "You've seen what she's done with the Blues."

"I have," I say. "Frankly that isn't rotting reassuring. I thought you were the one who couldn't bear the thought of a Kindre adept."

"I admit it still turns my stomach," she says, disgustingly cheerful. "But that's just my training. I'm a Ghul adept, I should know that better than anyone. If this is the only way . . ."

"It's still a rotting big risk. She's just . . ." I glance at the door and lower my voice. "She's just a *kid*. If she's wrong and screws this up, a lot of people are going to die. *I* could die. Or worse."

Meroe steps closer to me. "When you were hurt, on the march to the Garden, you asked me to heal you. Even though you saw . . . what happened to Berun." Her throat works. "You trusted me."

"That was different," I say weakly. "You're . . . different."

"I trust Tori," Meroe says. "You should, too."

There's a long pause.

"Well." I let out a breath. "Even if we assume this is going to work as planned, there's another problem we're going to have to deal with."

Meroe's grin returns. "Isn't there always?"

17

TORI

We start our work long before dawn, while a handful of stars still glitter overhead through gaps in the clouds. I've had time for only a few hours' sleep, but I was lying awake even before the Blues came to knock on my door. I should be exhausted, but instead I'm shot through with nervous energy.

This is it. One way or the other.

I'm getting dressed when I get the word that Kosura and her people have arrived. I hurry downstairs to meet them, and find a group of a dozen shaven-headed, white-robed Returners pointedly ignoring an equal number of armed Red Sashes. Kosura stands at their head. She gives me a bow as I come over, and I return it.

"Thank you for coming," I tell her.

"It was . . . the least I could do." A shadow passes across her face. "Do we have time for a moment alone?"

"Of course."

I wave the rebels aside and head to one of the back rooms. Kosura settles onto a cushion, and I sit across from her. It reminds me of our last meeting, though the battered, ugly barracks/headquarters has nothing in common with the ancient elegance of her temple. But Kosura looks as calm and as perfect as ever, in spite of her scars.

"I wanted to apologize to you," she says. "I have been . . . thinking, in the time since I spoke with Isoka and Meroe."

"You helped feed the people of the city," I say. "That's apology enough."

"To the people of the city, perhaps, or perhaps not." She shrugs. "The Blessed One will judge whether I have acted rightly. But I wanted to apologize to *you*. I . . ." Her calm demeanor fractures for a moment, and she looks down at her hands. "I have not behaved as I should."

"It's fine, Kosura. After what happened to you—"

"Please, Tori. It is *not* fine." She takes a deep breath. "We were . . . friends. Before. I don't know if I ever told you how much I valued that. I did not . . . have many friends."

Kosura was always so perfect, I'd assumed she was popular. But I certainly couldn't remember her spending time with anyone other than me. I have very little idea of what her life outside the hospital had been like, and it suddenly strikes me that she probably had a reason for not talking about it.

"After what happened," she goes on, with only a slight hitch in her voice. "You saved me. And I abandoned you. I was caught up in my revelation, and I thought it was all that mattered. But as Meroe reminded me, it is not enough to *know* the Blessed One's teachings. We must also *live* them. And loyalty to one's friends and kin is one of his most oft-repeated instructions."

My mouth is dry. What am I supposed to say to that? *No, wait, you've got it backward. I'm the one who screwed everything up.* Because it *was* my fault. Naga's Immortals had come to the hospital looking for *me*, because I'd been searching for the truth about Isoka. I'd inflamed the draft riots in the rebellion and drawn the remnants of the mage-blood sanctuary in after me. *It was all my fault.*

"I didn't know how to talk to you," I say quietly. "Afterward. You should have blamed me for what happened, I was ready for that, but you didn't. And I didn't know how to deal with it."

"How could I blame you?" She shakes her head. "Grandma lived her life knowing the risks she took, and accepting them. Everyone who worked in the sanctuary did the same. We always lived under the shadow of the Immortals."

"That doesn't mean . . ." I break off as a slight smile curves her lips. "What?"

"Look at us," she says. "Each determined to blame herself and absolve the other. I think we should call a truce."

I try a tentative smile in return. "All right, then. Truce."

Another pause, but a more comfortable one.

"Your people," I say. "Are they ready?"

"They are gathering, back at the temple. We will be in position by dawn."

"And they understand . . . what might happen? If things go wrong?"

"They accept the risk," Kosura says gently. "Though we have refused violence, this is still our city. We will do what we can, while abiding by the Blessed's law."

"But—"

"After all, the worst that can come to us is death, and reunion with the Blessed One," she says. "And that comes to us all, sooner or later."

Kosura and her Returners were the easy part. I could at least explain what I wanted them to do, even if it was difficult for them to understand why. For the volunteers who gather in the square outside the barracks, things are more complicated.

I'm surprised how many had answered the call. Giniva and her agents had spent half the night crisscrossing the city, explaining and recruiting. I'd worried that too many of the rebels had given up hope. But hope is a fickle thing, quick to vanish and just as quick to flare up again. Hundreds had jumped at the chance to put up a real fight against the Legion.

Now they stand in front of headquarters, illuminated by Blues with lanterns. Some wear red sashes, but most are civilians. Quite a few are people who hadn't been able to fight on the walls—old men and women, ex-soldiers missing an arm, a leg, or an eye. A woman with the shaking sickness, and a man born with twisted hands. They can't hold a spear or load a crossbow, but that isn't what we need now.

I step out in front of them. My palms are damp with sweat. Meroe stands beside me, and Giniva.

"Thank you for coming," I say. My voice sounds too small, like a little girl's. "We have a plan to turn back the Legion, but we need your help. It may not work, but it's the only hope we have." I take a deep breath. "I'm going to connect your minds, so you can pass thoughts to one another."

Dead silence for a moment. Finally, a young Red Sash in the front row steps forward and gestures at the flanking Blues. "Does that mean you're going to make us like them?"

"No," I say. "What I've done to them is much more . . . dramatic. This will only be the lightest touch." I think . . . I hope. I haven't done anything like this before. I hadn't even *known* I was doing it with the Blues, until I'd made enough of them that I'd realized what the network could do. "It should be entirely reversible. But it's going to feel . . . strange."

"And then what?" An old man, bald-pated and leather-skinned, limps forward with a cane. "Will this mind-whatever make us able to fight?" He glances around at the others. "I don't know about the rest of you, but my sword-swinging days are done."

Nervous laughter. I force a smile.

"You'll be able to fight," I tell them. *If it works.*

"Then sign me up," he says. "We'll show those Ward Guard rotscum, eh?"

There's a ragged cheer. I raise a hand for quiet.

"Anyone who has second thoughts can leave," I tell them. "The rest, form a line, and we'll get started."

The work, when I actually begin, is numbing, painstaking labor. The old man is first in line, by dint of whacking anyone who tries to get in front of him with his cane, and he lowers his head as though to receive a benediction. I reach out to him with Kindre, and feel a fleeting glimpse of his thoughts—crimson anger at the draft, which had taken his grandsons; cinnamon duty; an undercurrent of citrus fear, well-suppressed. I find the place I need and *twist*, leaving a narrow thread attached that leads back to me, like the links that connect the Blues to one another. He gives a little jerk, and his eyes widen. I feel his surprise at the press of my thoughts. Giniva escorts him aside, and the next person steps forward.

It takes *hours*. I told Isoka I would link as many as I could, but I had no idea how many that would be. Maintaining the connection takes power, but not much—my initial estimate of a few hundred proves to be about right. The more of them I connect, though, the more drained I feel, and not just from using Kindre. Each person comes up to me, and I reach out and get a brief look inside their skull. One after another, until their emotions seem to merge and blur together—a hundred rages, a thousand tiny griefs, a sickly river of fear. There's been precious little else in our poor city, lately.

Person by person, the network grows. As I assemble it, I feel the nodes flicker and pulse as they talk to one another, the fascinated volunteers testing their new connections. Thoughts ripple between them, fast as lightning. A whole group breaks out laughing, for no reason any outsider would be able to see.

Some of them don't take it as well. One young man sits apart from the others, eyes closed, hands pressed to his skull. An older woman vomits on the cobbles. But none of them asks me to undo the link.

By the time there's no one standing in front of me, the world is a blur. I straighten up, carefully. My head feels like it's made of glass, and one wrong move would send it cascading to the ground in pieces.

"We don't have much time," Giniva says in my ear. I blink and glance upward. The eastern horizon is pink with the approaching dawn. I look to one of the nearby Blues.

"Is the Legion moving?"

She goes distant, then says, "Yes. They are assembling outside the west wall."

No time to lose, then. I shake my head, trying to clear it, and send a pulse of thought to all my newly connected volunteers. *Wait. I'll explain everything soon.*

Back inside rebel headquarters, Isoka is pacing, dressed in her outlandish crab-shell armor, with Meroe, Jack, and Zarun waiting patiently beside her. She turns on her heel as I come in.

"Did it work?" she says.

I give a weary nod. "They're ready. And the Legion is coming."

"Then we'd better get things started." She halts in front of me, uncertain. "Do I need to . . . do anything?"

"Just stay still a moment." I take a deep breath and look up at my sister. "You're sure?"

"I'm sure." Isoka gives a weak smile. "Just try not to break anything while you're in there."

I return her smile. Then, before my nerve can fail me, I reach out for Isoka's mind.

I only need to touch it for a moment, just long enough to make the same tweak I've made hundreds of times today already, tying her in to the network. But that moment is long enough that her feelings roll over me. Familiar feelings, like all the rest of them—fear, and anger, and duty. But also love, a sweet scent and warm, indescribable sensation rolled together. For an instant I see myself through her eyes—a girl with her long hair tied up, in rough clothes, utterly different from the polished, perfumed creature she used to know, and yet still indisputably the same person.

At the same time, she sees *me*, not the way I present myself to the world but the way I fear I am in the dark of the night. All my sins ooze out of me, like pus from a wound. I see an innocent family reduced to slavering beasts to pull down an Immortal, I see a woman die at my mere command. I see the Sixteenth Ward burn, and I see the fear rolling off the girl, Krea, and all the others like her I'd turned into Blues. I see myself kissing Garo, and wanting more.

I know that Isoka sees all this, too. But she doesn't pull away.

ISOKA

When it's over, when the flood of images and guilt has washed over me and passed, I take a deep breath and open my eyes. Tori is standing in front of me, tears running down her cheeks. I smile, and thanks to our new link, I don't even need to speak.

I feel the others, at the edge of my mind. As I suspected, the Kindre network is reminiscent of the ones I can navigate with Eddica, the two different strains of sorcery playing alongside one another like music in two harmonious keys. Tori's Blues always reminded me of Prime and his corpses. Their network was driven by a single, dominating mind; here there are hundreds, flashing back and forth.

I hesitate, but there's no point in waiting. Either this is going to work, or it isn't. *And if it isn't, we're all going to rot.* I touch the piece of conduit, and reach out with Eddica. The connection to *Soliton* is fading, but it's still enough, for now, and I feel the ship's system respond.

Hagan?

Yes? Hagan's mental voice is curious. *Isoka, I can feel . . . something strange.*

It's all the others, crowding into my mind, fascinated by this new connection. I find myself grinning savagely.

Open the forward ramp, I tell Hagan. *And bring up every angel you can.*

I will, Hagan says. *But remember that I can't command them outside the ship itself. Have you figured out how to control more than one at once?*

Something like that.

I turn—not physically, but in my mind—to the mass of volunteers, Red Sashes, and citizens of Kahnzoka. I explain things to them. In words, it would have taken forever, with pauses for questions and reservations and debate. Here, through the network Tori has created, it takes no time at all, an idea passing wholesale from my mind to theirs. They understand what I want them to do, and they set to it.

I can watch, from any one of hundreds of blue crystal eyes. The front ramp of *Soliton* opens, metal groaning and shrieking, startling the Imperial troops guarding the shore. This time, they don't flee—not at first. But the end of the ramp is lined with huge, misshapen figures, hundreds of statues by a demented sculptor, a mass of bestial parts and human shapes. Things that skitter on hundreds of infant's arms, a one-winged owl with a human face and a squid's tentacles, a praying mantis with a woman's bare torso, wrapped round and round in her own wild hair. For a moment they just stand there, still and silent. The Imperials look up at them and shudder.

Then the boldest of the volunteers reaches out, through me, and slips into one of the constructs, guiding it forward. The thing, six-legged and ursine, wobbles, rights itself, and walks down the ramp. A few crossbow bolts hiss out, bouncing uselessly off its stony skin. By the time it reaches the bottom, a half-dozen more constructs are following. The Imperials break and run, militia and Ward Guard alike, refusing to face the mad horror disembarking from the ancient ghost ship.

For the first time in a century, the angels of *Soliton* are coming ashore.

At my silent urging, they turn left, streaming through the fire-blackened Sixteenth Ward toward the western wall. Debris is crushed under stone feet, and scorched beams shouldered aside. A thousand misshapen forms leave a trail a hundred yards wide.

It's a peculiar sensation, being the fulcrum of it all. Hundreds of minds, linked to me by Tori's power, and in turn connected by *mine* to *Soliton* and its angels. Reaching *through* me, issuing instructions in my name, paying attention in hundreds of places at once in a way I had never been able to master. When I return my attention to the real world, I still have the sense of vast energies in flux, like standing on a rope bridge in a windstorm.

"It's working," I say out loud. This is for the benefit of Giniva, Meroe, and the others. Tori already knows—she's connected to the network, like I am, and her eyes are wide with wonder.

One of the angels has split off from the others, heading north instead of west. Tori's Blues order the gate opened, and the dog-angel bounds past, galloping through empty streets. Tori is guiding it here, to our physical bodies. It's the same one Hagan once rode, coming ashore at the Harbor to help me stop Prime. Now it will carry her on our last desperate gamble.

"Worried Jack raises questions about this plan once again," Jack says. "Would it better for Isoka to stay with young Tori? Or for Jack and Zarun to go in her stead?"

"Isoka's going to be needed at the wall," Meroe says.

"And I need to talk to the Emperor myself," Tori says, eyes moving rapidly under closed eyelids.

"And I want Zarun with me," I add.

"But—" Jack sighs, and toys with the edge of her cloak. "Humble Jack is unaccustomed to this level of trust."

"Oh, please," Zarun says. "You've never been humble in your life. And Isoka has always trusted you."

"True!" Jack perks up, drawing the cloak around herself. "Very well, then. Decidedly-less-than-humble Jack will keep young Tori safe from any who might do her harm." She brandishes her spear. "To me, mighty steed!"

Whether by accident or design, her timing is perfect. The dog-angel gallops into the square, digging in all four legs and slewing to a halt in a spray of dirt. I raise an eyebrow at Jack, then turn to Tori, who opens her eyes.

"We'll keep it from getting bloody for as long as we can," I tell her. "But you have to hurry."

"I know."

Tori grins at me, and I can *feel* her determination, balanced over the yawning pit of fear. It makes me want to grab hold of her and never let go.

TORI

Oh, rot, rot, rot. What in the Blessed's name have I gotten myself into?

I'd ridden with Isoka on the double-humped angel, but it hadn't unsettled me like this. Maybe the difference was that this time I was on the *inside*, able to reach out through Isoka's link to *Soliton* and see myself approaching the angel in the black-and-white view from its crystal eye. I could feel the absurd power coiled inside its stone frame; a wrong twitch, and I would be *obliterated*, fragile flesh and bone smeared into the dirt with no more effort than stepping on a grape.

Jack, of course, is already on board, having swarmed up the dog-angel's side with no sign of fear. This, I gather, is how she approaches everything. I'm grateful she's there, though, and grab the hand she extends down to me.

"There appears to be no saddle," she says, as I settle in behind her. "So just hang on to Steady Jack, and she will hang on to . . . something."

I wrap my hands around her waist. I don't feel particularly unsteady on the angel, actually, but I'm going to be distracted. Jack grips the thing's sculpted mane and leans forward.

"Ready!" she says.

I close my eyes, letting the vision from the angel take over, and my thoughts flow through it. It's a strange feeling, reaching out *through* Isoka, using her Eddica link to give the angel orders and receiving its responses the same way. It doesn't feel quite natural, akin to having a conversation via a translator instead of face-to-face, but it's good enough. The angel mostly knows what to do anyway—how to walk and how to run—it just needs to be pushed in the right direction. Within a few moments, we're trotting out of the square toward the military highway, awed Red Sashes clearing rapidly out of the way.

Once we reach that long, straight road, I push the angel into a bounding run. If I'd been watching from the outside, I'm sure I would have been terrified, but the angel's movements are so regular and certain that it feels solid as a rock beneath me. The wind of our passage slashes at my face, drawing tears from my eyes. I hear Jack whoop with delight as we leap off a slight rise and hang in the air for long moments before returning to earth.

She looks back at me, frowning, and I pull my attention away from the angel a little. "Something wrong?"

"Foolish Jack should have thought harder about her positioning," she says. "With Young Tori in the way, her cape isn't fluttering as dramatically as it should. *However!* Together a dashing figure is still cut!"

I snort a laugh, then hurriedly close my eyes again, because the gates are coming up.

The Red Sashes at the Second Ward wall, warned via the Blues, have opened the gate well ahead of us. Past that, we're in Imperial territory. I keep the dog-angel moving at top speed, a couple of bounds taking us across the no-man's-land to the siege lines. A wall of wooden stakes rises up, and I cringe instinctively, but we land among them with a splintering crash and they have as little effect on the angel as all those crossbow bolts did. I get a glimpse of militia soldiers fleeing in all directions, and then we're bounding off again.

The Second Ward flashes past, its mansions set amongst willow and bamboo. All too quickly, the First Ward wall comes into view. The gate is still open—we've outrun news of our arrival, and that speed is our best protection. Ward Guard on the walls have time to do little more than gape as the dog-angel gallops past, their shouts fading in the slipstream behind us. I hear a few crossbows go off, far too late. Here the military highway is lined with the vast estates of the greatest nobles of the Empire, giving me blurred glimpses of elegant gardens and gilded luxury. Then the red-and-gold palace wall comes into view, and *this* gate is firmly closed.

"Young Tori!" Jack shouts. "Perhaps a reduction in speed is in order—the gate—"

Don't slow down. Angel or no angel, if they catch up with us, eventually bowmen will pick Jack and me off. Speed is our best defense. No doubt the angel could smash through the thick wooden gates, but I wouldn't want to be on its back at the time. Instead, I look to the wall itself. It's much lower than the stone walls of the wards, more decorative—no one *really* anticipates defending the Royal Ward from the First. Fantastic beasts, picked out in gold, crouch and snarl atop the wall-walk along with colorfully uniformed palace guards.

I feed instructions to the dog-angel, and it gathers itself, then *leaps*.

Eddica power, drawn up from *Soliton*, drives tons of stone into the air. The dog-angel's front legs hit the wall-walk hard enough to shatter the boards, while its hind legs scrape away huge swathes of the wall's red enamel. Stone claws dig into the wood, powering it over, destroying an eagle-headed statue with a casual blow. Jack and I experience a moment of weightlessness in mid-leap, then come crashing down again, hard enough to make my teeth crack painfully together.

At the base of the wall, I can see the courtyard where Isoka confronted Naga. Palace guards are rushing about in a panic, but no black-armored figures in chain-veils emerge to start pelting us with Myrkai fire. My hope is that Naga has his Immortals close by, at the battle. The angel leaps into the courtyard, and this time I remember to clench my jaw.

The palace is a maze, but fortunately the Imperial residence offers a polestar to navigate by, the huge gilded roof of its private temple rising over the lesser buildings clustered around it. Using that as a reference point, I guess roughly where the Pear Wing ought to be, and keep moving in that direction. Fences divide the grounds into meandering pathways, gardens, and courtyards, but I just plow through them, delicate carved wood exploding into splinters under the angel's paws.

"I always wanted to see the palace!" Jack shouts, as another fence shatters.

The angel skids to a halt, tearing a considerable furrow in a century-old lawn. I recognize this one from my time in captivity. *My room was over there, and the kitchen over there. So the library—*

There's shouting in our wake. *Not much time.* I duck my head as the angel crashes through a corridor, in one side and out the other, leaving bamboo-and-paper screens in tatters. Jack whoops again as we bound over an ornamental stream and splash through a tiny lake, scattering decorative fish. The library is up ahead, on the other side of another thin wall. I bring the angel to a halt, and have it tear a door-size hole with one swipe.

"He might be here," I tell Jack as I slide off the angel. "Or we might have to go further. Stay close."

I'm *hoping* Avyn is here. I've never been inside the Imperial residence, so if we have to go and find him in his bedroom it might take some searching. And, somewhere, the guards are rallying, telling Naga what's happened. *Kadi could be coming, running with Rhema speed—*

"What in the name of the Blessed One is going on?"

A knot loosens in my chest as we push through the library doors and Avyn gets up from his usual spot at the reading table. Dust sparkles and dances in shafts of sunlight, and the pile of books beside him is toppled over. He pulls up short at the sight of Jack— not unreasonably, since she's quite piratical-looking with her purple hair and leather armor—and takes a moment to recognize me standing beside her.

"Hello, Avyn," I say. "It's kind of a long story."

18

ISOKA

Once again, I find myself atop the double-humped angel, riding into battle.

This time, there's no army of Red Sashes following in my wake, just Zarun hanging from the harness beside me. The only army I'm going to need is streaming along the shore in a mass of stone and blue crystal eyes, scattering the Imperial pickets in what used to be the Sixteenth Ward. I'm going to meet them, following the military highway south from rebel headquarters and then turning west to thunder along the packed earth toward the gate opposite the Legion.

My awareness of my physical body is only a vague blur of jolting motion. Most of my attention is focused on the angel, seeing through its monochrome vision and keeping its off-kilter gait steady. When I have a spare moment, I touch the threads of Eddica and Kindre power connecting me to all the other volunteers, and to Tori.

The volunteers are back at headquarters, their bodies laid out in rows on the main floor, watched by a few anxious Red Sashes. Like mine, their minds are with their angels, which have now reached the outer wall at the western end of the Sixteenth Ward. This is the spot where Tori and the Red Sashes made their stand against the Imperials, soaking the cobbles in the blood of both sides before the Navy and the Immortals drove them back. The gate in the wall is a bottleneck, allowing only one or two angels through at a time, but fortunately the Imperials on the other side are keeping well back from the growing horde of bizarre stony creatures emerging onto the plain.

Tori, in the meantime, has nearly reached the palace. I send a flutter of anxiety her way, and receive a pulse of reassurance. I force myself not to interfere further. She doesn't need me looking over her shoulder. *And Jack is with her, if anything goes wrong.*

By the time I catch up with the rest of the angels, nearly all of them have passed through the gate. I join the queue, and I get the Kindre equivalent of a cheer from everyone whose crystal eye can see me. A few stragglers hurry through or move aside, and the double-humped angel carries me and Zarun through the gate and onto the flatlands outside the city. Behind us, the wall is thick with Red Sashes feverishly loading crossbows. If the Legion comes, it won't be enough, but I won't stop them from trying.

The Legion, for its part, is deployed on the plain a few hundred yards ahead of us. It's an impressive sight, an unbroken battle line of soldiers in full armor. Unit flags flap in the breeze at regular intervals, and officers marked out with silver helms wait a few steps behind the main line, ready to relay the orders of their superiors. On the flanks are the cavalry, formed up in disciplined wedges, each with its own colorful battle flag streaming from the tip of a long lance.

At the center of the line, a knot of officers and aides congregate around the Legion's battle standard. Lord General Gymoto, the commanding officer, is over there somewhere. And—as I'd both hoped and feared—there's a couple of dozen men and women in dark armor and chain-veils, too. It's a safe bet that Naga is over there. *If having the Legion here worries him, he'll be on hand to make sure he stays in control.*

That means less of a chance that there are any Immortals close to the Emperor to interfere with Tori's mission. *On the other hand, it means Kadi is probably somewhere over there as well.*

In accordance with the plan I'd pressed into their minds, the volunteers have driven their angels to the north, spreading out along the base of the wall until we make a line roughly as wide as the Legion's, with the gate at our backs. I pilot the double-humped angel to a spot in the center, and let it settle back on its haunches, opening my real eyes to take in the scene in color.

"Now what?" Zarun says. Apart from the flapping of the battle flags, the Imperial line is motionless.

"Now we wait," I tell him, letting the words roll out through the Kindre network, too. "Remember, we're trying to buy as much time as we can with as little bloodshed as possible. If they don't want to move, we shouldn't rush them."

The volunteers send me a collective ripple of assent. A human army might get tired, waiting all day in the sun, but not this strange agglomeration of stone and sorcery. Eddica energy flows into me from *Soliton's* reserves—the ship soaks up the energy of life and death wherever it travels, like a sponge. It passes through me, and breaks into hundreds of tiny threads, one per angel, each coordinated by one of the minds linked by Kindre to my own. *Soliton's* power is nowhere near full, but there's more than enough to drive the angels as far as we need them to go.

"Miss Gelmei!" Naga's voice echoes across the soon-to-be-battlefield. I can see him now, a tiny figure trotting forward on a white horse. He's an indifferent rider, and looks awkward compared to the Legion officers beside him. "I admit to being surprised. I had thought your threat to employ the angels entirely a bluff."

I cup my hands to my lips and shout, "You always did underestimate me."

"I think you are the one who has underestimated your opponent." Naga's voice is unstrained, augmented by some sorcerous trick. "The Legions are no strangers to battling monsters. But I would hate to damage the fighting power of the Navy's new flagship, so I give you this chance to stand aside."

"Likewise," I shout back. "I don't want to kill men and women who are only doing their duty to the Empire. Order them to retreat, and we can negotiate."

"I offered you a chance to negotiate, on quite generous terms,"

Naga says. "You chose to betray my trust. I will not make the same mistake a second time." He turns to the man riding beside him. "Lord General, destroy them."

Gymoto's response is lost to the distance, but the Legion starts moving all at once, as though every man were a small part of some monstrous clockwork engine. The front ranks of infantry lower their spears, presenting a dense thicket of wood and steel, and begin marching forward at an unhurried pace. Shouts drift on the breeze, ordering the soldiers to stay level and straighten up, but from where I'm standing they already look as regular as squares on a checkerboard.

We have to attack. I send my thoughts to the volunteers. *If they get too close to the wall, they can try to break through with Myrkai or Tartak. Let them come a little bit farther, then charge. But if they pull back or run, disengage.*

Another wave of assent. The unbroken phalanx keeps coming, closer and closer, until I send the command rippling out. *Now!*

The angels charge.

It's a strange sight, nothing like the lockstep perfection of the Legion. Each of the stone constructs is different, and the volunteers controlling them are hardly experts. Some of them wobble as they lurch into motion, or collide with their neighbors with a grinding *crunch* of stone. But the line moves forward, hundreds of stone feet coming down in a cavalcade that sounds like continuous thunder. Their blue crystal eyes flash as they crush the grass and weeds underfoot, half army and half avalanche.

I cringe, anticipating the moment of impact. The Legion troops are packed shoulder-to-shoulder, confronting the angels as if they were an army of barbarian horsemen. But spears will avail them little against tons of stone. *If they don't break and flee, it's going to be a slaughter—*

But Naga isn't wrong about the Legions.

At a barked command from their sergeants, a few men in each unit halt and throw up their hands. Bands of pale blue take shape, up and down the line, Tartak force forming in the air and rushing out to wrap around the limbs of the charging angels. No Tartak adept is strong enough to stop an angel, not alone, but here there are dozens of them, working together with the ease of long practice. They wrench one angel to a halt, leaving it sprawling in the dirt, and move on to the next. The front line is suddenly a mess, the monstrous constructs toppling and colliding with one another, stone chips flying.

At another command, more Legion soldiers start glowing with the orange-red shades of Myrkai. They work in small groups, concentrating their fire into a tightly packed orb, then hurling it like a sling-stone over the heads of the front ranks to explode among their enemies. Concussive blasts ring out, licking flames washing over the angels and drowning the blue of their eyes in a mass of crimson.

I hear panic in the minds of the volunteers, and I push my own thoughts out as forcefully as I can, the mental equivalent of shouting at the top of my lungs.

They can't hurt you!

That gets their attention. I sense sheepishness, even a little laughter.

Remember that you're safe, back in headquarters, I tell them. *And the angels are made of stone. They'll have to do better than this to stop us. Push them back!*

The Legions may be used to fighting monsters, but they've never met an army of angels. I can't imagine anything surviving amidst the hellscape of bursting fireballs and surging force just in front of the Legion lines—it makes me wish that we'd had their skill and coordination when we fought a horde of maddened crabs at the Garden—but the angels aren't alive in the first place. The Myrkai blasts are strong enough to smash chips from their hides, but no more than that. Under the volunteers' direction, the toppled constructs struggle back to their feet and press forward again. The legionary Tartak users move to stop them, and for a few moments a stalemate prevails, sorcerous force against tons of moving stone. But there are too many angels, and eventually one of them gets through, a six-legged, barrel-bellied thing with a dozen screaming faces. It reaches the line of spears and bulls through, smashing the weapons and sending them flying.

Even then, though, the Legion doesn't break and run. That section of the line backs away, leaving a gap, while the Tartak users on the other sides focus on driving the angel back. The same thing happens at another spot, and another. There's no breakthrough, no wholesale slaughter with men and women crushed underfoot, but slowly and surely we're driving the Legion backward. Fireballs still burst amid the angels, but the volunteers ignore them, pushing the great constructs onward in the face of everything the Emperor's soldiers can do to stop them.

We can do this. I'm grinning, sitting atop the double-humped angel well behind the lines. *They'll wear down, and we won't. Naga will have to retreat.*

"Isoka!" Zarun's voice is distant in my ear, my attention far from my physical body. "Look out!"

I open my real eyes, and catch sight of a figure high overhead, outlined against the morning sky in green and gold. She descends rapidly, and I just have time to throw myself aside, over the edge of the angel, my armor flaring to absorb the fall as I roll in the dirt. A moment later, and Kadi hits the ground in a crouch, her own armor sending arcs of crackling green lightning in all directions. She's left off her chain-veil, and I can see her twisted grin as she ignites her blades.

TORI

"You can't be here," the Emperor says. He gives Jack a long, curious look, then turns back to me. "If the guards find you—"

"The guards will be along soon, so we don't have much time," I tell him. "Please, listen to me. We can get you out of here, but we have to go *now*."

"Get me out of here?" He blinks. "You mean out of the palace?"

I nod. "You helped me escape. I'm here to return the favor."

"But . . ." He waves a hand helplessly. "I'm not a prisoner."

"That's not what you told me last time."

He takes a deep breath, and his expression settles a little. "Oh, Tori. You don't understand. It's different for me. Just *leaving* wouldn't mean anything. Naga would still be in command—"

"I do understand," I cut him off. By the look on his face, it's not something that happens to him often. "We have a chance to get rid of Naga for good, but we need your help. He's brought a Legion to the city, and he's going to turn it loose against the rebels. Thousands of people are going to die if we don't stop him. But if *you* appeal to the Legion, command them . . ."

His face changes as he understands. Just for a moment, I see the terror, quickly smoothed away and hidden under a mask. *He's afraid of Naga.* And no wonder. The head of the Immortals has been Avyn's bogeyman since childhood.

"It won't work." He gives an affected sigh. "I'm sorry, Tori. If Naga's brought a Legion here, he must be certain of their loyalty."

"That's just it. He didn't *want* to. He brought them in because we were *winning*." I try to suppress my frustration. "Please, Avyn. If we don't take this chance, we'll never get another one."

"I . . ." He shakes his head. "I thought about what you said. Emperor Curoa, for example. You're right that he was criticized at the time for his inaction, but looking from a modern perspective it's clear that he tried to—"

"I don't have time to debate history!" My control slips, my voice rising. "My sister is out there. My friends are out there. They could all die, anytime. They could be dead already."

He takes a step back against a bookshelf. I realize I've been advancing on him.

"You don't understand," he says again, looking at the ground.

"I do," I say quietly. "I told you that. You know my power. There are times I think everyone would have been better off if I'd stayed home, done nothing, pretended it doesn't exist. Certainly *I* would have been safer. I thought I had to help Isoka, but she didn't need me. I did things . . ." *Monster, monster, monster.* "But Grandma Tadeka once told me that you do what you can with what you have, even if it means you get covered in shit. I did what I thought was right. What I had to do. I may be sorry about the way it came out, but that doesn't mean it was wrong to try." I take a deep breath. "You may end up sorry, too. But that doesn't mean you don't have to try."

There's a long silence.

"For what it's worth," Jack says, "Thoughtful Jack agrees with young Tori."

"I'm sorry?" the Emperor says. "Who's thoughtful Jack?"

"She is," I say. "It's a long story. Are you rotting coming or not?"

"I mean . . ." He gives a weak laugh. "I suppose I don't have any choice."

"You always have a choice," Jack says. "A right one and a wrong one."

Avyn tightens his jaw, and nods. "So how are we getting out of here?"

"That . . . may also take some explaining." I can hear shouting from the courtyard, distant but getting closer. "Follow me, and just . . . don't ask too many questions, all right?"

"*That's* ominous," Avyn mutters, but he comes with me as Jack and I head back outside. His eyes widen at the sight of the torn-open hallway and the dog-angel, sitting on its haunches just outside. "I could have sworn," he says weakly, "there wasn't a statue there."

"It's not a statue." I direct the angel to lower its head, as though it were hoping for a scratch behind the ears.

"I was afraid of that," Avyn mutters, then stops as Jack pulls herself onto the angel's back. "Wait, we're going to *ride* it?"

"It's a long walk down to the city," Jack says. "Practical Jack recommends taking this route."

"Jack is clearly a person of many talents," Avyn says. "How do I even get . . . aboard?"

Jack holds out her hand, and the Emperor, after a moment of hesitation, takes it. She shifts backward and gets him settled in front of her, looking distinctly uncomfortable. I start clambering up myself when a door slams open and a young man in silks emerges at a run, stumbling in surprise at the sight of the angel. When he sees me, though, he stares, as if there's nothing else in the world, not even dog-angels and Emperors. *Garo.*

"Tori!"

Rot. I pause, halfway aboard, because what am I supposed to say to him now?

"Tori, please." Garo steps closer. "I don't know what's happening. But you can still come back. Stay here with me. I'll keep you safe." He swallows. "I love you."

I want to laugh and cry at the same time.

"I can't, Garo." I manage to keep my voice level. "Things have . . . changed."

"What do you mean?"

"She means she's just not that into you," Jack says, grabbing my wrist and pulling me onto the angel.

"Tori!"

Garo summons his Melos gauntlets, but we're already moving, the stone of the construct shifting smoothly underneath us. It bounds out of the courtyard the way we came, scattering a cohort of palace guards hurrying toward us. Jack lets out a whoop as the dog-angel jumps a low wall with a single bound, then crashes through another fence in a shower of splinters—

—and slews sideways, suddenly losing control. I struggle to keep us upright, fighting the unresponsive construct as it rips up a line of grass, spraying dirt. All thoughts of Garo go right out of my head, and I wrench at the Kindre link to the others.

Isoka! What's going on?

ISOKA

Kadi comes at me full force from the outset, and it takes everything I have just to stay alive.

I fight her with a shield in one hand and a blade in the other, like before. She slides from attack to attack, barely pausing to contemptuously parry my few ripostes. Blade meets blade with a sound like knives on glass, sparks arcing and popping. Her weapons slam against my shield, raising fresh waves of heat on my abused arm, and I give ground. Rhema glows around her, golden power worming through the green, and she's a blur.

"Tori has such faith in you," she says, as I jump backward again and catch both her blades on my shield. Sparks explode in a fountain. "But you're not a match for me, and you know it." I duck as a blade hums over my head, and manage to get in a shot to Kadi's midsection. She grins as her armor flares, ignoring the blow and trading me one that catches my shoulder in a painful bloom of heat. I disengage, backing away again, and she follows unhurriedly. "You never were."

"You're right." My breath comes fast, and sweat dampens my hair and drips off my chin. My shield arm is already throbbing painfully. I can feel alarm among the others, spreading through the Kindre network, but I don't dare take the time to pay attention. "I'm not."

"Then be a good girl and surrender." Kadi extends a blade to point at my face. " I'll let you keep some of your limbs."

"I'm not a match for you," I repeat, then force a smile. "I'm also not an idiot, so this time I brought a friend."

Pale blue light blooms around Kadi, Tartak bands materializing to grab her arms and legs. But with Rhema she's *fast*, and she's already twisting in place. Her left arm is caught in a vise, but she gets her right blade free and slashes through the force-bonds in an explosion of blue and green sparks. Another slash frees her legs, and she dances backward, trailing golden light.

"Well." Zarun hops down off the angel and ignites his own blades. "I guess we'll do this the hard way."

I shift my shield back to a blade. Kadi is no longer smiling. For a long moment, the three of us regard one another.

Then we come together in a mass of seething, crackling bolts of power. Kadi fights in both directions at once, using her speed to keep me and Zarun apart, matching me stroke for stroke then blurring away to push him back a step. But she can't keep it up forever, and now she's the one giving ground. Zarun fights with a showy flair, but his swordwork is solid, and he and I work together almost instinctively. When Kadi presses him too hard, he backs off, buying time to me to close in from behind. When I'm in danger, waves of Tartak hammer the Immortal, forcing her to dodge away.

Kadi shifts her ground, then shifts again, circling to the left to put her back against the bulk of the angel. It keeps us from flanking her, but she's out of room to run. Zarun and I come together for a moment, both breathing hard, blades humming.

"Push her back," I hiss. "Just for a second."

He nods. His Melos blades shift, melding into a single, longer weapon held in his linked hands. I last saw that technique from Karakoa, who'd died fighting off the last assault of *Soliton*'s crabs, and I'm willing to bet Kadi never has. She crosses her blades to stop Zarun's downward swing, and at the same time Tartak force lashes out, shoving her against the body of the angel.

Three Melos adepts. But not just that. We each have two Wells—Kadi has Rhema, Zarun has Tartak. *And I have Eddica.*

I reach out, and the angel moves. Just as Kadi is falling against it, expecting to put her back to a wall, the double-humped construct rears up, legs parting to let her tumble through. She tries to turn the fall into a roll, but Zarun hammers her with Tartak, leaving her flat on the ground. It's just a moment of vulnerability, but a moment is long enough. The angel shifts again, putting one broad, flat foot on Kadi's chest, her armor flaring and sparking. Bolts of Melos energy crackle across the construct's stony hide.

"Rotting *coward*," the Immortal says, half a scream. "Can't face me straight, and you know it!"

"You know," I tell her, "there was a time when that would have bothered me. I might have let you up to prove I was better." I shake my head. "You shouldn't have hurt my sister."

The angel settles its multi-ton weight on Kadi's chest. The Immortal's scream rises to a shriek, her armor flaring brighter and brighter. I step back, one hand in front of my eyes, as the glare goes from green to actinic white, outlining the bones in my hands. Then something finally breaks, with a *whump* of detonation, and I feel the pulse of a shockwave ripple past me. When I blink my eyes open again, there's nothing left under the angel's foot but a smear of ash.

"Give her that much," Zarun says contemplatively. "She took the heat to the end."

"Yeah." I glance at him. "Thanks."

"My pleasure." He lets the long blade fade away and stretches. "Now—Isoka?"

I've gone stiff, my blades dissipating, pulled away from my physical body by a very different kind of attack.

Seen with my Eddica senses, the assault is powerful but crude. Power flows from *Soliton* to me in a great gray stream, and from me out to the hundreds of angels in a multitude of tiny threads. The stranger's Eddica power lashes out, not a scalpel but a felling axe. Cutting each of those tiny threads would be tedious work. But the connection from me to *Soliton* is a large, tempting target.

I feel the blow coming, and position myself to meet it, power to power. In the immaterial world, lines of gray energy thrash and grind against one another, while my physical body stands stock-still. I'm stronger, I can *feel* that I'm stronger, but my position is intrinsically weaker, with my delicate place as the fulcrum of so much power to defend. It feels like standing on the polished top of a flagpole, while a child tries to shove you off—what matters isn't always strength, but *leverage*.

Or so my mind constructs the scene, at any rate, struggling to make sense of the clashing tides of spirit energy. I have little enough experience, just my single battle against Prime in the heart of the Harbor system, and I'd only won that with Silvoa's help. The attacker—she must be an Immortal, the one who'd shut down my angel back in the Fourth Ward—pushes harder, and I can't help but give way, losing my balance. The flood of energy from *Soliton* slows to a trickle, and I put all the concentration I can manage into hanging on to that much.

Across the front line, the angels facing the Legion go still. The soldiers hesitate, not sure what to make of this reprieve. Over the Kindre link, I can feel the volunteers demanding to know what's happened, and in the real world I catch the edge of Naga's barked order.

"*Now!* Attack!"

Isoka? What's going on?

Tori's voice. I struggle to hang on to a thin thread of Eddica energy, maintaining my connection to a single angel—hers. I feel her anxiety through the link, and try to send a pulse of reassurance, but my mind is shot through with worry.

I'm okay, I tell her. *Naga's Eddica user is interfering with the angels. The Legion is advancing. Where are you?*

Leaving the palace, she sends back.

We need more time, I tell her. *We need the Returners.*

But—

I know. But we have to take the risk.

There's a pause. I feel Tori's guilt, great waves of it. Guilt for what happened to Kosura. Guilt for putting innocent people in danger, again. For using them as tools.

They agreed to this, Tori, I tell her. *They want to save the city as much as we do.*

. . . I know. I feel her resolve. *I'll tell her to open the gate.*

Get here as fast as you can.

I will, she says.

You've really got the Emperor? I can't help but ask.

I do. I get a mental image of her smile. *If this all goes right, I'll introduce you.*

I open my eyes, and find the Legion advancing. Slowly, giving the motionless constructs a wide berth, the lines of armored soldiers move forward. They file around the angels, then re-form their ranks, spears bristling ahead and adepts waiting behind. Formation established, they march forward, steps synchronized to the steady heartbeat of drums.

"Back to the wall," I tell Zarun. When I try to walk, I wobble slightly, and he catches my arm. In the Eddica realm, I've established a new equilibrium, but it takes constant effort to keep Naga's Immortal from cutting me off completely. "Time for our last trick."

He grimaces, then nods. We take off at a jog, leaving the double-humped angel behind. Ahead of us, the gate has swung open, and the first ranks of white-robed, shaven-headed figures are marching out.

By the time we reach the gate, pushing past the outgoing tide of Returners, I'm stumbling like a drunk. Eddica power streams off me, not a quick flash of heat but an all-over warmth. I feel sweat soaking through at my armpits and across my chest, and it trickles down my cheeks and around my eyes.

Zarun helps me up the steps to the top of the wall, where Red Sash crossbowmen make way. I slump against the stone lip, breathing hard, and try to focus on what's happening down below. The Legion has made it most of the way across the field, leaving the line of angels behind. Having seen what they can do, I'm confirmed in my initial guess that a few crossbows on the wall wouldn't stop them—that many Tartak users could pull the wall down around our ears.

Instead, the only thing that stands in their way is Kosura and the Returners. Thousands of them have streamed through the gate and thousands more are still coming, spreading out along the base of the wall, forming a line of robed figures three or four deep in the Legion's path. Kosura herself stands slightly ahead of them, waiting calmly as the armed might of the Empire descends on her.

The Legion comes to a halt, well within range to annihilate the Returners with bolts of Myrkai fire. After a few moments, the front ranks part, and a small group of horsemen approach. I see Naga, flanked by several Immortals, and the silver-helmed Lord General Gymoto.

Tori, I send. *Where are you?*

Coming. Hold on.

"And what is this supposed to be?" Naga says, clearly audible now. "All you have left to send against us is unarmed fanatics?"

"We will not fight you," Kosura says. "That is against the Blessed One's teachings. But neither will we let you enter the city." She raises her voice. "Turn away, all of you, and look to your souls."

"Lord General Gymoto and his soldiers are loyal servants of the Empire," Naga says. "You think they'll hesitate if I order them to kill you?"

"I am sure they will do their duty."

"Then *stand aside.*"

Kosura pulls back her hood and stares up at Naga. "I received these scars at the hands of your Immortals, Lord Naga. I did not submit then, nor will I now. Burn us if you must. The Blessed One will know our devotion."

Returners are still pushing through the gate, thickening the line. Naga looks over them, distastefully, then glances up and spots me on the battlements. Zarun hovers by my side, protectively, but Naga only scowls.

"I'm surprised at you, Miss Gelmei," he says. "I knew you were ruthless, of course. But I always thought there was a hint of compassion as well. This"—he gestures at the mass of Returners—"I would have thought beyond the pale, even for you."

My head is still spinning, but I manage to speak up enough to be heard. "I guess your files aren't as accurate as you thought."

"You must know I won't stay my hand." Naga's pleasant mask is back. He thinks he's in control again. "I cannot, in the Emperor's name. He has ordered me to put down this rebellion, and I will do so with every means at my disposal." He adjusts his wire-rimmed spectacles. "You would send so many to their deaths, just to delay a few more moments?"

"The Returners volunteered," I tell him. "They want to defend our city, just as much as the rest of us. I haven't *sent* them anywhere."

He waves this aside. "They'll still die."

"They will, if you give the order." My head pounds, and I wipe away sweat. "Have you considered what happens next?"

"Next?" Naga laughs. "We take the city and crush your rebellion once and for all. You have nothing left to stop us. Without energy from *Soliton*, the angels are useless."

"Not . . . quite," I say. "You've forgotten where Eddica power comes from in the first place. It's *spirit* energy, the energy of life and death. I've felt that firsthand. If you turn the Legion loose on the Returners . . ." I summon the effort for an exaggerated shrug. "There might be plenty of energy for the angels after all."

"That's . . ."

Naga's mask cracks. He glances at one of the Immortals beside him, a slight woman on a slim mare, and they talk briefly in low tones. *That must be his Eddica user.* She must be as strained as I am, but it's hard to tell beneath the chain-veil. When Naga straightens up, it's clear he hasn't liked what he's heard. Gymoto is looking uncertain as well, glancing backward at the silent angels that litter the plain.

"Is *that* why you brought them out here?" Naga says. "So they could *fuel* your army with their deaths?"

He's talking to the Returners as well, hoping to damage their resolve. And, I admit, it would be a monstrous thing to do. Prime had something like it in mind, slaughtering the people of the world to provide power for his endless horde of corpses. For a moment, Naga gets a faraway look, almost admiring. *He just wishes he'd thought of it first.* Then he snaps back to cold calculation.

"You're bluffing," he says.

"Worse than that," I answer cheerfully. "I genuinely have no idea if it will work. But like you said, we're out of tricks, so . . ."

His expression flickers again, a quickly suppressed hint of rage. By the time he turns to Gymoto, he's all calm.

"If those . . . angels turn on us again, we will not be able to hold the line in both directions," the Lord General says. "I do not understand this talk of Eddica, but if you believe what she says, we should withdraw and regroup."

"No," Naga snarls. "Just . . . have your men disperse these *cultists*. But . . . carefully."

"That will take time."

"Then *get started*."

The Lord General bows slightly and turns his horse away, barking orders. Legionaries move forward, sheathing their weapons. The Returners gather more tightly around the gates, linking arms, as webs of Tartak force materialize to start prying them apart.

I let out a long breath. "It's working."

"Until Naga loses his temper," Zarun says. "But it's all for nothing unless Tori gets here soon."

Tori . . .

TORI

I'm coming, I send to Isoka. *As fast as I can.*

Which is not as fast as I would have liked, but it can't be helped. We have to take an alternate route out of the palace, avoiding the fully alerted guards. The dog-angel crashes through fences and bursts down corridors, stone paws tearing delicate carpets, lacquered doors fragmenting into a hundred pieces.

"Did you *make* this thing?" Avyn has a thousand questions, and he shouts them in my ear. His hands are linked around my waist, with no sign of embarrassment. Jack hangs on behind him. "How do you control it?"

"I didn't make it, my sister found it on *Soliton*," I mutter. "And controlling it is *quite difficult*, so try not to distract me."

"*Soliton*, as in the ghost ship?" The Emperor shakes his head. "It's not real!"

"You would be surprised how many things are real that aren't," Jack says cheerfully. "Duck!"

"Ducks aren't real?"

Fortunately, Jack puts one hand on Avyn's head and forces him to bend double as we pass under a stone archway. Another wooden fence shatters under the angel's paws, and then we're in the outer gardens, racing across a terraced lawn toward the red-painted outer wall. A few guards on the wall-walk have crossbows, but their terrified shots don't even come close.

Once again, the dog-angel gathers itself and leaps. It feels less sure-footed, and through the Kindre links I can sense the strain Isoka is under. But there's enough power left to propel us to the top of the wall, sending the guards fleeing in every direction, and another jump takes us down into the First Ward. The angel gallops through more gardens, cutting west across the great estates.

"Where are we going?" Avyn says. "We're well off the highway."

"There'll be more guards at the main gate," Jack says.

"We're not heading for the main gate," I tell them. "I have an idea."

On the west side of the First Ward, the outer wall reaches its terminus in a squat tower where the rocky side of the hill rises up to become part of the defenses. I can see that tower in front of us, and the line of the wall stretching down from it, sweeping all the way to distant shoreline and enclosing the western side of the city. The wall-walk atop it is like its own narrow highway.

There are guards here, too, but not so many—we're still well north of the rebel lines. And these are only militia, not palace troops. They flee at the first sight of the angel. Stone staircases run up the inner face of the wall, just wide enough for the dog-angel to scramble along. Jack whoops as we bound up one, tipped at a dangerous angle; I cling to the angel's sculpted fur, and the Emperor clings to me.

Then we're on top, and the path ahead of us is clear. I push the angel as fast as it will go, and its footsteps rattle and bang out a tattoo. Soldiers dive aside as we pass, or scramble down the stairs. Up ahead is the front line, the section of wall where Imperial and Red Sash troops have built opposing barricades. They hear us coming, and a few fire their crossbows. I duck behind the dog-angel's head, and the bolts ricochet off into oblivion.

The barricades fare little better than the palace furnishings did when the angel hits them, wood splintering and shattering with a resounding crash. We wobble as the dog-angel nearly loses its footing, but I keep control, concentrating harder. The rebel barricade shatters as well, and I send a silent apology to the Red Sashes who are now scrambling aside with just as much terror as their Imperial counterparts.

The circuit of Kahnzoka's walls is long, but the relentless power of the angel sweeps the distance away. It feels like no time at all before we're pounding along the top of the wall that borders the Fourth Ward, still scarred and stained from the battles fought there over the past week. Beyond that is the Tenth Ward, and the military highway, where the Legion is attacking and Isoka had planned to make her stand. Even from here, I can see pillars of smoke rising.

I have no idea what to expect. Isoka's alive—I can tell that much from the Kindre link—but there's no time to ask for details. My mind conjures all kinds of horror, a battlefield drenched in blood, the broken bodies of the Returners heaped in gory piles. Kosura, in all her courage and faith, ripped to pieces or burned alive.

Please. I close my eyes, just for a moment. *This city has suffered enough. I've done enough to it. Please.*

"Are they fighting?" the Emperor says, craning his neck over my shoulder. "I can't see."

I can't reach out to any of the angels on the field. But as we get closer, I can make out the scene through the smoke, and it's both better and worse than I feared. The angels lie where they fell, awkwardly frozen, and small fires still burn around them. The Legion has moved on, coming right up to the walls, trying to force a path to the gate. But the Returners have put themselves in the way, and the legionaries are pulling them aside with bare hands and Tartak, forcing them to kneel in long rows and binding their hands and feet.

It's not a slaughter, yet. We still have time.

We're getting close, and the Red Sashes on the wall see us coming. They clear out of the way, shouting and waving their crossbows. I wave back, and Jack answers the cheers with a whoop.

"Hold on!" I shout to the others. There's a clear space, just beyond the Returners and the line of legionaries. I can see men on horseback in important-looking uniforms. I can see Naga as he catches sight of me, points.

Now or never.

I reach out to the construct, and the dog-angel leaps, one more time. Eddica energy powers its indefatigable stone, sending us flying off the wall like a catapult-shot. Jack shrieks with delight, I hear shouts and screams as the struggling melee of Returners and legionaries passes below us, and then we're descending fast—too fast—and the grass is coming up—

The angel's legs flex on landing, absorbing much of the fall, but it's still hard enough to knock my teeth together and bruise my tailbone. The Emperor gives a yelp and slams into me from behind. The angel skids to a halt, its paws plowing furrows in the earth. Someone is screaming—Naga.

"*Kill them!* Fire! Now!"

I fill my lungs and shout, lashing out at the same time with all the Kindre power I can muster.

"*Stop!*"

For an instant, they all do. Crossbowmen freeze, Myrkai users halt without summoning their fire, Tartak adepts let their force bands fade away. Almost immediately, another Kindre user pushes me back, filling the mental realm with blanketing fog. I couldn't have held so many for longer than a moment anyway.

A moment, as it turns out, is all I needed.

I have to hand it to Avyn. I'd wondered, back in the library, if he'd be up to the job—if, in the end, his fear and indecision would overwhelm him. But now that we're here, among the smoke and screams, he's all decisive action. The Emperor, I think, is a role he's been taught to play since he was a boy, presiding over court ceremonies and military reviews. He may not like it, but it's been ground into his bones.

"Stop, all of you!" he shouts, he voice booming effortlessly through the clamor. He lets go of me and stands up on the back of the angel, long robes falling around him, billowing as he sweeps his arm in a dramatic gesture. "All violence is to cease this instant! Your Emperor commands it!"

Everyone freezes, almost as quickly as when they were under my mental compulsion. This time, though, they also turn and stare. Avyn is suddenly at the center of everything.

He hops down from the angel, and I swing hastily down beside him. Jack gives me a look, and I gesture for her to stay out of sight. She vanishes in a swirl of shadows.

Naga is staring at the Emperor, too, incomprehension gradually giving way to fury. Beside him, the officer I assume to be Lord General Gymoto hastily slides off his horse, falling to one knee in the dirt. His entourage scurry to do likewise.

"Kuon Naga," Avyn says, stalking forward. "You would remain mounted in the presence of your sovereign?"

"I—" Naga struggles to dismount, getting tangled in the reins. "Apologies, Your Majesty. But this place is not safe for you. Please, we must get you away before the rebels attack!"

"He is right, Your Majesty," Gymoto says. "Allow us to safe-guard you—"

"It is *unsafe*," Avyn says, "because of an attack on *our own city* that I neither ordered nor authorized. I want it to cease immediately, and I want to know who is responsible."

Gymoto bows his head deeper. "I had my orders from Master Naga, Your Majesty."

Naga shoots a brief look of fury at the general, who is apparently eager to throw him under the cart. Adjusting his spectacles, he composes himself. His voice is slick as oil. "I believe Your Majesty instructed me to deal with the situation in the city as I thought necessary—"

"I said no such thing," Avyn snaps.

"Perhaps not *directly,* but it falls under the course of my ordinary duties—"

"*Ordinary?* Half the capital rising in revolt is hardly an ordinary situation!" The Emperor looks from Naga to Gymoto. "I am displeased."

"Your Majesty—" Naga casts around, and spots me behind Avyn. "You!" He points. "That girl is a Kindre adept. She has influenced the Emperor—quickly, I want her captured and His Majesty rescued—"

Gymoto looks over his shoulder at one of his officers, who gives a quiet nod. The Lord General straightens slightly.

"Commander Ashiva is a Kindre talent," he says, "and she reports that there is no mental power in use apart from the fog coming from one of your entourage, Master Naga. And the Emperor's mind seems to be free of the taint of compulsion."

"Then she has lied to him," Naga says. "She's the rebel leader—"

"The rebel leader who escaped from your custody?" Gymoto says mildly.

"Enough," Avyn says. "Lord General Gymoto. Are you prepared to obey my orders?"

"Of course, Your Majesty." Gymoto falls back to one knee, head bowed. "My life is yours."

"Then I order you to place Kuon Naga under arrest."

"You wouldn't dare," Naga snarls, looking between the Emperor and the Lord General.

There's a long, dangerous moment. It feels like the world is a set of scales, balanced close to perfectly.

But not quite.

"As you command, Your Majesty." Gymoto gets to his feet. "Commander Ashiva, Commander Gao. Take Master Naga into custody."

Naga's Immortals form up around him, instinctively. But Gymoto raises a fist, and the small group is suddenly surrounded by a ring of legionaries, spears leveled and crossbows aimed, crackling sorcerous power at the ready. Very slowly, the men and women in chain-veils raise their hands.

"Go." All eyes are on Naga, and the Emperor bends down to whisper to me. "I will handle things from here."

"You're sure?" I meet Naga's gaze, his eyes full of mingled fury and despair.

"I'm sure." He gives me a smile. "And thank you. I think I needed to be rescued from myself most of all."

"Thank you, too," I whisper. "For everything."

There's a rush of shadow as Jack materializes beside me, cape billowing. She grins at me and takes my hand, and we hurry toward the gate to find my sister.

Epilogue

ISOKA

From the tower that rises over *Soliton*'s Garden, I watch the people come.

There's a good view out over the lowered bow ramp. The angels have cleared a path through the wreckage of the Sixteenth Ward, leaving a broad flat space of trampled ash and dirt. A queue snakes from the base of the ramp, winding and blurring until it mingles with the crowd beyond.

Some people are just here to gawk at the ghost ship, now that it's safe. With the siege lifted, food is flooding into the city, and vendors are here in full force, selling rice balls and fried dough and all the other staples of Kahnzoka fairs. Musicians stroll around, playing newly composed epics about the events of the last few days, shaking their hats for tips.

Other people shove through the crowd of merrymakers with a more serious purpose. They're heavily laden with bags, or pushing wheelbarrows laden with everything they own. Some have even brought donkeys. They come as families, parents and children, in larger groups, or alone. They come laughing and excited, or with heads lowered in grief. But they're coming.

At the base of the ramp, one of Tori's Blues asks a few basic questions. No one is turned away. We just want people to be clear what they're getting themselves into. Anyone who boards *Soliton*, here and now, is never going to see Kahnzoka again.

Almost all of them come aboard anyway.

I hear footsteps on the metal deck behind me. Meroe joins me at the rail, putting her arm around my waist and looking down at the crowd.

"There's more than I expected," she says.

"People are scared," I mutter.

"Do they have reason to be?" she says. "Your Emperor declared an amnesty."

He had, both for the rebels and any fugitive mage-bloods. The former were instructed to return to their homes, the latter to register and receive appropriate documentation to live in peace henceforth. The militia had dispersed, food flowed into the city, and Imperial edicts promised support for those left homeless and reform in the Ward Guard. The Navy draft had been quietly dropped, and there was no more talk of the coming war with Jyashtan.

"It depends," I say.

"On what?"

"On who you have faith in, I suppose. Naga's gone, and everyone who supported him is out of power. Now Lord General Gymoto is on the Council of State, and Lord Marka, and *their* allies. And they've made a lot of promises, but . . ." I shrug.

"The dance goes on," Meroe says quietly, "and there is no end to history."

"Is that a quote from one of your philosophers?"

"Something like that." She pulls me a little closer. "You don't want to stay?"

"No. Rot no. I'm going to head back to the Harbor with you and never leave again." I turn toward her and pull her into a kiss.

"And all these people?" Meroe says, when we pull apart again.

"They can come, too. There's plenty of room, plenty of food."

"You know they're going to expect you to be in charge. You're the one who controls the Harbor system."

"Ugh."

"And there'll be politics, and rivalries, and crime, and—"

"Meroe, please," I beg.

"Sorry." She pats my shoulder sympathetically. "On the upside, more people should help generate more Eddica energy, so the city won't need to go into stasis."

"It'll help, but it still won't be enough." I look over my shoulder at the bulk of *Soliton*. "We're going to have to send the ship back out to gather more. Maybe see if we can fix up the others, while we're at it. I'm sure Silvoa can help with that."

"I'm sure she can." Meroe's expression goes thoughtful. "I had a idea about that, actually. The ship won't demand sacrifices anymore—"

"Of course it won't!"

"But coming aboard wasn't always such a bad thing for everyone," she says. "Me, for instance."

"Your father kidnapped you."

"And probably would have killed me for what I can do, if he hadn't had an alternative." She spreads her hands. "It just occurred to me that if people *want* to come aboard, I don't see why we should stop them. There are a lot of places in the world where mage-bloods are treated badly, or ordinary people want to take a chance on a better life."

"I suppose. As long as we're not dragging them aboard in cages." I look back at Kahnzoka. "And if the people in charge knew that *Soliton* was coming back from time to time, it might help . . . keep them honest."

"Of course, someone would have to go along on these voyages, to keep an eye on things." Meroe snuggles close to me again. "It'd be a long trip, alone at sea. . . ."

"Sounds . . . relaxing."

"I thought you were never leaving the Harbor again?"

"Well," I murmur. "Maybe not *never*."

I hear the sound of feet on the ladder behind us, and half-turn to find Tori emerging onto the tower. She blinks in the afternoon sun, shading her eyes.

"I'll leave you two be," Meroe says, kissing me on the cheek.

I'd almost rather she stay. Tori and I haven't had a chance to . . . talk. The Kindre network she created has faded away, leaving only the echoes of the emotions it carried between us. From the look on her face as Meroe sweeps past, Tori has the same trepidation, but she squares her shoulders and comes over to join me at the rail.

"Hey," I manage.

"Hey," she responds weakly.

There's a long silence.

"All those people," Tori says. "You're really going to bring them all with us?"

"Why not?" Red Sashes and mage-bloods, rebels and criminals, anyone who doesn't trust the new regime and anyone looking to flee from an inconvenient past. *What could go wrong?*

"There's really room for everyone at the Harbor?"

"More or less." I think of the ancient, crumbling ziggurats, strewn with formerly living corpses. "It might requires a little fixing up, but we'll manage."

"That's good." Tori stares down at the crowd. "Giniva's coming. I just helped get her settled down below. I asked Hasaka and Jakibsa if they wanted to join us, but Hasaka said he was too tired to start again. They're going to take the amnesty and try to settle down somewhere."

"What about Kosura?"

"She's staying with the Returners. She told me that the Blessed One's return doesn't seem to be *quite* as imminent as they thought, but that just means there's more time to work on the state of their souls. Some of the supplicators came back to try and kick her people out of the temples, though."

"I imagine they'll get a nasty shock," I say.

"Indeed. Avyn will help them work something out."

Another silence, stretching on, broken by the distant chatter from far below.

"I'm going to try to fix the Blues," Tori says. "The ones that are left. I don't know if I can fully undo what I did to them but . . . I can try. Make them people again."

"Tori." I take a deep breath, looking away from her and out at the city. "Are you sure this is what you want? Coming with me?"

My jaw tightens. "The Emperor offered you a place in the palace. I think he might be sweet on you."

"Avyn?" Tori sounds as though she'd never considered the possibility. "Really?"

"Play your cards right, and you could be Empress."

She laughs. "That seems unlikely." Out of the corner of my eye, I see her turn to look up at me. "Besides. I'd rather live on a monster-infested ghost ship with you than in a palace by myself."

I swallow, eyes pricking.

"Are . . ." Tori's voice is very soft. "Are you sure you want me to stay? After everything I've done? I know that I'm not . . . what you wanted."

My throat is too thick to answer, but I turn and wrap my arms around her, pulling my little sister off her feet and into a tight embrace. We stay that way for a long time, while below us the gaping maw of *Soliton* takes aboard the citizens of a new world.

ACKNOWLEDGMENTS

As I write The End on another series, it occurs to me that it's my *third*, which scarcely seems possible. It wouldn't be possible at all without a long list of people helping me every step of the way. That starts with my wife, Casey Blair, who (in addition to her usual role of generally being brilliant with plots and characters) served as a YA expert and guide for me when I was fresh to the genre. As on previous volumes, Liz Bourke and Iori Kusano were my sensitivity readers, and the books are much better for their valuable contributions.

My editor, Ali Fisher, loved this series from the start, and I'm lucky to have been able to work with her. My thanks as well to everyone at Tor Teen: Devi Pillai, Fritz Foy, Isa Caban, Renata Sweeney, Anthony Parisi, Eileen Lawrence, Desirae Friesen, Sarah Reidy, Lucille Rettino, Jessica Katz, Steven Bucsok, and, as always, Tom Doherty. And thanks to Richard Anderson and Amir Zand, whose striking covers give this series its amazing look.

My agent, Seth Fishman, makes these things happen, and I'd be completely lost without him. As always, he and the team at The Gernert Company have all my gratitude: Jack Gernert, Will Roberts, Rebecca Gardner, and Ellen Goodson.

And for everyone out there: I hope you've had as much fun with Isoka, Tori, Meroe, and the rest as I have.